'T. M. Payne is one of the most exciting new voices in crime fiction. In *Long Time Dead*, she crafts a richly textured thriller that brims with authentic detail. I loved the humour, the poignancy and the intricate rendering of Liverpool in all its heart and grit. The comparisons to Val McDermid are well earned indeed.'

—Kia Abdullah

'T. M. Payne is one of the most talented storytellers of our time. The gripping and authentic storytelling, clever and deeply satisfying plot and superb characters make *This Ends Now* my standout novel of the year and puts Payne at the top table of crime writers.'

—Graham Bartlett

'Good twists, and plenty of red herrings, and the book builds to a very tense and unexpected conclusion, with some neat stings in the tale . . . a really quick and engaging read.'

—*Deadly Pleasure*

'Worth every interminable minute it takes to wind down.'

—*Kirkus Reviews*

PRAISE FOR THE DETECTIVE SHERIDAN HOLLER SERIES

'An excellent crime novel, full of humour and pathos as well as utterly realistic action. A stunning debut.'

—Elly Griffiths

'Make way for the brilliant Detective Sheridan Holler! Urgent and artful storytelling for die-hard fans of crime fiction and new blood alike.'

—A. J. West

'A thrilling debut . . . If you are a fan of police procedurals, this one set in the mean streets of Liverpool is for you.'

—Mari Hannah

'T. M. Payne has hit the ground running with *Long Time Dead*. Gritty, well-paced and packed with vividly drawn characters.'

—M. W. Craven

'A gripping and gritty start to what promises to be an excellent new police procedural series.'

—David Fennell

'An evocative, brilliantly plotted debut which I defy you to put down. I promise it will haunt you long after the end.'

—Graham Bartlett

'A brilliant debut.'

—Steve Cavanagh

'A twisty, compelling, page-turning cracker of a debut. Full of great characters, T. M. Payne's *Long Time Dead* is so absorbing you'll miss your bus stop AND stay up past your bedtime. Perfect for fans of Val McDermid and Michael Connelly.'

—Chris Merritt

'Dark and gripping, expertly plotted, and full of warmth and humour – you won't want this book to end.'

—Mel Sherratt

'A propulsive and character-driven mystery woven with authenticity and aplomb.'

—Victoria Selman

'A brilliant and compassionate new detective joins the scene.'

—Claire McGowan

'Such a great series. DI Sheridan Holler is one of my all-time favourite detectives. Written with warmth and humour, as well as a dark and twisty tale.'

—Jo Callaghan

'T. M. Payne's eighteen-year career in the criminal justice system brings authenticity to every page of *This Ends Now*. An expertly woven plot combined with the warmth and wit of the main character, DI Sheridan Holler, make this second book in the series a must-read for all crime fiction fans. A cracking police procedural. Don't miss this one!'

—D. S. Butler

ONE
BAD
DEED

ALSO BY T. M. PAYNE

Long Time Dead

This Ends Now

Play With Fire

Count The Dead

ONE BAD DEED

T. M. PAYNE

A DETECTIVE SHERIDAN HOLLER THRILLER

Published by Thomas & Mercer, Seattle

www.apub.com

Amazon, the Amazon logo, and Thomas & Mercer are trademarks of Amazon.com, Inc., or its affiliates.

EU Product Safety Contact:
Amazon Media EU S.à r.l.
38, avenue John F. Kennedy, L-1855 Luxembourg
amazonpublishing-gpsr@amazon.com

ISBN-13: 9781662532542
eISBN: 9781662532559

Cover design by Dan Mogford
Cover image: ©zhu difeng / Shutterstock; ©Maria Heyens / ArcAngel; ©John Davidson Photos / Alamy

Printed in the United States of America

For Susie.
Because without you, there would be no words.

He hides from you, for he knows how
He learned his lesson well
To seek him out, have not a doubt
He'll drag you first to hell

Of all the monsters gone before
You face this one alone
Which way to turn, which rule to burn
A promise carved in stone

He leads the dance, so take a chance
But be prepared to bleed
For what's revealed, when you don't yield
Is more than one bad deed

PROLOGUE

Monday 23 December 1974
Fire Service Control Room, Liverpool

Jimmy Turner settled down behind his desk and wrapped his hands around his mug of tea. The fire control room was bitterly cold.

'It's bloody freezing in here.' He looked across at Senior Control Operator Carrie Penhaligan, who was standing in the middle of the small room, grinning.

'This is only your third shift and you're already moaning,' Carrie said, shaking her head. 'It's going to be a long night.'

Jimmy took a sip of tea and sighed. 'I'm not moaning. I just think they need to get better heating in here.'

'Men,' Carrie muttered. 'Anyway, you all ready for Christmas?' she asked, attempting to lighten the conversation.

Jimmy leaned back in his seat. 'The kids are all sorted. I just need to get my wife's present. I'll probably get her some perfume.'

Carrie shook her head again. 'Bloody hell, it's Christmas Eve tomorrow, Jimmy. Why do you men always wait until the last minute?'

Jimmy looked at her over the top of his glasses. 'If I buy her present too early, she'll search the house from top to bottom until she finds it. She's like a big kid at Christmas. My two boys are better behaved.' He laughed.

'You've got twins, haven't you?' Carrie said.

'Yeah. Four-year-olds. Best thing that ever happened to us. We tried for a long time to have kids. When my wife finally got pregnant, it was a real worry right up until the boys were born. But then we were blessed with two.' Jimmy smiled. 'I know, I'm a big softie at heart.' He pressed a hand to his chest. 'You know what it's like, they get you right here. All the silly things they do and say.' He cleared his throat. 'Anyway, what about you? Big Christmas planned?'

Carrie smiled too, warming to her new colleague. 'Yeah, my parents are at mine at the moment, looking after the kids. They're staying with us until Boxing Day.' She glanced at the photograph proudly displayed in the frame on her desk. Her two children's animated faces beaming back at her.

'How old are your kids?' Jimmy asked, rubbing his hands together, trying to fend off the cold.

'Bradley's nine and Elizabeth's six.' Carrie felt warmed as she imagined them tucked up in bed, but probably wide awake with all the excitement of what presents they were going to get on Christmas morning.

She'd bought Elizabeth an art set. Her little girl loved to paint. Usually on the walls around the house.

Bradley had been asking for a penknife for the past two years. Carrie had always denied him; he was far too young to be playing with knives. But this year, she'd decided that he'd shown he could be a level-headed and responsible child, and so she'd bought him a beautiful penknife and had had it engraved. *Bradley. Christmas 1974*'

Her children were, in her eyes, perfect. Yes, they could be mischievous, but they were thoughtful and kind, just as she'd brought them up to be. Her parents often stayed over; having separated from her husband, she relied on them and they loved spoiling their grandchildren, always happy to stay at Carrie's house when she was at work. They lived in a little one-bedroom flat just down the road, so had no room for the children to stay. This was the first year that Carrie had allowed her parents to put the Christmas presents under the tree before Christmas morning. The children had 'crossed their hearts and hoped to die' that they wouldn't take a sneaky peek at them, and Carrie had tried to hide a grin at their little faces as they made the solemn promise.

At that moment, her thoughts were broken as the phone rang and Carrie nodded at it. 'Here we go.' She sat down to oversee Jimmy as he took the call.

'Fire service, what's the address?' Jimmy was sat upright. Being only his third shift, he still felt a flutter in his stomach with each call.

'How quickly can you get here? There's a house and it's completely on fire. I can see the flames through the windows,' the male caller said.

'Alright, sir. What's the address?' Jimmy asked, noting the panic in the caller's voice.

'It's so hot, I'm across the road and I can feel the heat from here . . . it's going up so quickly.'

'Sir, I need the address,' Jimmy pressed.

'I'm not sure. It's a house on its own – I'm across the road.'

'Which road?'

'I don't live around here.'

'Can you see the road name?'

'No. I can only see flames. There are people inside and I can see the curtains going up. It's spreading so quickly.'

'How many people are inside?'

'I can't be sure.'

'Can you see them?'

'No.'

'How do you know there are people inside?'

Silence at the end of the line.

'Sir?' Are you still there?' Jimmy asked, looking to Carrie who could only hear his side of the conversation and was contacting the GPO in an attempt to trace the call. This could take several minutes and Jimmy, under pressure, asked again. 'Sir?'

'There are children inside the house, but they won't be able to get out. Is there someone on the way?' the caller asked.

'I need the address and then we'll have engines coming. Please try to get me the address.' Jimmy tried to remain calm.

'Wait. I'm trying to see.'

'Can you describe the area to me?' Jimmy said, feeling as anxious as the caller sounded.

'It's a little house at the end of the road, it's on its own. The whole place is going up in flames.'

Jimmy suddenly felt out of his depth and looked to Carrie again. She took over the call.

'Sir, can you please give me the address where the fire is?' she asked, calmly and in total control, her experience evident in the way she spoke.

Then the caller did something she wasn't expecting. He suddenly burst out laughing loudly down the phone and Carrie's shoulders dropped. She mouthed to Jimmy, 'Hoax.'

The caller continued laughing hysterically, but even though Carrie had experienced hoax calls during her career, she knew to stay on the line. Listening.

Just then, another colleague at the back of the office raised her hand, indicating to Carrie that further calls were coming in. Although she couldn't immediately be sure they were about the same fire, she suddenly realised this call might *not* be a hoax. Carrie nodded at her colleague, still listening to the laughing man at the end of the line.

Then, abruptly the laughter ceased, and the call went silent for a moment. Carrie could hear him breathing heavily. And then he spoke.

'Send the fire engines . . . now,' he said slowly as an eeriness crept into his voice.

'Send them *where?*' Carrie asked.

There was a long silence before the caller said, deeply and calmly, 'To *your* house, Carrie Penhaligan. Send them to *your* house.'

CHAPTER 1

Present day
Saturday 8 January 2011
Liverpool

Detective Inspector Sheridan Holler was marching through Liverpool One shopping centre, a woman on a mission. She'd decided to sneak out of the office for twenty minutes and try to find a present for her colleague, Detective Sergeant Anna Markinson, whose birthday was looming.

The area was buzzing with shoppers hungrily snapping up bargains in the sales. Leftovers from Christmas. Some shops still had 'Happy New Year' banners draped in windows, and the remnants of Christmas decorations were visible everywhere. People were rushing, wrapped in scarves and hats to combat the chill in the air. Sheridan loved Liverpool in all its quirkiness. The guy selling Liverpool Football Club merchandise to foreign visitors, eager to take home a memento from their stay. Scouse women talking loudly to each other as they headed in and out of shops. The smell of coffee and warm doughnuts lingering in the air. It was *her* city. Her city to love and protect.

As she passed a sandwich shop, she spotted a homeless woman sitting outside, watching people. A tatty cardboard plaque was propped up against the window next to her, and Sheridan did a double take when the wording caught her eye.

HOMELESS AND HUNGRY. PLEASE GIVE GENEROUSLY. DON'T LIKE HARD ONS. SOFT PLEASE.

A little confused about the message, Sheridan approached the woman and slowly crouched down to her level. 'Hello.' She smiled.

'Hiya,' the woman replied, eyeing Sheridan sheepishly.

'Your sign.' Sheridan hesitated. 'It's a bit . . . misleading.'

The woman squinted at it. 'Why? What does it say?' Her crackly voice was drenched in a thick Scouse accent.

'You don't know what it says? Who wrote it for you?' Sheridan heard laughter nearby and turned to see two young lads with their phones out, about to take a picture.

She stood up and stepped over to them. 'Put them away, lads.'

'Who are you? The phone police?' one of them asked, looking at his mate, who was still laughing.

'No. I'm the *police* police.' She didn't bother showing her warrant card.

As the two lads looked her up and down, Sheridan simply crossed her arms defiantly. She had "copper" written all over her.

'Come on.' One of the lads quickly tugged on his mate's arm, before they wisely scurried away. Once they were a safe distance from Sheridan they looked back and laughed loudly, disappearing into a mobile phone shop.

Sheridan turned her attention back to the woman, who seemed oblivious as to what had just happened. She picked up the cardboard sign, keeping her voice low. 'Who made this sign for you?'

'Me mate. Can't remember his name. Funny fella, smelt of cheese. He used to have this spot before I took it over. He wasn't very happy at first, but he got over it and made me that sign. Haven't seen him for a while.'

Sheridan folded the sign in half. 'What did you ask him to write on it?'

The woman pinched her face into a frown. 'Homeless and hungry. And that I can't eat hard food. Got no teeth, you see?' She stuck a finger into her own mouth and wiped it along her gums. 'They fell out.' She gave a gummy smile.

Sheridan stood up. 'What sort of food *can* you eat?'

'Soup. I like soup. Soup and soft bread.'

Sheridan smiled. 'I'll be back shortly.'

Ten minutes later, she reappeared. After salvaging a cardboard box from a nearby shop, she'd written the woman a new sign.

HOMELESS AND HUNGRY. I ONLY ASK FOR SOUP AND BREAD. THANK YOU SO MUCH FOR TAKING THE TIME TO READ MY SIGN.

Sheridan read the words to the woman. 'Is that okay?' she asked, placing the sign next to her.

'Soft bread. I need soft bread,' she said.

Sheridan put her hands on her hips and grinned. 'All bread is soft, just take the crusts off and feed them to the pigeons.'

'You're a sweetheart.'

'You take care.' Sheridan checked her watch and headed back to Hale Street nick.

CHAPTER 2

Sheridan poked her head around the door to CID, checking that Detective Sergeant Anna Markinson wasn't walking up the corridor.

Having helped out the homeless lady, she'd run out of time to buy a present for Anna's birthday. And with literally no idea what to get her, she knew she'd have to scour the shops to find the perfect gift, so she was going to have to wait for another opportunity. But she did at least have a card, and had given the team strict instructions to write totally inappropriate comments in it.

Spotting DCI Hill Knowles coming out of her office, Sheridan beckoned her over.

'Have you heard?' Hill asked abruptly. Which wasn't unusual. Hill was always abrupt.

Sheridan ushered her into the CID office. 'Have I heard what?' she asked, and before Hill had a chance to reply, she produced the card.

'Can you write something in Anna's birthday card? Try to be funny. I know that might be hard for you, Hill . . . but . . .' Sheridan stopped talking, noticing the deep and familiar frown on her face. Hill frowned a lot.

'I didn't know it was Anna's birthday,' Hill responded with a confused look. 'Anyway, we've got a job come in.'

At that moment Anna walked in, and Sheridan threw the card at DC Rob Wills, who scurried it away in his desk drawer.

'Morning everyone,' Anna said cheerfully.

'Happy birthday,' Hill said flatly. Then, more animatedly: 'Right, listen up everyone.' Hill looked around the room, ensuring she had everyone's attention, and then caught Anna's confused expression.

'What?' Hill snapped.

'It's . . . not my birthday,' Anna said.

Sheridan raised a finger. 'Sorry, I meant to say . . . it's not Anna's birthday for another nine days.'

Anna tilted her head to one side. 'You're not all organising a surprise for me, are you?' She smiled broadly. 'I mean it's very sweet of you, but you don't need to make a fuss—'

'Jesus fucking Christ.' Hill's hands were on her hips. 'Did anyone hear me? We've got a job come in and it's all very jolly that you're planning some big birthday surprise for Anna, but can we—'

Sheridan interjected, 'We're not planning a big surprise.' She grimaced at Anna. 'Sorry mate, there's been some confusion, we're—'

'Oh, for fuck's sake. That's enough. Everyone shut up about this non-birthday bullshit.' Hill exhaled.

'Sorry, Hill. Right, what's the job?' Sheridan folded her arms and gave Hill her full attention, as did the whole team.

Hill made her way to the front of the room. 'Last night at 20.30 hours an elderly male was murdered on Buck's Road, in Liverpool. He'd just left the Buckstop Café along the street, and was approached from behind by the suspect, who appears to be a male dressed in dark clothing. As the suspect reaches him, he pulls the victim's head back and slashes his throat, before fleeing the scene. There's a seal on the area, which is currently being searched for any sign of the weapon, including at the back of the café where the bins are. Nothing found so far, but they'll keep us posted.'

'His throat was slashed?' Sheridan asked.

'Yes,' Hill replied.

'Jesus. Do we know who the victim is?'

'Possibly a male by the name of Dennis Canning. He had a bank card in his wallet with that name on it. No other ID.'

Hill went on to tell the team that the incident had been captured on CCTV and two witnesses, a young couple, had seen the attack, albeit from a distance, and had remained with the victim after the suspect fled the scene. By the brief description and the CCTV footage, the suspect looked more likely to be male. The young couple couldn't see his face as he was wearing what appeared to be a balaclava, so it was unknown if the suspect was black or white, and there was no indication of his approximate age. He was wearing a dark top and tracksuit bottoms, and was of medium build. The couple saw the suspect run back towards the café and disappear around a corner, but the CCTV coverage ended there. So far, no other images of him had been located.

Hill checked her notes. 'The last-known address for Dennis Canning is a flat about half a mile from the café. The key the victim had on his person fitted the lock, and officers attended with CSI. There was no one there, and the place was searched and sealed off. Nothing of relevance was found. In fact, the place was practically empty. A few bits of furniture and some personal belongings, but nothing to suggest anything happened there before the attack.' Hill paused. 'House-to-house enquiries were carried out and neighbours said that they knew an elderly man lived in the flat, but he never spoke. There's still some outstanding addresses to visit, so we'll see what comes of that. We're also checking CCTV from Canning's flat to the café from the last few weeks, just to see if he meets anyone or anyone's following him.'

'What about local patrols? We need to reassure the public that we've got boots on the ground,' Sheridan said.

'That's been organised. There's a uniform presence patrolling the area.'

'Do we think it's a robbery?' Anna asked.

'We don't know yet. The victim's wallet wasn't taken. The CCTV recording is being sent to me now,' Hill said. 'There were some checks done on the name, Dennis Canning, and there's a possible match on PNC. If it *is* him, then he was sentenced to life imprisonment in 1975 for murder. He set fire to a house where an elderly couple and two young girls died. He was released from prison two years ago, after serving a thirty-four-year sentence, and he's on life licence. I know we need to confirm it's him first, but I think we should speak to Probation sooner rather than later.'

Having viewed the CCTV of the incident, the team were allocated their tasks. Although they couldn't be absolutely certain that the victim *was* Dennis Canning, Sheridan agreed with Hill that it was highly likely, and they could get ahead of the game if they started looking into his background.

Sheridan was in her office when Anna walked in. 'Rob's trying to get hold of Dennis Canning's probation officer. It's a bit tricky though because Probation's closed today.' Anna sat opposite Sheridan. 'So, what are your thoughts? Do you think this was a pre-planned killing or an attempted robbery?'

Sheridan sat back. 'I'm keeping an open mind. It could be either. From the CCTV it looks like the suspect said something to the victim before he slashed him. Maybe the suspect told him to hand over his wallet and the victim said no. But, saying that, to kill him in that way was like an execution, so I wouldn't discount revenge. Hill's liaised with the press office and they're going to release an image of the suspect. Not that you can see his face.'

Anna put her hands behind her head. 'I'm going to do what *you* do. I'm going to think like Sheridan Holler and tell you *my* theory.'

'Go for it.' Sheridan grinned and settled back in her seat.

'Okay. So, if the victim *is* Dennis Canning – which I think we can safely say it is – I think it's *definitely* revenge.' Anna dipped her head once, indicating she'd said her piece.

'Is that it, or . . . ?' Sheridan said.

'Yep. That's it. It's revenge, not robbery.'

'Well, if that's the case, then someone has waited a very long time to kill him.' Sheridan raised her eyebrows.

'Yeah, but let's face it. Wouldn't *you*? Say it was Sam, what would you do if someone even laid a finger on her, let alone set fire to your house and killed her. How long would *you* wait? And what would you do to them if you had the opportunity to be alone with them?'

'I probably wouldn't slash their throat, too messy. But I would find them and . . . well. Anyway, let's change the subject. I can't think about anyone hurting Sam.' Sheridan looked at Anna. 'Or you for that matter. Or my mum and dad. Or Maud.' Sheridan shook the awful thought away, just as DC Rob Wills appeared at the door.

'I can't get hold of anyone in Probation, it'll have to wait until Monday,' he said.

Sheridan nodded. 'Okay, well, we should know by then if the victim really is Dennis Canning.'

CHAPTER 3

Anna was at the water cooler in CID, when Hill walked in, eating a packet of crisps for her breakfast.

Sheridan was sitting next to Rob, amused, listening as he and Dipesh were debating whose team was going to win the Liverpool versus Everton derby the following Sunday. Dipesh, being an avid Everton fan, was trying to entice Rob into a wager that Everton would slaughter Rob's beloved Liverpool, six–nil. The bet had started at a tenner and was gradually increasing when Hill butted in.

'I don't know a lot about football, but I do know that six–nil is an unlikely score. So, if you two buffoons want to keep upping the bet, I'll stick fifty quid on a two–two draw.'

Dipesh and Rob looked at each other, stunned that Hill would even contemplate betting on a game she knew little about.

'I'm going for three–nil Liverpool,' Rob said, opening his desk drawer and pulling out a notepad, scribbling down the bets.

DC Bridie Sexton sidled over, peering over Rob's shoulder. 'Can I put a bet on Liverpool winning one–nil?'

More stunned looks from Rob and Dipesh. Bridie was a long-standing DC on their team, quiet, diligent, and unassuming.

She'd never talked about football and certainly didn't seem the betting type.

'You sure?' Rob asked, his pen poised on the notepad.

'Yeah. I think Pepe Reina is on good form at the moment, Everton won't get a ball past him.' Bridie smiled, then nodded at the pad. 'Stick me down for fifty quid as well.'

Rob looked at her open-mouthed, before shrugging and noting her bet.

One by one, the team called out their predictions, oblivious to the fact that Hill's mobile was ringing. She answered it, walking over to the window, looking out at the Albert Dock.

A moment later, she turned to face the team who were listening to Bridie at the whiteboard trying to explain the offside rule to Anna, who looked completely confused, her face screwed up as Bridie drew little players all lined up.

Hill finished her call, then said loudly over the team's chatter, 'Alright, everyone. We've got a positive ID on the victim. It's definitely Dennis Canning.'

◆ ◆ ◆

Sheridan was at her desk, re-reading the initial details on the murder of Canning.

She read the statement from the Buckstop Café owner, Azriel Cass, taken on the night of the killing. Azriel stated that the man – whose name she didn't know – was a regular. He had first started coming into the café around a year earlier and went in most evenings, always sitting by the window, making his cup of tea last until closing time. She had tried talking to him, asking general questions, but he rarely spoke and certainly didn't want to engage in conversation. He was always alone and always paid cash. Azriel couldn't remember anyone ever joining him. She knew nothing else about him.

On Friday the 7th of January, the night of his death, he had entered the café at around 7.45 p.m., ordered his cup of tea and sat by the window. He behaved no differently than usual. He was alone the whole time, staring outside on to the dark street.

Just after the man arrived, Azriel's member of staff, Milo Adams, asked if he could go home as he felt unwell. Azriel started clearing up as the café closed at 8.30 p.m. Just before then, the man got up and left without a word, which again was not unusual.

A few moments later, Azriel became aware of something happening down the street as people started running past her window. She made her way to where a small crowd of around four or five people were gathered and spotted a male on the floor covered in blood, with a horrific wound to his neck. A young man, who appeared to be with his girlfriend, who was distraught, was on his mobile, calling for an ambulance. An elderly couple joined them and tried to calm the young woman down. Azriel remained on the scene in case police wanted to speak to her.

Azriel supplied police with a contact number for her employee, Milo, but the number was answered by a woman who had never heard of him. Sheridan made a note to check up on this.

She then read the statements from the four members of public who were there after the incident.

The elderly man and his wife had not seen the incident, but were aware of the young couple running and shouting and so went to see what had got them so worked up. They followed them and saw the male victim on the floor. They did not see the suspect, but remained with the victim. Neither of them touched him but both stated they knew he was very likely deceased. They stayed at the scene purely to console the young couple. The young woman was in extreme distress at the sight of the victim's injury.

The young couple had given statements. They had come around the corner and seen someone grabbing the victim from behind, and a few seconds later, they saw the victim fall to the floor. They described the suspect as male, medium build, dressed in dark clothing, wearing a cover over his face and head, possibly a balaclava. As they approached, the male turned and ran, heading towards the back of the café. They had not seen the suspect before the attack and did not follow him. Neither of them knew the identity of the victim.

The young female witness was treated for shock at the scene.

Sheridan stretched her back and flicked to the medical reports.

The ambulance had attended at 8.36 p.m., and paramedics confirmed the victim was already deceased. He was transported to the Royal Liverpool Hospital. Police were in attendance and the victim's clothing was seized and searched. In his pockets was a wallet containing only a bank card in the name of Dennis Canning. There was some loose change in his trouser pockets, amounting to two pounds and forty pence. He wore no jewellery, had no piercings or tattoos. He did not have a mobile phone. A house key on a key ring was found in his pocket.

The area around and behind the café was searched. There was a large refuse bin belonging to the café, which only contained one bag of rubbish as the bin had been collected that morning. House-to-house enquiries had been carried out, although the area mainly consisted of small firms which had closed for the day, and a short row of terraced houses that did not look out on to the area.

There was no CCTV in the café.

The seal around the area was lifted the next day, the 8th of January.

After they found no one present at Canning's flat, a seal was placed on the property as a precaution until it could be confirmed that the victim *was* Canning.

Sheridan looked up as Anna walked into her office. 'Rob's with Dennis Canning's probation officer now, so we should know more about him soon,' Anna said, perching herself on the edge of Sheridan's desk.

'Good,' Sheridan said. 'Have you read the file?'

'Yeah. I think it's definitely a revenge killing. Probably a family member,' Anna said emphatically.

Sheridan nodded. 'You could be right, but I don't want to discount an attempted robbery or even a random attack,' she said, taking a sip of her coffee and spitting it back into the mug, as it had gone cold an hour earlier.

'Nice,' Anna commented, screwing up her nose. 'I'm struggling with the robbery theory. The suspect cuts Dennis's throat too quickly. If it was a robbery, he'd at least make a demand and looking at the CCTV, I don't think he had time to say anything. He grabs Dennis, pulls his head back and a moment later, he slashes him.'

Rob Wills appeared in the doorway. 'Sorry to bother you. I've got some information from Dennis Canning's probation officer.'

'Great,' Sheridan said. 'We'll come through and you can update the team.' She followed Anna and Rob into CID.

CHAPTER 4

Sheridan and Anna stood in front of their assembled team in the CID office, with Rob beside them. Hill was sat at the back of the room, her arms crossed, chair tilted back.

'Okay, listen up,' Sheridan said. 'Rob has spoken to Dennis Canning's probation officer.' She pointed to Rob, and he addressed the room.

'Canning, as we know, was released from prison two years ago. Now, the details I've got so far of the arson attack that killed four occupants of the house are a bit scant, because it goes back to 1974 and a lot of Probation's records have been redacted. But his probation officer has given me *some* background into the case.'

Rob went on to tell the team that Dennis Canning had been in a relationship with a female called Carrie Penhaligan in the early 1970s. Carrie had two children from a previous relationship, a son called Bradley, and a daughter named Elizabeth. At the time of the fire, Bradley had been nine years old, and Elizabeth, six.

Bradley had survived the fire, but Elizabeth and her grandparents – Carrie's mother and father, who were looking after the children at the time – all perished.

Carrie had been a senior control operator in the fire service, based in Liverpool, and was on duty on the night of the fire. Two days before Christmas, 1974.

She had ended her relationship with Dennis Canning two years earlier in 1972 and was in a relationship with a local fireman called Vincent Royce. Vincent was also on duty on the night of the fire. His seven-year-old daughter, Melody, from a previous marriage, had been sleeping over at Carrie's house that night. She also perished in the fire.

The incident sent shock waves through the local community, further fuelled by the fact that the perpetrator, Dennis Canning, made the 999 call himself from a nearby public telephone, after setting the house alight by pouring petrol through the letter box. The fact that Carrie lost her parents and daughter, with only her son surviving, was tragedy enough, but it was even more tragic that Vincent Royce attended the address and was part of the firefighting team that tried to save his own daughter.

After making the call, Dennis Canning had remained at the scene and was there to watch Vincent as he collapsed on the front lawn when the bodies of the deceased were eventually recovered.

Carrie was taken to the hospital by police, where she was reunited with Bradley. He was treated for shock and smoke inhalation, having escaped the fire through an open back door.

Rob read from his notes. 'Now that we've confirmed the victim in our recent murder is in fact Dennis Canning, his probation officer will provide us with a Death Under Supervision report. This will tell us that Canning has been doing well since his release and was complying with his licence conditions. He has no drink or drug issues and hasn't reported any concerns about his own safety.'

'Does Canning have any family?' Sheridan asked.

'No. He's a bit of a loner as well. He'd never mentioned making any friends since his release.'

'Okay, anything else?'

'Only that Canning was hated in prison and spent a lot of it in segregation. No one likes a child killer and if it was someone looking for revenge, then there are plenty of inmates who would be on the list of suspects.'

Anna spoke. 'I know it could be an inmate, but I have to say, if it's revenge, it's more likely to be a family member.'

Sheridan turned to Rob. 'Were the family made aware of Canning's release?'

Rob shook his head. 'No. They weren't told. He wasn't deemed high risk when he was released, so there was no MAPPA meeting.'

'Okay, Bridie, can you speak to the prison intel unit and start looking at anyone who was in prison with Canning, who's since been released,' Sheridan said.

'Sure,' Bridie replied with a nod.

Sheridan spoke her thoughts aloud. 'If it is someone in the family that's got to him, then they found out about his release somehow. And if it wasn't one of them, they could have paid someone to carry out the killing.' She turned to Rob. 'I want you and Dipesh to locate the family, see what we can find out about them. When you've got their details, speak to the financial investigation team and let's get the family's bank accounts checked. You never know, something might come up to show they paid someone. Dennis Canning didn't have a mobile on him and there wasn't one in his flat. There is a landline, so let's get that checked out to see who he might have had contact with before he died. Anna and I will go and see Azriel Cass, the café owner, see if she can tell us any more about Dennis and we'll check the contact number for the member of staff who left early that night, Milo Adams.'

Hill said, 'CSI and a search team have already started working through Canning's flat.'

'Good,' Sheridan said. 'I'll go out there with Anna after we've been to see Azriel.' She nodded to the rest of her team. 'Right, everyone, let's crack on.'

CHAPTER 5

Azriel Cass ended the call from Sheridan Holler and peered around the door to check on her member of staff, who was busy serving customers. Usually, the café wasn't particularly busy on a Monday, but since the murder a few days earlier, the locals had been flocking to ask her all sorts of macabre questions as they ordered their cups of tea or coffee.

She made her way into the back room and dialled a number she knew off by heart.

'Hello?' said the voice on the other end.

'It's Azriel. Okay. Listen to me, Milo. Just listen *really* carefully. The police are on their way to the café to speak to me about what happened the other night.'

'But they've already talked to you.'

'I know, but they want to talk to me again. *Please* just listen. You know I gave them the wrong mobile number for you? Well, when they rang it, some woman answered saying she didn't know you, so they're probably going to ask me again for your number. I'm going to have to give it to them, or they're going to find it suspicious.' Azriel took a breath, her chest fluttering as she spoke. 'So, don't answer your phone unless it's from a number you recognise . . . and you need to stay put. And do *not* come to the café, Milo. I can't protect you if you don't do as I say.'

There was a silence at the other end of the line.

'Milo?'

'Yes. I understand. What if they come to the flat?'

'I don't think they'll need to. Don't worry, I'll tell them you've moved recently, and I don't know where you live.'

'Okay. So, what now?'

'Just sit tight.'

'Okay. Thank you, Azriel.'

'And remember to do the accent, like we practised.'

'I will.'

Sheridan pushed the door open to the Buckstop Café and held it open for Anna. The place was packed, with every seat taken and customers lined up in the aisle.

Sheridan spotted a young lad behind the counter, his face flushed as a large tea urn plumed out steam while he hurriedly served the waiting public.

Just then, an older woman appeared behind the counter, her face also flushed red, and she quickly wiped her hands down her apron. She looked up as Sheridan and Anna squeezed themselves past the queue and approached her.

'Azriel?' Sheridan asked, leaving her warrant card in her pocket.

'Yes . . . are you DI Holler?' she said quietly.

Sheridan nodded and Azriel lifted the countertop and ushered Sheridan and Anna into a back room.

'Busy place this,' Sheridan commented as Azriel pulled two chairs from behind the door and positioned them in front of a tiny desk covered in paperwork.

'It's not usually like this. It seems like the locals want to get a glimpse of the café that man was in before he was killed. Some sort of morbid fascination, I suppose.' She took a breath, and they all sat.

'This is my colleague, DS Markinson.' Sheridan introduced Anna and Azriel smiled at her.

'Firstly, we want to check on how you're doing. It must have been a terrible thing to have witnessed.' Sheridan rested her notebook on her lap.

'It was quite a shock if I'm honest, but I'm alright, thanks.' Azriel licked her lips and swallowed.

'Good.' Sheridan nodded once. 'Azriel, I know you've already given a statement to the police, but has anything else come to mind since then?'

Azriel shook her head. 'No. Nothing at all. I'm sorry.'

'It's fine. I take it the lad behind the counter is Milo Adams? We'd like to speak to him.'

'No. That's not Milo – he's just a temp. Only started today.'

'Was it just you and Milo that were here on Friday?' Sheridan said.

'Yes.'

'So, is it his day off today?'

'He only works a few hours here and there, he hasn't been here long and only comes in if I need an extra pair of hands.'

'But you're pretty busy today. How come he's not in?'

'He went home poorly on Friday and he's not due back in until next Friday.'

'We need to contact him. The number you gave my colleagues appears to be wrong.' Sheridan poised her pen.

'Oh. Hold on a minute.' Azriel pulled open a drawer in her desk and rifled through it. 'Sorry, I'm not very organised.' She produced a small, battered notepad and flicked through it.

'Here.' Azriel pointed to a phone number.

Sheridan wrote it down and checked it against the number Azriel had previously provided. 'There's one digit different, so that explains that.' She smiled. 'Don't you keep his number in your phone?'

'No, I'm not very good at putting contacts into my phone, I'm not very techie. I know how to make calls and text people, but anything more than that and my head goes to porridge.' She chuckled.

'Where does Milo live? Is he local?' Anna asked.

Azriel put the notepad back in the drawer. 'I actually don't know his new address. He only moved a few days ago and hasn't given it to me yet.'

'When you say a few days ago . . . when exactly did he move?'

Azriel lowered her head, looking at the floor. 'I think it was . . . possibly Saturday. He moves a lot, you know, sofa surfing.' She paused. 'He's looking for a flat.'

Sheridan nodded slowly. 'Okay. But I need the address he was staying at the night of the attack. You said he went home sick, so where did he go?'

Azriel hesitated before answering. 'I have to be honest, I don't know. Look, I pay him cash and he gets a free dinner. He's a good lad and I've kind of taken him under my wing.'

'Okay. Well, we'll give him a call.'

'Can I ask, why do you need to speak to him?' Azriel said, adding, 'He wouldn't have seen anything, he'd already left before the man was attacked.'

'We just need to ask if he saw anyone hanging around. Have you spoken to him since he left on Friday?'

'No.'

'You didn't call him to tell him what happened?'

'Oh, yes, I tried calling him but there was no reply, and I didn't want to leave a message, especially because of what the message would have been about . . .' Her voice trailed off.

'Are you okay?' Sheridan asked, leaning forward slightly.

Azriel wiped a hand across her forehead. 'Yes. I just think I'm still in shock. I'm sorry.'

'It's fine. We understand,' Sheridan said. 'It's a horrible thing for you to get your head around. Don't worry. We'll give Milo a call on this number.'

Azriel smiled. 'Okay.'

Sheridan readjusted her position. 'In your statement you said that the victim hardly ever spoke to you, and you didn't know anything about him.'

'Yes, that's right. He's been coming in for about a year. Not every day, but most days. He always orders a cup of tea and sits by the window. Always alone, and even when I tried to chat with him, he was never interested in talking. I didn't even get to know his name.' She looked between Sheridan and Anna. 'Do you know who he is?'

'Yes. He's been identified. There'll be a press release in the next day or so and then we'll be releasing his name,' Sheridan said.

'Of course, I understand.' Azriel looked down. 'He always seemed so sad. I often wondered what his story was. I hate seeing people on their own, or struggling; I like to help people if I can. Having the café is a way that I can do that. We have quite a few regulars and they come in for a cuppa and a chat, or just to get warm. It's a little sanctuary for them. But he was different; he looked like he had the weight of the world on his shoulders. And then he gets killed like that. It's so sad. That poor man, what a terrible way to go.' Her voice broke slightly as she spoke.

Sheridan stole a quick look at Anna. Dennis Canning may have been the victim of a brutal slaying, but he wasn't the sad old man Azriel had described. He was a killer. A killer who had set a house on fire and then relished in the aftermath, staying at the scene and watching as the flames took innocent lives with them.

There was a tap at the door, and the temp poked his head round. 'Sorry, but we've run out of cups.'

'Use the takeaway ones under the counter, love,' Azriel replied.

Sheridan stood up. 'We should go. Thanks, Azriel. If we need anything else, we'll let you know.' She handed her a card. 'My number's on there. Call me anytime if you think of anything else.'

Azriel took the card. 'I will.'

She showed Sheridan and Anna out, then watched as they walked along the road.

As soon as the two police officers were out of sight, she returned to the back room and called Milo.

'Hello?' he answered.

'It's only me. Right, I think you're okay. The police just want to ask you if you saw anyone hanging around when you left here early on Friday. So, you *can* answer your phone. I think it will look suspicious if you avoid them. I told them I haven't spoken to you since you left here on Friday.'

'Did they say anything about coming to the flat?'

'No. But if they ask where you're living . . . tell them you're sleeping on a mate's sofa. And if they need to see you, meet them somewhere . . . but not here in the café. I told them you've only worked here a few weeks, and I don't want one of the regulars to give it away that you've been here a lot longer. I said that you work a few hours here and there.'

He sighed heavily down the phone. 'Alright. So, I'll answer my phone and tell them the same thing you told them?'

'Yes.'

'We're not going to get caught, are we?'

'No. We're not.' Azriel hesitated. 'I'll do everything I can to protect you. But you have to lay low now and do as I say. You've done what they paid you to do and now it's over. We just have to wait until things settle down with the police.' She took a breath. 'Stay away from them now, Milo. Promise me.'

'I promise.'

'Good. Okay, look, I'd better go. Don't worry, it'll be okay.' Azriel ended the call, planted a smile on her face, and went back into the café.

CHAPTER 6

'Azriel seems sweet, doesn't she?' Anna said as they stood at the spot where Dennis Canning had been attacked.

'Yeah,' Sheridan replied vaguely.

'What's up?' Anna asked.

'Did you notice her face go red when she was talking about Milo?'

'Yeah,' Anna said, 'but I figured she was just getting jittery because she thought we were going to question her about paying him cash in hand. Maybe she was worried that we were going to check out his tax status?'

Sheridan looked back towards the café. 'Maybe.'

'You think she's dodgy?'

'I don't know. Possibly.'

'You really do suspect everyone, don't you?' Anna shook her head. Sheridan didn't respond and Anna looked at her. 'What's up?'

'Nothing, I'm just taking it all in.' She smiled at Anna. 'You know me.'

Anna smiled back. She *did* know Sheridan, especially how her mind operated. In every case they had worked on, Anna had watched as Sheridan attended each scene, and was able to somehow put herself there as both the victim and the perpetrator. It was like she was standing in the middle of a crime, watching as it unravelled before her while she observed, silent and invisible.

Her perception was like no one else's that Anna had ever known, and it was one of the reasons why she loved working with Sheridan so much – her insights were always unusual, and generally able to help them get to the heart of any case.

Anna was a good detective in her own right, too. She had been tempted to take the inspector's exam more than a few times in the past, but had binned the idea because working with Sheridan was more important to her than being promoted.

And now, as she watched Sheridan, she didn't speak, letting her do her thing. A moment later, Sheridan gently tugged her arm. 'Come on, let's walk the route the attacker took when he legged it.'

They walked side by side, slowly and purposefully, and as they came to the side of the café, where the suspect had run after killing Dennis Canning, Sheridan stopped again.

'It's very narrow down here,' she commented as they reached the rear of the café, where there was a large green commercial bin on wheels. She lifted the heavy lid and stood on tiptoe, trying to see inside, before letting the lid drop back down.

'What are you looking for?' Anna asked. 'Are you thinking that he could have hidden in the bin after the attack?'

'Possibly. But I think he more likely ran through here. The area was sealed off pretty quickly that night and the bin was checked, so he wouldn't have wanted to be anywhere nearby.'

Sheridan turned and walked towards an open archway built into a brick wall.

'He must have run through here, it's the only way out,' she commented as they walked under the archway in single file. As they came out on the other side, they found themselves in a narrow maze of alleyways, all leading in different directions.

'This is how he disappeared off camera and managed to get away.' She sighed. 'He knows this area well.'

After checking out several potential escape routes, they headed back to the car, both realising they were no further forward as they were still unable to ascertain where the suspect had run to after the attack.

◆ ◆ ◆

Sheridan handed Anna the car keys and climbed into the passenger seat. Taking out her mobile, she dialled Milo Adams' number.

'Hello?'

'Oh, hi, is that Milo?'

'Yes.'

'Milo, I'm sorry to bother you. My name's Detective Inspector Sheridan Holler from Hale Street CID, it's nothing at all to worry about but have you got a second?'

'Yes.'

Sheridan explained that they were investigating the killing of a regular customer to the café. She gave brief details of the time and date it had happened and asked him if, after he left work feeling ill the previous Friday, he had seen anyone hanging around.

Milo told her that he hadn't seen anyone. He'd just walked straight to the bus stop and gone home.

Sheridan asked where he lived at the time and he explained he'd been staying at a friend's house, a couple of miles from the café. She pressed him for the address, which he gave to her.

He confirmed Azriel's account that he had only worked at the café for a couple of weeks. Sheridan described the victim and asked if Milo remembered him coming into the café that evening or any previous evening. Milo claimed he had only seen the man a couple of times before, and confirmed what Azriel had already said, that he had been coming to the café for about a year and she had never seen him talk to anyone. Milo told Sheridan that Azriel had felt sorry for him, as he had seemed lonely and sad.

Sheridan put him on loudspeaker, so Anna could hear Milo's thick and overdone Scouse accent.

'Have you ever seen anyone hanging around the back of the café?' Sheridan asked. 'Or acting suspiciously nearby?'

'No,' Milo replied.

'What's your date of birth? Just for our records.'

He gave her the details.

'Okay, thank you. Well, you've got my number now, so please call me if anything comes to mind.'

'I will.' He hesitated. 'So, is that it? Or will you need to speak to me again?'

'I don't think so, unless anything else comes to light. Azriel said you've just moved, what's your new address?'

'I haven't actually got a proper address at the moment, I'm just staying on a friend's sofa for a couple of nights, until I find a flat. I'll let you know the address once I've found somewhere if that's okay.'

'Sure. And if you change your mobile number, can you let me know?'

'Yes.'

'You've got a very thick Scouse accent,' Sheridan said. 'Are you from Liverpool?'

He paused before answering. 'My family are Greek. I've always loved Liverpool, and I try to sound Scouse. I guess I'm overdoing it.'

Sheridan smiled, a little charmed by Milo's comment. 'Not at all. Anyway, thanks again, Milo.'

She ended the call and Anna pulled away, heading back to Hale Street.

'Bless him. Trying to sound more Scouse,' Anna said, chuckling.

'I'll get him run through PNC and see if Rob can confirm his account that he left work and went straight home.'

'You suspect him?'

'I suspect everyone.' Sheridan grinned. 'He left the café early, so we need to be sure he did go home and didn't hang around to kill Canning.'

'Jesus Sheridan, what motive would he have had?'

'I don't know.'

'It's a family member, I'm telling you. One hundred per cent. You can't suspect Milo, surely.'

'Okay, but if he's nothing to do with it, I'm going to nick him anyway.'

'What for?'

'Trying to impersonate a Scouser.'

CHAPTER 7

Anna parked up outside Dennis Canning's ground-floor flat, behind the crime scene investigators' van. Standing at the door was a uniformed police officer maintaining a seal on the property.

Recognising Sheridan and Anna, the officer nodded and pushed the door open.

Charlie, the senior CSI officer, smiled as he looked up to see them. 'My two favourite detectives.'

'Hi, Charlie. How's it going? Are we okay to come in?' Sheridan asked, acknowledging the officers who were searching the tiny flat.

'Yeah, please do. It's going to be a quick job, this one. The place is practically empty.'

The flat was grimly lit. Sheridan looked around the small living room and observed a single worn and battered armchair and a round wooden table, upon which sat the landline telephone. An empty bookcase stood against the wall and in the corner, on top of a box, was an old television. She noted the lack of personal items as she stepped into the kitchen, which was equally small and bare. In one cupboard were tins of beans, and a box of cereal. In the other, one plate, one bowl, a mug and a saucepan.

Sheridan snapped on a pair of latex gloves and opened the cutlery drawer. One knife, one fork, one dessert spoon and a teaspoon, along with a tin opener and two wooden spatulas. In the breadbin was half a loaf of sliced bread and next to the kettle was a box of teabags.

'Jesus,' Sheridan said, as Anna joined her. 'He literally has one of everything and it looks like he lived on beans and bread.'

She opened the fridge. A bottle of milk, butter and a packet of cheese.

They made their way to the bedroom. The bed was neatly made, and a standalone wardrobe was open, displaying three pairs of trousers hanging up, alongside four shirts and three jumpers. Two pairs of shoes were on the floor, next to the bed.

One of the search team officers was on his knees, pulling open the divan base drawer. Sheridan arched her neck to see and noted it was empty.

'There's literally nothing here,' he said as he got to his feet.

'Where else have you got to check?' Sheridan asked.

'Just the other divan drawer.'

Sheridan bent down and pulled it open. Inside was a stack of old newspapers, which she lifted out and placed on the bed.

The headline on the first newspaper read: *Family destroyed by cruel arsonist.*

She noted the papers dated back to 1974. 'These are from when he set the house on fire.'

Anna stood next to her and took the next paper from the pile. The headline read: *Killer called 999 after setting family house on fire.*

One by one, they read the articles, each one describing what Canning had done. Photographs of the burned-out house were splashed all over the front pages, alongside pictures of Canning.

Anna turned a page on one of the papers – dated 1975 – to an article reporting on Canning's court appearance. Eventually, she pointed to the piece. 'Well, well . . . Listen to this.'

'What?' Sheridan said.

Anna read the article aloud. '*Victims Carrie Penhaligan and Vincent Royce were among family members who were in court to see Dennis Canning be sentenced to life imprisonment. As Canning was led away, he was seen to smile and Vincent Royce, whose 7-year-old daughter Melody perished in the fire, tried to approach Canning from the public gallery, shouting that he would kill him if he was ever released. The distraught father was held back by police officers, repeating the threat over and over. Speaking to reporters outside the court building, Vincent Royce was still visibly upset as he described how Canning had destroyed his and Carrie's lives. When asked about the threat he had shouted at Canning, Royce said: "I told him I'd kill him, and I will if he ever gets out."*'

When she finished reading, Anna looked at Sheridan. 'I told you it was family who got to Canning.'

CHAPTER 8

Tuesday 11 January

Hill walked into CID with a face like thunder. She marched over to Sheridan, who was sat next to Rob.

'You okay, Hill?' Sheridan asked.

'Yes. Why do you ask?' Hill replied bluntly.

'You look pissed off.'

'I always look like this. Where's Anna?'

'She's in her office with Bridie, going through the list of prisoners who Canning was serving with, to see if any of them have been released.'

Hill reached out to Rob. 'Where's her birthday card?'

Rob produced Anna's card from his desk drawer and handed it to Hill, who read the inappropriate comments written inside, and allowed herself a rare smile.

She scribbled a message and handed the card back to Rob, who read it out loud. 'Happy birthday from Hill.'

Sheridan shook her head. 'I said be funny. Can you write something funny?'

'Fine.' Hill snatched the card back and scribbled another message. 'There.' She thrust the card under Sheridan's nose, who read the words aloud. 'Something funny.' She tilted her head to one side. 'I didn't mean for you to write the actual words "something funny", I meant—'

'I know what you meant,' Hill said, and grinned. 'That's me being funny.'

Sheridan stood up. 'I'm taking the team out for a meal tomorrow night, we'd love you to come.'

Hill frowned. 'No thank you.'

Sheridan sighed. The year before, after talking to some of her team – especially Rob, Dipesh and Bridie – she had realised how little she actually knew about them, even though they had worked together for some years. She knew how they worked, and that she could trust every one of them. She knew their strengths when it came to enquiries. But she knew very little about their private lives.

In the subsequent conversations she'd had with them all, she now knew Dipesh's wife collected Lego, that Bridie lived with her mother and was Catholic. She already knew Rob's wife, Jo, was deaf.

But that was pretty much it, and having chastised herself for not knowing her team as well as she should, she'd made a pact with herself to fix it. And she felt it would do Hill some good to try something similar.

'Oh, go on, Hill. It'll be nice for us all to get together, have a meal out and just . . . chat.' Sheridan noticed the expression on Hill's face. 'What?'

'That sounds fabulous, count me in,' Hill said.

'Really?' Sheridan's face lit up.

'No, Sheridan. It sounds like my idea of a nightmare,' she snapped, and then made her way to the front of the room just as Anna and Bridie walked in.

'Good timing you two,' Hill said. 'The chief wants an update, so let's have a catch-up.'

Sheridan joined her. 'You're all aware from the newspaper reports of the threats that Vincent Royce made when Canning was sentenced, so bear that in mind.' She indicated to Rob. 'What have you got, so far?'

Rob grabbed the papers on his desk and walked over to the whiteboard. 'Milo Adams is no trace on PNC. I've managed to find him on CCTV leaving the café on Friday night at 8.01 p.m.: he walks to the bus stop, and the bus turns up eleven minutes later at 8.12 p.m. I'm still working through it, but I'll see if I can locate him getting off the bus and if he's somewhere else at 8.30 p.m., when Canning is murdered, then I think we can eliminate him as a suspect.'

Sheridan flicked a look at Anna, hiding a grin, remembering Milo's terrible Scouse accent and her comment that she'd arrest him for it.

'Does Milo look like the killer? Height and build I mean,' Sheridan asked.

'Kind of.'

'Okay, let's try to establish as soon as that he definitely wasn't nearby at the time of the attack.'

Rob nodded and cleared his throat. 'We're still trying to locate the family members, but I've done a kind of family tree so that we all know who's who.' He started at the top of the whiteboard and wrote the names Carrie Penhaligan, Dennis Canning and Vincent Royce.

'I've had another conversation with Canning's probation offi-cer. A lot of the info I've got is from his meetings with Canning since his release two years ago. Luckily for us, he kept some really good, detailed notes about their meetings.' Rob cleared his throat. 'Right, so . . . Carrie Penhaligan was with Dennis Canning for a couple of years. She had two children, Bradley and Elizabeth, from a previous relationship with a man by the name of Raymond Penhaligan. Dennis moved in with Carrie and the relationship was going well, until Carrie started an affair with Vincent Royce.

Carrie and Vincent both worked at the same fire station, she was a senior controller and Vincent was a fireman. He was married with a daughter, Melody.'

Rob paused, ensuring the information was being absorbed by the team, before he continued.

'Once Canning found out about the affair, he moved out. And that's when he started planning to set the house on fire. Vincent left his wife and moved into a place of his own. His wife and him shared custody of their daughter, who happened to be staying over at Carrie's house on the night of the fire, as she had become good friends with Carrie's daughter, Elizabeth. So, on the night of the fire, Carrie was on duty in the control room and Vincent was on duty in his role as a fireman. Carrie's parents were staying for Christmas and were looking after the children.'

Rob stopped to update the names on the whiteboard. 'On the night of the fire, Canning went to the address with a washing-up liquid bottle, which he'd filled with petrol, and squirted it through the letter box, he then dropped a match and the place went up. Along the road was a phone box which, once the house was ablaze, Canning used to call 999. He never left the scene and by the time the fire brigade turned up, the house was totally engulfed in flames. So, Canning was there when Vincent Royce arrived in one of the fire engines and he watched the whole thing unfold. Apparently, when the fire was extinguished, Canning walked over to the fire truck and handed the washing-up bottle to Vincent and told him he'd set the house alight. Obviously, Vincent was distraught, knowing his daughter was inside and had to be restrained by his colleagues. Canning was arrested at the scene and made full admissions in his interview.'

'Did he ever say why he did it?' Sheridan asked. 'Was it just because Carrie had dumped him?'

'Basically, yes. Canning told his probation officer that he was angry when Carrie ended the relationship, but he pretended to her that he was fine about the break-up. He said he'd felt like he'd been part of the family and had settled in well with her kids. He was shocked when she started the affair with Vincent. He even went on to say that he was angry that he'd spent time decorating the house to make it nice for Carrie and the children, and he was delighted that the fire destroyed the place. He didn't want Carrie to live in a house that he'd worked so hard on.'

'So, Carrie's daughter, Elizabeth, died in the fire, along with her elderly parents,' Sheridan said and watched Rob as he wrote this on the whiteboard. 'I know that Canning's killer is very likely a male, but let's not rule anything out at this point.' She looked at Rob.

'Okay,' he replied.

'So, Carrie is a suspect,' Sheridan confirmed.

Rob updated the whiteboard, adding a note to reflect this.

'Vincent Royce's daughter Melody also died in the fire,' Sheridan added. 'Which makes *him* a suspect, especially due to the threats he made to Canning in court.'

Rob wrote 'suspect' next to Royce's name.

'And Bradley, Carrie's son, who survived the fire, is another suspect. He lost his grandparents and sister.' Anna directed her question to Rob. 'How old are all these people now?'

'Carrie and Vincent will be in their early to mid-sixties and Bradley will be in his forties.'

'What about Vincent's ex-wife? Her daughter died in the fire, are we looking at her too?' Hill asked.

'I guess so.' Sheridan sighed. 'And while we're at it, let's check out Carrie's ex-husband, Raymond Penhaligan. He lost his daughter in the fire.' She sighed again. 'Fucking hell, there's all of *them* and then we've got the possibility of ex-cons who hated Canning in prison.' She turned to Anna. 'How are you getting on with that?'

Anna stood up. 'So far, the prison can't find any that have been released, but they'll keep looking.' She paused. 'The other problem we have is that Canning didn't serve his whole sentence in one place, he was in four different prisons, so we need to decide how far back we go.'

'I think start with the last prison he was in, and we'll go from there.' Sheridan rubbed her temples.

Hill piped up, 'Let's hope the prisons don't throw up any other possibles – otherwise our list of suspects is going to be fucking enormous.'

The team remained silent, processing the fact that this job was going to be a complex nightmare.

A moment later, Sheridan spoke. 'I understand from the file that the back door of the house was open when the fire brigade turned up, and Canning denied that it was him who left it open. Bradley, the lad who survived, said the door was open when he came downstairs. Now, if Canning had access to the house via the back door, why did he go to the trouble of using a washing-up liquid bottle to squirt the petrol through the letter box? Why not just walk through the back door and set the house on fire that way?'

She looked at her team in turn, and Hill was the first to respond.

'Here we go. You're going to tear the original enquiry apart, aren't you.' She raised her eyebrows. 'Can we concentrate on who killed Canning before you go off on one, Sheridan?'

Sheridan pursed her lips. 'I'm just saying . . . according to Carrie's original account, the back door would have been locked by her parents when they all went to bed, without fail. Bradley said the door was open when he went downstairs, and Canning denied entering the house that way. Which means . . . one of them is lying.'

CHAPTER 9

At the end of a long day, Sheridan was ready for a glass of wine. As she drove through the Kingsway Tunnel heading home to the Wirral and her partner, Sam, a smile spread across her face. She imagined their cat Maud waiting on the window ledge until Sheridan pulled on to the drive. Her thoughts then turned to the enquiry. Having watched the recording of Canning's murder several times, she was becoming increasingly convinced that, like Anna had said, it looked like an execution. And if that was the case, then their suspect was likely to be a family member, or someone paid by one to carry out the killing.

As she turned off the engine, Sheridan could see Maud at the window, her paw pressed against the glass as Sheridan emerged from the car. She walked over and put her hand against the pane. Maud's mouth opened widely in a yawn.

Sam opened the front door and grinned. 'Hello, you.'

She kissed Sheridan gently on the lips as they stood in the hallway. Maud scurried through and wound around their feet.

Sheridan scooped Maud up and snuggled her face into the cat's fur, feeling the deep vibration from Maud's purring. 'How are my two favourite girls?' she asked as she carried Maud into the kitchen, followed by Sam.

'We're fine. And you are going to love me even more than you already do, when I show you what arrived today.' Sam opened the fridge and retrieved a bottle of wine, pouring out two glasses. Maud tapped her leg, and Sam reopened the fridge, taking out a slice of ham, sending Maud into a meowing frenzy, which only ceased when Sam rolled the slice up and Maud took it from her fingers, disappearing into the living room to devour it under the coffee table.

'How could I love you more?' Sheridan asked, sipping her wine and reaching out to pull Sam close to her. 'I already love you more than life.'

Sam looked a little puzzled. 'I . . . love you too,' she said softly. 'Are you okay? You look like you're going to cry.'

'I'm fine. It was just something Anna said the other day about what I'd do to someone if they ever hurt you.'

'You'd batter them, wouldn't you?' Sam kissed her lips.

'I'd do whatever I had to do.' She wrapped her arms around Sam and held her tightly.

'Hey,' Sam said. 'No one's going to hurt me, or anyone else, so don't even think about it.' She smiled. 'Right. First things first. How's the murder investigation going?' She rubbed Sheridan's shoulders.

'Slowly. We've got a shitload of potential suspects, which we're trying to trace, but . . . well . . . I think it's going to be a complex job.' She set her glass down. 'How was *your* day?'

'Fine,' Sam replied. Sam was a schoolteacher and although she loved her job, hearing about the cases Sheridan was working on was far more interesting than talking about what the kids in her class got up to. 'Anyway, have you managed to get Anna's birthday present yet?'

'No. And I have no idea what to buy her. I mean . . . what does she *need*?' Sheridan picked her glass back up and took a sip.

Sam put a finger in the air. 'Ah . . . maybe it's not something she *needs*, but something she doesn't even know she *wants*.' She disappeared into the living room, almost tripping over Maud who was heading back to the fridge expectantly.

A moment later, Sam emerged with a massive grin on her face. 'Check it out.' She handed Sheridan a remote-control device.

'What's this for?' Sheridan asked, inspecting it.

'This.' From behind her back, Sam produced a bright orange toy helicopter, placing it on the work surface. 'Try it.'

Sheridan looked at her. 'You bought Anna a remote-control helicopter for her birthday?'

'Yep. How cool is that?'

'What the fuck is she going to do with that?'

'Fly it. Trust me, she'll love it.' Sam beamed, taking the control unit from Sheridan. She pressed the 'on' button and moved the lever. The helicopter's rotor blades came to life, and it suddenly lifted into the air. Sam then made it change direction and Sheridan watched as the machine flew gracefully into the living room, where Sam deftly landed it on the coffee table. 'Isn't it brilliant?' she said excitedly.

Sheridan was a little stuck for words. 'It's . . . a helicopter.' She shook her head. 'Can't we just get her a bottle of bubbly or . . .'

'That's boring. Imagine the fun she'll have with this. Trust me, it's perfect.' Sam moved the controls again and the helicopter flew back into the kitchen, landing by the sink. Maud's eyes were wide like saucers as she scooted across the floor and stared up at where the helicopter had landed. Sam made it take off again and it whirred over Maud's head before Sam directed it back into the living room, flying it a bit too low. Maud had followed it and jumped into the air, bashing it with her enormous paw, bringing it crashing to the floor.

Sheridan puffed out her cheeks, placing her hands on her hips. 'You're bloody mental, do you know that?' she said.

'Do you want to try it?' Sam went to retrieve it, picking it up before Maud could smash it to pieces.

'Not right now. I don't think Maud likes it.' Sheridan laughed, pulling Sam towards her. 'It's a brilliant present. Weird, but brilliant.' She planted a kiss on Sam's cheek.

They settled on the sofa with their drinks and Sam asked about the case. 'So, you think it's a family member?'

'Possibly. It looks like a male on the CCTV and the way Canning had his throat slashed . . . I'm more inclined to think Anna's right – this was an execution.'

'Could it have just been a random attack? You know, some nutter?' Sam asked.

'Possibly . . .' Sheridan's voice trailed off, feeling Sam's comment hit home.

'You okay?'

'Yeah. I just realised that if it is random, then maybe this guy is going to strike again.' She pulled Sam close to her and laid her head on her chest. 'I love you.'

Sam kissed the top of her head. 'I love you, too . . . And I know what you're thinking. You're worried that if there is a fruitcake out there randomly slashing people's throats, then he might get *me*.'

Sheridan lifted her head. 'I wasn't thinking that.'

Sam smiled. 'Good. Because nothing bad is going to happen to me.'

'I *wasn't* thinking it. But I am *now*.' Sheridan crossed her eyes, trying to make light of the conversation. And trying to bury the thought of anyone hurting Sam.

'Let's change the subject.' Sam put her drink down and kissed Sheridan on the forehead. 'I know what will take your mind off those dark thoughts of yours.'

Sheridan lifted an eyebrow. 'Really? You . . . fancy it?'

'Absolutely. Let's do it.'

Two minutes later, they were back playing with Anna's helicopter.

CHAPTER 10

Wednesday 12 January

Sheridan walked into CID, having been called in by Rob and Dipesh. She made her way to the front of the room and called for everyone's attention.

Hill entered just as they were about to start. 'Update from Forensics: no other DNA was found on Canning.'

'Okay,' Sheridan said, before turning to Dipesh, who stood up, holding a piece of paper. Rob was at the whiteboard, ready to update the details against each suspect's name.

'Okay everyone. We've tracked down the following people.' He cleared his throat. 'Carrie Penhaligan, the mother of Elizabeth, who died in the fire, and Bradley, who survived, is now married to Vincent Royce, the fireman whose daughter, Melody, died. We've run them through PNC. Carrie's no trace, but Vincent has been arrested seven times in the last year for shoplifting. Carrie's son, Bradley is also on PNC – two arrests for criminal damage. His first arrest was six months ago and his second was the day that Canning was murdered. Bradley was booked in at Potters Road nick and we've checked the custody record, which shows that at the time Canning was murdered, Bradley was in his cell, so . . .' He turned to Sheridan. 'I think we can safely eliminate Bradley.'

Sheridan nodded and Rob updated the whiteboard with this information.

Dipesh continued. 'Carrie's ex-husband, Elizabeth and Bradley's father, died of sepsis in 1999. So, again, he's eliminated. Then we move to Vincent's ex-wife, mother to Melody, who died. We know she's very unlikely to have been the suspect on CCTV, but we checked her out anyway. She's in a nursing home in Manchester, suffering from dementia, so she's ruled out.'

'Great work, both of you.' Sheridan smiled. 'That narrows down our suspects quite nicely.'

Rob put the whiteboard pen down. 'I've been checking CCTV from when Milo Adams left the café that night. I haven't managed to see where he gets off the bus. But I know he didn't get off at the bus stop nearest to where he says he was living at the time.'

'Interesting. Okay, keep looking at it and let's see where he went that night. Cheers, Rob.'

'So . . .' Sheridan turned to the team. 'I'll go out with Anna to see Carrie and Vincent, see what they've got to say.'

Bridie Sexton raised her hand. 'Just a quick one – I'm still working through the list of prisons and prisoners that Canning was inside with. I'm not going to lie, it's going to take a while.'

'Thanks, Bridie. Keep me updated.' She turned to Anna. 'Let's go out and see Carrie and Vincent.'

Sheridan and Anna walked up the path to the Royces' house. It was a neat semi-detached property with a brick-weave drive, on which a black Mercedes was parked.

Sheridan rang the bell, and it was answered almost immediately by a woman in her sixties, her grey hair cut neatly around her thin face. She wore no make-up and was holding a tea towel.

'Can I help you?' the woman asked, looking from Sheridan to Anna.

Sheridan introduced herself and Anna and explained they were there to talk about Dennis Canning. The woman confirmed her name was Carrie Royce.

'My husband's at work at the moment, but please come in.' She showed them into the living room, and they all sat down.

Carrie still held the tea towel, and nervously wrapped it around her fist as she spoke. 'So, you want to talk about *him*, Dennis Canning, I mean. Please don't tell me he's being released.' Her head dropped momentarily, before she looked up at the picture of a young girl hanging on the wall.

Sheridan followed her gaze. She recognised the girl as Carrie's daughter, Elizabeth. Her face had appeared in the newspapers after the fire, and was now burned in Sheridan's memory.

'No, actually,' Sheridan said. 'Dennis was released two years ago.' She watched Carrie's reaction very closely. If Carrie was involved with Canning's death, she'd already know he'd been released and her reaction might give her away.

Carrie frowned. 'I . . . why weren't we told? So, he's been out for two years, and no one bothered telling us?' Her voice broke a little. 'He killed my little girl, my parents and Vincent's daughter. How *could* they let that monster out?'

Sheridan sat forward. 'You may have seen on the news that a man was attacked outside a café last Friday. He died from his injuries. We haven't released his name yet, but it was Dennis Canning.'

Carrie's face turned grey, and she swallowed. 'I see.' Her voice was barely audible.

Sheridan made a mental note that Carrie's reaction appeared too genuine not to be real.

Carrie looked past Sheridan towards the window. Sheridan turned and saw a small van parking up behind the Mercedes.

Carrie got to her feet. 'That's Vincent. I want him to hear this.'
She quickly left the room.

Sheridan heard the door open and Carrie's voice from the hall-way. 'The police are here. Something's happened to Canning.'

Vincent Royce appeared around the door. He was tall, his bald-ing head covered in dirt and his clothes equally grubby. He looked down at Sheridan, who stood and introduced herself and Anna.

'I'm Carrie's husband,' Vincent said. 'What's happened?'

Carrie sat back down, and Vincent stood behind her, placing an enormous hand gently on her shoulder. 'Don't tell me he's being released.'

Sheridan shook her head slightly. 'He was released two years ago. We know you weren't told at the time. But, last Friday, he was attacked after leaving a café and subsequently . . . died from his injuries.'

'Attacked by who?' Vincent asked, his eyes fixed on Sheridan. 'And why weren't we told he was out? He killed our children, and Carrie's parents. So, how could they have let him go?'

'He wasn't deemed high risk and so you weren't told. The probation service sometimes organises what's known as a MAPPA meeting.'

'What does that mean?'

'It's a multi-agency public protection meeting, where agencies discuss the risk someone poses to the public before they're released. Canning wasn't deemed high risk.'

'Wait,' Vincent interjected, his face flushed with anger. 'Not high risk? He set fire to Carrie's house and destroyed our lives. He watched as the whole place went up . . . you do know that, don't you?'

'Yes. We're aware of what happened and I'm . . . *so* sorry. I can't imagine what you've been through . . .'

'No. You *can't*. I had to watch as that house burned with our kids inside. Canning fucking ruined us and I'm glad he's dead. But I want to know how he was allowed two years of freedom before he died. He didn't deserve one single moment outside of a prison cell.' Vincent's voice was shaking with anger. 'He should have died behind bars.' He stared at Sheridan. 'So, who killed him, because trust me, I'd like to shake his hand.'

'We don't know yet. We've opened a murder enquiry and we're trying to locate the suspect.' Sheridan adjusted her position on the sofa. 'We're aware of the circumstances around the fire.' Her voice was drenched in sincerity.

'We've been to hell and back,' Vincent said, his chest rising and falling as he breathed deeply. 'Canning destroyed us, and he revelled in it. Am I glad he's dead? Yes.' His jaw tightened and he tilted his back as if to stop the flow of tears that streamed down his face.

Sheridan noticed Vincent's hands were shaking, but as she looked at him, he clasped them together.

She took a deep breath. 'I'm sorry, but I do need to ask you some questions and I hope you understand why. Can you think of anyone who would want Canning dead?' she asked, wondering as she did why neither Carrie nor Vincent had asked *how* Canning was killed.

'How long have you got?' Vincent spat his words out. 'He was hated by the whole community, I'm sure there's a list as long as your arm.' He wiped his sleeve down his face.

Sheridan took out her pocket notebook. 'We've got a team of detectives working on it.' She clicked her pen.

Vincent shook his head. 'I wouldn't waste your time. Canning doesn't deserve it. The only thing that man deserves is to burn in hell, and that's what I hope he's doing. Whoever did this deserves a medal.'

An uncomfortable silence followed as Sheridan allowed Vincent's fury to dissipate. Keeping her voice soft, she eventually said, 'I understand your anger, of course I do. But I won't pretend to know how you feel. However, the reality is that we *have* to investigate his killing.' Her eyes moved between the two broken people.

She knew that Carrie's son, Bradley, had been in police custody at the time Canning was murdered, but to eliminate Carrie and Vincent, she needed to know *their* whereabouts at the time.

But she didn't want to dive straight in, and so instead asked, 'How's Bradley doing?'

'He's wracked with guilt,' Carrie said. 'He never really got over the fire. They said at the time that the back door was left open, and that's why the fire spread so quickly. If the back door had been closed, the fire wouldn't have had a sudden dose of oxygen, it wouldn't have spread so quickly and everyone might have escaped.' She looked Sheridan in the eye. 'Bradley only survived because he heard a noise and came downstairs. He said that he went into the living room and the next thing he knew, the hallway and stairs were on fire. He couldn't save anyone, because the fire spread so quickly, and he was so frightened that he ran to the kitchen and saw the back door was open. Everyone assumed that he'd lied and had opened the door himself, but he swore he hadn't.' She paused. 'Then, when they did the investigation into the fire, and Canning was interviewed, he also denied going anywhere near the back door. He said he put the petrol through the letter box and lit the match, before watching the place go up. So, we never found out how the back door was opened, but Bradley swore it wasn't him.'

'Would your parents have locked the back door when they went to bed that night?' Sheridan asked.

'Yes. I'm absolutely sure they would have. And the keys were always kept in the kitchen drawer – they were still there when the fire was put out.'

'Did you change the locks when Canning moved out?'

Carrie sighed. 'No.'

'So, maybe Canning let himself in through the back door, possibly to look around the house while everyone was asleep and that's what Bradley heard. Maybe Canning then went out the back door, left it open, went to the front of the house and that's when he put the petrol through the letter box.'

'They did suggest something like that at the time. But Canning denied going near the back of the house.' Carrie clasped her hands together. 'We always wondered if he'd ever change his story and tell the truth, because I know Bradley wouldn't have lied. I know my own son, and he's not a liar.'

She talked openly about the fire and how all the neighbours had rallied around afterwards, offering them somewhere to stay, donating clothes for them all, as everything they'd owned had been destroyed. Canning had waited until the place was engulfed in flames before calling the fire brigade, ensuring that everyone inside had no chance of escape. He didn't know that Bradley had survived until he was interviewed later.

Immediately after the fire, Carrie and Vincent both left the fire service, unable to function in such an environment. Vincent eventually started up a gardening business, while Carrie trained as a hairdresser.

'We had a perfect life before the fire,' Carrie said. 'But Canning took everything away that night. I wouldn't call him evil. He was worse than that.' She held back tears. 'Like Vincent said, I hope he's burning in hell.'

Sheridan could feel their pain. She stole a sympathetic look at Anna. There were difficult questions to ask and there was never going to be a right moment to ask them.

But the atmosphere had softened, and Vincent appeared to have calmed down. So she chose to ask her questions then.

'I do have to ask you both some things, and I apologise if they're uncomfortable. But in every enquiry like this, we have to eliminate people, and so I need to mention the threat you made to Canning when he was sentenced.' She looked at Vincent as she spoke.

'I threatened to kill him if he ever got out,' Vincent said. 'I was angry, of course I was. He smiled at us when he was sentenced, and I wanted to put my hands around his throat and kill him. If they hadn't held me back that day, I would have done it.' His eyes were fixed on Sheridan. 'I hate him, I always have, but I didn't kill him. If I'd known he was out, maybe I would have got to him, I don't know.'

Sheridan waited for a moment before asking her next question. 'Again, I have to ask this question . . . where were you both last Friday evening?'

Vincent's shoulders dropped and Carrie shook her head slowly.

'Are you seriously thinking it was *us*?' Carrie said, clearly shocked at the question.

'I'm sorry.' Sheridan tilted her head to one side. 'But I wouldn't be doing my job if I avoided difficult questions.'

Vincent shrugged in resignation. 'It's alright. If you must know, we went out for a meal to celebrate our wedding anniversary on Friday evening.'

'Just the two of you?'

'No. We were with Roger and Marcia, Carrie's brother and his wife. You can speak to them if you need to.'

Sheridan wrote in her pocket notebook. 'What's their surname?'

'Yearwood,' Carrie said, giving Sheridan their contact number and address.

'Which restaurant did you go to?'

'Luigi's on Stanley Street. It's an Italian place, we go there quite often,' Carrie replied.

'I know the place. Great food. Do you remember what time you got to the restaurant?'

Carrie rubbed her forehead, looking to Vincent. 'We'd planned to meet them at eight, but we were a few minutes late, so around ten past, I think.'

Vincent nodded. 'They're sticklers for time, but we couldn't find a parking space, so we had to go to the car park on Victoria Street and walk down to the restaurant.'

So, you were in the restaurant at the time Canning was murdered, Sheridan thought. 'Thank you,' she said. Putting her pocket notebook down, she asked casually, 'How long have you two been married?'

'Twenty-seven years. We got married on the 7th of January 1984.' Carrie looked at Vincent again, and they briefly smiled.

Sheridan noted that they still hadn't asked how Canning had died. But for the moment, she continued with her questions. 'Do Roger and Marcia have any children?'

'Yes, a son,' Carrie said. 'Frankie. Although he's not a child anymore. He's forty-nine. They all grow up so quickly.'

'And where does he live?'

'Kirkdale.' Carrie frowned. 'I'm sorry, can I just check, you're not really thinking it was someone in the family who killed Canning, are you?'

'We just have to be sure that we cover everything, I'm sure you understand.' Sheridan picked up her pocket notebook again. 'Can I have Bradley and Frankie's contact details?'

Carrie provided their phone numbers and addresses. 'Bradley might find it difficult to talk about, so please be careful when you speak to him. He'll be angry that Dennis has been out for two years and he wasn't informed.'

Sheridan agreed to bear it in mind, the whole time weighing up how to broach the next subject. She knew that Vincent had been arrested several times for shoplifting in the last year and that Carrie was of good character, but looking at the house and Mercedes on the drive, it made no sense why he would need to steal. She also didn't know if Carrie was aware of his previous convictions.

'Can I ask, and I know it sounds like a strange question, but have either of you ever been arrested?'

Vincent's jaw tightened and Sheridan noted his head drop. 'I . . . I've been arrested, for shoplifting.'

'What were the circumstances?' Sheridan glanced at Carrie; this was clearly not news to her.

'I put some bottles of alcohol in my shopping basket and the next thing I know I was outside the shop. The alarm went off and I got stopped and the police were called.' He looked down at Carrie. 'I was so ashamed. But something inside me just clicked and I started doing it regularly. Carrie was amazing and we talked about why I'd suddenly started stealing and we realised I was having a breakdown. I've struggled a few times over the years, with everything that happened, and it finally just got to me.' He inhaled deeply. 'Anyway, I pulled myself together and I haven't been in trouble since.'

'Thank you for your honesty, Vincent.' Sheridan nodded, looking at Anna, who gave a slight shake of her head to indicate that she had no further questions. They both stood up.

'Well, thank you both for your time.' She handed Carrie a card. 'My contact details are on there if you need anything.'

Carrie took the card and tucked it into her cardigan pocket, getting to her feet to show them out.

As they reached the front door, Carrie turned to Sheridan. 'I take it you're not allowed to tell us *how* Canning died. You didn't mention it, so I wasn't sure if I was allowed to ask.'

Bollocks, thought Sheridan – she had been sure she'd found a reason to doubt the couple when they hadn't asked the question. But they'd just shot a hole in her theory.

'His throat was cut,' she said.

'Bloody hell,' Vincent responded. 'You said he was leaving a café, so . . . what actually happened?'

Sheridan gave them the brief details of the attack. Nothing that hadn't already been on the local news.

'I told you there was a list as long as your arm of people who'd wanted him dead,' Vincent said, 'I guess one of them got to him.' He placed his arm around Carrie.

'If you think of anyone who might have done this, please call me. I completely understand your feelings about Canning, but I do still have to investigate his murder,' Sheridan said.

A blank response was all she got back before she made her way to the car with Anna in tow.

As Carrie closed the front door, she broke down, holding her face in her hands and sobbing uncontrollably. Vincent took her in his arms and held her to his chest. 'It's okay, darling. It's okay.'

CHAPTER 11

'What did you make of them?' Anna asked, clipping her seat belt into place.

'Initially, I thought it was odd that they didn't ask how Canning died.'

'Me too. But then she *did* ask the question.'

'Yeah. Anyway, we'll check out their story about the restaurant.' Sheridan pulled away.

'You think they're involved?'

'Possibly. But only because I don't trust *anyone*.'

'Unlikely though, eh?'

Sheridan nodded. 'Yeah. Unlikely. But I'm not ruling out that they might have paid someone.'

Anna rested her head back. 'So, if the restaurant alibi pans out, then that rules out Vincent, Carrie, her brother and his wife. The only other person left is their son, Frankie. We'll have to add him to the list of suspects.'

'What are you smiling at?' Sheridan asked.

'Vincent's quite attractive. I always thought about dating a fireman. It's the uniform.'

'Why don't you join a dating website again? I mean a proper one. There are ones for professional people, you have to pay, but at least there's less chance of meeting some weirdo.'

Anna didn't respond, pursing her lips. The last time she'd joined a dating site she'd seen her ex-partner Steve's profile pop up, and had immediately cancelled her account.

'Oh my God, you've already joined one, haven't you?' Sheridan grinned, turning in her seat to face Anna.

'Maybe. Okay, yes, I have and that's all I'm saying.'

'Oh, you can't leave it there. Come on, have you met someone? Is he good-looking? What does he do for a living? Is he local? Tell me *everything*.'

'His name's Ben, he's attractive. He's twenty-two, from Liverpool and works as a lumberjack.'

Sheridan smacked Anna's leg. 'Don't be a dickhead. There's no way you found a lumberjack.' She laughed at her own joke.

'Seriously Sheridan, I'm not telling you anything. I'll let you know more about him when I feel the time is right. But so far, it's going well and we're chatting a lot.' Anna smiled, resting her head back.

'He's not twenty-two though, is he?'

'No.' Anna laughed.

'Well, he'd better be really fucking nice, because if he hurts you, I'll break his legs.'

Anna tilted her head. 'You have such a way with words.'

'Have you met him yet?'

'Not yet. And even if I was going to, I wouldn't tell *you*.'

'Why not?'

'Because you'd turn up and interrogate him.'

'No, I wouldn't. I just don't want you meeting another dickhead like Steve.'

Anna and Steve had been together for seven apparently happy years, until the day Anna threw him out.

Sheridan had always had her suspicions that he'd been violent, but Anna had continually denied it. In December 2007, Anna had confided in Sheridan that she was pregnant with Steve's child but hadn't told him. Sheridan had accompanied her to the hospital to have a termination, and had made Anna promise she would *never* tell Steve about what they had done. Even after all of Anna's denials that Steve had ever hit her, Sheridan was unable to bury her concerns and had always worried what he might do.

But Anna was keeping a secret from her. Steve *had* assaulted her and had regularly left her covered in bruises, once hitting her so hard in the face that she'd lost a tooth.

In 2008, after another assault, Anna had thrown him out of her house, still keeping the secret from Sheridan that he'd been violent.

Over the last three years, Sheridan was aware that Steve and Anna had met up on occasion, allegedly as friends. Anna knew that a part of her still loved him. And a part of her hated him for what he had done to her. Steve had apologised for his atrocious behaviour and had even given up drinking, alcohol having often been the catalyst for his uncontrollable anger.

Anna knew she could never trust Steve completely, but had always battled with her feelings towards him; love and hate in the same pot.

Steve had often told her that he knew their relationship was over, and all he wanted to be was friends, just friends. But the truth was, he didn't want to be her friend. He wanted her back and he was never letting go.

He'd sit outside her house at night and watch until the lights went out. He'd sit outside Sheridan's house when Anna visited there. He'd meet Anna for a friendly drink, always ordering a soft drink for himself to keep up the illusion that he no longer touched alcohol. And he didn't. Not in front of her.

He'd wait until he got home and crack open a bottle of whisky, drinking, thinking. Always thinking of ways to crowbar his way back into her life.

He even lied, saying he'd met another woman. But here was no other woman. Only Anna. And nothing else mattered, except getting her back. And he *would* get her back. She was *his*. She belonged to him. And no other man was ever going to have her.

◆   ◆   ◆

After briefing the team about what they had learned during their visit with Carrie and Vincent, Sheridan tasked Dipesh to confirm the Royces' alibi on the night Canning was murdered and tasked Rob to contact Bradley's cousin, Frankie.

She turned to Bridie. 'Can you pay a visit to Carrie's brother and his wife, Roger and Marcia, see if they can think of anyone who might have got to Canning? Anna can go with you.'

'No, it's fine. I'm happy to go on my own,' Bridie said. Bridie liked to work alone.

'Okay, if you're sure. And don't forget I'm taking you all out for a meal tonight.' Sheridan tilted her head towards Hill. 'You still not coming?'

'No thanks,' Hill replied, immediately returning to the job in hand. 'The chief wants me to keep him updated.' She paused, and looked around at her fellow officers. 'I know it goes without saying, but I'll say it anyway. Dennis Canning was hated, we know that. What he did was incredibly callous and that's an understatement. The public are unlikely to come forward and give us anything, so we're already up against it. But we can't be seen to pay any less attention to *his* murder than any other murder we've dealt with. I know the general consensus is that this was a revenge killing, an execution, aimed at him and him alone. But if it wasn't, then whoever was responsible could strike again. And in that case, we have to show that we're doing everything we can to catch this killer.' She took a sip of coffee. 'The chief is trying to bat away the press on this one as much as he can. They're starting to suggest that because of Canning's background, we might be dragging our heels. They're also saying that we need to reassure the public that there isn't some fucking lunatic out there randomly picking off his victims. The chief has given them a statement but he's really getting his bollocks in a twist over this one.'

She turned to Sheridan. 'Are you going to see Carrie's son, Bradley?'

'Yeah. We know he couldn't have killed Canning because he was locked up at Potters Road at the time. But I'd like to ask him if he can think of anyone who'd want Canning dead. Just to see what he says.'

'Fine. Keep me updated.' Hill turned to leave.

The desk phone rang. Rob answered it, looking at Sheridan and handing the phone to her.

'It's for you.'

Sheridan took the call and raised her eyebrows. 'Thanks, I'll be there in one minute.' She ended the call. 'Interesting.'

'What is?' Hill asked.

'Looks like we don't have to go out and see Bradley Penhaligan. He's downstairs in the public enquiry office, asking for me.'

Sheridan and Anna showed Bradley into a free interview room, and after declining a drink, he settled behind the table. He was in his forties, clean-shaven with sad eyes.

'My mum rang me and said you'd been to see her about Dennis Canning.' He swallowed. 'She told me to stay calm and not be angry that he's been out for two years and no one told us. I'm not going to deny that I *am* angry, and I don't understand why we weren't told. But me kicking off about it doesn't change anything.' He unzipped his coat and sat back in his chair. 'She said that you might think one of us, one of the family, killed Canning. Well, we didn't. Trust me, I'd have loved to have done it, but even though

I can't shift the hatred I had for him, I'm not capable of anything like that.' He looked at Sheridan. 'Did he suffer?' he asked blankly.

'It's hard to say. I believe the way he was killed would have been quick, but I can't say how much he knew about it.'

'Right. Well, I'm obviously a suspect seeing as he killed my sister and my grandma and grandpa, but I honestly didn't touch him.'

'We know.'

He frowned. 'How?'

'Because you were in police custody at the time.'

'My mum said that Canning was attacked last Friday evening, but she didn't say exactly what time. Was I in the police station when he was killed?'

'Yes. You were in your cell.'

Bradley exhaled. 'I was worried that you thought I had something to do with what happened to him. Not that I'm bothered that he's dead, he deserved everything he got.' He sat forward slightly and cleared his throat, wiping a hand across his mouth.

'Can you think of anyone who would want Canning dead?' Sheridan asked.

'Loads of people I suppose. When the fire happened, everyone who knew us hated him as much as we did. But I can't be specific and if I'm totally honest, I don't want you to catch whoever did this to him. He deserved it.'

'We can't be certain that Canning was killed out of revenge for what he did. I want you to bear that in mind, Bradley. If it wasn't revenge, then someone out there could do this again, they could attack a random stranger and next time, it could be someone completely innocent.'

Bradley pondered this for a moment. 'True. But whatever happened, I'm still glad he's dead.'

They talked for another half-hour. Bradley told Sheridan and Anna that he was a qualified car mechanic, running his business out of a small lock-up. He explained that the reason he'd been arrested for criminal damage was due to a customer, who owned a shop, not paying him for carrying out work on his van. After months of chasing up the payment, Bradley took it upon himself to smash the shopfront window on two occasions. He knew it was petty, but he'd worked hard to keep his business going and couldn't afford to lose money.

He'd been married, but the relationship was short-lived. He didn't have any children. He was still very close to his mum and knew she'd found love with Vincent. He didn't mention the details of the fire, until Sheridan prompted him. As he spoke she could see in his eyes that the pain of what happened still remained.

'Everyone thought I opened the back door to get out and that's why the fire swept through the house so quickly, but it wasn't like that. The door was already open when I got to it.'

'Do you think Canning got in through the back door?' The question had niggled Sheridan and although this had all been looked into during the original investigation, something didn't ring true.

'He must have done. It's the only explanation.' Bradley sighed.

After escorting Bradley out of the police station, Sheridan and Anna returned to CID and updated the team.

'We'll pick this up again in the morning, but for now, let's all switch off and get ready for our meal out tonight.' Sheridan smiled, checking again that Hill still didn't want to come. 'Sure you haven't changed your mind?'

'No. But I'm sure you'll all have fun,' Hill said as she turned to leave CID. 'Don't be late in tomorrow you lot.'

Sheridan was still in CID when Bridie walked in after visiting Carrie's brother and his wife.

'How did it go?' Sheridan asked.

'They're Jehovah's Witnesses.' Bridie dramatically dropped her bag on the desk.

'What's that got to do with anything?' Sheridan said, slightly amused by the blank expression on Bridie's face.

'They're Jehovah's Witnesses. If they said it once, they said it a thousand times.' Bridie exhaled. 'Basically, they knew Canning was dead because Carrie had rung and told them after your visit. They couldn't think of anyone specifically who would have killed him – although when pushed they said it was possibly someone who knew the family back then. But they said they're not in contact with any of those people anymore, and they thought it was unlikely that one of them would wait all these years to get to him. They confirmed that they were having dinner to celebrate Carrie and Vincent's wedding anniversary on Friday night and were quite specific about the fact that they arrived late.'

'What time did they say they'd planned to meet up at the restaurant?'

'Eight p.m. But Carrie and Vincent didn't get there until just gone ten past.'

'How did they seem when you told them what had happened to Canning?' Sheridan asked.

'Like I said, they already knew the details from talking to Carrie, but they seemed genuinely shocked.'

'What about their son, Frankie?'

'They don't have much contact with him, but they gave me the same mobile number and address that Rob's got. I got the feeling that they're not close to him. They didn't even know if he's working, or in a relationship. Apparently, he distanced himself from them a few years ago.'

'Okay, anything else?'

'Did I mention that they're Jehovah's Witnesses?'

CHAPTER 12

Hill arrived home and parked up, noticing a van parked on her elderly neighbour Gloria's drive.

Gloria had few visitors except her friend Doreen and although she'd never tell her, Hill was extremely protective of her neighbour. She walked across the road and, using the key Gloria had given her several years before, let herself in.

'Only me, Gloria,' she called as she pushed the living-room door open.

She expected to see Gloria sitting in her armchair, but finding it empty she went through to the kitchen. Gloria's dog was also missing. On the kitchen worktop was an empty mug and a half-eaten piece of cake.

Hill called out for Gloria again as she made her way upstairs. Hearing a noise coming from the bathroom, she turned and spotted a pair of legs sticking out from under the sink. And they certainly weren't Gloria's.

'Who are you?' Hill asked abruptly. No response. She nudged one of the legs with her foot and repeated the question.

The man lying on the floor jumped, banging his head on the wall. He sat up, pulling out his earpieces.

'Christ,' he said, 'you made me jump.'

Hill crossed her arms. 'Who are you, and what have you done with Gloria?'

The man rubbed his chin. 'I'm a serial killer. I've buried Gloria's body in the back garden and I'm just fixing her plumbing before I go on the run.' He got to his feet, smiling. 'Promise you won't call the police.'

Hill remained unamused. 'What's your name?' she asked bluntly.

'I'm Alan. Alan Rose, handyman. I have no previous convictions, I'm fully DBS checked, and Gloria gave me a key to let myself in which I will post back through the letter box when I leave. Gloria is out with her friend Doreen, they've taken her dog Barney to the vet's to have his nails clipped. I'm not charging Gloria to fix her leak because she's a pensioner and I don't charge pensioners.' He smiled again. 'That's everything Gloria told me to tell you so that you don't throw me out of her house.' He put his hands on his hips. 'You must be Hill. Would you like to interrogate me over a cuppa and a piece of cake?'

Hill didn't move. 'Alan Rose?'

'Yes. Would you like to see some identification?'

A rare grin worked its way across Hill's face as she realised why the man seemed familiar. 'Petal?'

Alan looked surprised. 'I haven't heard that nickname for more years than I care to remember,' he replied, leaning forward slightly, studying Hill's face. 'Do we know each other?'

Hill uncrossed her arms. 'St Bernard's Junior School, late sixties. We were ten and you picked a bunch of daisies for me from the school yard.'

'Oh my God. Hill Stanley.' Alan's face lit up. 'I can't believe it's you. You were my first kiss.' He laughed at the memory as they made their way downstairs.

Hill made them both a cup of tea while they sat in Gloria's kitchen reminiscing.

'I've just remembered you hated your real name – insisted that we all called you Hill.' Alan sipped his drink. 'Remind me of your real name?'

'Not a bloody chance.' Hill shook her head. 'As soon as I was old enough, I changed it to Hill, and that's what I've been called ever since.'

'Well, no one calls me "Petal" anymore. Was it you who first came up with that nickname?'

'No, it was . . .' Hill hesitated. 'Someone else.'

Alan talked about how he remembered Hill being the funniest kid in his class. How she was popular and pretty but studious and smart. They'd lost touch when they ended up in different senior schools. He told her how his parents had wanted to relocate, and they had ended up living in Norfolk. At the age of twenty, he'd joined Norfolk Police and become a firearms officer. He married a fellow officer, but the relationship didn't last. His wife had wanted children and Alan was against it, and that eventually led to their divorce. He took early retirement, having been seriously injured on duty, eventually moving back up north and starting his own handyman business. Alan lived alone and revelled in his own company.

'Anyway, enough about me. So, what have you been up to all these years? Gloria tells me you're a police officer,' he said, dabbing at the cake crumbs on the plate and popping them into his mouth.

'Yes, I'm a DCI.'

'I'm very impressed.' He tipped an imaginary cap in her direction. 'Do you still enjoy the job?'

'Yes, very much. I have a great team. I'm very lucky.'

'And what about . . . husband? Kids?'

Hill paused. She had known the question was going to come up at some point. She rarely talked about her late husband, Ralph, or her twin six-year-old girls, who had been killed in a car accident nearly twenty-eight years before, on Hill's twenty-sixth birthday.

She hadn't been with them in the car, and had never got over the loss. The day they died was the day she'd thrown up a barrier. Even after all these years, little had changed in her attitude to talking about it.

But the pain of losing them was still with her. Every day she woke up, they were there, and every night she went to sleep.

Alan picked up on her hesitation to answer. 'Would you like some more tea?' He got up and Hill watched him as he re-boiled the kettle.

'His name was Ralph,' Hill finally said.

Alan turned around. 'Who?'

'The kid who first started calling you "petal".'

'Ah, yes. I remember *him*. He was keen on you too. I wonder where he is now.'

The front door opened, and Barney came bouncing into the kitchen, wagging his tail furiously as he ran excitedly between Hill and Alan.

Gloria and Doreen walked in. 'She didn't throw you out then?' Gloria grinned.

'No. She didn't.' Alan smiled at Hill, which was reciprocated. 'Turns out we know each other.' Alan bent down to stroke Barney's head.

Gloria snapped a look at Hill. 'Really?'

'Yes. Well, anyway, I'd better be off.' Hill stood up. 'It was nice to see you again, Alan.' She nodded at him and made her way to the front door, closing it quietly behind her.

'That was weird,' Alan said, confused by Hill's sudden departure.

'What was?' Gloria asked, popping on the kettle.

'The way she just got up and left.' Alan was still looking at the door.

'That's just Hill for you. She's odd like that.' Gloria pulled three cups out of the cupboard. 'Cuppa?'

CHAPTER 13

Sheridan and her team were settled in the restaurant, drinks and conversation flowing. Sam was sat next to Dipesh's wife, Lina, listening in genuine fascination as she talked about her love of Lego. Bridie, usually quiet and unassuming, was on her third drink and keeping everyone entertained as she, Rob and Dipesh all discussed football tactics. Anna was listening to them, completely confused by the entire conversation.

Sheridan, meanwhile, was captivated by Rob's wife, Jo, who was profoundly deaf. Although she used sign language, she much preferred lip-reading, explaining to Sheridan that she could understand what anyone said as long as they kept their mouth visible, and didn't try to over-pronounce their words.

'So, can you see what people are saying from a distance?' Sheridan asked her.

'Yes, as long as I can see their lips moving. I can also pick up on body language. Rob doesn't bother lying to me anymore, because he knows that I can tell.' Jo laughed as Rob, having heard the comment, gently poked her in the ribs.

'That's amazing,' Sheridan said. 'It's like a superpower.'

'Not really. But see them?' Jo nodded towards a couple sitting two tables away. 'They're on a first date and he doesn't fancy her. She's a bit uncomfortable and . . .' Jo fell silent as the woman got up and headed to the toilets, watching as her date took out his mobile phone.

Sheridan was totally fascinated as Jo relayed to her what the man was saying.

'He's calling a mate. He just said, "Oh mate, this is a nightmare. I think it's pretty clear she doesn't fancy me, so I'll have to get her wrecked if there's any chance of giving her one. To be fair, I'll have to get wrecked too, she looks like a pig. Anyway, I'll talk to you later, after I've banged her and chucked her out."'

The man picked up his pint and sipped from it, keeping the glass near to his mouth.

'I can't see what he's saying now,' Jo said.

'What a complete prick,' Sheridan said, frowning at the man's comments. 'But I do have to say, that was remarkable. I literally had no idea that you could lip-read and pick up on body language as well. That's phenomenal.'

'Well, I've been deaf from birth and it's something I've learned over the years.'

'It's a gift. I'm sure you don't see it like that, but trust me, you really do have a gift.'

'Thank you,' Jo replied.

'Lip-readers are used by the police sometimes, but it's not an exact science, is it?'

'No, it's not. But I'm pretty accurate most of the time. Rob used to test me,' Jo said, smiling.

Sheridan placed a hand on her arm. 'Talking of Rob, tell me about all the times he's tried to lie to you.' She winked at Jo and the two women laughed.

By the end of the evening, everyone was full from the food, drink and easy, flowing conversation. Although Anna still had no idea how the offside rule worked.

As they all headed for the door, Sheridan whispered to Sam, 'I'll meet you outside.'

And then she headed over to the first-date couple, stopping beside the man, who looked up at her, confused as to who she was.

'Can I help you?' he asked, slurring his words.

'No.' She looked at the girl. 'But I can help *you*.' She turned her attention back to the man. 'Next time you take a woman out on a first date, there's two things you don't do. One, try to get them so drunk that they'll have sex with you. And two, you don't call your mate and describe your date the way you described *her*.'

The man opened his mouth to speak but struggled with his words. 'I . . . I just . . . how . . .'

Sheridan looked at the young woman. 'Do you want to stay, or would you like to leave?'

The woman frowned at her date. 'You thought I was going to have sex with you on a first date?' She stood up, scooping up her handbag. 'You're an idiot. And . . . you can pay the bill.'

And with that, she followed Sheridan outside.

'What did he say to his mate?' she asked as they waited to hail her a taxi.

Sheridan told her, missing out the horrendous reference to her being a 'pig'.

'Well, he lucked out there, didn't he? Because he's not getting a shag . . . and he has to pay the whole bill.' The woman grinned.

A taxi pulled up and she got in after thanking Sheridan.

Sam linked arms with her, and they walked to the car. 'What was that all about?' she asked.

She told her about Jo and how she could lip-read.

'That's amazing,' Sam said. 'Do I have any special gifts?'

'Yeah.' Sheridan smiled. 'You buy the best birthday presents.'

CHAPTER 14

Sheridan and the team were congregated in CID, discussing the Dennis Canning murder, and worrying over the lack of any new information. Which could mean the case would turn cold before they made any significant progress.

Canning's landline showed few outgoing or incoming calls. There were several from and to his probation officer, but none that gave the team anything to go on.

Financial checks had been carried out on Carrie, Vincent and Bradley, and again, nothing seemed out of place. Marcia and Roger's finances had also been looked into, as had their son Frankie's, with no evidence that they had paid someone to carry out the killing. Marcia, Roger and Frankie were all no trace on PNC.

Rob and Dipesh had confirmed that Carrie and Vincent's alibi panned out. CCTV clearly showed the time they arrived at the restaurant, 8.11 p.m., and the time they left, 10.18 p.m. They remained in the restaurant the entire time, as did Marcia and Roger, and their car was parked in the Victoria Street car park, which was also covered by CCTV.

'Okay.' Sheridan looked behind her at the whiteboard and amended it to show that Carrie, Vincent, Marcia and Roger were no longer suspects. 'So that just leaves Frankie, their son.'

'I haven't managed to get hold of him yet. He wasn't answering his phone, so we went to his house. But there was no answer at the door. I'll keep trying,' Rob said. 'Also, me and Dipesh spoke to some of the regulars at the café. They either don't remember seeing Canning in there, or, if they did, they can't recall him ever talking to anyone. We've basically drawn a blank there.'

'What about local shops?' Sheridan asked.

'Uniform have checked them out. Canning used to buy most of his food in a local convenience store, but they said he never spoke when he went in. We're looking to see if we can trace Canning on any CCTV. Maybe we can find evidence that he was being followed at some point.'

Bridie put her hand up. 'I'm still working with the prison service and so far there's no one that's been released with a connection to Canning. But I've got three other prisons to check.'

'Thanks, Bridie.' Sheridan sighed. 'We're getting nowhere fast here. We've had so few calls from the public since the press release, and no information yet that's going to help us. Okay, let's keep going, we'll get there.'

She headed back to her office.

Sheridan was packing up for the day and looked up to see Anna walking into her office. 'Right, I'm off. I'll see you tomorrow.'

She logged off her computer. 'Sam and I were talking about your birthday last night and we were wondering, if you're not doing anything, do you want to come to ours?'

'Yeah. That would be lovely.' Anna smiled – a smile that soon disintegrated into a grimace as a slight panic drifted into her voice. 'Sam's not baking a cake, is she?' Sam was notoriously the worst cook in the entire world.

Sheridan grinned. 'No. Don't worry, I'll get my mum to make one.' She grabbed her coat. 'Talking of birthdays, you haven't forgotten it's Maud's tomorrow? You still coming round?'

'Absolutely. I've bought her some Jaffa Cakes and some actual *normal* cat treats. And a card. Do you think she'll eat it?' said Anna. Maud ate *anything*.

'Highly likely. I'm just thinking, actually . . . we could make it a combined birthday for you and Maud,' Sheridan said.

'Absolutely *not*. Why have one party when we can have two?' Anna raised her eyebrows. 'No, we'll celebrate Maud's tomorrow and mine on Monday.'

Sheridan laughed. 'Okay, fair enough. Any excuse for two piss-ups.' She put her coat on. 'Anyway, have you got anything to tell me?'

'Like what?'

'How's the lumberjack?'

Anna shook her head. 'He's fine. That's all I'm saying.' She frowned. 'You do know he's not *actually* a lumberjack.'

Sheridan laughed. 'Of course, you muppet. Anyway, what are you up to tonight? You could come to ours and tell us all about him.'

'I can't come round tonight.'

'Why not?'

Anna hesitated. 'Steve wants to meet up for a drink. He says he's got me something for my birthday.' She cleared her throat. 'He might have to go away for work for a few days, so thought he'd give me my present now.'

'Okay, well, have a nice evening. I'll see you tomorrow.' Sheridan forced a smile.

After quickly checking in on the team, she made her way downstairs to the backyard and was about to get into her car when she spotted Anna's still parked up. As she pulled out on to the road, she saw Anna climbing into Steve's car. On her way home, she thought about Anna and Steve and had everything crossed that Anna would never get back with him.

CHAPTER 15

Steve ordered drinks at the bar as Anna settled down at a window seat. She took off her coat and draped it over the back of her chair. A moment later Steve was at the table, placing a glass of champagne in front of her, before sliding into the seat opposite and raising his glass of orange juice.

'Happy birthday.'

He smiled broadly as they clinked glasses. Anna smiled back at him, taking a sip of her drink and feeling bubbles up her nose. 'Ooh, that's lovely. Thank you.'

She set her glass down and Steve reached into his pocket, producing a small box wrapped in shiny silver paper, with a red bow on top.

'What's this?' Anna asked, taking it from him.

'Your birthday present.' Steve nodded at the box. 'Go on then, open it.'

He beamed as Anna carefully opened the package. She peered inside, her eyes widening as she lifted out a heavy gold chain with a beautiful angel pendant hanging from it. Her eyes filled with tears as she studied it.

'Where on earth did you get this?' she asked, touching it gently.

'I had it made for you.' Steve watched her face, knowing that she would be overwhelmed.

When they were together, their first holiday had been a trip to Lanzarote. They were so in love back then and had spent the entire time lying on the beach, their skin warm and salty. They'd swum in the sea and spent the evenings drinking wine and enjoying romantic meals out, before falling into bed and making love into the early hours. It was perfect. *They* were perfect. And that was the holiday where they had talked about spending the rest of their lives together. It was also the holiday where Anna had lost the necklace that her grandmother had left her. It was one that Anna had treasured, and she was heartbroken when she found it had slipped from her neck while she was in the sea. They had never managed to find a replacement and so Anna had resigned herself to the fact that it was gone. And now, as she stared at the angel necklace in her hand, tears dripped down her face. Steve stood up and stepped behind her, gently placing it around her neck.

'There you go,' he said cheerfully, before sitting back down.

Anna was searching for the words, before finally saying, 'It's beautiful, Steve. I can't believe you remembered.' She looked into his eyes. 'How did you get it made *exactly* like the original?'

'I was sorting out some old photographs of us recently . . .' He hesitated, his jaw tightening as he spoke. 'And I found some from that holiday in Lanzarote and remembered how much you loved that necklace, so I took the photograph into a jeweller's and he made it for me.' Steve picked up his drink and eyed Anna over the top of his glass.

'I'm speechless that you'd do that.' Anna's voice broke a little as she touched the angel, now safe against her skin.

'The chain's a bit thicker than the original, a lot thicker actually, but I just didn't want it to come off again,' Steve said.

'It must have cost you a fortune,' Anna replied. 'You didn't have to . . .'

'I know I didn't. But I guess it's a combined birthday present and . . . leaving gift.' He straightened himself up, waiting for her to respond.

'Leaving gift?'

'Yeah. I'm moving away. I'm getting more work in Glasgow and thought I might as well relocate.' He swallowed. 'I know you and I will never be together again, and I know what I did to you, but I wanted us to at least part ways on a nice memory.'

'Oh,' she said.

'You going to miss me?' he asked.

She grinned. 'No. Not one bit.'

'Well, Mrs Dobson will.'

'Who's Mrs Dobson?'

'My next-door neighbour. She told me yesterday that she hopes she gets another neighbour as nice as me.'

'What makes you a nice neighbour?'

'I do all sorts of things for her. Little odd jobs. She's an old lady, lives on her own and apparently her son never visits and she kind of relies on me. She bangs on the wall with her stick in the evenings if she wants me to go over there for a bit of company.'

'Why doesn't she just ring you?'

'Don't know. Maybe she enjoys banging her stick on the wall.'

'She sounds like a character. I hope you don't charge her when you do odd jobs.'

'Of course not. I'm not a monster.' He took a sip of his drink, and they sat in silence for a moment, before Steve brought the conversation back to the necklace and their holiday in Lanzarote.

He winked at her. 'That was a fantastic holiday, wasn't it?'

'It was.' Anna smiled at the memory of a wonderful time in their lives. Before his violence had ruined everything. The Steve sitting in front of her now reminded her of the man she'd fallen in love with. Cheeky and charming. The man who made her laugh. But it all seemed so very distant now.

'Was it that holiday when I jumped in the pool and my trunks came off?' Steve asked.

Anna laughed. 'Yes.' She threw her head back. 'Your bum was there for all to see.'

'That's when you started calling me "cheeks", do you remember?'

'I do. Oh God, I haven't thought about that for years.'

Steve ordered Anna another drink and as they chatted, he recalled all the good times in their relationship. He watched her face as she laughed out loud at some of the silly shit they'd got up to in the early days. All the while, he made sure her glass was never empty.

'I was thinking . . . how about I take you out to dinner tomorrow night?'

Anna tilted her head to one side. 'I can't. It's Maud's birthday and I'm going to Sheridan's to celebrate with them.'

Steve pulled a face. 'You're all celebrating a *cat's* birthday?' He laughed. 'I'd love to see *that*. Maybe I could come, too?'

Anna bit down on her bottom lip. 'I don't think that's a good idea. It's going to be a girly night.'

Steve sat back and let a huge smile cross his face. 'Come on, it'll be fun.'

'Sorry, Steve, I think maybe not.' Anna felt the alcohol had already gone to her head and remembered she hadn't eaten all day. But she still had the wherewithal to be cautious about Steve's suggestion to turn up at Sheridan's. Even though she had never admitted Steve's violent past, Anna knew Sheridan's previous comments suggested that she didn't like him.

A moment's silence hung between them, but Steve maintained his expression, thinking. Wanting the conversation to turn back

to his move away, he let the smile drift. He was playing Anna
and could see the alcohol was taking effect. He felt she was making excuses not to see him and didn't believe for a second that
she was going to Sheridan's the following night to celebrate her
cat's birthday.

He cleared his throat. 'God. I'm going to miss you so much.'

Anna suddenly looked visibly upset and Steve took the opportunity to use this, reaching across the table for her hand. 'Hey. It's
for the best,' he said. 'I want you to move on, Anna. I want you to
find someone who loves you like I loved you. Someone who takes
care of you and sees you for the incredible woman that you are. I
never deserved you and I know I fucked up the best thing that ever
happened to me.' He paused, putting his head down and squeezing
tears from his eyes. 'I also need to move on. I want to have children
one day and settle down. I'm a different person to the man I was
back then, and I think I'd make a great dad.' He wiped a hand
down his face and sniffed.

Anna could see the emotion in his expression and went to
change the subject. She slowly got up, her head feeling a little
woozy. 'I'm just popping to the loo.'

When she returned, he'd ordered her another drink. A double.

'You trying to get me drunk?' she grinned.

'Absolutely. I'm going to get you drunk, take you home, have
a farewell shag, get you pregnant and we're going to live happily
ever after.' He lifted his glass to his mouth, trying to hide a smile,
before bursting out laughing.

Anna shook her head, laughing with him.

'Can I tell you a secret?' Steve asked.

'Sure.'

He leaned forward, keeping his voice low. 'As much as I wanted
to have children with you, I'm glad we didn't. Is that terrible of me?'

Anna slowly shook her head. 'No, it's not terrible.' Her words were slurred, and her head swayed a little. 'Why are you glad that we didn't?'

He clasped his hands together. 'I just think that we'd be another one of those families where the kids get dragged through the mill, split between mum and dad.' He shook his head. 'That's not what I ever wanted.' He looked at her, noticing tears in her eyes.

'What's wrong?' he asked, his voice soft.

'Nothing.' Anna cleared her throat, taking a large sip of her drink.

'Come on. I know when you've got something on your mind. Whatever it is, just say it.' Steve gave a reassuring squeeze of her hand.

'I . . . got pregnant when we were together.' Anna felt a little sick and took a breath.

Steve didn't respond at first, his eyes wide as he studied her face. 'Really?'

'Yeah.'

'What happened?'

'I had a termination.' Her voice was barely audible.

Steve felt a rock form in his stomach, his heart thumping furiously in his chest. He slowly inhaled through his nose, trying to keep himself calm. 'Why?' he said, his voice breaking.

'I just didn't want kids. I was always honest with you about that, Steve.'

There was a moment's silence before he spoke. 'Oh, God, my darling Anna.' He reached for her hand, and she let him take it. 'Why didn't you tell me? I could have been there for you,' he said softly.

'I thought you'd kick off.'

'No, I wouldn't have kicked off. And now I just ache knowing that you went through something like that on your own. I'm so glad you've told me now.' He squeezed her hand a little tighter, running his thumb gently across her knuckles.

'You're not mad?' Anna asked sheepishly.

'Of *course* I'm not mad. I'm just sad that you felt you had to keep it from me.' He sighed. 'Does . . . Sheridan know?'

'Yeah. But she's the only one who does.'

Steve kept his voice low. 'Did you ever tell Sheridan that I hit you?'

'You've still got your legs, so I think you know the answer to that is no.' Anna raised an eyebrow.

'But you tell each other everything.'

'Not *everything*.'

'I always got the feeling that Sheridan never really liked me.' Steve sighed. 'Maybe in her own way, she guessed what was going on when we were together, even if you didn't tell her.'

Anna recalled the times that Sheridan had asked her about Steve and how she'd always denied it. 'Maybe,' she said.

'Does she know you're here with me tonight?'

'Yeah.'

Steve nodded and cleared his throat. 'Anyway, let's change the subject. I think you should concentrate on finding someone. You're such a catch and any man would be lucky to have you. Please don't stay single, just get out there and find someone who's worthy of you. Promise me you'll do that. It would genuinely make me happy to know you've met someone.'

Anna looked down, took a sip of her drink and placed the glass down. 'I haven't actually met him, but I've been chatting to a guy online.'

Steve sat back, forcing a smile. 'Well, that is *great* news. So, come on, tell me about him.'

'Not much to tell. He's nice.' Anna didn't want to tell Steve anything personal about Ben. She couldn't be sure how he'd react.

'So, you haven't physically met him yet?'

'No.'

'Well, don't wait too long. And I know it's none of my business, but please keep me posted on how it's going. We're mates if nothing else and I honestly want you to be happy.'

Anna smiled. 'Thanks.'

They talked a while longer, as Steve steered the conversation away from new relationships.

As it got later, Anna realised she'd drunk far too much, and told him she really should head home. 'I just need another wee before we go.' She got up and Steve watched her make her way across the pub to the toilets a little unsteadily. Then, checking no one was watching, he leaned over and reached inside her coat, and, feeling her warrant card, pulled it out and slipped it into his own pocket.

When she emerged from the toilets he got up and, after she had put her coat on, walked her to his car. 'Are you going to be okay getting up in the morning for work?'

'I'm on a late shift, I don't have to be in until twelve, so I can have a lie-in.' Anna yawned.

'What time do you finish?'

'Around eight.'

'So how are you going to make Maud's birthday party?'

'I'm going straight from work.'

Later, pulling up outside her house, Steve turned to her. 'I've had a great evening.' He lifted her hand and kissed it. 'I'm glad we've been honest with each other about . . . well, you know.' He forced another smile. 'I'll try to get to see you before I make the move to Glasgow.'

'That would be nice.' Anna burped. 'Sorry about that. I've had way too much to drink.' She went to open the car door, but struggled to focus.

'Here, let me help you.' Steve undid his seat belt and got out. Opening Anna's door, he held her arm and eased her out of the car.

He kept a tight hold on her as they walked up her path and watched as she tried to unlock the door, unsuccessfully. Then he took her keys from her and helped her inside.

'Let's get you some coffee, shall we?' Steve sat her on the sofa, and she immediately laid her head down. He went into the kitchen to put the kettle on. Five minutes later, he woke her up and, after drinking half a cup of coffee, Anna told him she needed to go to bed.

As they stood at the front door, he asked if she was going to be alright.

'I'll be fine. Thanks, Steve. I really love the necklace.'

'You're welcome.'

'See you . . . cheeks.' She grinned drunkenly.

As he stepped out on to the path, he turned. 'Oh, I meant to say, my phone's playing up. I should be getting a new one, so I'll let you know the number when I get it.'

'Why do you have to change your number?' Anna asked, feeling her eyes closing as she clung on to the front door.

'Well, apart from my phone playing up, I keep getting hassle from some woman I got chatting to, and she keeps calling me. I've blocked her number, but she just uses other ones to call me from. Anyway, I'll text you my new number when I get it.'

'Okay.' Anna gave him the thumbs up before she closed the door.

He drove away slowly. The fury that he had hidden so well since she'd told him about the abortion and that she was seeing a new guy was now boiling over. The moment she'd mentioned meeting someone else, the anger had started inside of him. He didn't believe for one minute that Anna was going to Sheridan's to celebrate a cat's birthday. She was meeting *him*. Then the bombshell that she'd aborted his child. His hands shook as tears of rage stung his eyes and he slammed on the accelerator, hearing the engine roar as he took the corner at the top of her road before suddenly braking, his tyres burning rubber on the tarmac.

When Steve came to a halt, he closed his eyes. 'You fucking bitch,' he said through clenched teeth. 'How dare you fucking kill my child.' He began to sob.

CHAPTER 16

Saturday 15 January

Sitting at her desk, Sheridan was going over the Canning murder, checking and re-checking the evidence and where the investigation was going, realising that they were getting nowhere fast. Dead ends at every turn and the list of suspects diminishing by the day. Taking a sip of her coffee, she looked up to see Anna plonking herself down on the chair opposite Sheridan.

'New necklace?' Sheridan said, nodding towards her.

Anna instinctively touched the angel around her neck. 'Yeah. Steve gave it to me for my birthday.'

'You never wear jewellery.'

'I do now.'

Anna told Sheridan how she had lost the original one that had belonged to her grandmother, and how Steve had had a new one made, designed from an old photograph he'd found of her wearing it. She also told Sheridan that Steve was moving to Glasgow.

'How do you feel about that?' Sheridan asked, secretly hoping that Steve really *was* moving away. Her instinct still told her that he had been violent to Anna in the past.

'I'm fine with it.' Anna hesitated, remembering that Sheridan had previously made her promise never to disclose the abortion to Steve. She took a deep breath. 'I told him about the abortion.'

Sheridan's shoulders dropped. 'Jesus, Anna. Why did you tell him *that?*'

'Because I was really drunk and a bit emotional, and it just came out.' Anna flicked her hand dismissively. 'He was fine about it. He even said that he was glad we never had kids. Anyway, he's moving on.'

'So, is that it? Is that the last time you're going to see him?' Sheridan asked, hoping for a swift 'yes'.

'We might meet up before he moves to Glasgow,' Anna replied. 'Maybe just for a farewell shag.' She grinned.

'You've been sleeping with him?'

'No. I was joking.'

'I think Steve leaving is for the best if I'm honest,' Sheridan said. 'And anyway, you're on a dating site now, and maybe this Ben turns out to be someone amazing. Did you tell Steve about him?'

'I told him I'd met someone online and we were just chatting, but I didn't tell him his name or anything about him.' Anna paused. 'I . . . . know you never really liked Steve, and that's fine.' She put her palm up to indicate that Sheridan didn't need to deny it. 'So, you can relax, it's definitely over between us. He's going to get on with his life . . . and so am I.'

'I never said I didn't like him.' Sheridan felt her face flush.

'He's not a bad person, you know. He does all sorts of nice things for his next-door neighbour. She's elderly and lives on her own. All she has to do is bang on the wall and he goes round there. He's got a good heart.'

'I'm sure he has,' Sheridan said, but knew she couldn't stop herself saying what had been on her mind for so long. 'I was just always worried that he'd been hitting you and you couldn't tell me.'

Anna put her head down. She had wanted to tell Sheridan so many times that Steve had hit her in the past, but the time was never right. Was this it? Was this the moment when she finally admitted it? Was it now or never?

She raised her head. 'Yes. He hit me.'

Sheridan felt her eyes fill with tears, partly from anger, but also relief that she had been right all along, and hadn't misjudged Steve. And relief that her best friend had finally spoken the truth.

'Come here.' She took Anna in her arms. 'I knew. I always knew,' she whispered.

'I know you did. And I'm so sorry I didn't tell you before.'

'You have nothing to apologise for. *He* does. Not you. Fucking bastard.' She held Anna's face in her hands, locking eyes with her. 'You know you can tell me everything and if you give me a statement, I'll have him nicked.'

Anna shook her head slightly. 'None of it was ever more than a common assault and so we're out of time to prosecute. Anyway, I wouldn't want to go through that.' She sighed. 'I don't want anyone knowing. Can you imagine? I'm a police officer, I'm not supposed to be a victim.'

'It doesn't matter about you being a copper. Anyone can be a victim Anna, you know that. There's no shame in it.'

'I know,' Anna said. 'But like I said, there's nothing more than common assault and he's changed anyway. He made a mistake. Let's leave it at that.'

Sheridan held her tightly. 'I just can't bear the thought of him hurting you.'

Anna closed her eyes. She knew that the time Steve had punched her in the face and knocked her tooth out was a more serious offence and if she admitted it to Sheridan and made a statement, Steve could be arrested. But he was moving on with his life and in the years since they'd split, he had changed, and

Anna had practically convinced herself that he would never hit another woman.

Rob Wills appeared at Sheridan's door. 'Sorry, am I disturbing a moment?'

Sheridan let go of Anna. 'No. What's up?'

'Frankie Yearwood, Marcia and Roger's son, is proving to be elusive. I've been trying to get hold of him, been to his house and then a few minutes ago, I rang his number again and he answered it. I started to talk about Canning and he cut me off. So, I rang back, and he answered again, and said he wanted nothing to do with it and told me not to contact him again.'

'Right. Let's look at him very closely. I want his phone checked, see where he was at the time Canning was killed. Find out if he owns a vehicle and get a marker on it, look at CCTV around his home address, see if we can place him there on the night. Let's find out if he works,' Sheridan said. 'Let's also find out what he looks like, height and build, and compare it to the images of the killer.'

'Will do.'

'We might actually be getting somewhere.' Sheridan smiled, glancing at Anna. 'And you might be right about this being a family member getting revenge.'

CHAPTER 17

Sheridan, Sam and her best friend Joni were in the kitchen, opening the first bottle of wine in celebration of Maud's birthday. Maud and Joni's cat, Newman, were tearing around the house, chasing each other and playing a cat version of hide-and-seek.

The doorbell rang and Sam answered it, finding Anna standing there holding a gift bag with cat paws printed on it and a bottle of wine. 'Hey. Where's the birthday girl?' Anna asked, kissing Sam on the cheek and following her into the kitchen, just as Maud flew in, being chased by Newman, both skidding across the kitchen floor.

'Jesus, how big is that scarf?' Sheridan laughed as Anna gave her a hug.

'What's wrong with it? It's lovely and warm. You just have no fashion sense,' Anna said, unravelling the enormous scarf and dropping it on to a kitchen chair.

After Anna handed Maud one of her birthday Jaffa Cakes, the four women toasted her with their full glasses of wine and settled in the living room, awaiting the pizza that Sam had ordered.

Five minutes later, the doorbell rang, and Sam jumped up. 'Bloody hell, that was quick.' She grabbed the money from the sideboard and answered the door.

Sheridan, Joni and Anna had gone back into the kitchen to get the plates ready when Sam entered.

Followed by Steve.

Anna put her hands on her hips, a little annoyed that he had turned up after she had expressively told him not to come.

As he entered, he put his hands up. 'Sorry to disturb the celebrations. Don't worry, I'm not staying, I just came round to give you *this* back, you must have dropped it when I took you home last night.' He handed Anna her warrant card.

'Cheers, where did you find that?' she asked as she took the black wallet from him.

'In the footwell of my car.'

Sheridan took the lead, feeling the sudden awkwardness in the air. 'Do you want to stay for a quick drink?' she asked. *Please say no,* she thought.

'I could stay for one. Just a soft drink for me.' He leaned against the door frame and crossed his arms, nodding at Joni and Sam.

Neither of them had met Steve before, but Sam was fully aware of Sheridan's concerns about him.

'Nice to meet you,' he said.

'You too,' Sam replied, tentatively.

Joni, on the other hand, had absolutely no idea of how Sheridan felt about Steve. 'I'm Joni. So, you're Anna's ex?' The half glass of wine that Joni had consumed had clearly gone to her head already as she rambled. 'I'm Sam's best friend. We met at school. It's Maud's birthday.' She beamed at Steve.

As if on cue, Maud appeared and tried to step past Steve as he leaned down and picked her up.

'You must be the famous Maud.' He held her high above his head and then pulled her to his chest, kissing the top of her head, and then bringing her face towards his. 'Give us a kiss.' He puckered his lips.

A low growl came from Maud's throat and Steve laughed. 'You're a bit grumpy, aren't you?'

And then Maud did something that Sheridan and Sam had *never* seen her do before.

She took a swipe across Steve's face so hard that she drew blood.

'Shit.' Steve dropped her back on the floor and instinctively put a hand to his cheek.

Sheridan pulled off a few sheets of kitchen roll and handed them to him. 'I'm so sorry, I've never seen her do that to anyone. Are you okay?' she asked. Trying to sound concerned but finding the whole thing rather amusing.

'It's fine, it's just a scratch.' Steve looked at his hand and wiped it, noticing more blood than he expected.

Joni piped up, 'It's okay, I'm a nurse and Sam's a first-aider.' She nodded at Sam, who leaned forward to look at Steve's injuries, while Anna tore off more kitchen roll and ran it under the cold tap.

Steve pulled out a chair and sat down while Anna dabbed the deep scratches on his face.

'It's quite deep,' Sam said. 'But I think you'll be fine. Just keep it clean and I'd lay off the aftershave for a few days, cos that'll sting like fuck.'

Sam stepped back, picking up her wine glass and taking a sip. She stole a quick look at Sheridan, who put her head down, trying to hide her grin.

Steve was holding the wet tissue to his cheek when the doorbell rang.

Sam set her glass down and went to the door. 'That'll be the pizza.'

'Forget the drink, I'd better be off. Leave you ladies in peace.' Steve stood up and after saying a brief goodbye to Sheridan and Joni, he followed Anna to the door, passing Sam in the living room as she carried the hot pizzas into the kitchen.

'Bye, Steve,' she said.

'Bye, Sam,' Steve mumbled and as Anna opened the front door, he smiled at her. 'I really didn't mean to turn up unannounced, I just knew you'd need your warrant card.'

'It's okay.' Anna smiled back. 'You could have just called me though.'

'I told you last night, my phone's playing up, I can't get into my contacts, and I don't know your number off by heart. As I said, I'm getting a new phone in the next few days.'

'When did you tell me that?' Anna asked.

'Last night.'

'Oh. I was a bit drunk last night.'

Steve leaned forward and kissed her on the cheek. 'Have a great time tonight. Speak soon.'

He got back into his car, looking back at the house. So, Anna wasn't seeing *him* tonight, the new guy she'd been chatting to online, she really *was* at Sheridan's for Maud's birthday. He checked his face in the interior mirror.

'Fucking cat,' he said under his breath, touching the deep red lines down his cheek and wincing at the stinging sensation.

'Fucking cat,' he repeated, as he started the engine and drove away.

CHAPTER 18

Sheridan dialled Anna's number.

'Birthday girl speaking, how can I help you?' Anna answered cheerfully.

'Happy birthday, mate. So, how are you spending your day off?'

'I'm going to pamper myself. I'm at the hairdresser's in an hour, then I'm going to get my nails done, might get some fancy false ones and then treat myself to a posh lunch. Then I'm going to get ready to come over to yours tonight, where you're going to spoil me rotten and give me amazing presents.'

'About your present . . . all I'm going to say is Sam got it for you.'

'Oh God, that's not good.' Anna laughed. 'Is Joni coming?'

'Yeah, she'll be there about half six. You getting to ours at seven?'

'Certainly am.'

'You can come earlier if you want.'

'No, it's okay. Seven suits me.'

'Okay. Well, have a fab day, don't worry about us slogging our guts out here trying to solve a murder.' Sheridan looked up to see Hill at her door.

'Anything new happening?' Anna asked on the other end of the line.

'Nah. And anyway, you need to switch off and go enjoy your day. See you tonight. Love ya.'

'Love ya, too.'

Sheridan ended the call and gave Hill a smile. 'Morning, boss.'

'Morning. Was that Anna?'

'Yeah.' Sheridan puckered her lips. 'I know you're going to say "no", but we're having a little party at ours tonight for her birthday, and you're more than—'

'No thank you.'

'Well, if you change your mind . . .'

'I won't.' Hill folded her arms. 'I'm off to see the chief, he wants an update on the Canning case. I'll be back later.' She turned to leave, before stopping. 'By the way, what have you got Anna for her birthday?'

'A remote-control helicopter.'

Hill shook her head once. 'Fine. Be sarcastic. I'll see you later.' And with that, she stomped off down the corridor.

◆ ◆ ◆

Sheridan walked into CID where Rob and Dipesh were both scrutinising a sheet of paper.

'What's that?' Sheridan asked.

'Un-fucking-believable,' Dipesh said, shaking his head. 'Hill has only gone and won the bet on the Liverpool–Everton game yesterday. Two–two draw.'

'She knows nothing about football. It's not fair,' Rob added.

Sheridan laughed, just as Andrea, the public enquiry officer, walked in holding an enormous bouquet of flowers.

'Who are those for?' Sheridan asked.

'Hill. But she's not in her office, shall I leave them here?'

Rob jumped up. 'Bloody hell, she's won a hundred and fifty quid and now she gets flowers.' He sighed. 'I'll look after them.' He walked over and took the bouquet from Andrea, peeking inside.

When Andrea had gone, the team gathered round, and Rob took out the card.

'It just says "To Hill". It's not sealed. Shall we open it?' Rob grinned.

'Absolutely *not*.' Sheridan snapped up the bouquet and walked to the door with it.

'Oh, come on Sheridan,' Dipesh piped up. 'They might be from an admirer . . . maybe she's got a secret lover?'

'We're not opening the card. I'm locking these in my office. You lot are so childish.' She quickly made her way down the corridor, placing the flowers on her desk after closing the door.

She stared at the beautiful array of pink-and-white roses, drumming her fingers on the desk. The angel on one shoulder told her not to peek at the card as it was none of her business who they were from. The devil on her other shoulder was shouting at her to open it immediately because no one would ever know.

She took a deep breath. Then her mobile pinged with a message from Anna. Attached was a photo of her new nails, with the message: *How lush are these beauties?*

Sheridan texted back: *Lovely. Hill's been sent some flowers and there's a card. She's out at the moment. Shall I open it?*

Her phone rang almost as soon as the message was sent.

'Oh my God, so you don't know who they're from?' Anna said excitedly.

'Nope. Shall I open the card? Is that bad of me?'

'Yes, it's very bad of you. Is it sealed?'

'No.'

There was a momentary silence down the line.

'Open it, but stay on the phone and tell me what it says.'

Sheridan placed her mobile on the desk. 'Okay. I'm going in.'

'What does it say?'

'*To Hill, it was so lovely to see you again after so many years. If you ever fancy going out to dinner, or just for a drink, here's my number. Alan.*'

'Any kisses?' Anna asked.

'Nope.'

'Well, well . . . Hill's got an admirer. Do you think it's an old flame?'

'I doubt it, she married young and . . . Anyway, don't tell anyone that I opened the card. Our secret.'

'Our secret.'

'Okay, I better go. See you at seven.'

'Alan, eh? Interesting.' Anna chuckled.

Sheridan ended the call, carefully placing the card in the envelope before locking her office door and heading back to CID.

As she walked in, Rob squinted at her, got up and joined her at the whiteboard, whispering 'So, who are they from?'

Sheridan carried on writing. 'I have no idea. I have morals Rob and opening that card goes against everything I stand for. Honesty and integrity.'

'What a load of bollocks, you opened it, didn't you?'

At that moment, Hill walked in. 'Have I missed anything?'

Sheridan snatched a look at Rob before answering. 'You won the football bet, a hundred and fifty quid.'

Hill walked over to Rob and put her hand out. 'Cough up.'

Rob took the money out of his drawer and tried not to cry as he handed it over.

'Oh and . . . some flowers came for you. They're in my office.' Sheridan put the whiteboard marker down and Hill followed her along the corridor. She unlocked her office door and pointed to the bouquet. 'There you go.'

Hill stepped over to the desk, lifted the bouquet and, without a word, she left.

CHAPTER 19

Sheridan was counting the candles on the birthday cake that her mum had made for Anna. 'Shit. There's only forty-five. We're one short. Where are the spare candles?'

Sam and Joni were fastening a 'happy birthday' bow tie around Newman's neck. Sam looked up. 'We haven't got any more. There's some big candles in the cupboard under the stairs.'

Sheridan smiled at Newman as she passed him. Rifling in the cupboard, she emerged with a ten-inch bright red candle, left over from Christmas. Pushing it down into the middle of the cake, she stood back. 'It's a bit big, but I think it works.'

Joni patted Newman on the head, then turned to Maud, who was sitting next to him. 'Your turn.' She held up the bow tie she'd bought for Maud and let her sniff it. Maud whipped it out of Joni's hand with a swipe of her paw, picked it up with her teeth and legged it into the living room.

Sam poured them all a drink as she checked the clock on the wall. 'Anna's late, do you think we should call her?'

'Nah. She'll be here soon.' Sheridan took a sip of her wine and checked she'd put the champagne in the fridge.

Just then, the doorbell rang.

'Here she is, better late than never.' Sheridan put her glass down and went to open the front door, surprised to see Hill standing there.

'Hill, you changed your mind? Welcome to the party.' Sheridan stepped back, smiling.

Hill stepped into the hallway, and it was then that Sheridan noticed how awful she looked.

'Are you okay?' she asked, just as Sam and Joni appeared with party poppers in their hands.

'I'm not here for the party,' Hill said, her voice broken and almost inaudible. Her eyes filled with tears which ran down her face. 'It's . . . Anna.'

CHAPTER 20

As they pulled into the hospital car park, Sheridan yanked off her seat belt and was out of the car the moment Hill applied the brakes. Hill followed Sheridan as they ran through the main doors and stopped at the reception desk.

'Can I help you?' the reception nurse asked.

'Anna Markinson was brought in by ambulance, do you know where she is?' Sheridan could hardly speak. Images of Anna being so horrifically injured made her want to be sick.

Hill had explained on the drive there that Anna had been found unconscious on a pathway leading to a pub car park. Two witnesses had pulled in and caught a male figure in their headlights kneeling next to Anna, a weapon of some sort raised above his head. When the headlights hit him, he stood up and ran. The two witnesses – both male – didn't see his face, but immediately went to help Anna.

She had been hit on the back and side of her head several times with an unknown weapon and was unconscious when she was found. Having been identified by the warrant card secured in her inside coat pocket, the control room had been informed, and they'd contacted Hill.

After a few minutes of waiting in the hospital, a doctor appeared and talked to Hill and Sheridan.

'How is she? Can I see her?' Sheridan asked frantically.

'She's having a scan at the moment. Do you know if next of kin have been informed?'

'I'm her next of kin. She's my sister,' Sheridan lied. 'And this is my DCI.'

'Alright, please come with me.' The doctor led them to a small office.

'Is she going to be alright?' Sheridan asked, ignoring the doctor's offer for them to sit.

'It's too soon to say. It looks like she has a skull fracture, a fractured cheekbone, a fractured arm and a broken nose. The scan will show if there's any bleed to the brain.'

Sheridan felt sick. 'Can I see her after she's had her scan?' she pleaded.

'We'll see.' The doctor's bleeper went off and he stood. 'I'm sorry, I have to go.'

Sheridan and Hill watched as the doctor ran down the corridor.

'Oh my God, Hill.' Sheridan put a hand over her mouth. 'She's not going to die, is she?'

'No. She's not.' Hill's normally stoic tone was gone, and she blinked down on a tear. 'She's tough and she'll get through this.'

'Who would do this to her?' Sheridan said, choking on her own words. 'What was she doing there? I thought she was coming straight to my house from hers.'

A female uniformed police officer appeared at the door. 'Ma'am, I'm PC Jo Walker. I was first on scene.'

Sheridan recognised the officer. She was long in service and had a reputation for being dedicated and efficient. Seeing her there gave Sheridan a sense of confidence. If Jo Walker had been the first officer to arrive at the scene where Anna was found, then nothing would have been missed.

'Hello, Jo. Please tell me what happened.' Sheridan tried to compose herself but couldn't stop shaking.

Jo put her hand on Sheridan's arm. 'Why don't we all sit down, eh?'

Sheridan and Hill sat.

'Like I said, I was first on scene, ambulance arrived a couple of minutes later. DS Markinson was on the ground, there were a few people from the pub with her as well as the two witnesses. They hadn't moved her. I didn't recognise who it was to start with, I know Anna from the nick, but it was only when I found her warrant card that I realised who she was.'

'Was she unconscious the whole time?' Sheridan asked.

'Yes. Once the ambulance arrived, I started gathering witnesses with other uniform, we searched and sealed the scene. I found a thick woollen scarf nearby which I seized, but I don't know if it's Anna's.'

'Is it blue? Really long?'

'Yes.'

'That's Anna's. She was wearing it the other day.'

'Okay, I'll get it sent for forensics.'

'Weapon?' Hill asked.

'Nothing found on the first search, but the area will be thoroughly searched again. Her car was parked in the pub car park and she had her car keys and her mobile on her. Witnesses from the pub said they saw her sitting on her own shortly before the incident, looking at the door as if she was waiting for someone. She started looking at her phone, and shortly after that, she left. Apparently, she'd been in the pub for around fifteen minutes. We're getting all the CCTV from the pub, the car park and surrounding area. The actual place she was assaulted isn't covered by CCTV.' Jo Walker handed Anna's keys and mobile phone to Sheridan. 'I had a quick look in her car, just in case there was anything in there to suggest what she was doing at the pub – if she was meeting anyone. There's a small case in the boot, which had some clothes and toiletries in it, so she might have been planning to go away.'

Sheridan swallowed, holding back the tears that threatened. 'She was supposed to be staying at my house tonight.' Her voice broke.

'Oh. I see. Well, I'll arrange for her car to be removed and get CSI on to it,' Jo said.

'Thanks Jo. What about the clothes she was wearing, anything in her pockets?' Hill pressed.

'Just her warrant card, keys and mobile. Her clothes have been seized and bagged for CSI.'

'Good.' Sheridan took several deep breaths. 'Did anyone actually see what happened?'

'No one saw the assault. The two male witnesses who pulled into the car park and saw a male kneeling down next to her said he had something in his hand, but they couldn't be sure what it was.'

'But she was already on the ground?' Sheridan said, wiping her face with her sleeve. She wanted so badly to let out her emotions and cry openly, but her police head had taken over.

'Yeah,' Jo said.

'So, whoever did this . . .' Sheridan had to stop for a second as her voice broke again. '. . . was going to finish her off.'

Jo nodded once. 'Possibly. The two witnesses couldn't really describe the suspect, just that it looked like a white male.'

'Is her purse missing?' Sheridan said.

'No. It was in her bag, which was found next to her. I've checked through it, nothing in there to suggest who she was meeting. As her bag wasn't taken, I'm guessing whoever attacked her wasn't interested in robbing her. She didn't have any jewellery on, do you know if she wears any?'

Sheridan closed her eyes, her mind working overtime. 'Yes, a necklace with an angel on it.'

'She wasn't wearing a necklace,' Jo replied.

'Okay.' Sheridan looked at Anna's mobile and typed in her password. Thankful that Anna had a habit of rarely, if ever, changing it. She looked through her messages and noticed several from 'Ben'.

The first message was timed at 1 p.m. that day. It read: *Still okay to meet at 5.30?*

Anna replied: *Yes. Looking forward to it.*

Ben: *Me too*

Then a further message from Ben at 3.15 p.m.: *Sorry, need to change the pub we're meeting at, there's a private function on at the Seven Horses, how about The Blacksmith? Same time?*

Anna: *That's fine. I'll see you there.*

Sheridan's heart sank. This must be the same Ben who Anna had mentioned meeting online. Then as she scrolled down, the next message screamed back at her.

Sent by Ben at 5.40 p.m.: *I'm sorry, something has come up. I won't be able to make it.*

Anna hadn't replied.

'Christ,' Sheridan said under her breath, showing the messages to Hill.

'Who's Ben?' Hill asked.

'Some guy Anna met online,' Sheridan said, taking out her phone.

'Who are you calling?'

'I'm looking up the number for The Seven Horses,' Sheridan said and a moment later she dialled the number and asked if they'd had a private function on that night. Once she had her answer, she ended the call and turned to Hill.

'There was no private function on.'

Sheridan rang Ben's number. The phone was switched off.

'I'll get enquiries done around Ben's phone,' Hill said. 'Let's see if we can trace him.'

At that moment, the door opened and the doctor from earlier walked in. 'Okay, we've done the scan. There's no bleed on the brain but we're moving her to intensive care.'

'What does that mean? Is she going to be okay?' Sheridan felt a sickness in the pit of her stomach.

'It's hard to tell at this stage, she might need surgery.' The doctor put a reassuring hand on Sheridan's arm. 'We're looking after her, but I will say, she's very poorly.'

'Can I see her?' Sheridan's jaw tightened.

'I'd like to get her settled first. Then, maybe . . . just for a few minutes,' the doctor said.

'What do you think she was hit with?' Sheridan could hardly bear to think about what had happened to Anna. But she needed the question answered if they were going to find the person responsible.

'From the shape of her injuries, and from my experience, although I can't be totally sure, I'd say it was possibly a hammer.'

'What about her arm fracture, could that have been when she hit the ground?' Sheridan was choking on her words.

'I don't think so. It looks like the weapon was used . . .' The doctor's voice trailed off as he noticed the horrified look on Sheridan's face. 'I'm sorry, I know this must be very upsetting . . .'

The doctor apologised for having to go and quietly left the room, after assuring Sheridan that he'd let her know when she could see Anna.

'She tried to defend herself. She put her arm up and he hit it with the hammer.' Sheridan felt tears sting her eyes, but she continued to force them back. She looked to Hill.

'Sounds like it,' Hill said.

Sheridan put her hands on her head and tried to stop herself from breaking down. She stepped out into the corridor and tried to calm her breathing. Hill joined her, placing a reassuring hand on her shoulder. As Sheridan turned, she looked past Hill to see Rob Wills running towards them. He grabbed Sheridan as soon as he reached her and she buried herself in his arms.

'It's okay. It's okay,' he said, holding her and looking at Hill. 'How's Anna?'

'We're not sure,' Hill said, before briefly telling Rob what the doctor had told them.

At that moment, Dipesh and Bridie appeared around the corner. The team were there. Together. Always facing everything together. Because they were a family. And one of them had fallen.

CHAPTER 21

It was almost midnight, and the team were still sat outside ICU when Sheridan was finally allowed in to see Anna.

She was shaking as she was shown into intensive care. The doctor had warned her that Anna had severe swelling around her face, and not to be alarmed by the tubes and wires that were attached to her. Sheridan had seen hundreds of victims of crime lying in their hospital beds, having suffered horrific injuries. But this was different. This was Anna.

As she was taken to Anna's bed, Sheridan cleared her throat and took a breath.

Anna's face was horribly swollen and heavily bruised, to the point that at first glance she was unrecognisable. There was a wound above her right eye and dried blood in her hair.

Sheridan's eyes moved to Anna's hands, one of which had a cannula inserted in it. Sheridan's impulse was to take Anna's hand in hers, tell her to wake up and that everything would be alright. As she went to touch Anna's finger, she looked at the new false nails that Anna had been so proud to show off earlier that day.

Tilting her head to one side, Sheridan leaned in closer and noticed two of the nails were broken off.

Her mind started racing as she tried to piece together what must have happened.

Anna was meeting Ben at The Blacksmith pub. He changed the venue. He knew she'd be there and at what time. Then he cancelled. Did he wait outside for her to leave? Did she grab him and that's how her nails got broken?

Her recent conversation with Anna came back to her:

'Have you met him yet?'

'Not yet. And even if I was going to, I wouldn't tell you.'

'Why not?'

'Because you'd turn up and interrogate him.'

So that was it, Anna had planned to meet with this Ben but hadn't told Sheridan.

Sheridan closed her eyes, thinking: *Anna had been wearing the long, thick scarf which was found nearby.*

She didn't want to leave Anna's side but this thought made her stand up, and she was buzzed out by the nurse.

Hill, Rob, Dipesh and Bridie were all stood in the corridor, turning to see Sheridan emerge. 'How is she?' Hill asked.

Sheridan paused. 'I need to know if she was wearing the scarf when she left the pub.'

'Why?' Hill took out her phone.

'I just need to know.'

Hill contacted PC Jo Walker, who confirmed from the accounts taken by witnesses that Anna had put her scarf back on before leaving the pub. One commented that they only noticed because the scarf was so long and Anna had wrapped it around her neck several times.

Sheridan looked up and down the corridor. There were too many people around, so she ushered the team into a nearby room, taking a deep breath before she spoke. 'I think we need to speak to Anna's ex – Steve.'

Hill's eyes widened. 'Why?'

'He bought her a necklace for her birthday. Jo Walker said that Anna wasn't wearing any jewellery, and her scarf was found nearby. So, if she was wearing the necklace tonight, then whoever attacked her went to the trouble of taking off the scarf to get to the necklace.'

'So – it could have been a robbery? Maybe someone in the pub saw the necklace and followed her outside,' Hill said.

'She wasn't robbed. They would have taken her phone and wallet if that was the case. This was a sustained attack and if it was Ben, then why would he take her scarf off to remove the necklace? Maybe Steve knew about Anna meeting up with Ben and followed her, attacked her and took the necklace back. He's angry.'

'About what?'

'I'll explain on the way, but I want to go and see Steve.'

'You're not making any sense, Sheridan. Where does Steve come into it?' Hill said.

'I don't have time to explain the whole story, but I think Anna might have managed to grab her attacker. She had her nails done today. They were new false ones and some of them have snapped off. Maybe she managed to fight back. I want CSI here to take swabs, and I'm going to pay Steve a visit.'

'We don't have anything to arrest him on, Sheridan.' Hill sighed.

'I know that. But I want to see his reaction when we tell him what's happened.' Sheridan wanted nothing more than to stay at Anna's bedside, but the urge to find her attacker was as strong. She was no use to Anna if she faltered now.

CHAPTER 22

Sheridan left Rob to carry out phone enquiries into Ben's mobile, while Dipesh arranged for CSI to take swabs from Anna. Hill had organised uniformed officers to be stationed outside ICU to ensure no one was allowed to see Anna. Bridie was tasked with starting background checks on Steve, with the little information they had on him. PC Jo Walker was to search Anna's car thoroughly and look for the necklace.

'So, explain your concerns about Steve,' Hill said as they drove to his house.

'It's a long story and I don't want this repeated to *anyone*. Not yet.' Sheridan sighed, her head was thumping and she still felt sick to her stomach. 'But basically . . . Steve hit Anna when they were together. She never admitted it to me until a couple of days ago, but I'd always suspected it . . . and she . . . she got pregnant with his child and had an abortion. I made her promise that she'd never tell him, but they met up the other night and she had too much to drink and let it slip. According to her, he was fine about it. But I have to wonder if he really was.'

'Let's not lose our focus on this Ben character, though. He planned to meet Anna tonight at the pub she ended up being attacked at, Sheridan,' Hill said.

'I know. But I'm going to do what I always do, go with my gut. I never trusted Steve, and I always suspected he'd been violent to Anna. But now I know I was right. I know this Ben is seriously in the frame, but I don't want to miss a trick if Steve has something to do with this.'

'Okay. How do you want to play it?' Hill asked. 'With Steve, I mean.'

'I don't want him to think for a second that we suspect him. If we do that, he might run. He's moving to Glasgow, so if he gets wind that we think he might have done this, he could disappear.' Sheridan put her head down. 'But I do want him to agree to give a DNA sample, that way we can hopefully match it to any DNA we might find under Anna's fingernails.' She paused, thinking. 'And I really want to search his house, because if that angel necklace is there, then we've got him.'

'We'll never get a warrant to search the place. There's absolutely no evidence to indicate Steve's the attacker, he's not under arrest . . .'

'I know the law, Hill, you don't have to remind me of the grounds to get a warrant issued . . .' Sheridan took a breath. 'I'm just saying I want the place searched.'

'Have you considered that the necklace could have come off in the struggle? It looks like Anna put up some sort of fight, so maybe it came off and just hasn't been found yet. Or the attacker took it with him? Or maybe she wasn't even wearing it tonight.' Hill looked at Sheridan. 'We just need to ask Steve's permission to search the house, and then we'll know if it's there or not. Maybe we'll find the hammer too, if that's what was used. Or something else that links Steve to the attack.'

Sheridan took a moment to answer. 'No. We're not going to ask his permission. If he says yes, then we know he's got rid of any evidence. And if he says no, then we've alerted him to the fact that we suspect him and he'll then get rid of anything that proves he did this. He could have hidden the necklace anywhere. We can't watch him twenty-four seven, so he'll have plenty of time to get rid of it and anything else.'

'I think you're wrong, Sheridan. If we don't ask him about searching the house, and we find out later that there was evidence inside, then I'll have to explain to the chief how we had the opportunity and didn't take it.'

Sheridan inhaled. 'Please trust me on this, Hill. I don't want him to leg it and I think he will if he gets even a sniff that we suspect him.'

'I hate to pull rank, but I think I'm going to on this one. Plus, I don't want you to lose focus on this Ben fella. It was clearly him that Anna was meeting tonight, Sheridan.'

'I know. But I'm trusting my gut here. I'm happy to ask Steve to volunteer a DNA sample, but nothing else.' She turned to Hill. 'I know you want to play this differently, but I don't want to. And if I'm wrong and we find out later that we should have asked Steve's permission to search the place, then I'll put my hands up and tell the chief it was my fault.'

Hill shook her head slightly. 'I know you're emotional and so I need to be the level-headed one here.' She turned to Sheridan. 'We play it my way. And if I'm wrong, then I'll put *my* hands up.'

It was 1.30 a.m. when they reached Steve's house. The living-room light was on downstairs.

'Looks like he's up,' Hill said, turning off the engine.

'Maybe he's getting rid of any evidence to link him to Anna's attack.' Sheridan inhaled deeply.

Hill looked straight ahead. 'Hence why we ask him if we can search the place.'

'For fuck's sake, Hill.' Sheridan closed her eyes for a moment. 'We're going to have to convince him that we don't suspect he has anything to do with the attack. That way, he'll feel confident and then he might make a mistake.'

Hill didn't respond.

Sheridan stared at the house. 'I hate this man so much but I have to make sure I don't show it.'

Before they walked up the path, Sheridan noted the blue BMW parked outside the address, remembering seeing Anna get into the same car when Steve had picked her up from work a few days earlier. She noted down the index number, so she could get the team to start making enquiries as to where he had driven to that night.

When they reached the door, she rang the bell, her hands trembling with the adrenaline pumping through her body.

Eventually the door opened, and Steve frowned as he saw Sheridan standing there with Hill.

'Sheridan, what are you doing here?' His frame was silhouetted in the darkness of the hallway.

Sheridan wanted to grab him round the throat, and it took everything inside of her not to. She had to play the police officer who was here to give bad news. Trying to keep the image of Anna in the hospital out of her head, she took a breath. This had to be the performance of her life.

'Steve, we need to come in.' Sheridan could hear her voice shaking with anger, but hoped that Steve wouldn't notice.

'Why? What's happened?' Steve asked, looking from Sheridan to Hill, before stepping back, allowing them into the hallway.

As they followed him into the living room, he turned to face them. 'You're scaring me. What's going on?' He was unsteady on his feet, and Sheridan could smell alcohol on his breath. His hair was dishevelled, and he looked like he hadn't shaved since he came to her house two days earlier. The whole place smelt strongly of bleach.

'Anna was attacked earlier this evening, she's in hospital.' Sheridan kept her focus on Steve's face, watching his reaction very carefully. It was then that she noticed the scratches on his cheek, through the stubble. An image of Maud swiping her claws across his face came into her mind.

'Oh my God. What happened?' Steve asked, placing his hands on his head. 'Is she going to be alright?'

Sheridan opened her mouth to speak, but no words came. Struggling to hold back on what she wanted to say.

Hill stepped in. 'I'm DCI Hill Knowles. Anna is very poorly, we don't know much else at this stage, but being her ex-partner, we thought we should inform you.'

Steve slowly shook his head. 'I can't believe this. Is she conscious?' He'd directed his question at Hill, slurring his words. 'Do you know who did this to her? Christ, she's not going to die, is she?'

'She's . . . not conscious and we don't know what's going to happen,' Hill said.

'Can I see her? I need to see her.' He suddenly turned. 'I'm getting my coat.'

The second he was out of sight, Hill grabbed Sheridan's arm and pointed to her own cheek, having noticed the marks on Steve's.

Sheridan shook her head and whispered, 'I'll explain later.'

Steve appeared, pulling his coat on. 'I want to see her. Can you drive me to the hospital . . . I've had a drink.'

'They're not allowing visitors at the moment. We haven't even been allowed to see her,' Hill lied. They didn't want him anywhere near Anna. If he'd had anything to do with the attack, allowing him to be near her could risk cross-contamination of evidence.

Steve dropped his head. 'Have they said they think she'll die?' He raised his face. 'Please tell me she's not going to die, Sheridan.

I know we're not together anymore, but I still love her.' Tears filled his eyes.

Sheridan felt her jaw tighten. *You fucking bastard*, she thought. 'I don't know,' she said.

Steve placed his hand on the back of the sofa, steadying himself, and Sheridan took it as a chance to ask him where he'd been that evening.

'You been out for a drink tonight?' she said, desperately trying not to sound like it was a probing question.

Steve wiped a hand across his mouth. 'Yeah, I went out earlier. Then I got home and carried on cleaning. I'm moving to Glasgow. I've been having a clear-out.' He flicked a hand indicating two boxes by the window. The rest of the room was empty, apart from the sofa and an armchair.

Getting rid of evidence, Sheridan thought.

'Where did you go for a drink? Anywhere nice?' Hill hoped he would give the name of a pub, so they could check out his alibi.

'Can't remember the name of it. It's in Cheshire.'

'How did you get there?' Hill asked.

'I drove.' He looked at Sheridan. 'I didn't have a drink until I got home, if you're thinking I was drink-driving.'

Sheridan knew that Steve was no fool. As casual as she and Hill were trying to come across to him, he likely knew why they were asking questions about where he'd been. She looked at the boxes on the floor. 'You *have* been busy,' she said.

'Yeah. It's a rented property and I have to leave it spotless, or I'll lose my deposit. So, I've been scrubbing every inch of the place.' Steve held Sheridan's stare.

'So, where's all your stuff?' Hill asked.

'I've taken most of it to charity shops or the tip. I thought I'd make a new start, new things.'

'Glasgow's lovely,' Hill said. 'Have you got family there?'

'No, just a few friends. I get quite a lot of work there, so it was the obvious choice.'

'What kind of work do you do?'

'I'm in the building trade.'

'Where are your family? If you don't mind me asking.'

'Not at all. I don't have any contact with them really. My mum died when I was a kid and my dad remarried and lives in Nottingham. We don't really talk. And I'm an only child.'

Hill nodded, consciously trying not to sound like she was interviewing him, probing, trying to find out everything she could about the man Sheridan had her suspicions about. 'Do you have somewhere to stay in Glasgow?'

'Not yet. But I'll probably be able to crash with a mate until I find somewhere to live.'

Hill pushed a little harder. 'I've been to Glasgow a few times, whereabouts are you staying?'

'Like I said, I'm not sure yet. I'm just going to get there and figure it out then.' Steve ran a hand through his hair. 'So, what happens now, about Anna I mean.'

'We'll keep you updated as soon as we know anything more. What's your contact number?' Sheridan asked, noting that Steve had asked very few, if any, questions about Anna's attack.

Steve gave her his mobile number, and Sheridan gave him hers.

'When you last saw Anna, did she mention that she was meeting anyone tonight?' Sheridan asked.

Steve shook his head, taking an age to answer. 'No. Sorry, my head's all over the place. I can't think straight.' He pressed the palm of his hand to his forehead. 'Actually, she did mention she'd met someone online recently, and they'd been chatting.'

'Do you know who?' Hill asked.

'No, she didn't say.'

Sheridan felt her jaw tighten. 'Steve, what's your date of birth?'

'Why do you need to know *that*?' He crossed his arms defensively.

'We have to keep a record of everyone we've spoken to, it's just routine.'

Steve hesitated before giving her his details.

'I'll also need to arrange to get a voluntary DNA sample from you,' Sheridan said, again keeping her tone as matter-of-fact as she could.

'What for? I'm not a bloody suspect, am I?' He stepped back.

'No, of course not. It's just because you and Anna have had recent close contact and we need your DNA to eliminate any that might be found on her. You're not a suspect, don't worry,' she said. *Except you fucking are,* she thought.

Steve swallowed, looking between Sheridan and Hill. 'I don't think I want to give a DNA sample.'

'Why not?' Sheridan asked.

Steve shook his head and looked to the floor. 'I've heard horror stories about the police planting DNA at crime scenes to set innocent people up . . . I just don't trust the system.' He looked at Sheridan. 'Sorry. No offence.'

'That doesn't happen. We simply take a sample—'

Steve put his hand up. 'Sorry, but the answer's no. I don't have anything to hide but I'm not giving you a DNA sample.'

And that makes you look even more guilty, thought Sheridan. 'Okay,' she said, keeping her tone calm. 'Well, if you change your mind, just let me know,' she said.

An awkward silence hung in the air. Sheridan asked to use the toilet. Making her way upstairs, she could hear Hill talking – keeping Steve engaged while Sheridan looked for any indication that Steve could have been involved in Anna's attack. The main bedroom door was ajar, the bed had been stripped. The mattress was bare. There was no bedding and no pillows. A pile of clothes spewed out of a suitcase and on to the floor.

She crept into the room, taking out her mobile. She pressed record and filmed the scene, focusing on the pile of clothes. Then she moved her phone slowly around, noticing the large, fitted wardrobe that took up the entire wall. The front of the wardrobe was fully mirrored, one door slightly open, revealing mostly empty hangers. The bedside table had nothing on top of it. Standing in the corner was a vacuum cleaner.

She stepped across the landing into the spare room, which was equally bare. Carefully opening the wardrobe, she noted it had been emptied and then, still filming, she walked across the landing into the bathroom. There were no toiletries on the shelves and she opened the bathroom cabinet. Empty. She carefully pulled back the shower curtain that was closed around the bath and spotted a bottle of body wash. No toothbrush, no razor, nothing. He'd cleared the place out. And scrubbed it clean. Not wanting to raise Steve's suspicions, she flushed the toilet before making her way back downstairs.

Steve had taken his coat off, draping it over the back of the sofa where he now sat with his back to her. Sheridan indicated to Hill to keep Steve's attention while she surreptitiously checked the pockets, hoping to find Anna's necklace. Her thought process being that after finding out about the abortion, he had somehow found out where she was going to be that night, attacked her and taken the gift back.

Finding nothing, she looked around the room for anything else that could provide a clue. Her eyes roamed over an empty bookcase and TV cabinet, sofa and armchair. There were two boxes on the floor by the window. That was it. She wanted to tear the place apart but had no authority to do so. So far, Hill hadn't asked him if they could search the property, much to Sheridan's relief. But Hill had been so insistent that Sheridan feared she would still ask. Would Hill go against her? Pull rank? Or would she trust Sheridan's instinct?

Steve was telling Hill about how he and Anna had met and while he spoke, Sheridan put her hand to her mouth in a drinking motion and Hill got the hint. Sheridan wanted to look in the kitchen.

'Steve, can we make you a coffee or anything?' Hill asked.

'No. I'm good thanks.' He turned to look at Sheridan.

'Can I grab myself a glass of water?' she asked. 'Then we should be going.'

Steve flicked a drunken hand at her. 'Sure. Help yourself.'

Walking into the kitchen, Sheridan flicked the light on, the empty surfaces reflecting back at her. By the sink was a bottle of bleach, several cloths and a kitchen roll. Next to the bin was a full black bag, tied at the top. She opened a cupboard and finding it empty she tried another; inside were two glasses and a plate. Taking one, she filled it with water from the tap and immediately poured it down the sink, and placing the glass on the draining board, she went back into the living room.

'You will let me know when I can go and see Anna, won't you?' Steve asked as he walked with them to the front door.

'Of course,' Hill replied.

Steve watched as they went down the path back to their car, before closing his front door.

Sheridan sat in the passenger seat.

As Hill started the engine, Sheridan held up a hand to stop her from driving away.

'Give me a second.' She got out of the car and, watching to make sure Steve wasn't looking out of the window, quickly made her way down the side of his house. Lifting the bin lids, she peered inside. Both were empty. As she made her way back to Hill's car, she peered into Steve's BMW but couldn't see anything inside. Not really knowing what she was looking for, she looked up at Steve's house and noticed his bedroom light come on. 'Bastard. He's literally cleared the place out,' she said, climbing into Hill's car.

'Do you think he's really moving to Glasgow?' Hill asked as they pulled away.

'I don't know. Possibly. I mean, there's literally nothing left in the house, his bedroom's empty apart from a few clothes and there are no toiletries in the bathroom. Looks like he's cleared the kitchen out too.'

'And scrubbed the place to within an inch of its life,' Hill added.

Sheridan rested her head back. 'I think he knows we suspect him.'

'What's with the scratches on his face?'

Sheridan sighed. 'He turned up at my house the other day and my cat took a swipe at him.'

'Do you still think he had something to do with it?'

'I'm trying not to let my feelings towards him cloud my judgement, but I wouldn't put it past him. He didn't ask enough questions about Anna. Not *where* she was attacked, *how* she was attacked. Nothing.'

'Agreed.' Hill nodded once.

Sheridan turned to face her. 'Really?'

'Really. But Ben is still our main suspect. What do you want to do now?'

'Go and get Anna's laptop.' Sheridan turned to Hill. 'Why didn't you ask him if we could search the house? What made you change your mind?'

Hill tapped the steering wheel. 'It was when he declined to give us a DNA sample. I thought about what you'd said. If he declined *that*, then he certainly wasn't going to let us search the place. It was a judgement call.'

'Thank you. For trusting me.'

'Oh, I'm sure I'll live to regret it. The chief will go fucking mental if I've got it wrong.'

'I'll back you up all the way, Hill. We're a team, remember.'

'Oh, the chief doesn't scare me.' Hill threw a look at Sheridan, the slightest of grins on her face. '*You* scare me.'

CHAPTER 23

En route to Anna's house, Sheridan called Rob and gave him the
details of Steve's car, so he could check if it had been picked up
on ANPR. She also asked him to check out Steve's phone number, along with Anna's landline, having left Anna's mobile with
him already so they could carry on looking through her messages
and calls.

They let themselves inside, and Sheridan reached up to grab
Anna's laptop from the top of the bookcase, knowing she always
hid it there when she left the house.

'Do you know her password?' Hill asked.

'Yeah. She never changes it,' Sheridan replied, logging on, her
hands shaking as she typed. She took a deep breath and clicked
on the chat history between Anna and Ben on the dating site.
Ben's profile showed his picture and full name. Ben Harper. He
was white, clean-shaven with a bright white smile, wearing a suit
and tie. His profile description read that he was forty-six, slim
build, five foot seven, originally from Manchester but now lived in
Liverpool and had his own accountancy business. He was a non-
smoker, never married and had no children. He enjoyed socialising
and drinking fine wines. He loved animals, especially cats.

The first few messages between him and Anna seemed like simple introductions. Ben was the one who had instigated contact with a simple 'Hi'. Anna had replied back with the same.

Sheridan and Hill read through the contact log. Anna had told Ben that she worked in criminal justice, leaving out the details of what she actually did for a living.

His response: *So I'm guessing you're a police officer?*

Anna had replied with a laughing face emoji.

Ben: *I understand if you don't want to say. I'm sure you have to be careful. My granddad was a police officer. Served twenty years. He always wanted me to join, but I'm too much of a geek. I'm better with numbers.*

The conversation moved to their likes and dislikes and their shared love of cats. Ben had three, and clearly adored them. Anna mentioned that her best friend had a cat called Maud who ate Jaffa Cakes, and had a boyfriend called Newman.

They chatted about holidays they'd been on and places they'd visited. Their favourite films and favourite wines. From the content of the conversation, they had a lot in common.

Ben talked about how he had an office set up in his house and how he loved working from home as he got to spend time with his beloved cats.

Sheridan and Hill read every message carefully, Sheridan wondering if Hill felt as guilty as she did prying into Anna's personal and private conversations. But knowing they had no choice. They had to find out everything they could about Ben Harper, and they had to *find* him.

She carried on reading.

Ben: *Do you know the Seven Horses pub in Liverpool?*

Anna: *Yes, I've been there before. It's a nice place. Live music on Fridays. Why?*

Ben: *Well, if you're free on Monday evening, I'd love to meet up. No pressure at all and I completely understand if you say no.*

Anna: *I can't on Monday, it's my birthday and I'm spending it with friends. Sorry. Maybe another time?*

Ben: *Oh. Happy birthday for Monday.*

Anna: *Thanks. I'm sure copious amounts of alcohol will be consumed.*

Ben: *I think you'll find it's obligatory on your birthday!!*

Anna responded twenty minutes later. *We could meet up before I go to my friends. Say around 4?*

Ben: *I can do 5.30, does that work? It means it will be a quick drink, but nothing like taking things slowly eh?*

Anna: *Sounds good and taking things slowly works for me.*

Ben: *You'll recognise me immediately, I'll be the one wearing a jumper with cat paws on it.*

Anna replied with three laughing emojis.

Ben: *You think I'm joking?*

Anna: *Not now I don't.*

Ben: *Here's my mobile number.*

Anna replied with hers.

Ben: *Great, see you on Monday. Looking forward to it.*

Anna: *Me too.*

Sheridan kept scrolling down, but that was the last online message sent between them. 'He sounds really nice,' she said, sitting back. 'But has he put on a facade to lure her to the pub and then attack her?'

'Highly likely. He's a suspect, but only because he knew where she was going to be tonight. I'm not going to dismiss your theory about Steve. I've doubted you in the past and you've been right, so I have to trust that instinct of yours now,' Hill said.

Sheridan called Dipesh and gave him Ben's surname, age and an image of his profile picture, along with his number, tasking him to contact the dating site to see if they held any information on him. After which they'd start making enquiries into his call data and where his phone had been at the time of Anna's attack.

After speaking to Dipesh, Sheridan and Hill checked each room carefully, looking for the necklace.

It felt so strange to Sheridan walking through the house; the emptiness, the silence. Standing in Anna's bedroom with the freshly made empty bed filled her with desolation and despair. Anna should be lying *there,* not in a clinical hospital bed, surrounded by wires and tubes, with machines bleeping every few seconds. She took a deep breath and started sifting through Anna's bedside drawer, the en-suite bathroom, anywhere that Anna might have left the necklace had she not been wearing it. Opposite Anna's bed was a bookcase with a TV on top, next to a photo frame. Sheridan stepped closer and picked it up. A picture of herself, Anna, Sam and Joni, all pulling ridiculous faces at the camera. She felt her chest heave and held the picture close to her, aching for Anna to be there. She placed the photograph back and made her way downstairs, where Hill was checking through cupboards in the kitchen.

'Anything?' Sheridan asked.

'No,' Hill said.

They stood in silence. The only sound coming from the ticking of the clock on the wall. Sheridan stepped into the living room and noticed Anna had no birthday cards on display anywhere. A sadness washed over her as Hill joined her.

'She hasn't got *one* birthday card,' Sheridan said, swallowing back tears. 'Not one.'

Hill tried to console her. 'Maybe she has and maybe she was saving them to open when she got to yours.'

Sheridan wiped a hand down her face, her voice at a whisper. 'My mum made her a cake, we put candles on it. She should be celebrating with us, not lying in a fucking hospital bed . . .' She closed her eyes.

'You can celebrate her birthday when she's home,' Hill said stiffly, trying to sound positive.

Sheridan turned to her. 'She's going to be alright, isn't she?'

'Yes. She is.' Hill felt herself welling up and turned away, refusing to let Sheridan see the pain she was feeling inside.

Sheridan's mobile rang – it was Jo Walker.

'Ma'am, I've searched Anna's car thoroughly. There's no necklace in there and nothing found on the initial search of the area where Anna was attacked. We've sealed the area off and will search again in daylight.'

'Good work, Jo. Thank you.'

'Any update on Anna?'

'No.' Sheridan pinched her forehead between her thumb and forefinger. 'Can we seize her car? Let's get it checked by CSI.'

'Yes, no problem.' She ended the call and looked at Hill. 'Let's head back to the hospital.'

At that moment, Hill's mobile rang.

'DCI Knowles.'

'Ma'am, sorry to bother you but I've got a lady on the phone who won't give her name, she's calling from a withheld number, says she has some information on the Dennis Canning murder.'

Hill frowned at Sheridan. The call had thrown her for a second. She was still reeling from the night's events, and it took her a moment to realise what the control room officer was referring to.

'Okay, put her through.' Hill put the call on loudspeaker so Sheridan could listen in.

'This is DCI Knowles, how can I help you?'

'I've been watching the news, and I see you haven't arrested anyone for killing Dennis Canning,' said the woman on the line.

'It's an ongoing enquiry.' Hill watched as Sheridan walked over to the window and looked out.

'Well, you need to look very closely at Bradley Penhaligan. Please look at him very, very closely.'

'What makes you say that?' Hill pressed.

'Just trust me. It was Bradley Penhaligan. And you're running out of time.'

'What do you mean?'

The line went dead.

Putting her mobile in her pocket Hill said, 'We've eliminated Bradley as a suspect in the Canning case, haven't we?'

'Yeah,' Sheridan replied vaguely, still staring out of the window.

'What did she mean . . .we're running out of time? Dennis Canning's already dead.'

'I don't know.'

'Hoax call do you think? Strange to call the control room at this time in the morning—'

'I don't care,' Sheridan butted in.

'What?' Hill walked over to her.

Sheridan turned around. 'I said I don't care.' She inhaled long and hard. 'I don't fucking care who killed Dennis Canning. I don't fucking care if we never catch his killer, he set fire to a house and killed four people, he destroyed a family and . . .' She struggled to speak as emotion seeped into her voice. 'And I can't think about anything else right now except who attacked Anna and the fact that she might not survive. So, whoever this woman is that thinks Bradley killed Canning can just fuck off, because I . . . don't . . . care.'

Hill looked at Sheridan. 'I know you're emotional, we all are, but I can't ignore that call. Especially the part where she said we're running out of time. If she's not a crank caller, then we need to know what she means by that statement.' She folded her arms and quickly unfolded them. 'We can have the Canning case handed over to Potters Road if you want. That way, we can concentrate on Anna.'

'Do whatever you want.' Sheridan dropped her head and put her hands over her face. 'I'm sorry, I just can't . . .'

'Sheridan, it's fine. You're exhausted and emotional. Forget about Canning and let me sort it.'

They stood in silence while Sheridan composed herself. Eventually she spoke. 'It wasn't Bradley . . . so this anonymous caller *is* either a hoax or she's trying to set him up. Like you say, we can't be running out of time if Canning's already dead . . . unless she means there are more victims to come, but that doesn't make sense if this was a targeted attack.'

'I thought you didn't care about the Canning case?' Hill raised an eyebrow as a brief smile crossed her face.

Sheridan closed her eyes for a moment. 'Of course I care about it.' She sighed heavily, then looked at Hill. 'I'm sorry about airing off. I'm just . . .'

'You don't need to apologise. I know Anna's at the forefront of your mind right now, so I can give you some slack. But we still need to catch Canning's killer. The press aren't letting up and the chief is on my back every five fucking minutes.' Hill shook her head. 'I think I know what you're going to say, but I can hand either Anna's case or the Canning murder over to Potters Road . . .'

'Don't even think about it. We're keeping both jobs, Hill. Ignore what I said about not caring about Canning's murder. Of course I care. I'm just tired.'

Hill smiled. 'Okay.'

CHAPTER 24

Sheridan and Hill were sitting outside ICU. Sheridan had been allowed to see Anna for a few minutes but had been asked to step outside while the doctors were with her.

On the way back to the hospital, Hill had questioned Sheridan about Anna's family, Sheridan having told the doctors that she was Anna's sister and next of kin. Sheridan explained that Anna's circumstances were not unlike Steve's: she was estranged from her parents and had no siblings. She had never talked about any extended family. Sheridan had given Hill more background into Anna's relationship with Steve. Guilt kicked in when she spoke about all the times she'd asked Anna if he'd ever been violent and she was beating herself up at every turn that she hadn't pushed Anna harder on the subject.

'You can't blame yourself for any of this, Sheridan. If, and it's a big if, Steve was the one that attacked her, then he would have done it anyway, whether you'd known for sure if he'd ever hit her or not.'

'I don't know why I can't let it go. Something's telling me that it was Steve. I *know* it was him. Fucking piece of shit. I swear to God, I'm going to get him Hill, whatever it takes.' Sheridan rested her head back as warm tears of anger stung her tired eyes.

Hill remained silent while Sheridan continued.

'If Anna did grab him, then he knows we might get DNA from her. That's why he's cleaning the house with bleach and refused to give us a DNA sample. He lived with her long enough to know how these things work.'

Hill finally spoke. 'Before I say this, I want you to know that I'm *completely* with you. But why do you think for absolute sure it was Steve? It could have been a random attack. Maybe it wasn't either Steve or Ben, we have to consider that.'

Sheridan shook her head. 'The scarf that Anna was wearing when she left the pub was really long and thick. I even commented on it when she wore it the other day. So, if she had it on before she was attacked, then whoever did this took the time to take the scarf off to get to the necklace. It *has* to be Steve.' Sheridan caught herself, suddenly overwhelmed by what had happened. She closed her eyes, but images of Anna in the hospital bed flashed through her mind. 'I can't lose her, Hill.' She choked out the words.

Hill moved closer, awkwardly placing an arm around her shoulder. She didn't do emotion, and she certainly didn't show it physically. But this was one of her own.

Sheridan had been holding back, but now tears tumbled down her face and Hill pulled her closer.

It was an unfamiliar feeling to Hill, the warmth of another human being, witnessing grief as Sheridan crumbled in her arms. The last time Hill had held anyone that closely, it had been her own children. Just before they got into the car on the day they died.

Several moments passed before Sheridan composed herself and Hill unravelled her arms. 'I want to prove it was Steve so badly, Hill. I want to throw everything at him.'

Hill hesitated before responding. 'Let's see what the phone enquiries and CCTV throw up, if we can get something on him, then we'll take it from there. But for now, we need to find Ben Harper.'

'What if there is no Ben Harper? I know that Steve's been on a dating site in the past. What if he logged on pretending to be someone else? Steve could have been the one who instigated meeting up, and if you think about it, the first pub he suggested, The Seven Horses, is on the main road – it's busy and well lit. Then he changed it to The Blacksmith, which is set back off the road, and where the car park has no CCTV. Oh God, the more I think about it, the more convinced I am. Steve has set this up.' She turned to Hill. 'Ben Harper doesn't exist.'

Hill crossed her arms. 'Sheridan, I know you're tired and you want all of this to be true, but it doesn't change the messages we saw on Anna's phone from Ben. I think he's a real person. He could have changed the location and attacked Anna. None of this proves it was Steve.'

The door to ICU opened and a nurse came out. 'You can see her now – just for a few minutes.'

Sheridan was on her feet and followed the nurse into the unit.

As she stood at Anna's bedside, her heart felt heavy. Gently taking Anna's hand, Sheridan leaned down, her lips an inch away from her ear. 'I love you,' she whispered. 'You're safe now, no one's going to hurt you ever again. I swear to God. You need to get well because I need you. I'll be back soon. I love you.' She gently kissed Anna's forehead, before quietly leaving.

When Sheridan went back to the waiting area, Hill stood up.

'What do you want to do now?' She touched Sheridan's arm, expecting her to want to get right back to the nick and help the team.

'Can you take me home?' Sheridan said.

Hill frowned, a little surprised at the response. 'Of course . . . I just thought you might want to . . .'

'Just take me home. Please.'

Hill sighed. 'I know you, Sheridan. And I know your emotions are wrecked, but I'm going to say one thing. Please don't do anything stupid. We'll get Steve if it was him, but we'll do it the right way. Okay?'

'Okay.' Sheridan nodded.

Hill drove her home and as Sheridan got out of the car, she popped her head back in. 'Thanks Hill.'

'You going to get some sleep?' Hill asked.

'Yeah.' Sheridan closed the car door and walked up the path.

She wasn't going to get any sleep. She needed time to think about what she was going to do next. And the only person she wanted to see right now was Sam.

CHAPTER 25

Sam could see the exhaustion on Sheridan's face as they sat at the kitchen table. Once Sheridan had arrived home and updated Sam and Joni on Anna's condition, Joni had taken herself and Newman off home.

Sheridan had replayed the recordings she'd made on her phone from her visit to Steve's house but hadn't seen anything of use.

She took Sam's hand in her own. 'I can't believe this has happened.'

'Me neither,' Sam replied.

'It was definitely Steve.'

Sam sat back slightly. 'Has he been arrested?'

Sheridan swallowed. 'No. We don't have anything on him yet, but I know it was him.'

'*How* do you know?'

Sheridan told Sam her theory about Anna's scarf and the missing necklace. She also told her about Ben Harper and the arrangement to meet Anna at the pub.

'So, if this Ben was the one Anna was meeting, why is he not a suspect?' Sam asked.

'He is. But I still think it was Steve . . . and that Ben Harper doesn't exist.' Sheridan sighed, swallowing a yawn, while Sam got up to make them another coffee.

'What evidence do you need before you can arrest Steve?'

Sheridan told Sam about the conversation she'd had with Hill and how they'd decided not to ask his permission to search his house. And their reasons why.

'And there's no way you can get a warrant?' Sam asked.

'No.'

'So, what are you going to do?'

'I don't know. I just wish I could get into his house without him knowing and look for that necklace.'

Sam processed this for a moment. 'But, there's no way you can do that.'

'No . . . I don't know. God, I can't think straight right now.' Sheridan closed her eyes. 'And to top it all, while we were at Anna's going through her laptop, Hill got a call from some woman to say that we need to look at Bradley Penhaligan for the murder of Dennis Canning and that we're running out of time . . . It didn't make any sense, but . . .' She opened her eyes and looked at Sam. 'I told Hill I didn't give a fuck about the Canning case. But I *do*. I want to catch his killer; I just know that the team are going to struggle now, with what's happened to Anna . . .' Her voice trailed off.

'Can't someone else, like another team, deal with the Canning enquiry now, or doesn't it work like that?'

'We could pass it over to another CID unit, but we've already put so much work in, and I think the team will want to see it through,' Sheridan said.

'But they'll also want to catch whoever did this to Anna. And I know *you* do. You desperately want to prove it's Steve, but . . . I don't want you to burn out.' Sam frowned and put her hands on Sheridan's shoulders, gently massaging them. 'Why don't you go and get some sleep, maybe after some rest things will be clearer. Anna's attack is personal and I know it's going to take its toll on you and the whole team. Maybe you need to hand that one over to another CID unit.'

'I *can't*. Because I'll never convince them that it's Steve. They'll probably look at the evidence we have and dismiss him. Just because my gut is telling me it was him, that won't be enough for them for take me seriously.' Sheridan rested her head back. 'I *have* to get into Steve's house.'

They sat in silence for a moment, before Sheridan suddenly looked up at the clock on the wall. 6.33 a.m.

'I've just had an idea.'

Five minutes later, she was heading out of the door.

She'd spent her career pushing the boundaries to get a result. But this time, it was different. This time, it was Anna. And Sheridan was not about to bend the rules.

She was about to break the law.

CHAPTER 26

Sheridan had sat outside the house for an hour, her heart thumping in her chest. She'd rung the hospital for an update on Anna and had been told there was no change.

Tapping the steering wheel nervously, she battled with herself over and over. Was there any other way to do this? But she kept coming back to the same answer. There *was* no other way.

She had to get into Steve's house without him knowing. And the only person who could help her was someone she and Anna had dealt with two years earlier. A criminal like no other that Sheridan had ever encountered in her career.

He was, on the face of it, a simple burglar. But he was much more than that. He could get into any house without being seen or heard and leave without a trace that he had ever been there. Even with the occupants inside.

He was also someone who, Sheridan believed, had taken his revenge on two men who had wronged him years earlier. But nothing had ever been proved. Because he was *that* good.

As Sheridan sat in her car outside his house, she knew that she was risking everything by coming to him to ask for help. Her head was full of every doubt imaginable, and her body was trembling, not just from exhaustion and emotion, but from the realisation of what she was contemplating.

She stared at his front door and imagined what she would say to him. And at that moment, it opened. And there he was. He looked at her for a moment before stepping back, leaving the door open for her.

Taking deep breaths, she got out of the car, walked up the path to the front door and stepped inside, hesitating in the doorway, where he stood, his head tilted to one side. He looked the same as when she'd last seen him. The man before her . . . was Gabriel Howard.

◆ ◆ ◆

'I thought, seeing as you've been sitting outside for an hour, that you might want a cup of coffee.' His familiar voice was strangely calming.

'Are you alone?' she asked, her voice breaking a little. She knew that he shared the house with his sister, or at least he had two years earlier.

'Yes, I'm alone. Denise moved out.'

A silence hung in the air for a moment.

'I need your help, Gabriel.' She could feel her eyes welling up even as she spoke, and she hoped he hadn't noticed.

'Hey, it's okay. Whatever it is, it's okay.' He tried to reassure her, his voice low and deep. He patiently waited until she had composed herself before putting his hands gently on her shoulders. 'What's happened?'

Sheridan's tear-soaked face turned to him. 'It's Anna. Someone attacked her with a hammer. She's in intensive care.'

'Shit,' Gabriel said softly. 'Let's go and sit down.'

Sheridan followed him into the kitchen, and he pulled a chair back for her. He listened silently as she told him how Anna had been found and about the horrific injuries she'd sustained. How witnesses had described the man kneeling next to her, his arm raised above his head, ready to hail blows down on her as she lay helpless and unconscious on the ground.

When she'd finished, Gabriel said. 'I'm so . . . so sorry. I don't know what to say, Sheridan. You said . . . you needed my help?'

Sheridan knew that what she was about to say would sound ridiculous. She was a high-ranking and highly respected police officer and Gabriel Howard was a man with a criminal record.

'I'm just going to ask you outright, because I don't have time to fuck about.' She paused. 'I need you to teach me how to get into someone's house, search it and get out without anyone seeing me.'

Gabriel put his hands behind his head and puffed out his cheeks. 'Well . . . I wasn't expecting *that*. But, why do you need to get into the house?'

'I need to get in because I think there's evidence in there to prove this person attacked Anna.'

'And I'm assuming there's a reason why you can't get a warrant. Otherwise, you wouldn't be here.'

'I can't get a warrant, because there's no evidence against this person.' She looked him in the eye. 'So, will you do it? Will you teach me?'

Gabriel shook his head slightly. 'It doesn't work like that, Sheridan. I always spent months studying people, their routines, entry points, exit points.'

Sheridan felt hot tears sting her eyes again. 'I don't have months, Gabriel. At best, I have *hours*. The longer I wait to do this, the more chance there is that he'll get rid of any evidence.'

'What about a voluntary search?' Gabriel pulled a face. 'Sorry, I'm sure you've considered that. I don't need to know.' He took a deep breath. 'Who is it?'

Sheridan hesitated before answering. 'Anna's ex-partner.'

Gabriel looked at the broken Sheridan Holler before him. He knew that for her to come to him meant one thing, and one thing only. Her back was against the wall. She had no other choice. But *he* did. And now he battled with it. If he agreed to help her, and it went wrong, he could end up losing all he had worked for.

When he'd been released from prison two years earlier, he'd turned to a skill he'd learned many years before. He was a carpenter and a brilliant one, making bespoke pieces of furniture for his clients, a job he was doing very well out of. Could he risk it all now?

Even though Sheridan had been the OIC in the case that had seen him sent down, he still had the utmost respect for her. She was so different to other police officers he'd come across in his time. She was brilliant, smart. And the most beautiful woman he had ever seen. But he'd respectfully buried his feelings for her the very moment his sister had informed him that Sheridan was very happily in a relationship with another woman.

As she sat at his kitchen table, he felt himself being pulled in so many directions. He could agree to help her out of respect that she had turned to him, of all people. The fact that she'd come to him proved that she trusted him. But it was an unthinkable risk for them both. But she needed him. And she needed an answer.

'If you get caught, you'll lose your job,' he said.

'I know.'

'Why would you risk everything you've worked for your whole life? There must be another way.'

'No. There isn't. And I'm risking everything because Anna is practically my sister. I love her and I'll break every fucking rule in every fucking book to get this done.' She looked him in the eye. 'You'd do it for *your* sister, wouldn't you?'

'Of course . . . but.' He dropped his head. 'I have every respect for you, you know that. And that's why I think you need to figure out another way. To put your whole career at risk to do this, is . . .

look, I get it, but I think maybe you're so emotionally involved because it's Anna that you're not thinking straight. Let's talk about it and maybe we can think of another way.'

'I'm telling you, Gabriel, there is no other way. And I have to do this *now*. Every minute that passes is giving him the time to get rid of evidence. He knows how the law works, he knows what I need in order to catch him out and so I have to be smarter than him.' Sheridan sighed. 'In all my years in the job, I've never dealt with anyone like you. A criminal, yes. But you're smart and the way you get into people's houses is . . . genius. I'm not condoning it, of course I'm not, but there's no one else who can do what you do. I know what I'm asking of you sounds ludicrous, but right now, I don't have any other choice.'

Gabriel leaned back in his seat, taking a moment to respond. 'I'm sorry, Sheridan. I'm really sorry, but I can't help you destroy what you've worked for all these years. You're the smartest police officer I've ever known. You'll think of a way, I know you will, but you'll do it the right way. By the right side of law.' He felt his jaw tighten as she stood up.

'I don't have time for any of that, Gabriel. But . . . thank you anyway.' She nodded once and made her way to the front door, stopping before she opened it. 'I hope I can trust that you won't tell anyone that I was here.' Sheridan turned to look at him.

'Of course I won't. So, what are you going to do?'

'I'm going to see Anna and then I'm going to get into his house, one way or another.'

And with that, she left.

Gabriel watched as she got into her car, before going back inside.

'Jesus, Sheridan,' he said under his breath.

CHAPTER 27

Hill sat at her kitchen table, nursing a cold coffee that she'd been staring at for the past hour. Her head was swamped with emotions she hadn't allowed herself to experience since she'd lost her family. The familiarity of those feelings overwhelmed her suddenly, as if she couldn't breathe. She gasped once and stood up, holding her chest. Heavy tears came freely, and she went over to the sink, running the cold tap and splashing her face with water, looking down at the bouquet that Alan had sent to the police station, which was lying on the draining board and still in its wrapper. Lifting it up, she closed her eyes and smelt the flowers, inhaling their sweetness.

Having not been given flowers since her husband, Ralph, had died, she didn't own a vase. Looking through her cupboards for a receptacle, and finding nothing adequate, she took the lid off her food blender and filled it with water, arranging the flowers, which now just looked awkward and ridiculous. Standing back, she crossed her arms and shook her head.

She flicked the kettle on and made herself another coffee. Tiredness had descended on her, but she wanted to get to the nick, having not bothered trying to get any sleep, the evening's events haunting her every thought.

She knew grief, she knew how in the darkness of night it would come and consume her. When Ralph and the girls had died, she'd wanted to be with them. Always telling herself that she should have been in the car, they were all meant to go together. But God had other plans. And so she was left, alone and terrified of the path before her.

She'd considered ending it all so many times because what was the point in carrying on? Why even get out of bed? For what? To face the day without her beautiful family. To face a life of despair, guilt and loneliness. If she couldn't have her family, then she wanted no one. No one could get close to her and so she threw up a wall. She would never love again, never let anyone love her, and she'd maintained that stance for all the years since the accident. Until she'd been put on Sheridan's team.

They weren't just a group of colleagues, working together. They were a family who had each other's backs. They loved each other in a way that only true friends could. Sheridan's reaction to what had happened to Anna was tangible; grief in its rawest form.

Hill looked skywards. 'I don't believe in you,' she whispered. 'I stopped doing that. But . . . if you are real and you are listening, then don't let Sheridan lose Anna. Don't let *us* lose Anna. That's all I'll ever ask of you.'

There was a knock at her front door. She checked her watch: 7.18 a.m.

She opened it to find Gloria standing there, leaning on her walking frame.

'What are you doing here? Is everything alright?' Hill asked.

'I came to ask you the same question.'

'Why?'

'Are *you* alright? You went out yesterday evening and didn't come home all night, so I thought I'd check if everything's okay. Can I come in, or do I have to stand here freezing me bits off? Get the kettle on and tell me what's going on.'

Hill shook her head. 'I'm fine and I don't have time to—'

145

'Oh, be quiet you miserable old cow. Come on, let me in.' Gloria lifted her walking frame over the doorstep, catching Hill in the leg.

Gloria barged past her into the kitchen, where she put the kettle on, before pulling out a chair and plonking herself down. 'Right then. Why were you out all night?'

'It's none of your business.'

'Was it work?'

Hill took an exaggerated breath. 'Yes. It was work. And no, I don't want to talk about it.' She felt her voice breaking as she spoke.

'Something bad happened, I can see it in your face. You might be a miserable old bat, Hill. But you're still my friend and friends talk to each other. You only have *me*, so . . . talk.'

Hill crossed her arms protectively across her chest. 'One of my team was attacked last night. She's in hospital . . . and I don't know if she's going to be okay.'

Gloria slowly pulled herself up and shuffled over to where Hill was standing, placing a hand on her arm. 'Have you caught the person who did it?' Her voice was low and calm.

'We have an idea. But it's . . . complicated.'

'I know you can't go into detail and that's fine. But you need to let it out, Hill. I know you, I know you better than anyone and you keep everything inside.' Gloria gently poked at Hill's chest. 'Sometimes, just sometimes, you need to let that brick wall crumble a little bit.'

Hill felt tears filling her eyes and she looked down. 'I can't.' She let out a sob. 'I can't.'

Gloria wiped a tear from Hill's face. 'I've got news for you. You *can*. Because what you're doing now, by letting it out just a tiny bit, is the first step.' She reached out for Hill's head and gently rested it on her shoulder. 'Come on, kid. Let it out.'

Hill Knowles felt the foundations of her wall begin to crack. Just a little.

After a few moments, she raised her head, kissed Gloria on the cheek and turned to make them both a cup of tea.

Gloria looked at the flowers that Alan had sent to the nick, stuffed into the food blender. 'Bloody hell, Hill. Are those the flowers that Alan sent you?'

Hill poured water into the cups. 'How did you know he'd sent me flowers?'

'Because he said he wanted to.' Gloria shook her head. 'Why are they in the blender? What are you doing with them? Making a feckin' smoothie?'

Hill explained that she didn't own a vase. As they sat drinking their tea, Gloria admitted that when Alan had mentioned wanting to buy Hill some flowers, he'd originally planned to leave them on her doorstep, but Gloria had told him to have them sent to Hill at the police station.

'Why did you do that?' Hill asked.

'Because I thought it would be much more fun if your colleagues thought you had a secret admirer. Not that I told Alan. He thought he'd upset you because you left so quickly.' Gloria sipped her tea. 'I told him he hadn't upset you and that it's just the way you are – miserable and moody. Have you got any biscuits?'

Hill got up and retrieved a packet of Rich Tea from the cupboard, handing them to Gloria. 'I'm not miserable and moody. I just didn't want to talk anymore, that's why I left.'

'He told me about your conversation. And I know you left because he asked about Ralph.' Gloria tore the biscuit packed open. 'I know Ralph was the love of your life and you don't want to be with anyone else. I know you've never gotten over losing the girls and you're terrified of letting anyone get close to you. But if you spend the rest of your life grieving for them, then your life is a wasted one.

You adored them, nothing will ever change that. But I worry about you, Hill. I worry that you're so angry all the time and if Ralph was here now, he'd tell you the same thing. I never met him, but I know he was a good man, and he'd want you to be happy.'

When Hill didn't respond, Gloria took the opportunity to continue. 'When I lost my Jack, I swore I'd never be with another man, and I was only in my fifties. Then, I met Cyril, and I fell in love. The three years I had with him were the best years of my life, and it didn't mean I stopped loving Jack. I just fell in love again.' Gloria bit into her biscuit. 'Well, that was until he turned into a manic depressive and took all them pills.' She shrugged her shoulders. 'Silly old bugger. Anyway, what I'm trying to say is, life goes on. But only if you let it.'

Hill didn't reply, finishing her tea in silence before telling Gloria that she needed to get showered and get back to work. 'You can stay and finish the biscuits while I'm getting ready if you like,' she called as she made her way upstairs.

Fifteen minutes later, she came down and found the kitchen empty. She grabbed her keys from the kitchen counter, called the hospital and was told that Anna was stable. It was when she ended the call that she spotted Alan's flowers, now beautifully displayed in a vase with a note beside them.

> *You only have one life. It's not too late to start living it. P.S. It wouldn't kill you to buy some decent biscuits. And I want the vase back when the flowers die. Love Gloria. xx*

Hill stared at the note and allowed herself a brief smile. As she made her way to the front door, she hesitated, before returning to the kitchen and flicking the bin lid open. She reached inside, taking out the card that Alan had written. Hill smoothed it out and re-read it, before placing it down on the counter.

CHAPTER 28

Sheridan was walking into the hospital when her phone rang. It was Steve.

'Hello, Steve.' Her stomach turned as she spoke.

'How's Anna? I tried ringing the hospital, but they won't tell me anything.'

'There's no change, I'm afraid.'

'So, she hasn't come round?'

'No.'

'I want to see her. I'm her ex-partner, so I have the right to see her, surely. I'm coming to the hospital.'

'They won't let you in, Steve. They're not letting anyone see her. Even me. She's too poorly.'

'That doesn't make any sense. Why is she not allowed visitors?'

'She's got so many doctors around her, they need to do their job, and we have to respect that.'

'But they can't expect me to not want to see her. If I just turn up, they'll have to let me in eventually.'

'Steve, please just stay away for now. I'll let you know as soon as she's allowed visitors, I promise.'

Steve hung up and Sheridan's jaw tightened. 'Don't you dare come anywhere fucking near her,' she said under her breath, before making her way to ICU, stopping at the vending machine to buy a coffee for the uniformed officer stationed outside the unit.

He gratefully took a sip. 'Thanks, ma'am.'

'I'll be in with Anna for an hour or so, so why don't you go and take a break,' Sheridan said.

'That would be great, thanks ma'am. Just shout if you need me.' The officer walked off down the corridor.

After being buzzed back into the ward, Sheridan sat at Anna's bedside. The doctors had updated her that she was comfortable and although there was no change in her condition, she hadn't deteriorated.

She held Anna's hand gently, hoping that maybe, just maybe, the touch would be enough for Anna to wake up. Sheridan whispered, 'You're going to be fine. I'm here.'

She spent the next half an hour telling stories of all the good times they had shared. She talked about Sam's cooking, how Maud and Newman were probably falling in love. She talked about anything that might spark a reaction, not knowing if Anna could even hear her. Sheridan had stood up to stretch her back when a nurse approached her.

'There's a guy outside asking to see you.'

Shit. Steve, you fucker, thought Sheridan. 'Okay, thanks,' she said, before making her way to the door.

She peered through the glass but couldn't see anyone, and pressed the buzzer to let herself out. Sheridan checked up and down the corridor, looking at the people walking past, but still couldn't spot him. As she went to go back into ICU, she noticed a figure out of the corner of her eye and turned her head.

Stepping out in front of her, his head tilted to one side, was Gabriel Howard.

◆　◆　◆

Sheridan buzzed to be let back into the ward and quietly ushered Gabriel towards Anna's bed.

He stood, silently looking down at her, and Sheridan thought for a moment that she could see tears in his eyes. Gabriel stayed back, as if respectfully not invading Anna's space, but he didn't take his eyes off her. Sheridan could see he was visibly shocked at the sight before him. After a few moments, he looked around, checking the staff were out of earshot, before turning to Sheridan, nodding slowly.

'Let's go and break the law, shall we?' he whispered.

CHAPTER 29

Hill walked up the corridor to CID, carrying a box. The team were already there, busy working on their tasks.

'Good morning, everyone,' she said, placing the box on Rob's desk.

A sombre good morning was returned by all.

'I've been on the phone to the hospital, Anna had a comfortable night and although there's no change, she's not shown any signs of deterioration. So, help yourself to cakes,' she said, nodding at the box and noticing confusion on the faces before her.

Rob was the first to speak. 'What are they for?'

Hill cleared her throat. 'Well, I know that Sheridan brings cakes in and as she's not here, I thought I'd bring them in.'

Rob looked at Dipesh and Bridie in turn, an unexpected smile creeping over his face.

'What?' Hill asked.

'We . . . usually get cakes when we've *solved* a case,' he said tentatively.

'Oh. Right.' Hill paused. 'Anyway. I know you're all exhausted and shocked about what's happened to Anna, and I also know we still have the Dennis Canning case.' She told the team about the anonymous caller who had pointed the finger at Bradley Penhaligan as being Canning's killer and had intimated that the police were running out of time.

The team discussed what the caller could have meant by this, and it was agreed that although it might well be a hoax, they couldn't dismiss it.

'I've agreed with Sheridan that we're going to be dealing with Anna's attack, *and* carrying on with the Canning murder. Is everyone agreed?' Hill looked around the room.

Rob was the first to respond. 'We all spoke this morning and thought you might suggest we don't take on Anna's case because it's too close to home. But we want to keep it. Her case *and* the Canning job. We're all over that. All our background checks are pretty much done and we're concentrating on Frankie Yearwood. He's the only one who's being elusive and not engaging with us, so at the moment, he doesn't have an alibi. We're getting his phone data, looking into any vehicles he owns, we're going to be checking CCTV around his home address and trying to establish if we can place him at the scene. We're also looking at Milo Adams . . .'

Hill put her hand up. 'Okay, point taken.'

Rob continued. 'And as far as Anna's case goes, we're already making a shitload of enquiries.' He threw a look at Dipesh and Bridie, who were both nodding, before focusing back on Hill.

Hill put her hands on her hips, thinking for a moment. 'Fine. But I will say this. With Anna's case, we have to do everything by the book. Our enquiries will be monitored by a DI from another team, just to make sure we're doing everything right.'

'We *will* do everything right,' Rob said, before asking, 'is Sheridan coming in today?'

'I don't know. I spoke to her briefly earlier, she's at the hospital with Anna.'

She cleared her throat and went on to tell the team Sheridan's theory that Ben Harper didn't exist and Steve had somehow set himself up on the dating site to lure Anna to the pub.

'We're looking into Ben Harper, so we'll soon know if Sheridan's right,' Rob said. 'And let's face it, she usually is.'

'True,' Hill agreed. 'Rob, can I see you in my office?'

Rob followed her down the corridor.

'Close the door,' Hill said, sitting at her desk.

'As the longest-serving officer on the team, you're now acting detective sergeant. Just until Anna's back with us.'

Rob was taken aback. 'I don't know what to say. I mean, yes of course I'll act up. I just wish it was for a different reason.'

'So do I.'

There was a knock on Hill's door.

'Come in,' she called out.

Dipesh appeared. 'We've got an update on Milo Adams, the guy who works at the café.' He glanced at the sheet of paper in his hand. 'The address he told Sheridan he was living at when Dennis Canning was murdered was derelict.'

'So, he was living rough inside? What's suspicious about that?' Hill asked, noticing the chief constable's number flash up on her desk phone. She picked it up and put it straight back down.

Dipesh continued. 'It *was* derelict. But it was demolished two weeks before the murder. He *couldn't* have been living there.'

Hill sat back. 'Interesting. Anything else?'

'We're still checking through the CCTV from when he got on the bus after he left work early that evening. We know he didn't get off where he said he did.'

'Remind me what he said.' Hill ignored the phone which started ringing again.

'He said he'd got off at the stop near to his home address, which we know isn't true because we've got CCTV to prove he didn't. And now we know that address was just a pile of rubble.'

'Good. Okay, let's concentrate on seeing where he did get off. Once we know that, we can establish if he had time to get back to the crime scene and kill Canning.' Hill paused. 'We have no idea what his motive would be, but he's lied to us, and he must have a reason to do that.' She looked at Rob. 'Put him up on the whiteboard as a suspect.'

CHAPTER 30

Sheridan and Gabriel left the hospital separately so as not to be seen together by any police officers that might be around.

As Sheridan was coming down the stairs, anxiety took over as the enormity of what she was about to do suddenly hit her.

She spotted Gabriel walking slowly towards the car park and caught up with him.

'Meet me back at your house,' Sheridan said. 'We need to come up with a plan.'

He smiled at her as he went to get into his car. 'I've already got a plan.'

Sheridan watched as Gabriel made two cups of coffee, noticing for the first time how immaculate his kitchen was. As was he. He looked after himself, keeping fit by running. He had an aura about him that made Sheridan feel calm in his presence, somehow knowing that with him on board they might just get away with whatever he had in mind.

He placed her coffee on the kitchen table and sat opposite her, blowing the steam off his own.

'So, what's your plan?' she asked.

Gabriel cleared his throat. 'We don't have time for me to teach you how to get into this guy's house. So, I need you to get *me* in.'

Sheridan inhaled. 'Okay.' She sipped her coffee, and started thinking out loud. 'Steve wants to see Anna, so if I go to his house now to speak to him, what's the easiest way to get you inside without him seeing you?'

'Can you describe the place, or draw me a quick plan? Have you been upstairs?' He stood up and grabbed a pad and pen from the kitchen drawer, placing them in front of Sheridan.

'Yeah. I know the layout of the place.' Sheridan took another sip of her coffee, before reaching into her pocket for her mobile. 'Actually, I videoed the upstairs rooms when I was there last night. Would it help if you watched the recording?'

'Absolutely.' Gabriel smiled as Sheridan found it and slid her phone across the table towards him. 'I won't ask why you made this recording.' He watched intently, stopping and rewinding every now and then to memorise the layout of Steve's house. While he watched, Sheridan sketched the plan of the downstairs.

'The place looks pretty empty,' Gabriel said.

'Yeah. He's moving out.'

He looked up. 'Moving out or doing a runner?'

Sheridan raised an eyebrow. 'The latter I think.'

Gabriel handed Sheridan's mobile back and fetched his laptop from the coffee table.

'What are you doing?' she asked.

'Normally I like to check a place out by physically being there and spending time checking the area, but we don't have time for that. So, I'll look on Google Earth.'

After studying the images, Gabriel switched off his laptop. 'Okay. I think this could work. When you arrive at his house, you need to make sure he walks into the property in front of you. So, maybe suggest that you'd like a cup of coffee and get him to go straight to the kitchen. Don't close the front door fully, and I'll get in that way. I need a few seconds to get upstairs, and I'll stay there until you get him out of the house.' Gabriel hesitated. 'Did you notice if any of the stairs or floorboards creak?'

Sheridan thought for a moment. 'I don't think so. I managed to walk into his bedroom, the spare room and across the landing to the bathroom and I don't remember making much noise.'

'Good.'

'How long will you need to be inside?' Sheridan asked.

'As long as you can give me. What am I looking for?'

'In particular, a gold necklace.' Sheridan described the angel pendant that Steve had given Anna for her birthday.

'Okay. Anything else?'

Sheridan closed her eyes for a moment. 'I don't know.' Exhaustion was kicking in and she rubbed her temple, trying to think. 'I basically need anything that can link him to Anna's attack, but you won't know what that is and I won't be there to see it. Unless you find a hammer, but if you do, don't touch it . . .' She looked at him and noticed he was grinning. She didn't need to tell Gabriel the obvious and quickly shook her head.

He nodded. 'Okay. Well, I can get out of a window and leave through the back garden. No worries on that score. I'll take a good look around and I'll take pictures of anything I think's important. I'll then send them to you. If I do find anything, I'll make sure I make it look like a burglary and make enough noise when I'm leaving so that hopefully a neighbour calls the police, and then your lot will turn up and find whatever I leave out for them to see. Do you need me to make it look like a burglary anyway, even if I don't find anything?'

'Yes. Because that way, I can get into the property and have a look around myself, and maybe I'll spot something that you don't see.'

'That suits me.' Gabriel grinned. 'Plus, I get to smash his windows.'

'How will I know when you're inside the house?'

'I'll text you a smiley face.'

Sheridan smiled wearily, before swallowing. 'I hope this works. I mean, what if it goes wrong?'

Gabriel leaned a little closer to her. 'You're the smartest police officer I've ever known, Sheridan. And you know what *I'm* capable of. You have to trust me. It'll work.'

Sheridan put her elbows on the table and rubbed her forehead. She knew that trusting Gabriel meant risking everything. She also knew about his previous feelings towards her and suddenly doubted her own morals about turning to him.

She studied his face for a moment. 'Why are you helping me? You're taking a huge risk here.'

'I know. It's fine. I just don't want him to get away with it.'

'Is that the only reason? Or is it because you like me?'

'I *did* like you, and yes, there was a time when I wanted to ask you out. But I know you're with a woman and if I'm totally honest, the minute I found that out, whatever feelings I had for you disappeared. Look, forget about all that now. I'm not doing this because I was attracted to you once, I'm doing it because I want to help. It's that simple.' He grinned. 'Anyway, the more I look at you, the more I find you very unattractive.'

Sheridan shook her head, allowing herself a smile. 'If it goes tits up, we'll both end up in the shit.'

'Stop doubting it. It'll work. Does he have a car?'

'Yeah, a blue BMW, he parks it outside the house.'

'And one last question . . . Does he have a massive fucking dog?' Gabriel grinned again.

'No,' Sheridan replied. 'You know we're trusting each other completely here, don't you?'

'Yes. I know. And I want you to know that you *can* trust me.' Gabriel stood up. 'I just need to grab a few things, get changed and then we'll go and stage a burglary, shall we?'

Ten minutes later, Gabriel came back downstairs. 'I'll take my car. I need to do a quick drive around the area before you go to his house. Once I'm in position, I'll text you a thumbs up and you can then knock on his door.'

Sheridan stood up, feeling her legs shaking slightly, holding the table to steady herself.

'You okay?' Gabriel asked.

'Yeah. Fine, just tired . . . and beginning to doubt this plan.'

He placed a reassuring hand on her arm. 'I wouldn't think about doing it if I didn't think it would work. This is what I do, Sheridan. Remember that.'

'Okay.' She forced a smile. Now it was real. Now it was really happening.

CHAPTER 31

Sheridan sat in her car, just up the road from Steve's house. She could see his car parked outside and knew that Gabriel would be somewhere around, watching. All she had to wait for was the message that he was in position and then she'd knock on Steve's door. The plan kept going round in her head and the doubts began to creep in every now and then. But then she thought about Anna and the reason she was taking such a risk.

Her thoughts were broken when her phone pinged. The thumbs-up message from Gabriel appeared on her screen. She felt her heart race and took a deep breath. 'Here we go,' she said under her breath. 'Goodbye career.'

She started the engine and drove nearer to Steve's house, parking behind his BMW.

Getting out of the car, she resisted looking around to see if she could spot Gabriel. But she already knew that wherever he was, he'd have made himself invisible.

She knocked on Steve's door.

A few moments later, the door opened, and Steve appeared. 'Sheridan. Oh, God, has something happened?' he asked. 'Is it Anna?'

Sheridan nodded. 'Can I come in?' she asked.

Steve swallowed. 'Of course.' He stepped back and Sheridan put her hand on the door. She had to get Steve to turn his back and walk into the house so she could leave the door ajar for Gabriel to get in. But Steve remained where he was, and Sheridan suddenly panicked. The first part of the plan had already failed, and she hesitated for a moment, trying to think of what to do. Her mobile rang, and she took it out of her pocket. Steve stood there waiting while she answered the call. 'DI Holler.'

'Stay on the phone,' Gabriel whispered. 'Tell him you need to take this call and hover in the doorway, tell him you won't be a second. He'll go into the house and then you can leave the door very slightly ajar.'

'Right,' Sheridan replied, and put her hand over the mouthpiece. 'Sorry, Steve, I need to take this. I won't be a sec.' Steve nodded and turned, walking into the living room.

'Good. That's good. Okay, so now just say a few policey things,' Gabriel said.

Sheridan put her head down. 'That's all received. Thank you.'

'Now end the call and get him to go into the kitchen. Then let me do the rest. And don't worry. We've got this. You'll know I'm inside when I text you the smiley face. My phone will be off except when I send the text.'

'Thanks. Thanks for everything,' Sheridan replied and pressed the end call button, making her way into the living room, where Steve was waiting for her.

'What's happened?' he asked.

'Let's go into the kitchen, shall we. I could do with a coffee, it's been a long night.'

She felt a wave of relief wash over her as Steve stepped into the kitchen and started filling the kettle.

'What's happening? What's the latest on Anna?' he asked.

'I was going to call you, because I know you're desperate to see her. But I thought it was better to come and see you in person,' Sheridan said, bracing herself for what she was about to say. She knew she'd hate herself for it, but it was the only way she'd be able to convince Steve to leave the house. She took a deep breath. 'Steve. Anna hasn't regained consciousness, and the doctors aren't sure she ever will.' She felt a pang in her chest.

'Jesus,' Steve said. 'I can't believe it. Is she going to die?'

'I don't know.'

'I want to see her. I really want to see her.'

'And that's why I came. I'll take you to see her, I think the doctors will allow it. But I want you to be prepared, she's in a bad way.'

'So, you've seen her?'

'Very briefly.' She went on to explain to Steve that there were no witnesses to Anna's assault, wanting him to believe that he was going to get away with it. She knew if he believed that, then he'd make a mistake. As she talked, her senses were on full alert, wondering if she'd hear Gabriel when he came in the front door. Having not heard a sound, she guessed that he wasn't inside yet.

Her mobile pinged. The smiley face emoji from Gabriel. *Christ, he's good,* she thought to herself.

As Steve made the coffee, Sheridan noticed that he hadn't made himself one. He talked about how devastated he was and how much he loved Anna, wishing they could have worked things out, his head down most of the time. All the while, Sheridan was thinking about Gabriel and felt apprehensive, wondering where he was hiding up and praying that wherever it was, Steve didn't go upstairs and catch him.

This is it, she thought, holding her mobile up. 'That was the message I've been waiting for. We can head to the hospital. I'll drive you there.'

'Okay,' Steve said.

Now all Sheridan had to do was get Steve out of the house. But he had to be with her; she had no intention of letting him actually see Anna, and keeping him close meant she had complete control of him.

Her mobile rang again. It was Hill.

'Sheridan, I'm sorry to call you. Were you asleep?' she asked.

'No.' Sheridan realised Hill would assume she was at home, having dropped her off the night before.

'I'm sorry, Sheridan, you were wrong, Steve didn't invent Ben Harper. He's a real person.'

CHAPTER 32

Sheridan's eyes widened. 'Right.'

She tried not to look at Steve as she got up and made her way through to the living room.

'We're heading out to his house shortly. I thought you'd probably want to be there,' Hill said.

'I . . . can't.' Sheridan's mind was racing. She couldn't abandon the plan now. Gabriel was upstairs and she *had* to get Steve out of the house. She literally couldn't leave without him.

'You sound . . . strange. Are you okay?' Hill asked.

'I'm fine. I just . . . I can't come.'

'Why? Are you still at home? I can send someone to pick you up if you're too tired to drive.'

'No, I'm not at home.' Sheridan lowered her voice. 'I'm at Steve's house.'

'What the hell are you doing there?'

'I'm taking him to the hospital to see Anna.'

'What are you up to, Sheridan? I thought you didn't want Steve anywhere near her.'

'I'll explain later. Look, I have to go. Keep me fully posted.' Sheridan ended the call and prayed Hill didn't call back. She closed her eyes momentarily, trying to slow her heart rate down. Then she took a calming breath and went back into the kitchen.

'Everything okay?' Steve asked, putting his coat on.

'Yeah.' She looked at him. Could she have been wrong? Was Steve innocent? Was she focusing on him so much that she had become blinded to any other possibility? Almost every part of her was convinced that Steve was guilty, but now Ben Harper was real, and depending on what he told the police, he really could be the main suspect. She couldn't change the plan now. Gabriel was already in the house, and she had to get Steve out and in her car.

'Are you ready to go?' Sheridan asked.

Steve nodded. 'Yeah. I just need the loo first,' he said, before heading upstairs.

Shit. Please don't get caught Gabriel, Sheridan thought, the panic making her feel dizzy. Taking slow, deep breaths, she closed her eyes, trying to listen as Steve moved around.

A moment later, she heard the toilet flush, and Steve came back downstairs. 'I've been thinking. You don't need to take me to the hospital, I'll drive myself there.'

No, no, no, she thought. This wasn't part of the plan. For it to work, she needed to keep Steve close to ensure he didn't return home and catch Gabriel in the house. 'No, really, I'll drive you.'

Steve flicked his keys around his fingers. 'I'd rather drive myself there.'

At that point, Sheridan's mobile rang. She looked at the screen: unknown number.

'DI Holler,' she answered.

'Hi, it's Dr Forsyth. I thought you'd be pleased to know that Anna has just regained consciousness.'

Sheridan's eyes widened. 'Right. Okay. Thank you. I'll be there soon.' Desperate not to alert Steve to the fact that Anna was awake, Sheridan resisted asking the doctor if Anna had said anything.

The doctor ended the call, but Sheridan kept her phone next to her ear as if it was still live. Giving herself a moment to think, as

Steve stood, ready and waiting. She was working blind now. How could she *make* Steve get into her car? He was insisting on driving himself to the hospital and if he arrived there before her, he'd find out Anna was awake. What if he was on his way to the hospital and suddenly changed his mind and returned to the house while Gabriel was still inside? She felt sick. But she couldn't stall him any longer.

Her only choice now was to get to the hospital first and once she was there, think of a reason why Steve couldn't see Anna.

'Right, well thank you for the update,' she said into her phone, before pretending to end the call.

Steve was putting on his coat. 'Was that about Anna?'

'Yeah. They just wanted to tell me there's no change.' Sheridan stood up. 'I'll follow you to the hospital. They won't let you in if I'm not there.'

Steve swiped his mobile from the counter and Sheridan followed him out of the house.

As she unlocked her car door, she heard Steve say, 'Shit.'

'What's wrong?' she asked, looking up.

'I've got a fucking flat tyre.' He spat the words out.

'Oh. I'll . . . *have* to drive you then.' Sheridan bit down on a grin. *Nice one, Gabriel,* she thought.

Steve put his hands on his hips and stared at his car. 'Yeah. I suppose you'll have to. I'll sort this out later.' He glared at the tyre.

'You coming?' Sheridan said, eager to get going.

'I've just remembered something, I'll be back in a sec.' Steve walked back down the path and let himself in.

'Oh God. Oh God,' Sheridan said under her breath, now panicking so much that she thought she was going to throw up.

A thousand questions went through her head. The first being: *What if Steve catches Gabriel this time?*

She swallowed, trying to keep the bile down that felt trapped in her throat.

As the seconds passed, she convinced herself more and more that the plan had failed. *What was I thinking? How was this ever going to work? And how the fuck can I explain Gabriel Howard being in Steve's house?*

At that moment, Steve reappeared, and she watched as he locked the front door.

'Okay, let's go,' he said, before climbing into Sheridan's car.

Now she had him. And all she had to do was keep him with her long enough for Gabriel to work his magic and find the evidence she was looking for; anything that could connect Steve to Anna's attack.

If he was actually involved. After learning that the mysterious 'Ben Harper' was real, she was seriously starting to doubt herself.

She needed to go to the nick first to pick up her radio. If Gabriel got it right and managed to make it look like a real burglary by making enough noise smashing a window, then she had to hope that Steve's neighbours or someone passing would call the police. Sheridan would be listening on her police radio, ready for when the call came in. She would then tell the control room that the occupant of the house was with her, and she'd drive him home. That way, she'd get in the house and if Gabriel had found the necklace, Steve would be arrested. That was the plan. But that was before she'd been told that Anna had regained consciousness. And that Ben Harper was real. Now it might be even simpler. Maybe Anna would tell her it was Steve who'd attacked her. Or she might identify Ben as the guilty one. But what if Anna *hadn't* seen anyone? So many questions buzzed round Sheridan's head.

As Steve put his seat belt on, Sheridan took out her phone and texted Rob: *Anna is awake. Go to the hospital right now and see if she can tell you who attacked her. Text me back. Don't call me. Text only.*

Rob texted back: *I'm on my way.*

She texted Rob back: *I'm bringing Anna's ex Steve to the hospital. When we get there, you need to tell me that Anna is still unconscious and we can't see her at the moment, I'll take it from there*

Rob replied: *Everything ok?*

Sheridan responded: *All good just trust me, and tell Hill that I have specifically asked that only you go to the hospital*

Rob sent back a thumbs-up emoji.

Sheridan started the engine. 'I need to pop to the nick first and grab something. Then we'll go straight to the hospital.' She didn't look at Steve.

'Okay,' he said.

As she pulled away from the house, Sheridan could feel her heart pounding. The plan could work perfectly. Or it could cost her and Gabriel everything.

Ten minutes later, she pulled into the backyard at Hale Street. She'd spend as much time as she could retrieving her police radio, as the longer she kept Steve with her, the longer it would give Gabriel inside the house.

'Stay here, I won't be a minute,' she said as she got out of the car.

Sheridan made her way upstairs and as she reached the top, Hill was coming out of CID.

'Sheridan.' There was a look of concern on Hill's face. 'What's happening? Rob said that Anna's regained consciousness but why do you only want *him* at the hospital?'

'I've got Steve in the car. I've just come to grab my radio.' Sheridan didn't want to face a barrage of questions from Hill and avoided answering her actual question.

'You need to tell me what's going on,' Hill said, crossing her arms.

'Steve wants to see Anna. I just thought it best that I take him myself. Anyway, what's going on with the mystery man, Ben Harper?'

Hill walked to her office and Sheridan followed.

Hill looked at her notes. 'Benjamin James Harper – runs his own accountancy business, works from his home address. He's no trace on PNC, looks like he lives alone. The dating site he's on told us that to register, you just need a photo and email address. They don't hold any personal information. We're checking to see if he subscribes to the dating site, so we'll know for absolute certain that it was him who set up the profile and not Steve. Dipesh, me and uniform are going out to his house now.'

'Good. And you'll keep me posted?'

'That's what I'm confused about. And that's also why I know that something's not right. You choose to take a man you hate and suspect of attacking Anna to see her in hospital. This isn't like you, so I want to know why you're more interested in doing that, than coming to Ben Harper's house.'

'You don't need me to come to Harper's house. Just let me know what he says.'

'I get it. Of course.' Hill shook her head. 'You still don't think Harper had anything to do with Anna's attack. You're so convinced it's Steve that you're ignoring all the signs that this was Harper. Jesus, Sheridan.'

Sheridan couldn't think of anything better to explain what she was doing with Steve and so chose to agree with Hill's theory. Even though it was wrong. But how could she tell Hill the truth? *Oh yeah so, I've been planning with a known criminal to get into Steve's house, ransack it and then smash his windows to make it look like a burglary on the off chance there's something in there to prove Steve's involved. All because we can't get a warrant.* No. She couldn't tell Hill. Ever.

'Yeah I guess you're right, Hill,' she said, shrugging her shoulders before turning to walk down the corridor to get her radio from the locker.

After retrieving it, she stopped in the corridor to look out of the window, checking Steve was still in the car. The longer he had to wait, the more he might become suspicious that something was wrong, but Sheridan was desperate to keep him away from the hospital for as long as she could.

Her phone pinged with a text from Rob, and it wasn't what she wanted to hear: *Anna very drowsy. Didn't see who attacked her.*

'Shit,' Sheridan said under her breath. She called Rob's number.

'Hi, Sheridan.'

'Is she awake now?'

'No. But they said she'll be in and out for a while.'

'Are you positive that she doesn't know who did this?'

'As positive as I can be. She was quite drowsy though and I can't be sure she even understood me.'

'Did she say anything about Ben Harper?'

'No. She's pretty out of it.'

'Okay, I'm on my way with Steve. When we get there, I need you to be outside ICU and as we arrive, you tell me she still hasn't come round, and they've taken her for another scan.'

'Okay, but . . . can I ask what's going on?' Rob asked tentatively.

'I don't want Steve to see her. I don't want him anywhere near her.'

Rob hesitated before answering. 'But if she does see him, maybe it might spark something, and she'll remember if it was him.'

'You're right, I know you are, I just want him as far away from her as possible. Just trust me.'

CHAPTER 33

Sheridan spotted Rob outside ICU as she and Steve walked up the corridor.

'How is she?' Sheridan asked.

'She's still unconscious, they've taken her for another scan,' Rob replied, using the scripted response she had given him earlier.

'This is Steve, Anna's ex-partner,' Sheridan said.

Rob nodded at Steve, and said, 'I'm DS Wills.'

'Hello,' Steve said, looking past Rob to the uniformed officer standing at the door to ICU. 'Why is there a policeman here?'

'It's a precaution. Because Anna's a police officer, we've got her guarded in case whoever attacked her tries to get into ICU and cause her further harm. It's standard practice,' Sheridan responded.

It wasn't standard practice. It was her way of telling Steve that even if he did turn up alone to see Anna, he'd still have eyes on him.

'How long will the scan take?' Steve asked, leaning against the wall.

'I'm not sure, they said it could be a while,' Rob replied, having already briefed the uniformed officer to go along with the pretence that Anna had been taken for another scan.

Steve sat down on a chair and folded his arms, sighing heavily. 'Fine,' he said, resting his head back and closing his eyes.

Sheridan turned to Rob, mouthing, 'Stay close.'

Rob nodded, unsure of what was going on, but trusting that whatever Sheridan had planned, there must be good reason for it.

Now all Sheridan had to do was wait for Gabriel to contact her. She turned away from Steve, who still had his head back and his eyes closed. She placed her radio earpiece in and turned the volume up, winking at Rob who was frowning, questioning her without speaking.

Her phone pinged, and her heart fluttered in her chest. She looked at the screen. A picture from Gabriel.

Sheridan opened the message, and her eyes widened as she saw the image. Was it enough? Was what Gabriel had found *enough*? She put her phone back in her pocket and looked at Rob, who was still frowning, and Sheridan gave a slight shake of her head, indicating that she couldn't share with him what was happening. She knew Rob trusted her and she in turn trusted him implicitly. Now she had to wait again. This time for the call to come into the control room that there was a burglary in progress at Steve's house. Once that call came, she just had to hold on a little longer for officers to get there and find what Gabriel had left in plain sight. Then, and only then, could she hope that Steve would agree to them forensically examining the house to establish if the burglar had left any prints or DNA. That way, they would inevitably ask Steve for his DNA again, purely for elimination purposes.

Steve suddenly opened his eyes and stretched out his legs before standing up, arching his back. 'How much longer do we have to wait?' he asked, stepping over to the uniformed officer, who shrugged his shoulders.

'I'm not sure,' the officer replied.

'You got to stay here all day?'

'No.' The officer checked his watch. 'Someone's taking over shortly.'

Steve yawned. 'I'm going to get a coffee, do you want one?' He looked at Sheridan and Rob, who both declined.

Sheridan watched as he walked down the corridor and turned the corner heading for the vending machine.

Then the call she'd been waiting for came over the airwaves.

'All units, burglary in progress, 46 Juliet Close, Wavertree.'

This was it. Gabriel had done it. Sheridan knew he'd be well away by now. Patrol cars would be assigned to attend Steve's address. She was so close.

She spoke into her radio. 'Charlie Delta six-six, re that burglary, can you repeat the address please?'

'Yes, Charlie Delta six-six, the address is 46 Juliet Close, Wavertree, called in by a neighbour, two units attending.'

'Thank you. I'm actually with the occupant of that address now. We're at the hospital on an unrelated matter. Keep me fully updated on this job. I'll bring him to the location.'

'Will do, ma'am.'

'What's going on?' Rob asked.

'Steve's house has been burgled. Units are on their way. We'll take him back to his address, you and me.'

'He's been burgled? What are the chances . . .' Rob stopped halfway through his sentence. A slight grin crossed his face. 'Okay. I . . . don't need to know, do I?'

'I don't know what you're talking about.' Sheridan looked up to see a uniformed officer walking towards them.

'Hello, ma'am,' he said as he approached.

'Hi. Everything okay?' Sheridan asked.

'Yeah. I'm just here to relieve PC Nune.' He nodded at the officer standing guard at the door to ICU. 'I just heard over the airwaves about that burglary. You've got the victim here?'

'Yes. He's just gone to get a coffee. I'm taking him back to his home address.' Sheridan looked at Rob. 'You ready?'

'Sure. Let's go.' Rob threw his coat on.

Sheridan and Rob made their way down the corridor towards the vending machine, but there was no sign of Steve.

'Maybe he's gone to the loo,' Rob said. 'I'll go and check.'

Sheridan watched as Rob headed into the gents' toilet.

Then she saw it.

'Shit.' She shook her head just as Rob reappeared.

'He's not in there,' Rob said.

Sheridan turned and walked at a pace back to the uniformed officer who had just arrived, with Rob in tow.

'Did you pass a guy at the vending machine round the corner when you just arrived?' Sheridan asked.

'I think so. Yeah, yeah I did.'

'Did you have your radio up loud?'

'Yes. Why?'

'Christ.' Sheridan's head dropped and she walked away, back towards the vending machine, where she stood staring at the cup of coffee still sitting in the tray. 'He overheard the message about the burglary at his house.' She looked at Rob. 'He's fucking legged it.'

They ran down the stairs, searching the reception area and outside, with no sign of Steve.

Sheridan put out a message to the control room, advising officers to keep a lookout for him. He wasn't to be arrested, but Sheridan was to be updated if he was found as she needed to speak to him.

Sheridan gave Rob instructions as they walked towards the taxi rank. 'If we don't find him, I want you to stay with Anna and get the uniform to check the CCTV, see if we can spot where he's gone. He's on foot so he won't be far away.'

'Where are *you* going?' Rob asked.

'I'm going to his house.'

After finding no sign of Steve in the immediate area, Rob headed back into the hospital.

Sheridan called Steve's number, which was switched off.

'You bastard,' she said as she climbed into her car and headed to his house.

CHAPTER 34

Sheridan pulled up behind a marked police car, spotting Hill emerging from the house. She got out of her car and cleared her throat. Now she had to put on another performance.

'Hello, boss, what are you doing here?' she said, casually. 'I thought you were going to Harper's place.'

'I was, but I heard this job come in and so I've sent Dipesh, Bridie and uniform to Harper's place. Can I have a word?' Hill said as she walked down the path.

'Sure.' Sheridan was desperate to get inside and see for herself what Gabriel had found. Because she knew at that moment she could throw suspicion back on Steve.

Hill walked along the road a few doors, stopping with her arms folded, her voice low.

'Let me get this straight. You asked me to get a warrant to search Steve's house, and I explained that we'd never get one based on what we had. You then pick Steve up from his home address and get him away from the place on the pretence that you're taking him to see Anna. Then, hey fucking presto, while he's with *you*, his house gets burgled. And now he's done a fucking runner.'

Sheridan puffed out her cheeks. 'I know. You couldn't make it up, could you? So, has anything been found?' She nodded towards the house.

Hill shook her head. 'Let's go and see, shall we?' She turned and walked back towards the house, with Sheridan shadowing her.

Sheridan knew that what Gabriel had left in relatively plain sight was upstairs in Steve's bedroom, but she couldn't head straight there, that would be far too obvious. Instead, she walked into the living room, glancing at the two boxes by the window, their contents having been emptied out. A few books and ornaments were scattered across the floor.

She walked into the kitchen, where all the cupboards and drawers had been left open.

'Ma'am?' A uniformed officer appeared behind her and Hill, and they both turned. 'There's something upstairs you need to see.'

Sheridan and Hill made their way up the stairs. The crime scene officer, Charlie, was photographing something on the floor in the bedroom.

'What have you got?' she asked, stepping around the bed, immediately spotting the photograph that Gabriel had sent her a picture of. The crime scene investigator picked it up with gloved hands and showed it to Sheridan and Hill.

It was a photograph of Anna, her smiling face, likely taken with a long-lens camera. And drawn on it was a target.

'Christ,' Hill said, squinting at the picture. 'When do you think it was taken?'

'I don't know.' Sheridan studied the photograph. 'Looks quite recent.'

'Where exactly was this photo found?' Hill asked the uniformed officer.

'Sticking out from under the bed.'

'Let's lift it up.' Sheridan and the uniformed officer grabbed a corner each and hoisted the bed up.

Hill crouched. 'There's nothing there,' she said, and Sheridan and the officer set it back down.

'Let's get this place and his car searched,' Sheridan said.

Hill nodded. 'Sure.'

'Have we got a point of entry?' Sheridan asked. It was a question she didn't need answering, but one that she would have asked had she not set this whole situation up.

'Yeah, downstairs back door,' Charlie replied, and Sheridan followed him downstairs, as did Hill.

As Sheridan walked into the kitchen, she could see the smashed glass bottom panel.

'That's the point of entry and also exit. All other doors and windows were shut.'

Charlie continued. 'There's this broken window, too.' He pointed to another glass panel. 'I'm guessing that the suspect smashed that window first, then realised he couldn't get through it, so he smashed the larger panel instead, gained entry and left the same way.'

Hill stepped over so she was beside Sheridan. 'The neighbour who called it in said she heard several loud smashes. As she couldn't see over the garden fence, she went upstairs. She didn't notice anything at first, but a minute or so later, she saw a male in the back garden, he climbed over the fence and was gone. That's when she called the police,' Hill said.

'Right.' Sheridan nodded, imagining Gabriel with his ingenious mind. He'd smashed both panels to ensure he made enough noise to alert the neighbour.

'The suspect didn't spend more than a minute or so in the house by the sounds of it,' the uniformed officer chipped in.

Sheridan nodded. 'Most burglars don't hang around too long. Plus, the place is practically empty, so whoever it was probably realised there wasn't anything worth stealing, and it wouldn't have taken them long to go through the cupboards and drawers,' Sheridan replied, avoiding looking at Hill as she spoke.

'Let's hope the suspect cut himself on that glass,' the uniform said.

No bloody chance. Gabriel's too good for that, Sheridan thought. 'Yeah, hopefully,' she said.

'The whole place smells quite strongly of bleach – any idea why?' Charlie asked.

'The occupant's moving out and he's been cleaning the place down.' Sheridan sighed.

'Okay, well, depending on how thorough he's been, we might get lucky.' Charlie looked around.

'What do you mean?' Sheridan asked.

'If the occupant has cleaned the place to a high level, then whatever fingerprints and DNA we get are more likely to be the suspect's, unless he was careful of course.'

Sheridan knew that Gabriel would have left no prints or DNA. The problem she had now was that Steve had probably erased most of his own DNA from the house, making it highly unlikely that they could match a sample to the DNA swab taken from Anna.

'I really need the occupant's DNA.' Sheridan looked at Charlie.

Hill's phone rang. 'DCI Knowles.' She stepped into the living room, emerging a moment later. 'How's that for timing? Forensics have just confirmed that they've found DNA under Anna's fingernails and it's not hers. So now we just have to hope we can get Steve's DNA and it matches.'

'I'm going to speak to the neighbour. I'll leave you to it, Charlie.'

Sheridan made her way outside, followed by Hill.

'I need to get a seal on the place,' Hill said as they walked down the path. 'Do you think Steve will come here?'

'No. He's gone, Hill. He'll be miles away by now.'

'I've got an all-ports alert on his passport. We're going to seize his car and get it forensically examined and financial checks are being done to see if he withdraws money somewhere, or makes any purchases,' Hill said.

'Bloody hell, you are on the ball,' Sheridan replied.

'Yeah, surprisingly I'm not completely useless.' Hill raised her eyes skyward. 'Why do you think he's done a runner?'

'Because he's guilty. I think once his house had been broken into he knew that we'd attend and get it forensically checked, and that way we might get his DNA. And he really doesn't want us to have it. I think he knows we're on to him and it's only a matter of time. He's no fool. He lived with Anna long enough to know we'd suspect him.'

Sheridan's mobile rang. 'DI Holler.'

'Ma'am, it's Jo Walker, are you free to speak?'

'Yes, Jo.'

'We've found a hammer in the bushes a little distance away from where Anna was found. There's quite a lot of blood on it. I'll send you a picture and we'll get it sent off for forensics.'

'Thank you, Jo. Great work.'

Sheridan ended the call and updated Hill, just as the image came through from Jo. Sheridan's stomach turned. The picture showed a lot of blood on the head of the hammer. 'Jesus,' she said under her breath, showing Hill the image.

Just then, Hill's mobile rang. 'DCI Knowles.'

'Boss, it's Dipesh.'

'Go ahead.' Hill put the call on loudspeaker.

'We're at Ben Harper's house. You need to get here.'

CHAPTER 35

Sheridan again found herself with a massive headache. She was desperate to speak to the neighbour who had called in the burglary at Steve's house. She had to know if she'd seen anything that could compromise her and Gabriel. But now the call from Dipesh had changed everything and Hill would be highly suspicious if Sheridan didn't go with her.

'Let's get to Harper's place,' Sheridan said, making her way to her car and watching as Hill got into hers and drove away. As soon as she was out of sight, Sheridan walked up to the neighbour's house.

The door was opened by an elderly lady holding a heavy wooden walking stick.

'Hello. Mrs Dobson?'

Mrs Dobson invited her inside. Knowing she didn't have long, Sheridan stepped into the hallway and followed the older woman into the cramped living room. 'I don't want to take up too much of your time, but firstly I just wanted to say thank you for calling the police about the burglary next door.' Sheridan smiled reassuringly. She wanted to know exactly what the elderly woman had to say about the man seen leaving the property. And she had to play it very carefully.

'Did you catch him? The fella who jumped over the fence?' Mrs Dobson asked as she sat with her legs slightly apart, holding her hefty walking stick between them.

'Not yet,' Sheridan replied. 'But I don't want you to worry. This was what we call a targeted incident. Basically, the burglar was only interested in the house next door, and he won't be coming back to the area. I can't really say much more than that, but I hope that puts your mind at ease.' She tried to reassure the old lady. Technically it was a targeted incident. Set up by Sheridan.

'Oh, I'm not scared if that's what you're thinking.' Mrs Dobson tapped her stick on the floor.

'That's good to hear.' Sheridan smiled again. 'I know my uniformed colleagues have spoken to you about what you saw, but can you describe to me exactly what happened?'

'I was sitting here eating my lunch, when I heard a loud smash and then another. I thought it was probably coming from Steven's house, so I went out the back and tried to look over the fence, but I couldn't see anything. I then went upstairs and looked out of the back bedroom window and that's when I saw the fella climbing over the back fence. So, I called the police.'

'Can you describe the man?' Sheridan asked.

'Not really. I only caught a glimpse of him.' Mrs Dobson tapped her stick on the floor again. 'He was gone before I could get a decent look at him.'

'Was he white?'

'I'm not sure. I think so. It happened so quickly.'

'What about what he was wearing?'

'I couldn't tell you, I'm afraid. I'm not much help, am I?' Mrs Dobson shrugged her shoulders.

'Yes, you are,' Sheridan said, looking around the living room and noticing thick net curtains across the front room window. 'Is there anything you remember about him?'

'Not really. My eyes aren't too good and it just happened so quickly. I'm sorry.'

'Don't worry. Do you spend most of your time in this room?'

'Yes, I watch a lot of television. You say that Steven's house was targeted. Do you know what was taken? I mean, he can't have that much left in there.'

'What do you mean?' Sheridan asked.

'Well, he's been emptying the place out for weeks now. I see him going out all hours of the day and night, loading his car up with boxes and bags and driving off.'

'Do you know where he goes?'

'No. I assume it's to wherever he's moving to.'

'How long is he usually away for after he's loaded the car up?'

'A few hours.'

'When you say a few hours . . . can you think how many?'

'I can't be certain, but I'd say at least three or four.'

Sheridan absorbed this information. 'Is it *mainly* during the day or at night?'

'Mainly night time.'

'That's very helpful.' Sheridan looked towards the window. 'So, you look out of your window a lot?'

'Not all the time, but when I hear his front door slam, I tend to have a peek.'

Sheridan smiled. 'I expect you saw *me* turn up earlier.'

'No. Why do you ask?'

Because I need to know if you saw Gabriel Howard walk into Steve's bloody house, she thought. 'Just wondered. I came to see Steve and we left in my car together. I just wondered if at any time you saw anyone hanging around? Maybe acting suspiciously?'

'No. I didn't.'

'Well, I should leave you in peace. Thank you for your time.' Sheridan needed to get to Harper's house, so Hill didn't wonder where the hell she was. She stood up to leave and Mrs Dobson got to her feet, following her into the hallway. Remembering what Anna had told her about Steve's relationship with Mrs Dobson, Sheridan stopped at the door.

'I understand you and Steve get along well. He helps you out doing odd jobs and comes over to sit with you, if you need a bit of company. Is it right that you bang your walking stick on the wall to let him know you'd like a bit of company?'

'Where did you hear that load of old nonsense?' Mrs Dobson frowned.

'I . . . heard it from someone who knows him.'

'Well, he's never done an odd job for me, and the reason I have to bang my stick on the wall is to stop him making all that bloody noise day and night.'

Sheridan's eyes were fixed on Mrs Dobson. 'What noise?' she asked.

'All that shouting and throwing things around. God knows what he gets up to in there, drives me potty. He wakes me up with it all and I hammer on the wall and shout for him to shut up. He's a bloody nuisance.' She shook her head slightly. 'And you can tell him that from me.'

Sheridan stood there in silence.

Mrs Dobson continued. 'I'd try to get him evicted but I know he's moving out soon, so then I'll get some peace and quiet.'

'Has he told you where he's moving to?'

'No. But I hope it's far away.'

'When you hear him shouting, can you make out what he's saying?'

'Not really. He just shouts,' Mrs Dobson replied, leaning forward slightly. 'What's he done?'

'What do you mean?'

'Well, he's been burgled and you're asking me questions about *him*. Has he set this burglary up? You know, as an insurance scam or something?'

'We don't know. But we do need to speak to him about an incident that happened last night. Do you have a contact number for him?' Sheridan wanted to check if Steve was using burner phones.

'No, I don't. So . . . what's he done? Go on, tell us.'

'We just need to speak to him, so if he comes to the house or tries to contact you, I need you to call 999.'

'I knew he was a wrong 'un.' Mrs Dobson tapped her own forehead. 'Not right in the head if you ask me. All that screaming and shouting. It's not normal.'

CHAPTER 36

Sheridan jumped back into her car and made her way to Ben Harper's house.

Hill would be spitting her dummy out and wanting to know what had taken Sheridan so long, and she already had a speech planned. She'd tell Hill that she wanted to put Mrs Dobson's mind at ease and thought a quick visit would do the trick. She'd also learned more about Steve and was convinced he wasn't moving to Glasgow. He was either storing his stuff somewhere, or moving into a new place that he was able to get back and forth from in a few hours. Steve had previously told Sheridan and Hill that he'd been taking items to the tip or charity shops. But based on what Mrs Dobson had told her, this didn't make sense. Charity shops and tips weren't open at night.

Half an hour later, Sheridan pulled into Ben Harper's drive, where she parked next to Hill's car. She noted that Dipesh's job car was also present, alongside a marked vehicle. The front door to the house was ajar. She pushed it open.

Hill appeared in the hallway. 'Where have you been? Is everything okay?'

'Yeah fine, sorry I just popped in to see Steve's neighbour before I headed here. She's elderly and I wanted to put her mind at ease. I found out more about Steve too. He's . . .'

Hill put her hand up. 'Before you continue, you need to hear this.' Hill ushered Sheridan outside. 'Ben Harper's cleaner, Kathleen, is inside. She comes every other day. On Sunday when she arrived, Harper wasn't here, which wasn't particularly unusual. She's got her own key and let herself in, cleaned upstairs and left a few hours later. She didn't come on Monday, but turned up today to find the cats haven't been fed and there's no sign that Harper has been here.'

'Has she tried contacting him?'

'Yes. And you need to see the messages between them.' Hill took a deep breath. 'It was him, Sheridan. Ben Harper was the man who attacked Anna, not Steve.'

Sheridan peered through into the living room and saw Kathleen sitting rigidly on the enormous sofa, with Bridie next to her. She was a petite woman in her sixties, dressed in jeans and a thick white jumper, her grey hair neatly tied in a ponytail.

Hill showed Sheridan into the kitchen and handed her Kathleen's mobile.

'She's worked for Ben Harper for a year. Her husband, Colin, also works for him doing odd jobs. He's on his way here now. We haven't mentioned anything about a hammer. Just told her we need to know if anything's missing from the house or shed. According to Kathleen, Colin knows every tool in the shed. He's a bit OCD and likes to keep everything meticulously clean and tidy. Everything in its place. If anyone can tell us if there's a hammer missing, it's him. When Kathleen found the place empty today, she tried calling Harper, but his phone was switched off. She tried again and there was no reply. So, she sent a text asking where he was and if he was okay.' Hill nodded at the mobile in Sheridan's hand. 'You can see the conversation.'

Sheridan looked at the screen and read the messages.

Kathleen: *Hi Ben. I'm at the house, are you okay? Have you been home in the last few days?*

Ben: *No I haven't. Are the cats okay?*

Kathleen: *Yes, I've fed them, they seem fine. When will you be back?*

Ben: *I don't know. I can't explain right now, but I've had to get away, something's happened and I might not be back for a while. Can you keep an eye on the place and make sure the cats are alright?*

Kathleen: *You want me to come every day?*

Ben: *Yes please*

Kathleen: *Are you in trouble? I'm worried about you*

Ben: *No, I'm not in trouble, just stuff to sort out. But don't worry*

Kathleen: *How long will you be gone?*

Ben: *I don't know. Please just look after the cats and I'll call you when I can*

That was the last message between them.

Sheridan looked at Hill. 'Have we checked the house and grounds?'

'It's being done now. We've tried calling his phone; it's switched off. He doesn't own a car, just a motorbike. And that's in the garage.' Sheridan followed Hill out of the house and as they headed over to the garage, a small black van pulled on to the drive and out climbed a short, portly man, who came over to them.

'I'm Colin, Ben's handyman,' he said. 'Is everything alright?'

Sheridan introduced herself and Hill. 'We were hoping you could help us. We need to know if anything's missing.'

'Anything in particular?' Colin asked.

'We can't say, but are you able to look in the shed and house and see if you can spot anything?'

'Sure.' Colin nodded. 'Is Ben alright?'

'We're trying to find out,' Sheridan said. 'Can I ask that you just look and don't touch anything?'

They walked over to the shed situated to the left of the gravel drive. Colin stepped inside as Sheridan stood in the doorway and looked around. Everything was in its place. Gardening tools were hung in size order, and an immaculate lawnmower stood in the corner, its cable coiled neatly to one side. Colin took his time, looking at the shelves and tools hanging up. He bent down to check under the heavy wooden bench, where pots of varnish and paints stood, perfectly placed like a shop display. He turned and walked over to the corner, his hands studiously crossed behind his back.

Sheridan and Hill waited patiently until, eventually, he turned back to face them. 'Well, for starters, there's a hammer missing.'

Sheridan swallowed. 'Really? Are you sure?'

'Positive. I know every tool and every screw in this place. Ben's never been any good at DIY – that's why he employs me to do all the jobs around the house and garden. If I need anything, he gives me the money and I go and buy it. He wouldn't have a clue about what's in here, I don't think he ever steps foot in the shed, so everything is just as I left it.'

'When were you last here?'

'A couple of weeks ago. He asked me to take down his outside Christmas lights.'

'Can you describe the hammer?' Sheridan took her phone out and clicked on the picture that Jo Walker had sent her.

'Yeah, it's a claw hammer. Quite new. It's got a blue rubber handle with a black stripe around it.'

Sheridan showed Hill the image on her phone. It was exactly as Colin had described.

Colin turned and made his way to the back of the shed. 'The plastic sheeting's gone, too.'

Sheridan joined him. 'Can you describe it?'

'It's about six feet wide, and I'd say . . . twenty foot long? I use it when I trim the hedges, saves raking up the cuttings.'

Sheridan threw a look at Hill.

'And a couple of rolls of Gorilla tape.' Colin was pointing to a neat stack of various adhesive tapes. 'There were three of them before, and now two are missing. And some rope. Quite a lot of rope's gone, too. There was also a suitcase over there – an old one – that's gone as well.'

Colin described each missing item and Sheridan noted down the details before they all headed into the house, where Colin went over to his wife and hugged her.

'I take it Ben's in some sort of trouble?' Colin asked.

Sheridan kept her answer vague, only confirming that they needed to speak to him.

'Shall we take a look around inside?' Sheridan said. 'I need to see if anything else is missing or out of place.'

Kathleen, Colin and Hill made their way through the house with her.

After checking each room, but finding nothing missing, Sheridan opened the door to the last room upstairs, which had been turned into a home gym.

'Is Ben into his fitness?' Sheridan asked.

'Not at all,' Kathleen answered. 'He bought all this stuff ages ago, but he's never used it.' Kathleen looked into the room. 'I only come in here to dust the equipment. The cats like to sleep on the treadmill.' She glanced at Sheridan. 'Ben's a lovely man, you know.'

'Describe him to me, what sort of person he is.'

'Quiet, unassuming. He keeps himself to himself, he's very private. And he adores his cats.'

'Does he have any family?'

'I don't know, he's never talked about any.'

Kathleen stepped over to the bench press before turning, her eyes scanning the room. 'The weights are missing.'

'What?' Sheridan said.

'There's some weights missing. A few of the medium-sized ones.'

They all headed downstairs and while Dipesh and Bridie took statements from Colin and Kathleen, Sheridan talked to Hill in the kitchen.

'I assume we're both thinking the same thing,' Sheridan said, feeling something brush against her leg and looking down to see one of Ben's cats rubbing his face against her.

'Absolutely. Ben went to the pub prepared. With everything that's missing, I think he was going to kill Anna and wrap her body up, use the weights to weigh her down and dispose of her in the Mersey.' Hill put her head down. 'But why? He doesn't have any previous. He's got a good job, a beautiful house, and he clearly loves and cares about his cats. Why do something like this out of the blue?'

'I don't know,' Sheridan said. 'And the other question is . . . if he was planning to kill Anna and take her body somewhere, how was he going to do that if he doesn't have a car. Unless he's hired one. I'll get local hire companies checked out.' Sheridan reached down, letting the cat sniff her hand, before gently scratching the top of its head, causing it to purr loudly.

'Sorry, Hill, I know you hate cats.' Sheridan crouched and the cat looked at her. She closed her eyes and slowly opened them, the slow, reassuring blink that cats usually respond well to. After a few moments the cat pushed its head against Sheridan's knee and she gently picked it up, encouraging it to nuzzle its face into hers.

'I don't hate them. I just don't want to be near them.' Hill felt her jaw tighten. It was a cat that had run out in front of her husband's car, making him swerve that day. The day her family had all died. She walked over to the kitchen window and looked out. 'The other question is, if Steve has got nothing to do with any of this, then why has he done a runner? It doesn't make any sense.' She sighed with clear frustration. But then, a moment later, she turned around. 'I've just thought of something. And it's to do with a certain cat.'

'What do you mean?' Sheridan asked, gently stroking the cat in her arms.

'We need Steve's DNA to see if it matches the DNA found under Anna's fingernails.'

Sheridan's eyes widened. 'Of course. Maud. She bloody scratched him. Why didn't I think of that?'

Hill raised an eyebrow. 'You need to get her nails clipped. Get her to the vet, I'll get CSI to meet you there.' She walked over to Sheridan and did something she hadn't done since her family were killed. She touched the top of the cat's head.

CHAPTER 37

Sheridan sent a text to Sam: *Hey beautiful. Looks like Maud is a fucking genius. Can't explain right now, but we need to get her nails clipped, so I'm taking her to the vet, just in case you get home and she's not there. XX*

Sam texted back: *I'm intrigued. Oh my god. It is something to do with when she scratched Steve?*

Sheridan replied: *Yep. She might have his DNA under her claws . . . let's hope*

Sam typed back: *That is so cool. Will she get a medal or something?*

Sheridan texted back a laughing face emoji.

◆ ◆ ◆

Sam came through the door just as Sheridan was about to head back out.

'How did it go?' Sam picked Maud up and kissed her head. 'Did our girl come good?'

'We'll find out tomorrow, hopefully.'

'How's Anna doing?'

'I'm going to the hospital now, but then I have to go and see someone.'

'You look exhausted. Is there anything I can do?' Sam put her hands on Sheridan's shoulders and pulled her close.

Sheridan kissed her. 'Just be here when I get home tonight and pour me a very large drink.'

'Now, *that* I can do.'

'Right, I'd better go. I'll text you when I'm on my way home and in the meantime, give Maud whatever she wants.'

Sam watched as Sheridan climbed into her car and waved her off before heading back inside, scooping Maud up. 'Let's get you a Jaffa Cake, shall we?'

◆ ◆ ◆

An hour later, Sheridan was back at Anna's bedside. Since she'd arrived, Anna had opened her eyes twice and responded when Sheridan had squeezed her hand, but she hadn't spoken.

'Can you hear me?' Sheridan whispered, her face an inch from Anna's. No response.

'I have to go. I love you,' Sheridan said, kissing Anna gently on the cheek, before making her way out of the ward and back to her car.

Taking out her mobile, she sent a text to Gabriel Howard: *You at home? All clear to come round?*

He responded: *Yes and yes.*

Sheridan started the engine, closing her eyes for just a moment. She wanted to sleep, she wanted to be at home wrapped in Sam's arms. She wanted to cry from exhaustion and the emotions surging through her body. She was running on empty, but she desperately wanted to see Gabriel. After the set-up burglary at Steve's house, she needed a debrief with him. Sleep would have to wait.

As she pulled away, Hill rang her.

'Hi Sheridan. Where are you?'

'At the hospital,' Sheridan said hesitantly, stopping the car.

'How's Anna?'

'The same.'

'Are you okay to speak?'

'Yeah, go ahead.'

'When you get back to the nick, I've got an update on the Canning case. How long are you going to be?'

Sheridan put her head back. She wanted to get to Gabriel's house and didn't know how long she'd be with him. 'I'm not sure . . . what's the update?'

'Milo Adams is fast becoming a real suspect.'

'Really? What's happened?' Sheridan sat upright. She took a moment to mentally place the café worker with his bad Scouse impersonation.

'We know he left the café at 8.01 p.m. on the night Canning was murdered. We also know that he got on the bus to go home at 8.12. The address he gave you, the one he said he was living at, at the time Canning was killed, had been demolished two weeks earlier. We've now found him on CCTV getting off the bus at 8.20 hours, two miles away from the café.'

'So, he probably didn't have time to get back on the bus and get back to the scene at half eight, when Canning was killed,' Sheridan said, remembering the details as she always did, even with her head filled with Anna's attack. 'So, why is he such a suspect?' she asked.

'The CCTV shows him getting off the bus and straight into a car being driven by another male.'

'Do we know where he goes?'

'No, but we do know the car, a silver Mercedes, is carrying false plates.'

Sheridan processed this new information. 'Shit. So, he could have been driven back to the scene, he'd have easily made it back in time for eight thirty, and maybe the balaclava was in the car.' She paused. 'We need to place that Mercedes or him near the scene.'

'I've got the team looking at the CCTV,' Hill said.

'Great. I'll be there . . . in a bit. I just want to spend a bit more time with Anna, if that's okay?'

'Sure,' Hill replied and ended the call.

Sheridan pulled away and headed to Gabriel's house.

CHAPTER 38

Gabriel put a mug of coffee in front of Sheridan as she sat at his kitchen table.

'You look exhausted,' he said, taking the seat opposite her.

'I'm fine.' She took a deep breath. 'But I literally shat myself when Steve went back into the house. I take it there's no way he saw you?'

'No. But it was a close one. I was in the big wardrobe, the one in his room with the sliding mirrored doors. I heard the front door open, and he came back up the stairs. He took a set of keys that were on a hook inside the wardrobe.'

'Fuck. You were right *there*. Are you positive he didn't see you?'

'Trust me. He didn't. He literally reached in and took the keys. To see me, he'd have had to have put his head in and look left, then move the clothes that were hanging up. He didn't see me, Sheridan.'

'So why did he need to get back in and get those keys?' Sheridan put her elbows on the table and rested her head in her hands.

Gabriel nodded. 'He's moving out and I think they're to his new place. On the key ring was a round blue ball with the word "SOLD" written on it. I could see it clearly. I think there's something else written on the ball as well, something ending in E, written round it.'

'Sold?' Sheridan thought for a moment. 'That could be really helpful, maybe he's got a new place like you say.'

'There was also a kind of Allen key.'

'Okay.' Sheridan rolled her shoulders. 'The only problem is, I can't share this with anyone. Because the only way I'd know about the keys is if I'd seen them in the wardrobe.'

'Can't you just say that you *did* see them? Pretend they were in plain sight? Even if, or when, Steve's arrested, it'll be your word against his and no one's going to believe *him*.' Gabriel pursed his lips.

Sheridan stared at him. 'Of course. Christ, I'm really not on the ball at the moment.'

'You're exhausted, Sheridan. Anyway, what about the photograph of Anna? I left that in plain sight, was that helpful?'

'Absolutely.'

Gabriel nodded. 'Do you think there are more pictures somewhere?'

'Highly likely. But if there are, he'll have got rid of them by now. Where did you find the photo?'

'Behind his bedroom cabinet, so I put it under his bed, but left it sticking out, so you'd find it.' Gabriel cleared his throat. 'Has he been arrested?'

'No. He's done a runner.'

Sheridan went on to explain how Steve had likely overheard the message over the police radio about the burglary. And that after Sheridan had spoken to his neighbour, Mrs Dobson, and she had given a very different account of the sort of person Steve was. She explained to Gabriel how the elderly lady had seen Steve leaving the house with boxes and bags at all times of the day and night, and Sheridan's belief that he had no intention of moving to Glasgow. Wherever Steve drove to, it took him a few hours to return.

'Where do you think he is?' Gabriel asked.

'I have no idea. We can do checks on where his car and his phone have been, but that'll take time, and he might have even changed his plans by now. He could be anywhere.'

'Do you know any areas he visits? Family? Friends?'

Sheridan smiled. 'You really sound like a copper now. All he told us was that he'd been out for a drink in Cheshire last night. He couldn't remember the name of the pub.'

'What a prick. How's Anna?'

'In and out of consciousness . . .' Sheridan felt her voice waver. Tiredness, emotion and frustration took over and she buried her face in her hands.

Gabriel reached across the table and gently touched her arm. 'It's okay. She'll be okay.'

Sheridan wiped a hand down her face and looked at him. 'I hope so.' She took a sip of her coffee and tried to pull herself together. 'So, tell me. What happened once you were in the house?'

Gabriel placed his palms down on the table. 'Once you'd driven off, I searched the place, that's when I found the photograph of Anna. I didn't find the necklace, I'm sorry.'

'You can't find what's not there,' Sheridan said.

'I didn't go into the loft. Has it been checked?' Gabriel asked.

'Yeah. Nothing found. I like the way you think, you'd have made a great police officer.'

'Maybe. But as you well know, my life was never going to pan out like that.'

'How did you get out of the house?'

'I opened the bathroom window, climbed down the gutter and into the back garden. That's when I smashed the back window and door, made as much noise as I could. Then I climbed through and went back upstairs to lock the bathroom window. I waited for another two minutes before climbing back outside and over the fence.' He looked at Sheridan. 'I knew someone called the police because I waited until they turned up.'

'The elderly lady next door saw you, but she can't describe you.'

'I saw her looking out of her upstairs window, she was on the phone, I guessed, to the police. I needed her to see a glimpse of me, so she knew the breaking glass was a burglary. I didn't frighten her, did I?'

'No. She's pretty feisty.' Sheridan rubbed her forehead. 'Where were you hiding when the police turned up?'

'Nearby.' He smiled.

'And no one saw you? I need to ask because they'll do house-to-house enquiries, and I need to know if there's a chance that someone saw you in the area.'

Gabriel shook his head. 'Don't worry about that. I'm not boasting here, but I can make myself invisible.'

'That's impossible.'

'Trust me, your house-to-house enquiries will come up blank.'

'How can you be so sure?'

'What was I wearing when I got in the house?'

Sheridan closed her eyes. 'Grey trousers, trainers and a thick dark grey jacket.'

Gabriel nodded. 'And when I left the house, I was wearing black tracksuit bottoms, a blue jacket, green cap and was carrying a black rucksack. Listening to my music.'

Sheridan frowned. 'You got changed?'

'I went prepared. It's just illusion, Sheridan. And it only takes a second to change your appearance. People *see* but they don't really *look*.'

'Fucking hell – that's *my* saying. *I* say that.'

'Great minds.' Gabriel raised his coffee cup.

'I like the way you think. Like waiting two minutes after you'd smashed the glass. If you'd smashed it and left seconds later, the police would question how you had time to go through the house.'

'It's not my first disco, to be fair.'

'When did you let his tyre down?'

'Just before I got into the house.'

'What made you do that?'

'I knew you had to get him into *your* car, that was the only way you could be sure he didn't drive himself and come home and catch me inside.'

Sheridan took a deep breath and smiled. 'Jesus. You're almost as good as me at thinking like that. That was genius.'

Gabriel tilted his head to one side. 'I'll take that as a compliment.'

He made them another coffee, and the subject turned to how he loved his life and the carpentry business, and how he had everything he wanted, except a partner to share it with.

'Surely you don't have problems getting girlfriends. I mean, obviously you're not *my* type, but you're attractive and you keep yourself fit. So, what's stopping you?'

Gabriel sighed. 'I want what my parents had. The perfect relationship. They loved each other so much, they hardly ever argued, and they were together practically every minute of every day.' A sadness swept over his face as he thought about them. How they had lived and died together. Gabriel had been twenty-three when his parents had gone on a boating holiday in Turkey. His mother had fallen in and his father, never a strong swimmer, had jumped in after her. They both drowned.

Gabriel had told Sheridan the story before and she noticed the pain in his eyes, even after all these years.

'I should have been there with them. They wouldn't have drowned if I was there.' He sighed. 'They used to take us on boating trips all the time. My dad taught me everything he knew about boats. From sailing boats to canal boats and cruisers. We used to go to the Norfolk Broads in the summer, and they always made sure we wore our life jackets. Mum was so strict about it. That's why I don't understand why they weren't wearing them that day.' He shook his head slightly as if to rid himself of the memory.

'I'm so sorry, Gabriel,' Sheridan said.

'It was a long time ago. But, thank you.' He stood up, stretching his back. 'And as for me finding a girlfriend, I'm in no rush. She's out there, and I'm sure one day I'll find her. I just hope she accepts me for who I am.'

'What do you mean?'

'I want my relationship to be an honest and open one. But, with a criminal record and a history of violence, getting someone to see past that isn't going to be easy.' He put his hand up. 'Anyway, what happens now, about Steve?'

'We'll keep looking for him.'

'Will he get life?'

Sheridan raised her eyebrows. 'Probably not. It's hard to tell, maybe ten years, maybe less, maybe more.'

'That's not enough for what he did.' Gabriel picked up Sheridan's empty mug. 'He could have killed her.'

Sheridan fell short of telling Gabriel about Ben Harper and how he was now their main suspect.

'I know.' Sheridan got to her feet. 'I'd better go. I want to see Anna before I go home.'

'What do you need me to do?'

Sheridan stood in front of him. 'Nothing. You've done everything I asked you to do, and I can't thank you enough. I couldn't have got into that house without you. You took a huge risk for me.'

She put her hand on his shoulder for a moment, before making her way to the front door. As she went to open it, she stopped and turned around.

'What made you change your mind about helping me?'

Gabriel folded his arms across his chest. 'I realised that for someone like *you* to come to someone like *me* for help, meant you had no other choice. You were prepared to put everything on the line and the only person you could turn to was *me*. It doesn't get any more desperate than that. Plus, you'd never have got over that back fence.' He grinned.

Sheridan smiled. 'Good point.' She hesitated. 'I . . .we have to trust each other, Gabriel. What we did today was a huge risk. For both of us. If it ever came out, then any prosecution against Steve would be thrown out. The way we got into his house wouldn't only ruin us, it would completely destroy the case.'

'I know. And I don't want you to ever worry about that. It's done now, Sheridan. We did it and we got away with it. Let it rest there. I know that you'd do anything for Anna; like you said, she's practically your sister and you love her. But let's make a promise to each other, that you never tell her what we did.'

'I won't be telling anyone. Especially Anna. She'd literally kill me if she knew I'd risked everything for her.'

CHAPTER 39

Wednesday 19 January

Sheridan opened her eyes, having been woken by her work mobile ringing on the bedside table. She blinked at the clock. 4.03 a.m. She sat bolt upright and Sam, also now awake, turned on the lamp.

'It's from an unknown number.' Sheridan swallowed. 'It could be the hospital.' She felt her head spinning with the sudden realisation that this could be the worst news. In the two days since Anna's attack, she had remained stable, but Sheridan knew that could change. Her hands shook as she tried to hit the answer button.

'Here.' Sam gently took the phone from her. 'Let me answer it.' She put the call on loudspeaker. 'Hello?'

'Oh, hello. Is that Sheridan Holler?' the male voice said.

'Yes,' Sheridan said.

'Sheridan, I'm Dr John Stoker from ICU. I'm one of the consultants who's been looking after Anna.'

'Is she okay?' Sheridan asked, noting the sombre tone of the doctor's voice, her heart pounding uncontrollably in her chest.

'I'm so very sorry to have to tell you this. Anna passed away a few minutes ago.'

◆ ◆ ◆

Sam pulled into the hospital car park and turned off the engine. Having been told by Dr Stoker that Sheridan would be allowed to see Anna before her body was taken to the mortuary, she and Sam had got dressed and made their way there. Sheridan had been inconsolable when she'd got off the phone and Sam was desperately worried about her. She knew the love that Sheridan had for Anna and how this news would have the most detrimental effect on her. This day and always.

Sheridan hadn't spoken a single word on the journey and now, as they sat in the car, Sam had no words herself. She looked at the totally broken Sheridan next to her and reached for her hand, and Sheridan turned to her.

'I can't believe it, Sam. I can't believe she's gone.' Sheridan's voice was barely audible. 'What am I going to do? I don't know what to do.'

Sam took her seat belt off and moved closer, pulling Sheridan towards her. 'We'll get through this. I promise you.' Sam could barely talk herself.

'Will we?' Sheridan buried her head in Sam's chest. 'How? How do we carry on? She's gone and I can't think about our life without her.'

They cried together. They held each other. Sam could feel Sheridan's heartbeat and wanted to wrap her up in love and take the pain away.

After several moments, Sheridan lifted her head. 'I have to tell Hill. How am I going to tell her? How am I going to tell the team? Oh God.' She burst out crying again and shook her head. 'I can't do this. I don't think I can do this.'

Sam gave her the time she needed, patiently waiting for Sheridan to find the strength to get out of the car. When she did, Sam held her arm, worried that Sheridan's legs would buckle beneath her.

As they headed slowly towards the main doors, Sheridan spotted Hill's car.

'Hill's here,' she said. 'They must have already called her.'

They took the lift, Sam holding Sheridan's hand the whole time and as the doors opened, they stepped out.

Hill was coming out of a side door near to ICU, her mobile to her ear. There was no uniformed police officer outside ICU, a presence that Sheridan had got used to. They no longer needed to protect Anna. She was gone.

Sheridan walked slowly towards Hill, dreading what was to come. As they reached her, she turned around.

'Sheridan.' She pressed a button on her phone. 'I was just about to call you.'

'The hospital rang me, we came straight here. Did they call you first?' Sheridan asked.

'Yes. I told them not to ring you. They shouldn't have called you at this hour. Anyway, you're here now.'

Sheridan knew Hill well enough to know that her stoicism didn't mean she didn't care, or wasn't affected by Anna's death; she was more likely in self-preservation mode. Putting up that wall to protect herself.

'Shall we go in?' Hill said, turning round and holding the door for Sheridan.

Sam let go of Sheridan's hand. 'Maybe best I wait out here?'

She nodded, kissed her gently on the cheek and followed Hill inside.

A heavy curtain was drawn around Anna's bed and Sheridan felt sick as Hill pulled it back.

Sheridan prepared herself, firstly looking to the floor, before slowly raising her head.

But nothing could have prepared her for how she felt as she looked at Anna lying there. Still. So very still.

CHAPTER 40

Sam stood awkwardly in the corridor, not knowing what to do or how to deal with the feeling of helplessness. In the years she'd known and loved Sheridan, nothing compared to the way she had seen her this night. How would she ever get over it? Maybe she wouldn't. Maybe losing Anna was the one thing that would finally break Sheridan. They'd loved each other, laughed and cried together. Worked on cases together and shared their triumphs and supported each other when the job could have broken them. And now Anna was gone.

Sam went to sit down, but instead, walked slowly down the corridor, aimlessly looking at the paintings hanging on the walls. A picture of Liverpool Cathedral, painted by 'Amy, aged 8'. Another, of the Liver Building, by 'Joshua, aged 10'. Pictures of all the places Anna probably once walked past or visited in her life. Sam felt hot tears fill her eyes and she quickly wiped them away. The hospital seemed deathly quiet. No nurses or doctors racing into or out of wards, no visitors carrying bags filled with clean clothes, magazines or packets of biscuits. Sam felt intolerably lonely, and it took everything inside of her not to scream out. Just to hear a sound. Any sound.

She knew that everything would change now – life without Anna would be too hard to bear for Sheridan, Sam was sure of it.

She turned and walked back towards ICU, stopping momentarily to look out of the window, staring at the car park below. She could see Sheridan's car and remembered the silence of the journey here.

She didn't see the car parked over by the trees, hidden in the shadows.

But he saw *her*.

CHAPTER 41

Sheridan held Anna's hand and couldn't help but kiss it. Over and over. Her other hand moved to her face, and she used the back of it to gently touch her cheek.

At that moment, Anna smiled. 'What are you crying about?' she asked.

'Nothing,' Sheridan replied. 'I just love you. You muppet.'

'You're a muppet,' Anna said, before coughing, holding her head. 'Shit. That hurts.'

Hill was stood with her arms across her chest. 'I think we need to let Sam know,' she whispered.

'Oh Christ, yes. I'll go and see her.' Sheridan stood up.

'Sam's here?' Anna said, a look of confusion on her face.

'Yeah,' Sheridan replied. 'I'll explain later.' And with that, she left the ward.

As soon as the door to the side room opened, Sam took a deep breath, ready to grab Sheridan and hold her.

'I don't know quite how to say this . . .' Sheridan put her hands on Sam's shoulders. 'Anna's alive. Very much alive.'

Sam almost fell over. 'What?' She placed her hands on her head, her mouth dropped open. 'What about the phone call? I . . . I don't understand.'

Sheridan explained that, having recovered from the initial shock of realising Anna was alive, she'd pulled Hill to one side and described the phone call she'd had from Dr Stoker. They'd quickly established that there was no Dr Stoker and that Sheridan had clearly been the victim of a cruel and malicious call. Her immediate thought was it had been Steve, although she hadn't recognised his voice, describing it to Hill as much deeper than Steve's.

They had decided between them not to tell Anna about the call.

Hill had explained to Sheridan that she'd received an *actual* call from the ward at just gone midnight: Anna had regained consciousness and was lucid, asking over and over if they could call Sheridan as she wanted to see her. Hill had informed the staff earlier that Sheridan wasn't to be called if anything changed during the night, as Hill was growing more concerned about her by the day. Sheridan had hardly slept since Anna's attack, working around the clock trying to establish who was responsible.

When Hill had arrived, she'd been informed that the doctors were going to be moving her out of ICU and on to a normal ward. But first, they'd placed her in a side room so that Sheridan and Hill could have some privacy with her. Hill had stayed with Anna for a few hours before Anna insisted on seeing Sheridan and that was when Hill had stepped outside to call her, just as Sheridan had arrived.

'I can't believe it,' Sam said, the shock on her face apparent. 'I mean, who would do that? Who would call and say she'd died . . .' She tilted her head to one side. 'You think it was Steve?'

'No. I'd have recognised his voice. But I'm going to find whoever it was, and I swear to God I'm going to . . .' Sheridan's face flushed red with anger.

'Hey, it's okay.' Sam squeezed her hand.

'No, it's not okay. How could someone do that? To make me think she was dead? It's beyond fucking cruel. It's just evil.' She took a breath. 'But I can't let Anna see how mad I am.'

'If it wasn't Steve who made the call then maybe he put someone up to it?' Sam said, still holding Sheridan's hand.

'Maybe.'

'Are you going to tell Anna about the call?'

'No. I don't want to upset her.'

'Look, just think about the positive for now. She's alive, that's all that matters,' Sam said.

Sheridan sighed. 'You're right. Anyway, I'd better get back in there. Do you want to go home?'

'Yeah.' Sam pulled Sheridan towards her and held her tightly. 'I can't tell you how bloody happy I am right now. That was awful.'

'Promise me you'll drive carefully. You must be knackered.'

'I will. I promise. Will Hill bring you home later?'

'Yeah.' Sheridan kissed her. 'I love you so much.'

'I love you too. Say hi to Anna for me.'

Sam made her way back to the car.

CHAPTER 42

Sheridan took Anna's hand and settled down in the chair next to her bed. Hill had gone to get them a coffee.

'Tell me what you remember about what happened.' Sheridan kept her voice calm, even though she was still reeling from the horror of the call earlier and the realisation that it had all been some sick joke.

Anna swallowed. 'I've told Hill everything I can remember.'

'I know. But if you feel up to it, I want to hear it.'

'I remember getting to the pub to meet Ben, the guy I told you about who I met online. I went in, got a drink and waited for him. Then I got a text back to say he had to cancel.'

'Then what happened?'

'I left.' Anna's voice croaked, and she licked her lips. Sheridan helped her take a sip of water.

'What about the attack?'

'I was on my way back to the car and I heard something behind me. I went to turn and all I felt was this awful pain in the back of my head. I think I knew I'd been hit with something, and I was aware of someone being there. I put my hand up and something hit me on the arm, and I just reached out with my other hand and tried to grab him. I say *him*, but I didn't see who it was. I managed to grab him around the back of his neck, but then I just went down on the floor, and I think he hit me again. That's all I remember. Until I woke up here.' Tears filled her eyes.

Sheridan reached over to wipe them gently away. 'It's okay. You're safe now.'

'Hill told me I've been out of it for a couple of days and that you've been working around the clock trying to find out who did it.'

'Yeah. And we're still working on it. But we'll get him, I promise you that.'

'Do you have any ideas?'

Sheridan wanted to say that she highly suspected Steve. But with what they now knew, it was looking more likely to be Ben Harper and Sheridan didn't want to confuse or upset Anna at this stage. She told Anna about the items missing from Ben's house and the texts between him and his cleaner, Kathleen. Along with the fact that a hammer had been found nearby. As she spoke, Sheridan kept thinking of how she could broach the subject that she had suspected Steve.

'We need to find Ben. But I want to check something with you. When you left the pub, witnesses said that you were wearing that long scarf.'

Anna nodded. 'Yeah, the one you took the piss out of.'

'That's the one. Do you remember if it came off at all when you were being attacked?'

'No. I don't think it came off. Why?'

'Were you wearing the necklace that Steve bought you?'

'Yeah.'

'Well, it's gone, and we can't find it.'

Anna absorbed this information. 'Was I wearing the scarf when they found me?'

'No. It was found nearby.'

'So, whoever hit me . . . took the scarf off . . . and took the necklace?'

'I think so.'

'You think it was a robbery?'

'I don't know. Nothing else was taken.' Sheridan hesitated. She really hadn't wanted to mention Steve but now felt she had no choice. 'Did you tell Steve that you were meeting Ben?'

'No. Of course not. I told him I'd met someone online, but I didn't tell him anything else and I certainly didn't tell him I was meeting him. I didn't even tell *you*.' Anna frowned. 'How do you know his surname's Harper? Did I tell you that?'

'No. We had to log on to your laptop and look through your online contact with him.'

'How do you know my password?'

'I know it, because you're shit at changing it and you always use Sheridan Sherlock.'

Anna gave a faint smile and then her eyes widened. 'Do you think Ben did this?'

'It looks that way.'

'Christ.' Anna paused. 'He led me to the pub and then texted me to cancel, waited until I left and then attacked me.' Her voice broke and she squeezed tears from her eyes. 'I've been such an idiot.'

Sheridan gave her time.

'Does Steve know what's happened?' Anna asked.

'Yeah. Hill and I went to see him.'

'Has he been to see me?'

'No.' Sheridan used a tissue to wipe the sides of Anna's mouth where she'd dribbled some of the water she'd sipped. 'Look, I'm going to say it. I told Steve that you weren't allowed visitors. Oh, and by the way, if the staff ask you, you're my sister. I had to pretend to be your next of kin. Talking of which, I don't know if you want your parents informed.'

'No. And don't change the subject. Why did you tell Steve I wasn't allowed visitors?'

Sheridan thought of the right words, the right way to tell her best friend that she had doubts about Steve.

'I . . . just . . .'

'You think he had something to do with this, don't you?' Anna closed her eyes for a second. 'He had no idea I was even going to be at the pub. It wasn't him, Sheridan. Please tell me he's not a suspect.'

Sheridan moved a strand away from Anna's face. 'He's a person of interest.'

'Why?'

Sheridan told Anna that she believed Steve might have been angry after Anna told him about the abortion. If that was the case, then he might have somehow found out she was going to meet Ben at the pub, perhaps Anna had told him but had forgotten. Maybe Steve removed her scarf and took back the necklace he'd given her. She went on to explain that when she and Hill had visited Steve, he'd been scrubbing the house and had bleached most of it down. He'd also refused to give a voluntary DNA sample.

Sheridan was careful, just giving Anna the facts as she knew them. She finished by telling Anna that when she'd eventually arranged to bring him to the hospital to see her, he'd been burgled. When they'd looked inside his house, they'd found a photograph of Anna with a target drawn on it.

'And now he's done a runner. He left the hospital . . . and now he's disappeared.' Sheridan noticed the look of horror on Anna's face when she described the target drawn on the photograph.

Anna's eyes widened. 'He . . . he's moving away, maybe he just decided to go and he's in Glasgow,' she said, sounding unconvinced by her own words. 'I just don't think he'd hurt me this badly. He's changed, he used to drink and gave it up, he doesn't touch a drop anymore and he's so kind to his neighbour . . .'

'He was drunk when Hill and I went to see him. He'd been drinking in a pub in Chester. And Mrs Dobson described him as a pain in the arse. She doesn't bang her stick on the wall to get his attention for him to go over and have a friendly chat. She does it to stop him from making so much noise banging around the house and shouting to himself.'

Anna closed her eyes. 'Shit,' she said under her breath.

'I'm sorry mate. I know you have a different opinion of Steve, but he's not the changed man you think he is.'

They talked for an hour, candidly, Anna agreeing that Steve's disappearance had to make him a person of interest. She asked about the burglary and that was the only part Sheridan left out. The fact that she and Gabriel Howard had orchestrated the break-in. A fact she would never share with Anna, or anyone else.

It had crossed Sheridan's mind several times if she would ever tell Sam. They had no secrets and it didn't come down to a lack of trust; that was never in question when it came to Sam. It came down to protecting her. If Sam knew, then she could never unknow, and that would lie heavily on Sheridan's shoulders. Keeping the secret from Sam was an act of love. This was Sheridan's cross to bear. Hers and hers alone.

She asked Anna if she could think of anyone, including family, that Steve might go to, any place he might be hiding. The last Anna knew was that Steve's father lived in Nottingham. She had only visited there once in all the time she had been in a relationship with Steve, as he and his father didn't get on and very rarely spoke. She couldn't think of anyone or anywhere he would go to.

It was gone 6 a.m. by the time exhaustion kicked in and Anna needed to get some rest. As Sheridan got up to leave, Anna asked if she could see herself in a mirror.

'You look lovely.' Sheridan grinned.

'Liar.' Anna grinned back. 'Bring me a mirror later.' She sounded sleepy, now, barely able to keep her eyes open. 'How's it going?' she asked, her voice now a little slurred.

'How's what going?'

'The Canning case.'

Sheridan shook her head. 'It's going fine. Now you get some rest.' She kissed Anna on the cheek and quietly made her way out of the room.

Hill was waiting on the seat outside. The uniformed officer that Hill had sent for a break earlier was back in position.

'How is she?' Hill asked, standing and stretching her back.

'She's okay. Why didn't you come back in?'

'I thought you two would like some time together. I'll take you home, you need to get some sleep. You can fill me in on the way.'

'I don't want to go home. I want to get to work.' Sheridan yawned loudly. 'We need to crack on with finding out if Milo Adams went back to the scene where Canning was killed.'

CHAPTER 43

Sheridan and her team congregated in CID. Hill updated them with Anna's account of the attack. A wave of shock rippled through the room when Sheridan told them about the phone call she'd received, someone impersonating a doctor telling her that Anna had died.

'I want to go around the room for updates on where we are with Anna's case, and then we need to discuss the Canning job,' Sheridan said.

She took a sip of coffee as Rob stood up to speak.

'Firstly, we've looked at CCTV from The Blacksmith pub, and so far, we can't see anyone hanging around before or after Anna was attacked. Anna's clothes, including her scarf, have been to Forensics and nothing was found, the same with her car. CCTV from the hospital at the time Steve did a runner shows him leaving by the main door, he walks across the car park and disappears. We don't know where he went after that. CSI haven't managed to get any DNA from Steve's house, so let's hope Maud comes up trumps.'

Rob smiled before clearing his throat and turning to Dipesh, who took to his feet. 'We've looked at Steve closely. We know he's no trace on PNC. He only has the BMW registered to him, no other vehicle and local hire companies have come up blank. We're looking at train stations, starting with Lime Street to see if we can spot him, but it's a slow process. We've checked ANPR cameras for the BMW and in the last few weeks, it's seen leaving the area near to his house but then it disappears. We know from what Mrs Dobson, his neighbour, told you that he's usually gone a few hours, but without a direction of travel, he could have been going *anywhere*.'

Sheridan nodded. 'Cheers, guys. We've got Ben Harper's laptop and computer from his house, the tech team are looking to see if he's had contact with any other women.'

Bridie put her hand up. 'We've spoken to Steve's landlord. He can confirm that Steve gave notice to vacate the property a few weeks ago and the landlord told him to leave the place in good order or he'd lose his deposit. He said Steve told him he was moving to Glasgow. That's all he knows.'

'So, that's consistent with what Steve told Anna,' Hill said.

'What did he say about the break-in?' Sheridan asked.

'He wasn't too happy about the broken glass, but said his nephew will get it fixed so he won't be out of pocket.'

Hill stepped up. 'How are we doing in relation to the burglary at Steve's house?'

Sheridan put her head down for a moment. She could only hope that no other neighbour had seen Gabriel Howard enter or leave the address. She felt a flutter in her stomach.

'CSI haven't found anything in relation to the suspect. House to house was done by uniform and a couple of the neighbours have cameras. So far, they've only found one camera that captured a few people in the area at the time. I've got the images.' Bridie turned to her computer and the team gathered round.

Sheridan felt her face flush and realised this could be the moment that Gabriel Howard had been seen on CCTV. She stood behind Bridie while everyone focused on the screen. *Please don't have fucked it up, Gabriel,* she thought.

'Okay, let's see it,' she said.

Bridie pressed play and they all watched the screen intently. The first person to appear was a woman walking her dog, the next was a couple carrying shopping bags. The third was a guy wearing a large set of headphones, jogging slowly in his running gear, stopping at one point to stretch out his calf muscle, before continuing. Bridie pressed stop. 'That's it.'

'No one suss there,' Dipesh said. 'The only possible could be the guy in the running gear, but I've never seen a burglar wearing headphones and jogging calmly away from the scene of the crime.' He smiled and the team, including Sheridan, joined in his amusement. *You clever fucker, Gabriel,* she thought. A moment of guilt washed over her as she realised she had fooled her colleagues, and that didn't sit well with her. Then she gave herself a mental slap, remembering the reason why she had done it. For Anna.

'Okay,' Hill said. 'So, what's outstanding?'

'We're looking at Steve's mobile phone data. His mobile has gone offline and isn't currently signalling. We'll contact Steve's father in Nottingham this morning to see if he's been in touch,' Rob said.

'Good job everyone.' Hill put her thumb up.

Sheridan took another sip of coffee. 'Thanks so much for all your hard work.' She turned to the whiteboard behind her. 'Now, let's move to the Canning murder.' She cleared her throat.

'We know that of the main suspects, Carrie Penhaligan, whose parents and daughter died in the fire, was with her husband Vincent Royce at the time of the murder, having dinner with Carrie's brother and his wife, Roger and Marcia Yearwood. Financial checks have drawn a blank, with no evidence to suggest the family have paid someone to kill Canning. Carrie's son, Bradley, also has an alibi as he'd been in police custody at the time of the killing. But now we have this unknown female who's called in to say we need to look at Bradley and we're running out of time.' Sheridan sighed, giving herself a moment. 'Okay, so the only person still on the list of suspects is Frankie Yearwood, the son of Roger and Marcia. And Milo Adams, but I'll come to him in a minute.' She looked at Rob. 'So, Frankie's refusing to cooperate with police and has now gone off radar. So, he's still a suspect.'

Sheridan looked at the whiteboard again. 'His grandparents and cousin, Elizabeth, died in the fire and he's the only one who hasn't given us an alibi. Let's find him. Have you managed to get a description of him yet? I'd like to compare him to the CCTV image of Canning's killer.'

'I'm going to be speaking to his parents,' Rob said. 'Sorry, I know you asked me a few days ago to sort that . . .'

Sheridan put her hand up. 'Don't worry, it's been mental. As long as it gets done now.' Sheridan smiled. 'Right . . .' She pointed to Milo Adams' name on the board. 'This little fucker has lied to us. We need to place him at the scene. We know he got off the bus and got into a car which was carrying false plates. So, where did he go once he got picked up? And who was driving that car?'

Rob piped up. 'The images of the driver aren't clear, but we're working on it.' He frowned. 'Maybe . . . the driver is Frankie and him and Milo are working together?'

Sheridan nodded slowly. 'Maybe. So, we need to find a link between them. I think we should pay Azriel's café another visit, maybe Milo's working today.'

Sheridan went back to her office to grab her coat and realised she felt more upbeat than she had of late. Anna was out of danger, and they were now making headway in the Canning case. The team were still under immense pressure to get a result, but she felt for the first time that things were moving in the right direction.

◆ ◆ ◆

Sheridan hadn't called ahead to let Azriel know that she and Rob were coming back to the café. As they entered, Azriel was serving a customer and looked up. The smile left her face and she appeared agitated, spilling the customer's cup of tea before apologising and wiping the counter down.

Sheridan waited with Rob, looking around and noting the café was practically empty. And there was no sign of Milo Adams.

Once Azriel had finished serving her customer, she wiped her hands together and the smile was back.

'DI Holler, this is a nice surprise. Can I get you a cuppa?' she asked cheerfully.

'No thanks,' Sheridan replied, and introduced her to Rob. 'Is Milo in today?' she asked, keeping her voice low.

'No. He . . . doesn't work here anymore. I don't know where he is.'

'How come he left?'

'He wanted to go travelling. I don't know where he is.' Azriel spoke quickly. 'Can I help?'

'When was the last time you spoke to him?' Sheridan asked, noting that Azriel had twice said that she didn't know where Milo was.

Azriel looked down, thinking. 'Not since he left.'

'I need to speak to him. I'll give him a call.' Sheridan took out her mobile phone and walked to the front door, stepping outside.

Rob was eyeing up the cakes that were temptingly displayed under a clear plastic cover on the counter.

'Would you like one? On the house?' Azriel said.

Rob tapped his stomach. 'I shouldn't really. The wife thinks I'm getting chunky.' He grinned.

Rob had picked up that Azriel appeared a little uncomfortable with their presence. He hadn't met Azriel before, but he could sniff out anxiety in a person and Azriel was oozing it.

'Is . . . Milo in trouble?' she asked, flicking a look towards the door, where Sheridan stood outside, her mobile to her ear.

'We just need to check something with him. Does he drive?' Rob kept his voice light.

'I don't think so, he always got the bus into work.'

'Did he ever get picked up or dropped off by someone in a car?' Rob asked, trying to ignore the cake display.

'No. I don't think so.' Azriel appeared distracted as she continued to watch Sheridan.

'I might have one of those cakes actually,' Rob said, pointing to an enormous fresh cream scone. 'Don't tell the missus.' He winked, getting his wallet out.

Azriel lifted the cover. 'Eat in or take away? And I don't want any money for it. It's on the house. I like to look after the police, you all do such a great job, protecting the public.'

'That's very kind of you, but I'm not allowed to take freebies. Can you pop it in a bag for me?' Rob handed over a five-pound note, noticing Azriel was still watching Sheridan. While she rang Rob's purchase through the till, he turned to see Sheridan, who appeared to be deep in conversation.

'How's the investigation going?' Azriel asked as she handed Rob his cake in a white paper bag and a napkin.

'I can't say too much, but we're getting there,' Rob said, peering inside the bag and scooping some of the cream out with his finger. 'Wow, that's delicious. Do you make these yourself?'

'No. I order them in.' Azriel smiled. 'Has anyone been arrested?' she asked.

'I really can't say, I'm sorry.' Rob scooped more cream out of his cake. 'Did Milo say where he was travelling to?'

'No. He's a free spirit, you know what youngsters are like.'

'Did he say he'd stay in touch with you?'

'No. I didn't know him that long. He wasn't a friend or anything.' Azriel looked up as Sheridan opened the door.

'Thanks, Azriel.' Sheridan lifted her hand. 'Rob, we have to go.'

Rob wiped his mouth with the napkin. 'No rest for the wicked.' He smiled at Azriel before turning.

'Did you get hold of Milo?' Azriel called to Sheridan, who appeared not to have heard her as she walked away.

Rob caught up with Sheridan outside. 'Well?' he asked.

'No reply.' She squinted at the bag in his hand.

'Who were you talking to then?'

'No one. But I wanted Azriel to think I was talking to Milo. How did she seem?'

'Nervous. And she couldn't take her eyes off *you*.'

Azriel made her way into the back office and dialled Milo's number. He answered immediately.

'Did the police just call you?' she asked, poking her head around the door to make sure Sheridan and Rob hadn't returned.

'Someone did, but I didn't answer. What's going on?'

'They were here asking where you are. I told them you've gone travelling and I haven't heard from you.'

'What do they want?'

'Milo . . . I think they know something about the car. They asked if you ever got picked up or dropped off in a car.'

'Shit. They're going to find out, aren't they? I'm going to get caught.'

Azriel could hear the panic in his voice. 'Look, do as I say. Get rid of your phone, destroy it. Stay in the flat and don't go anywhere. And I mean *anywhere*.'

'Then what?'

'I don't know. I need time to think. I need to get you away from here, but I need time to figure out how to do it.'

'I could ask *them* to help me. I could do another job for them, they said there were more . . .'

'No, Milo. No more. Stay away from them now. You did what they asked you to do and they paid you. No more. If you contact them the police will find out and I won't be able to protect you next time.'

CHAPTER 44

The day was exhaustingly long, and Sheridan felt her eyes closing as she stared at her computer screen. Emails and reports stared back at her, and she desperately wanted to log off and go to see Anna. She looked at the clock. 4.15 p.m.

The team had been updated about the visit to Azriel. They had tried Milo's mobile again, but the call wouldn't connect. The suspicion was that Azriel may have warned him, and he'd got rid of his phone, which meant the team now had no way of tracing his movements. Enquiries were in hand to find out the last time it was used and where. CCTV was still being checked to establish if Milo had returned to the scene in the Mercedes.

Sheridan tasked Bridie to make checks on Azriel Cass, and it was quickly ascertained that she was no trace on PNC and therefore had never been in trouble with the police. Enquiries were being made around her mobile phone and background checks were being looked at in relation to Milo Adams, but initial results found no trace of him.

Sheridan was aware that Hill was under pressure from the chief who wanted a swift result as he was coming under scrutiny from the press, convinced that the police were dragging their heels.

Questions were being asked as to whether the police were taking Canning's murder seriously, considering his own conviction for murder.

Sheridan sighed and sent a text to Sam to say she was going to see Anna and then head home. After checking in on the team, she went downstairs, and met Hill, who was on the way up.

'You off?' Hill asked.

'I'm going to the hospital.'

'I spoke to them a little while ago, Anna's still in the side room. And uniform are still keeping an eye on her.'

'Thanks Hill. I'm surprised the chief has authorised all that overtime.'

'He hasn't.' Hill carried on up the stairs and Sheridan turned.

'What do you mean?' she asked.

Hill stopped. 'The chief didn't authorise overtime. I got the patrol sergeants to speak to their teams and ask if anyone would volunteer to watch over Anna on their rest days. They all volunteered, every single one of them. No overtime.'

Sheridan felt herself welling up. 'Really?'

'Yes. Really.' Hill tapped the banister and carried on. 'That's what families do. They look after each other.'

Sheridan stood motionless and speechless as Hill disappeared at the top of the stairs.

◆ ◆ ◆

Sheridan spent an hour with Anna, noticing a remarkable improvement in her. Apart from the horrific bruising to her face, she was alert, sitting up and chatting lucidly.

'I can't wait to get out of here and get back to work. The doctor reckons I could be discharged in a couple of days.'

'You're fucking joking,' Sheridan said with a mouth full of the grapes she'd brought with her.

'No. I'm not. I want to get stuck into the Canning case. I've been thinking about it. The only person who doesn't have an alibi is Frankie and he's not playing ball. So, it has to be him . . .'

Sheridan brought her up to speed with the suspicions they now had around Azriel Cass and Milo Adams.

'Really?' Anna said. 'So, where are we with that?'

'We're all over it, so you don't need to fill your head with it; you need to rest,' Sheridan said, chomping on another grape.

'I want to get back on the case. So, Milo Adams—'

'What are you doing?' Sheridan asked.

'What do you mean?'

'Have you forgotten that someone tried to kill you?'

Anna put her head back on the pillow. 'No. Of course I haven't forgotten. I saw myself in the mirror and I know how lucky I am to be here.' She paused as tears filled her eyes. 'But I don't want to think about it. I want to think about something else, anything else.' She turned her head to look at Sheridan. 'So, you catch who did this to me, and I'll catch whoever killed Dennis Canning.'

'Or how about, you rest and let us do both?'

'I'm . . . struggling.' Anna choked a little on her words and Sheridan took her hand. 'I'm struggling with it all and I just want to take my mind off it. If you don't let me work on the Canning case when I get out of here, then I think I'll have a meltdown.'

'Shit. I'm so sorry, mate. I didn't even think about how it was going to get to you. Let's see how you feel when you're discharged and if you still feel the same way, then I'll sneak you out the case file. You're going to be officially off duty for a while, but you can still do some work from my house.' Sheridan knew that working from home meant Anna wouldn't have access to the various systems she would need to make any enquiries, but letting her read through the case file would at least make her feel she was being of some use.

'Your house?'

'Yeah.' Sheridan tilted her head to one side. 'You do know you're not going to be able to go home until we get who did this. I want to keep you safe.'

Anna closed her eyes for a moment. 'I can't hide forever and anyway, if I stay at yours, am I not putting you and Sam in danger?'

'I'm all ears if you've got a better suggestion,' Sheridan said, popping another grape into her mouth.

'Smartarse,' Anna replied, swiping the bag of grapes from her.

CHAPTER 45

Thursday 20 January

Sheridan was at her desk when her phone pinged with a text from Gabriel: *How's Anna?*

She replied: *Doing well. Had a hoax call about her. Horrible. But she's ok*

Gabriel: *Ok to call you?*

Sheridan sent back a thumbs up and closed her office door, just as her phone rang.

'Hi.'

'Hoax call?' Gabriel asked.

'Yeah. Someone rang me in the early hours of the morning pretending to be a doctor, saying that Anna had died.'

'Jesus. That's awful. Are you okay?'

'Yeah. I am *now*. She's doing really well. Are you alright?'

'I'm fine. Do you think it was Steve who made the hoax call?'

'No. I'd have recognised his voice.'

Sheridan looked up as Rob appeared at her door. 'Anyway, I've got to go. Thanks again and I'll speak to you soon.' She ended the call.

Rob came in. 'Got some updates for you.'

'Go for it.'

'Nottinghamshire Police have been to see Steve's dad. He hasn't seen or heard from him in years and has no idea where he could be. According to the officers who went out, his dad pretty much hates him and said he wouldn't hesitate to call us if Steve makes contact, which he said is highly unlikely.'

'Did he say why he feels that way about his own son?'

'Just said they were never close, and he thinks Steve's a loser.'

'Okay. What else?'

'Steve's mobile has gone completely offline.'

'So, he's binned it. He knows we can track him.' Sheridan sighed. 'Any good news?'

'Nope.' Rob grimaced. 'We've also got a lot of data back on Ben Harper's mobile. He makes and receives a lot of calls, but none since Anna's attack. We'll start going through the phone numbers to see if we can find him that way.'

'So, he's also binned his phone and is using another one. Great,' Sheridan said. 'So, now we just have two missing men.' She put her hands behind her head. 'And we don't know which of them is Anna's attacker.'

Rob perched on the edge of the desk. 'Who do you suspect the most?' he said.

'Ben Harper,' Sheridan said. 'All the evidence points to him. The hammer we found near to where Anna was attacked matches the one that's missing from his shed, along with the sheeting, rope, tape and weights. I fucking dread to think what he was planning to do with Anna if he'd managed to kill her.' Sheridan's jaw tightened as she spoke.

'You don't think Steve's involved now, then?' Rob asked.

'I don't know. I mean, the photo of Anna is pretty threatening, and the fact that he's legged it but nothing else helps our case against him.'

'I think you're right. I hate to say it, but I can't see how Steve would have known that Anna was even going to the pub that night.'

'I know. But I still keep coming back to two things. Her scarf was removed after the attack, and her necklace is missing, which makes me think Steve took the necklace back. Also, I have to ask why he did a runner from the hospital and disappeared off the face of the planet?' Sheridan raised her hands.

'He legged it when he knew his house had been burgled, and that's where we found the photo of Anna with the target drawn on it,' Rob said.

'I also think he ran because he didn't want us having his DNA; he refused a voluntary sample. Which again confuses me if he's innocent.' Sheridan sighed heavily. 'Oh, I don't know. My head's fucked. Shall we go and raid the vending machine? Maybe chocolate will help.' She got up and Rob followed her.

As Sheridan fed the machine, she looked around to make sure no one was nearby, before whispering, 'Can you do me a favour?'

Rob smiled. 'One of your off-the-record favours?'

'Yeah. Can you get me a copy of the Canning murder case file? Anna's probably being discharged tomorrow, and she wants to go through it. Take her mind off what happened.'

'Sure. No problem. Is she doing okay? I feel terrible that I haven't been to see her.'

'Don't worry mate, you've all been bogged down with work. She's going to be staying at mine. I'll feel better that she's not on her own. Especially as we haven't caught her attacker yet.'

Sheridan's mobile rang. It was Hill.

'Yes, boss,' Sheridan said.

'Are you in the nick?'

'Yeah.'

'You need to come to CID. We've got the results back on the hammer and the DNA found under Maud's claws.'

Sheridan couldn't help but smile. 'Maud's claws,' she repeated Hill's words.

'There's something else,' Hill said.

'On my way.'

They headed into CID and Sheridan joined Hill at the front of the room.

'Right,' Hill addressed the team. 'Although no conclusive fingerprints were found on the hammer that we believe was used in the attack on Anna, the blood found on it matches her DNA.' She turned to Sheridan. 'So, we now know that this hammer is the one Ben Harper used.'

Sheridan nodded. 'We've got him.'

'Not exactly.' Hill looked down at the sheet of paper in her hand. 'We've also got the DNA which was found under Maud's claws. It matches the DNA found under Anna's fingernails. So, the person Anna managed to scratch when she was attacked is the same person who Maud scratched.'

Sheridan nodded emphatically. 'Steve.'

'Yes, it looks that way.'

'So, he was the one who attacked Anna . . . but where does Ben Harper come into it then?' Sheridan asked.

'And there's another thing.' Hill looked at the piece of paper. 'Ben Harper bought a transit van two weeks before Anna was attacked, private sale. We're trying to locate the person he bought it from.'

'But his cleaner said he only has a motorbike. She never mentioned a van. So, where is it now?' Sheridan looked completely confused.

'We don't know. But I wonder if Ben was involved with Steve somehow, that they were going to use the van to move Anna's body if they were successful in killing her,' Hill replied.

CHAPTER 46

Anna didn't speak as Sheridan told her about the DNA results and how they thought maybe Steve and Ben were linked somehow. Bearing in mind they'd proved that it was definitely Steve's blood under Anna's fingernails, and the fact Ben Harper had bought a vehicle big enough to move a body. She took a sip of water, resting her fractured arm across her stomach. Sheridan had written her name on the cast with a drawing of a cat's paw and 'I love Maud' next to it.

'You okay?' Sheridan asked.

'Yeah. I'm just a bit numb with it all.' She touched her face. 'Do you think they know each other?'

'I don't know. We're looking at everything. What we do know is they've both vanished. Literally.' Sheridan pulled a face at the green-coloured smoothie on Anna's bedside table. 'What the fuck is that?'

Anna pulled a face. 'I'm on mashed up food. It tastes as bad as it looks. Do you want it?'

'No, I bloody don't. Anyway, Sam's getting your room ready at ours. I thought I'd take you home first to pick up some bits and then get you settled at our place. You definitely being discharged tomorrow?'

'Yeah. And tell Sam not to go to too much trouble. Did you manage to get the case file on the Canning job?'

'It's being sorted.'

'Good, because I need something to work on, take my mind off Steve and Ben.'

'We will find them. You know that, don't you?'

'Of course I do, Sheridan Sherlock's on the case.' Anna shifted her position. 'I need a poo. Can you give me a hand?'

Sheridan stood up. 'Sure. What do you need me to do?'

'Just come into the loo with me and pull my pants down and then wipe my bum when I've finished.'

Sheridan swallowed. 'Of . . . course I can.'

Anna burst out laughing and held her head. 'Don't make me laugh, it hurts.'

'You dickhead.' Sheridan sat back down and crossed her arms. 'I hope you shit yourself before you get there.'

They talked for an hour, and Sheridan noticed a brightness in Anna. Bearing in mind what she'd been through, her spirits were high, and Sheridan hoped this was going to be the way it was. Unless Anna was just off her tits on painkillers.

As Sheridan got up to leave, she kissed Anna on the forehead.

'I'll come tomorrow morning and pick you up. You're doing great by the way. Now get some rest. Love ya.'

'Love ya, too.'

Sheridan made her way to her car and pulled out of the hospital car park. She was a mile down the road when she got a call from Anna.

'Yes, mate?'

'I've just realised something . . . and . . . it might be an issue.'

'What is it?' Sheridan pulled the car over.

'When Maud scratched Steve's face, I cleaned the blood off. Is there any chance that that's how Steve's blood got under my fingernails?'

Sheridan closed her eyes. *Shit*, she thought. 'I doubt it. But . . . leave it with me, I'll have a think,' she said.

'It could explain it though, couldn't it?' Anna said.

'Maybe. Anyway, let's not worry about it for now,' Sheridan said with as much conviction as she could muster.

'Okay. See you tomorrow,' Anna replied and ended the call.

'Fuck. Fuck, fuck, fuck,' Sheridan said out loud. She knew that this really was an issue. If Steve was arrested and his defence got hold of this information, the whole case could be thrown out. She had already broken the law by involving Gabriel Howard and knew she could never divulge that they had set up the burglary at Steve's house. That would always have to remain a secret, but she could live with that. She had no choice. And no regrets. She'd do it again if she had to.

But now that Anna had identified a problem with the DNA evidence, it changed everything. Because to cover this up would mean asking Anna to lie. As much as Sheridan trusted her implicitly, she couldn't and wouldn't ask *her* to break the law too.

If Sheridan was going to prove that Steve had anything to do with Anna's attack, she needed something solid. Something that would prove beyond *any* doubt that he was responsible. Or at least something to throw suspicion at him. As she drove through the Kingsway Tunnel, her mind went over the evidence. And it dawned on her again that maybe her hatred of Steve was such that she'd ignored the mountain of evidence against Ben Harper. Her head hurt as she emerged from the tunnel.

Her mobile rang.

'DI Holler,' she answered with a heavy heart.

'Sheridan, it's Hill. Guess what?'

'What?'

'We've got the financial checks back on Steve's bank accounts.'

'And?'

'He's cleared them out. Every penny.'

Sheridan smiled. 'What a fucker. When?'

'He's been doing it gradually over the last few months. A few grand here and there. Thirty-two thousand in total.'

'Why would he do that if he was just moving to Glasgow?'

'He wouldn't. He's been planning to run and go off grid for months.'

CHAPTER 47

Friday 21 January

Sheridan helped Anna out of the car, after driving slower than she could ever remember, being careful not to hit any potholes on the way. Having confirmed with Anna that she'd changed the locks after Steve had moved out nearly three years earlier, Sheridan had arranged for a police alarm to be installed in Anna's house, even though she was going to be staying at Sheridan's. The alarm worked as a combined intruder and personal attack alarm. So the only way Steve could get into Anna's place was to break in and if he did, he'd set off the alarm which would alert the control room and police would immediately be deployed.

After settling Anna on the sofa, Sheridan went into the kitchen to put the kettle on.

Maud jumped up and sniffed Anna's cast, licking it vigorously.

'How does it feel to be out?' Sheridan called from the kitchen.

'Bloody lovely. Thank you for this. I think it'll do me good to be here. But I will have to go home eventually. I can't hide here forever.'

'It won't be forever. Just until we find Ben and Steve.' Sheridan stood in the doorway.

'That could be months. Once I feel stronger, I'm going home. I'm not scared, Sheridan.' Anna stroked Maud's back and the cat settled down next to her, resting her head on Anna's now slightly wet cast. 'I'm worried about putting you and Sam in danger. Ben doesn't know where you live, but Steve does, and if it was him then he might come here. You can't be here twenty-four seven, you have to go to work and so does Sam.'

'We'll be fine. Don't worry. Anyway, I've talked to Sam, and she knows the risks. The control room supervisors have briefed every-one. They know that any calls from this address are to be treated as an urgent response.'

◆ ◆ ◆

It was gone 5 p.m. when Sam walked into the house carrying two bulging shopping bags.

After kissing Anna, she unpacked the bags on the kitchen worktop. 'I'm doing pasta for dinner. I'll put yours in the blender, Anna.' She opened the fridge and took out a bottle of wine, walk-ing back into the living room. 'I got this yesterday. It's alcohol free, so it won't stop your painkillers working. Joni told me you need to be good.'

Anna grimaced at the thought of going so long without a decent drink.

Headlights appeared through the blinds and Sheridan peered out. 'Joni's here.'

An hour later, they all settled down to eat, with Anna spooning her pasta smoothie into her mouth. 'It actually tastes okay. Maybe you should mash up all your meals, Sam, this is almost edible.'

Sam smiled. 'Really?'

'No. It tastes like sick.'

Sam laughed. 'Well as soon as your jaw's working properly, you can have real food again.'

'God, I hope that happens quickly,' Anna said, sipping her non-alcoholic wine. 'I'm only joking by the way. It's lovely of you to go to all this trouble.'

'It's no trouble. You spend half your life here anyway, so it's not putting us out.'

After dinner, they all settled in the living room and Anna rested her head back, falling asleep almost instantly. Sheridan woke her and helped her into bed.

'Sleep well. If you need anything in the night, just ring this.' She held up a bell that Sam had placed on the bedside table. One she'd stolen from a hotel reception desk a few years earlier.

Anna smiled. 'Thank you. I'll be fine.' She yawned and was asleep by the time Sheridan closed the blinds, glancing out into the darkness. The street light opposite cast shadows from the trees in her neighbour's garden. She pulled the blinds tight to stop any light coming in and disturbing Anna.

She didn't see him.

But he saw *her.* And now he knew Anna was out of hospital. All he had to do was carry on with his plan.

CHAPTER 48

Sunday 23 January

Sheridan was at her desk, having gone through all the evidence in the Canning case again. She'd given a copy to Anna who, in between bouts of sleeping, was picking out anything she could find to try to solve his murder. The phone enquiries into Milo Adams' and Azriel Cass's phones showed that Azriel had called his number one minute after Sheridan and Rob had left the café, on the previous Wednesday.

Azriel was visited, and eventually admitted that she had called him, but said the phone had been answered by a male who told her that Milo had sold him the phone. The male had refused to give Azriel his name, telling her that he had no idea where Milo was, but he was annoyed because the phone wasn't working properly. Sheridan and the team surmised that if this were true, it might explain why the mobile was no longer in service.

Mobile data showed that the phone had been in the area near to the café when Azriel called it, and there had been several calls between them in the days leading up to Sheridan and Rob's visit. Azriel told the police that she had tried calling Milo and although the calls were answered, Milo hadn't spoken. When asked why she hadn't told Sheridan that she'd tried to contact Milo, Azriel said that she was only asked if she'd spoken to him, not whether she'd *tried* to call him. Azriel was asked if she had any photos of Milo, as although he had been captured on CCTV, his facial details weren't particularly clear. She said she had none. Background checks on Azriel showed she was of good character and gave the police no evidence that she was involved in the Canning murder.

Checks carried out on Milo Adams were ongoing, and so far, no trace of him had been found. No trace that Adams even existed.

The case of Anna's attack had gone cold and there had been no sign of Steve or Ben Harper. Harper hadn't used his bank cards. Steve's phone records had been examined and nothing suspicious was found, and it remained offline. The team were still waiting for Ben Harper's phone records to be sent to them. They had tried his mobile several times, but it had remained switched off.

Sheridan yawned, having lain awake most of the night listening out in case Anna stirred or needed help. But she'd still been asleep when she left for work that morning. Sam and Joni were staying with her, Joni having taken three days off work to play 'nurse'. Sheridan had left strict instructions that Sam had to text her every hour to let her know everything was okay.

Rob appeared in the doorway. 'You look shattered. Why don't you take some time off?'

'I can't. We've got two cases to solve.'

Her desk phone rang.

'DI Holler.'

'Ma'am, it's the control room. I've got a lady on the phone, she won't give her name but says she wants to talk to the OIC in the Dennis Canning murder. Can I put her through?'

'Yes, please do.' Sheridan put the phone on speaker so Rob could hear, suddenly remembering the anonymous female that Hill had previously spoken to.

'DI Holler speaking.'

'Have you looked at Bradley Penhaligan yet?' said the female voice. The same woman who had called Hill, telling the police they were running out of time.

'Who am I speaking to?'

'I'd rather not give my name. But have you looked at Bradley?'

'I'm afraid I can't discuss the case, but if you have information, I'd be happy to hear it.'

'I want to help. If you haven't looked at him, you really need to. Please, just think about Bradley. You need to stop him, before there are more killings.'

The line went dead.

Sheridan called the control room back and they confirmed the number had been withheld. She looked at Rob.

'Did Hill tell you this woman has called before?' she asked.

'Yeah,' Rob said. 'And Bradley *was* a suspect until we found out he was in police custody at the time of the murder. You think this was a malicious call?'

'Probably,' Sheridan replied, staring at her phone. 'What does she mean, there will be more killings?'

Sheridan was about to ring Hill and call an urgent team briefing when her desk phone rang again.

'DI Holler.'

'I'm sorry for hanging up on you a moment ago. I have information about Bradley Penhaligan that you won't know about. It was never made public, and only I know about its existence. I'm not a crank and I have nothing to gain by telling you this. But you really need to concentrate on him. I don't know if you've spoken to him, but I've been watching the news, and I haven't seen anything to say that you've caught Dennis Canning's killer.'

'It's an ongoing enquiry,' Sheridan said.

'So, you're still looking?'

'Yes. But I'm interested to hear what you have to say.'

'Alright, I'll say it. Bradley Penhaligan killed Dennis Canning. He planned it and he waited, like he said he would.'

'When did he say this?'

'A long time ago. And the way Canning died was exactly how Bradley said he'd die.' There was a pause. 'Like I said, I have nothing to gain by telling you this. I know what Canning did and how that poor family suffered as a consequence, but I couldn't live with myself if I withheld information about it.'

'I take it you've met Bradley for him to have told you about killing Canning.'

'Yes. Many years ago. Please just look carefully. Dennis Canning won't be the only one, more will get murdered.'

The line went dead.

'Who the fuck is this woman? Why is she saying that Canning won't be the only one?' Sheridan looked at Rob who shrugged. She sat back. 'Whoever she is, she's pretty adamant about Bradley.' Sheridan sighed, rubbing her temples. 'Bradley was definitely in the cells when Canning was killed, wasn't he?'

'Yeah. I'll double-check if you want, but there's no doubt,' Rob said.

'Yeah,' Sheridan said, thoughtfully. 'But double-check. Just in case.'

'Shit,' Rob said.

'What's wrong?'

'What if she meant by other murders that this wasn't just an attack on Canning? What if someone is going to target other murderers who've been released from prison?'

Sheridan sat back, her mouth slightly open. 'Fuck. Of course. Someone who hates killers.' She let out a heavy sigh.

'But it might not just be in the Merseyside area, it could be anywhere in the country,' Rob said. 'I'll put Bridie on it, see if we can find out if there's been any other killings like Canning's.'

Sheridan nodded slowly. 'I fucking hope there hasn't been. Because if there has, the chief will haul Hill over the coals for letting us keep the Canning case . . . and Anna's.'

CHAPTER 49

Sheridan was in the kitchen with Sam, while Joni made coffee for everyone. Anna was asleep on the sofa with Maud, who was snoring, stretched out on her stomach. The three women had made a pact that while Anna wasn't allowed to drink alcohol, they'd abstain.

The doorbell rang and Sheridan looked at the clock. 8 p.m.

Sam put the milk down and turned to head to the door.

Sheridan grabbed her arm, pulling her back. 'Stay here. I'll go.' She felt a flutter in her chest as she peered through the blind and was surprised to see Hill standing there.

She opened the door. 'Hello, Hill. Come on in.'

'I won't stay, I just wanted to see how Anna's doing.' She thrust a bunch of flowers at Sheridan. 'These need to go in water, I bought them yesterday and they've been in my office by the radiator.'

Sheridan smiled. 'Come in, Anna's asleep but she'll be happy to see you.'

'Well don't wake her. Just let her know I was here.' Hill turned to leave, but Sheridan put a hand on her arm.

'Please don't go.'

Hill reluctantly obliged and followed Sheridan inside. They went to the living room. As Anna woke, Hill peered at her.

'Hi Hill,' Anna said croakily.

'Anna. How are you feeling?'

Anna sat up, causing Maud to jump down and immediately head over to Hill, sniffing her trousers.

Anna wiped her dry mouth. 'I'm good.' She looked at the flowers in Sheridan's hand. 'Are they for me? They're . . . lovely,' she said politely, smiling at the half-dead bunch of nondescript flowers.

'I didn't know what else to get.'

Hill looked up to see Sam and Joni emerge from the kitchen. Joni introduced herself with a firm shake of Hill's hand.

They all sat around the kitchen table, drinking coffee, with Sheridan trying to keep Maud and Newman away from Hill, who insisted she didn't mind them being in the same room. As if hearing this, Maud promptly jumped on to her lap and pushed her head into Hill's chest.

Sheridan didn't know whether to laugh or try to rescue her. So she watched Hill's reaction, and to her amazement, Hill touched the top of Maud's head with her finger. Maud obliged by licking it and Hill wiped her hand down her top.

'Maud, get down,' Sheridan said.

'It's alright. She can stay. As long as she doesn't keep *licking* me,' Hill said with an air of disgust.

And that was the moment that Sheridan lost it and burst out laughing.

An hour later, Hill left, and Sheridan walked her to her car, parked a few yards up the road.

'See you tomorrow. Thanks for coming, I know it meant a lot to Anna.'

'No problem.' Hill got into her car and Sheridan waited until she disappeared down the road.

He was in the shadows, watching, and saw Sheridan glance around before going back into the house and locking the door behind her.

He wasn't in any hurry. He'd watch and wait. For as long as it took.

CHAPTER 50

Sheridan walked into CID. Little progress had been made on Anna's case over the last two days. There was still no sign of Ben Harper or Steve, and frustration was taking over. With nothing new to go on, Sheridan knew she had to keep the team focused and positive. The two cases were now weighing heavily on their shoulders: the killing of Dennis Canning and the attack on Anna. All they needed was that one break, that slither of information that could help bring the suspects to justice.

Bridie had started enquiries to check if any other released murderers had been killed. With time against them, Hill had tasked two other officers to help.

Dipesh beckoned Sheridan over. 'Boss, got some info on the transit van that Ben Harper purchased.'

Sheridan sat next to him. 'Go for it.'

'It was bought at auction, two weeks before Anna was attacked. He paid cash, two grand, and drove it away that day.'

'So where is it now?'

'No idea. I'll get the index number circulated and see if it gets picked up on ANPR.'

'Okay, thanks.'

Sheridan plonked herself next to Rob just as he stood up, grabbing his jacket from the back of his chair.

'Where are you going?' she asked.

'To visit Frankie Yearwood, see if he's home. I can't get hold of his parents, and Dipesh has been out to his house a couple of times, but no answer. So I thought I'd try. Wanna come?'

'Sure.'

Twenty minutes later, they parked down the road from Frankie's house. The unkempt front garden was full of old cars and car parts, none of them being a silver Mercedes, the car seen on CCTV that had picked up Milo Adams just before Dennis Canning was murdered.

Rob spotted Frankie with his head under the bonnet of an old Ford Escort. 'We're in luck – he's home. Hello, Frankie,' he said, making him jump. 'I'm DS Wills, we've spoken on the phone. This is my colleague, DI Holler. Have you got a sec?'

Frankie wiped his hands on a filthy cloth, covered in oil. 'I'm a bit busy.' He looked around. 'Can we talk another time?'

'Not really,' Rob said and Frankie agreed to let them into the house.

Frankie, Bradley's cousin, hadn't been at the house when the fire broke out that night, and there was no evidence to suggest that he was involved in Dennis Canning's murder. But along with Milo Adams, he was the only person who had been elusive during the enquiry.

Canning's killer had been wearing a balaclava when he was caught on CCTV slashing Canning's throat, so they had no facial recognition to go on, but if his height and weight matched Frankie's, then they could look at him a little closer. Everyone in the family they had spoken to had provided a solid alibi. Except Frankie.

They stood in the kitchen while Frankie washed his hands at the sink. 'Sorry if I've been hard to get hold of. And I'm sorry

I said before that I didn't want anything to do with this. It's just that I didn't really want to be reminded about what happened. It was a long time ago and I've seen how Bradley and his mum have suffered over the years.'

'It's fine. We just need to ask you a few questions,' Rob said, taking out his pocket notebook. 'You're not in any trouble.'

Frankie leaned back against the sink. 'You want to know where I was the night Dennis Canning was killed? Well, I was here, all night. I don't go out much. So if you think I had something to do with it, I didn't. I wasn't there.'

'Were you on your own?'

'Yeah. I spend most of my time fixing up old cars and then I stayed in all night. I wasn't there.' He scratched the stubble on his chin. 'Sorry I can't be any more help.'

Rob took the lead and asked Frankie how he'd been affected by the fire. Frankie told them that he remembered being woken by his parents and that they left him with a neighbour while they went to the house. When they came home, they explained that his Aunt Carrie's house had caught fire and that his grandparents and cousin Elizabeth had all died, along with Vincent's daughter, Melody. Frankie's parents tried to protect him from the horror of what had happened and kept him away from the reporters and subsequent court case. Frankie and Bradley were close, more like brothers than cousins, and Frankie described Bradley as having been devastated by what happened. They had remained close over the years.

'We understand that Bradley never got over what happened,' Rob said. 'And neither did Carrie and Vincent.'

'Not at first, but over time they all just got on with their lives. Once Canning was in prison, everyone just forgot about him.'

Sheridan took note of this comment. It was a very different account than the one Carrie, Vincent and Bradley had given. They had never forgotten Canning and were still reeling from the fire even after all these years. Sheridan watched Frankie's body language, picking up on how he scratched his face when he spoke. He had the beginnings of a beard which hadn't been trimmed or cared for. He had an air of confidence about him and spoke well, with a soft Scouse accent.

'You're into your cars then?' Sheridan asked.

'Yeah. It's been a hobby of mine for years. I wanted to be a car mechanic, but my parents wanted me to get an office job.'

'Is that anything to do with being Jehovah's Witnesses?' Sheridan remembered the comments from Bridie Sexton after she'd visited Frankie's parents and how they'd mentioned their religion several times.

'Not really. They were just strict and wanted me to be some high-flyer. I did work in an office for a few years after I left school, but I hated it. Then I went to uni and walked away with first-class honours in science. Just to keep my parents happy really. But I didn't really use it for anything, so just did a few different jobs. Then a couple of years ago, I decided to follow my dream and work on cars, doing them up and selling them on.'

'Do you own a silver Mercedes, or have you worked on one recently?' Sheridan asked.

'No.' Frankie shook his head. 'Why do you ask?'

'Just something that came up.'

They talked a while longer before Sheridan and Rob left.

As they made their way back to the car, Rob asked, 'What do you think?'

'I think we need to look at the CCTV of Canning's killing again, because I think it could have been Frankie on that footage.'

'Did you notice how many times he said "I wasn't there"?'

'Yeah,' Sheridan said. 'Let's check out the local cameras, see if Frankie's telling the truth about being home all night.'

CHAPTER 51

Saturday 29 January

Rob walked into Sheridan's office to find her on the phone. She looked up and gestured for him to come in.

She put the call on loudspeaker. 'Sorry, can you say that again?'

'I want to help you, I can't stress that enough. Have you checked Bradley out yet?' said the woman on the other end of the line.

'Like I told you before, it's an ongoing enquiry and I can't discuss the details. But I want to assure you—'

'It was Bradley Penhaligan. That's all you need to know.'

The line went dead.

'She's persistent. I'll give her that.' Sheridan put the phone down.

Rob smiled. 'It wasn't Bradley. Frankie Yearwood lied to us about being home at the time Canning was murdered.'

Sheridan sat back. 'Really? Tell me more.'

'We've been through the CCTV. I've just emailed you the footage. But basically, Frankie left his house at 4.32 p.m. on Friday the 7th of January, he's in a dark Toyota which is registered to him. So, it's not the same car that Milo Adams got into. We haven't managed to track where Frankie drove to yet, but he doesn't return until 9.37 p.m.'

'So,' Sheridan said, 'he's away from his house for long enough to get to the café, carry out the killing, and get home. Or pick someone up and take them to the location, they carry out the killing and he drops them somewhere before he goes home.' Sheridan paused. 'Unless he got the date wrong?'

'No. He knows the date. Trust me. He lied.'

Sheridan clicked on the link to the CCTV and watched Frankie walking along the street where his car was parked a little way from his house. He was wearing a long dark coat down to his ankles, carrying something in a bag.

She then found the CCTV footage of the killing. The suspect wasn't wearing the same coat. But they re-looked at the footage and the height and build matched Frankie's stature.

'So, he went out wearing the coat, took it off and what we see is what he's wearing underneath, plus the balaclava. But why take the coat off?'

'Maybe just to change his appearance,' Rob said. 'We're going through the CCTV from around the area that covers the café. It's taking a while, but if we can place Frankie in the area, then I think we could have him in.'

'At least we're making progress in one of our jobs,' Sheridan said, just as Hill appeared in the doorway.

Sheridan updated her with the information on Frankie.

'Good,' Hill said, letting out a sigh of relief, having just got off the phone from the chief, who had totally lost his shit about the lack of arrests in the Canning murder.

Bridie and the two detectives working with her had not, as yet, found any other related killings that the anonymous female caller had appeared to warn them about.

Sheridan's desk phone rang.

'DI Holler.'

'Ma'am, it's the control room.'

'Hold on one second.' Sheridan put the call on speaker and covered the mouthpiece. 'This will be that woman who keeps calling me about Bradley Penhaligan.'

Hill and Rob moved closer.

'Go ahead,' Sheridan said.

'We've got a male caller on the line, won't give his name and it's from a withheld number. He says he's got important information about the suspect in connection with the attack on Anna Markinson.'

Sheridan looked at Hill and Rob, who both shrugged. 'Put him through,' Sheridan said.

'Hello?' the male voice said.

'Hello, this is Detective Inspector Holler, how can I help?'

'The man who attacked Anna Markinson is in Cheshire. Head to The Key Keeper pub car park. Once you get there, I'll tell you exactly where to go. I'll need a number to contact you on for further instructions. Please don't ignore this.'

'Is he in the pub?' Sheridan asked, getting to her feet.

'No. But he's nearby.'

'We get a lot of hoax calls – can you tell me something that will prove this isn't one of them?'

'This isn't a hoax. Go to the place I've just told you. Wait there and I'll be in touch.'

The caller wouldn't elaborate any further and Sheridan gave him her work mobile number. 'It's going to take us a while to get there. Will he still be there in a couple of hours?'

'Yes.'

The line went dead.

Sheridan hung up. 'We need to go.'

Hill raised her eyebrows. 'You think it's real?'

'We've got no choice but to get there. If it's a hoax, then at least we didn't ignore it. Steve told us he went for a drink in Cheshire the night Anna was attacked, so there's a connection with the area.'

'True. But something sounded off with his voice,' Hill said. 'Like it was muffled.'

Sheridan nodded. 'Yeah, it did sound odd . . .' She put her coat on. 'Anyway, let's contact Cheshire Police, let them know what's going to be happening on their patch; but I want to make it clear that we're dealing with it. Can we get firearms organised?'

'Sure,' Hill replied.

'Shit,' Sheridan suddenly said.

'What's wrong?'

'The voice on the phone. It's like the one that called me to say Anna had died. It's not exactly the same and it wasn't until I got to the hospital and found out she was okay that I remembered the voice was weird.'

'Do you think it's the same guy?'

'I don't know.' Sheridan shook her head. 'I don't know.'

CHAPTER 52

Steve took the bags out of the car and walked along the pathway, the bottles clinking as he reached the canal boat. Climbing on board, he lifted the bags up then stepped over to the back door, and put the key in the padlock. Once inside, he took off his coat and threw it over the chair, reaching into the first bag and pulling out a bottle of bourbon. He grabbed a glass and poured himself a large one before tearing open a bag of crisps and shoving a handful into his mouth. Finally, he switched the radio on. He stretched his back out and sat on the sofa, taking a slug of his drink and closing his eyes.

Ten minutes later, he got to his feet, and went towards the bedroom, flicking on the light.

And that's when he saw him.

Steve didn't move, thinking about what was nearby that he could grab to protect himself with.

'Don't bother, Steve. Just sit down. You need to listen to me.'

Steve swallowed, feeling warm urine soak his groin.

◆ ◆ ◆

Still reeling from his unexpected visitor, who had left two minutes earlier, Steve wiped tears from his face and made his way towards the front of the boat. 'What the fuck?' he said under his breath, as he reached the middle of the cabin and stared at the heavy wooden battens that had been screwed across the door. Placing his hand on the top one, he tried to pull it off with his bare hands, his fingers slipping each time. He turned, heading back towards the kitchen, kneeling down to retrieve the toolbox kept under the sofa. Dragging it out, he opened it and found the screwdriver, ignoring the wetness between his legs. A moment later, he could feel the boat rocking slightly and stood deathly still. Was he back? Had he returned to do as he'd threatened and shoot Steve?

Steve's heart was pounding as he closed his eyes, trying to think. He gripped the screwdriver in his hand and slowly stepped towards the back of the boat. If he *had* come back, then the only way he'd get into the boat was through the rear door. The boat was moving from side to side more now and Steve gripped the screwdriver tightly in his hand.

Then came the shout: 'Armed police! We have the area surrounded. Come out with your hands in plain sight.'

'Fuck,' Steve said under his breath.

Dropping the screwdriver, he shouted back, 'I'm coming out, don't shoot.' He reached the back door and put his hand against it, pushing it slowly open.

'Keep your hands in plain sight.'

Steve complied. Putting his hands outside the door, he stepped up and could see the gun pointed at his head. 'Don't shoot, don't shoot.'

The officer instructed him to keep his hands visible and the next moment he was being restrained and handcuffed to the rear. Once he was off the boat, he was searched and as he looked over, he spotted Sheridan Holler standing there. Smiling broadly.

She walked over to him, hesitating momentarily as she took in how different he looked. His head was shaved bald and thick stubble covered his chin. 'Steven Templeton. You're under arrest on suspicion of the attempted murder of Anna Markinson. You do not have to say anything, but it may harm your defence if you do not mention when questioned, something which you later rely on in court. Anything you do say may be given in evidence.' She leaned in closer and dropped her voice to a mere whisper. 'You fucking piece of shit.'

Steve shook his head. 'Sheridan, you've got it all wrong. I swear it wasn't me. I can explain everything. Please Sheridan, you have to believe me,' he pleaded with her.

'We're taking you to Hale Street custody, where you'll be interviewed—'

Steve butted in. 'Listen to me, Anna's in danger, you need to make sure she's safe. He'll find her.'

Sheridan exhaled impatiently. 'Who'll find her?'

Steve looked her in the eye. 'Ben Harper.'

CHAPTER 53

As Sheridan and Rob followed the police van back to Liverpool, she arranged for a police unit to go to her house before ringing Sam.

'Hey, you okay?' Sam answered.

'Yeah, fine,' Sheridan said. 'Is Anna awake?'

'Yeah . . . you want to talk to her?'

'I need to talk to you both, can you put me on loudspeaker?'

'Okay. We can both hear you.'

'Look I don't want you to worry, but I need you both to stay inside the house with the doors locked. There's a marked police car coming round. It's just a precaution.'

'What's happening?' Anna asked.

'We've arrested Steve.' Sheridan let that sink in for a moment before continuing. 'But we're still looking for Ben Harper and it might be that he's looking for you. I'll know more once we get Steve into custody.'

'Has he admitted anything?'

'No,' Sheridan said. 'I take it Joni's not there?'

'No,' Sam replied. 'I'll let her know not to come.'

Sheridan sighed. 'I love you. Both of you.'

'We love you too. Stay safe,' Sam said.

'I'll call you later.'

◆ ◆ ◆

It was late by the time they arrived at Hale Street custody suite. Hill was already there when Sheridan and Rob presented Steve to the custody sergeant.

'This is a huge mistake. I haven't done anything wrong,' Steve said.

'You'll have an opportunity to give your account when you're interviewed, and I'll remind you, you're still under caution,' the custody sergeant said.

After going through the booking-in procedure and risk assessment, Steve was led away to have his fingerprints, photograph and DNA sample taken. Sheridan had noted that Steve had wet himself and ensured she informed the custody staff in front of Steve. Loudly.

Sheridan, Hill and Rob went upstairs to CID for a debrief.

'So now we know the anonymous call wasn't a hoax,' Hill said, turning to Sheridan. 'Fill me in with what happened when you got to the car park.'

'We got to The Key Keeper pub and waited. I got a text to ask if we were in place and I responded with a yes. Then ten minutes later, I got another text with the name of the canal boat, *Soldier Blue*, and its exact location, which was two minutes from where we were parked up. After we arrested him, he kept pleading that we'd made a mistake and that Anna was in danger from Ben Harper.'

'Okay. Well, seeing as he's named Ben Harper, let's put an interview into him. Does he want a solicitor?'

'No.'

'Fine. Let's see what he's got to say.' As they made their way downstairs, Hill stopped. 'Rob and Dipesh will interview him.'

Sheridan went to protest. 'Why not me?'

'Because you're too close to Anna. I don't want your feelings towards Steve to show in interview. We'll monitor it from next door.'

'Dipesh isn't here, so me and Rob can do it.'

'Dipesh is on his way, he'll be here in five minutes.' Hill turned to Rob. 'Get yourself prepped.'

CHAPTER 54

As Sheridan was unable to interview Steve, she fully briefed Rob and Dipesh as to how she wanted the interview conducted. Rob and Dipesh were experienced detectives, which meant she had no concerns about their technique and skills. But she reiterated that, at this point, she didn't want them to mention the angel necklace. She knew that whoever had attacked Anna had gone to a lot of trouble to remove her scarf and get to it. So that person *had* to know she was wearing it. If Steve slipped up and referred to the necklace, it would give him away.

Sheridan sat down and looked at the screen, making sure the volume was turned up so she could hear the interview. Hill joined her, placing a coffee on the table, and they watched as Steve was brought into the room.

'Fucking bastard,' Sheridan said under her breath.

'And *that's* why I didn't want *you* interviewing him.' Hill sipped her coffee.

Sheridan threw her a look and then focused back on the monitor.

Steve took his seat and after the initial introductions and reminder that he was still under caution, Rob began.

'Is it okay to call you Steve?'

'Yes.'

'Good. So, tell us how long you've known Anna Markinson for.'

'You know how long I've known her. She's my ex-partner, and I know who attacked her.'

'Who was that?'

'His name is Ben Harper. And he's dangerous.'

'Why is he dangerous?'

'He's threatened me.' Steve leaned forward. 'I've known Ben for a few years now – he did some accountancy work for me, and we became friends.'

'Does Anna know him?'

'No. I met Ben after Anna and I split up.'

'Okay, carry on.'

'Last year I was having some major cash-flow problems and spoke to Ben about it. He offered to lend me fifty grand as long as I could pay it back in six months. I snapped his hand off for it. I thought he'd probably give me more time to pay him back, but a couple of weeks ago, he called me and asked if I had the money and I told him I didn't have it all, so he asked me to go to his house and discuss it.'

'So, you went to his house?'

'Yeah. He's got a massive place out in Crosby. He lives on his own, well, apart from his cats. So, I turned up and he was really fucked off that I couldn't pay him back and started threatening all sorts. He's been on at me lately, asking for the money and because I didn't want him to know how much I had, I've been clearing out my accounts. But he was so angry that I told him I'd give him what I had, which was about thirty grand, but he just went mental.'

'In what way?'

'He threatened to hurt everyone I loved. Ben knew about Anna, that we'd split up a few years ago. In the past, I'd told him about the fact I really wanted to get back with her. I told him that I was working on getting her back. Then I told him that she'd been on a dating site and was probably chatting to other blokes, and even he said that wasn't a good sign. He was like a really good mate before the problem with the money, so I didn't see the harm in confiding in him. Anyway, when I was at his house, he demanded his money back and said he wanted it in cash. I told him I only had thirty grand, and he said it wasn't good enough. That's when he said that if he didn't get the full amount, he was going to hurt people. He didn't say Anna specifically, but he intimated that he'd hurt people that I love, and he knows the only person I love is Anna.' Steve cleared his throat. 'Anyway, at one point he came right up to me and grabbed me around the back of the neck and said he'd snap it if I didn't pay him back the money.' Steve turned his head and pulled his collar down, showing a faded scratch mark. 'He left his mark.'

Sheridan, watching from the next room, took to her feet. 'Little fucker. He's making this up to cover himself for when Anna scratched him. He's had all this time to get his story straight.'

Hill touched her arm, and she sat back down. 'Let's see what else he says.'

'Where's the money now?' Rob asked.

'It's on the boat.'

'Describe Ben. Physically, I mean.'

'He's around five seven, five eight, slim, brown hair, white.'

'Does he work out?'

'I don't know. He's never mentioned going to the gym or any-thing. Why?'

'You're well-built and look like you can take care of yourself. I just wondered why you'd be intimidated by him.'

'It's not his build that bothers me, he's a skinny guy, it's what he's capable of.'

Rob turned the page of his interview notes. 'Why didn't you report the threats to the police?' he asked.

'Because if Ben found out, he'd kill me. I'm not joking when I say how dangerous this guy is,' Steve said.

'Did Anna tell you she'd met anyone online?'

'Yeah, but she wouldn't tell me anything about him. I think recently I've realised that we'll never get back together and that's why I was making the move to Glasgow, you know, for a fresh start. But I knew if I gave Ben all the money I had, I wouldn't be able to afford to move. I didn't tell Anna, I just kept up the pretence that I was still going to Glasgow and everything was fine.'

'Where's Ben Harper now?' Dipesh asked.

'He left just before you lot turned up.'

Rob looked up from his notes. 'He was at the boat?'

'Yeah. I'd been out to get some shopping and when I came back, he was inside, frightened the shit out of me. He had a gun and said that he wanted the rest of the money, or I'd regret it. I told him I didn't have it and that's when he said that while I was out shopping, he'd planted things around the boat that would make it look like I was the one who attacked Anna.'

'What things?'

'I don't know. He just said there were things he'd hidden and if the police found them, they'd think it was me who hit her and not him. He mentioned some photographs of Anna.'

'Did he say that it was him who attacked Anna Markinson?'

'Yeah. He said he did it to prove to me that he could get to any-one he wanted. Then he told me he'd put himself on the dating site to look for her and then they'd got chatting and he set up a meet-ing with her at some pub. Then he said that he left her half dead, even though he'd planned to kill her. He'll kill me if he knows I'm telling you any of this. I'm not embarrassed to say that I'm bloody terrified of him.' Steve's hands were shaking as he picked up the cup of water and took a sip, wiping his mouth with the back of his hand. 'I did everything I could to hide from him. I changed my appearance, got rid of my mobile phone because he kept ringing me and I kept ignoring him, so I ditched it and got another one. I did everything to keep away from him. I know I should have given him all the money I had. If I'd have done that, he wouldn't have hurt Anna. It's all my fault.' Steve put his head down.

While Rob asked the questions, Dipesh took out his mobile phone and sent a text to Sheridan. He knew she was watching and listening to the interview from the room next door, but wanted to ensure that she'd heard the mention of a gun.

Sheridan *had* heard and had immediately spoken to the control room, telling them to update the officers attending her house that Harper was likely to be armed.

'Whose canal boat is it?' Rob asked.

'A friend of mine – Martin Styler. He's in Afghanistan, he's in the forces and got deployed a few weeks ago. He asked me a while back if I wanted to save myself some rent money and stay on his boat while he was away. I agreed because it was a win-win for me. I could save some money, and I had somewhere to go where Ben wouldn't find me. I was going to hide out there until I figured out what to do next. But Ben found me anyway.'

'We're going to need to contact this Martin Styler,' Dipesh said.

'No problem,' Steve said, nodding once.

'You said that Ben threatened you with a gun tonight. Can you describe it?'

'I didn't see it, he had it under his jacket. But I could see it was definitely a gun.'

'Why did you screw wooden battens against the door of the boat?'

Steve slumped back. 'I didn't. Ben did that before I got back.'

'Why would he do that?'

'I don't know. I guessed that he didn't want me to get through the door before the police got there. I assume he's left something behind there that he wanted you to find.' He looked between Rob and Dipesh. 'Did you find something?'

'My colleagues are still searching the boat.'

'Good. And will I be told if you find anything?'

'Yes.' Rob checked his interview notes. 'So, when Ben left tonight what was the last thing he said?'

'He told me that because I didn't have the money, things were about to get bad for me.'

'What do you think he meant by that?'

'Well now I'm guessing he meant he'd called the police. Like I said, he's planted things on the boat, so now you're going to find whatever it is and think I attacked Anna.'

'After Anna was attacked, Detective Inspector Holler took you to the hospital to see her?' Rob said.

'Yes.'

'So why did you run from the hospital?'

'I was going to get a coffee and a police officer walked past with his radio up, and I heard someone saying my house had been burgled, and I panicked. I thought it must be something to do with Ben. I just . . . panicked.'

'And you didn't think to tell me or DI Holler? We were both there with you,' Rob said.

'No. I just wanted to get away. Plus, Ben would have killed me if he found out I'd said anything. I knew the break-in was something to do with him. When me and Sheridan . . . sorry, DI Holler, left my house that day, my car tyre was flat and I guessed Ben must have done it. I took it as a warning.'

'When DI Holler picked you up to take you to the hospital to see Anna, you went back inside the house to get something. What was it?'

'I went to get the keys to the boat. Like I said, I thought Ben had slashed my tyre and I realised I might need to run and hide at the boat, so I grabbed the keys.'

Rob put his hand up to stifle a sneeze. 'Did Ben ever go to your house?'

'No.'

'How does he know your address?'

'I don't know. He must have found out somehow and then broke in.'

'After the break-in at your house, we found a photograph of Anna. Do you know anything about that?'

'Yeah. Ben sent me some photos of her a while ago, with a round sort of target drawn around her face. Like the ones on an archery board.'

'Why did he send them?'

'He was making a point that he'd managed to follow her, and that she was a target, I guess.'

'How many photographs did he send you?'

'About five or six, I think.'

'Could you tell *when* they were taken?'

'Not really. I mean they're fairly recent ones I think, but I can't say exactly when they were taken.'

'What did you do with them?'

'I put them away. I can't remember where.' He looked at Rob. 'You said one was found in the house?'

'Yes.'

'I've been packing to move. I think I put them in a box. Is that where it was?'

'Which room was the box in?'

'I can't remember. My head's been battered the last few months.' Steve puffed out his cheeks and closed his eyes. 'I'm really tired. Is there any way we can carry on in the morning? I'd really like to get some sleep.'

Rob looked at Dipesh, who nodded, and the interview was terminated.

Steve was led to the cells and Rob and Dipesh joined Sheridan and Hill.

Sheridan had spoken to Anna, who was now aware that Ben Harper might be looking for her and was very likely to be armed. She'd confirmed that Ben wasn't aware of Sheridan's address, not from *her* at least. Sheridan had suggested that Anna and Sam were taken to another location, but they had both declined.

'What do you think?' Rob asked.

'I think we've got a problem. Steve's story makes sense so far, and I can't find any holes in it.' Hill looked at Sheridan. 'Sorry, Sheridan.'

'Me neither,' Rob replied. 'I'm sorry too Sheridan, but I have to say – and I hate saying it – it's all credible. He even described Harper's house and cats. They know each other and he's explained everything we know about what's happened.'

Hill crossed her arms. 'And we know Steve cleared out his bank accounts. So it makes sense what he said about wanting to hide the money from Harper. *Was* his tyre slashed when you left the house?'

'I don't know if it was slashed, but it was flat,' Sheridan said. *Gabriel Howard did that*, she thought, but clearly couldn't say anything. 'Maybe I made a mistake. Maybe I hate Steve so much that I got blinkered,' she said, defeated.

'It's been a long day. Let's all go home and pick this up first thing in the morning,' Hill said. 'The search team and CSI will let me know if they find anything.'

◆ ◆ ◆

After the team had left, Sheridan walked down the empty corridor to her office. She stared out of her window across to the Albert Dock, strangely comforted by the red-brick buildings that stood strong and familiar before her, their lights reflecting like Christmas decorations across the Mersey.

Then her head was back in the case. She had been so sure that Steve was the one who had attacked Anna. But now the realisation kicked in that she'd got it wrong. The moment she'd seen Anna in the hospital was the moment everything changed. She'd called upon a criminal for help. She'd broken the law. And the case against Steve was falling apart – not through her mistake, but because she'd practically ignored the facts that proved beyond much doubt that Ben Harper was the guilty one.

As she stood there, she heard a faint noise behind her and turned to see Rob, his shoulder touching hers.

'My dad was a police officer, as you know,' Rob said. 'He was a DS in CID, here at Hale Street. He did his thirty years.'

Sheridan carried on looking out of the window.

'Many years ago,' Rob continued, 'he was dealing with a case of a woman found half beaten to death in a flat. He convinced himself that it was a guy he'd always hated, just like you hate Steve. This guy had been arrested a few times for violence against women, and my dad was convinced he'd been responsible for an almost identical attack on another woman a few months earlier. He almost drove himself into the ground trying to gather evidence against this guy, but the longer it went on, the more he realised he might have been wrong. But it consumed him, and it was all he could think about. Then, when the real perpetrator was arrested and convicted, my dad started to doubt himself. He started to question everything about the way his mind worked. He was a brilliant detective, but after that case, he came to the realisation that he was only human. He wasn't Superman. He was just a person. And people make mistakes.'

Sheridan rested her head on his shoulder.

CHAPTER 55

Sheridan was heading downstairs, ready to go home, when her mobile rang.

'DI Holler.'

'Hi Sheridan, it's Sergeant James from custody, are you still in the nick?'

'Yeah, what's up?'

'Steve Templeton wants to speak to you.'

'Okay.' Sheridan made her way to the custody suite and was let in by the detention officer, who escorted her down the cell corridor and dropped Steve's wicket.

'DI Holler is here to see you.' The DO turned to Sheridan. 'Do you want the door open or shut?'

'Open, please.'

'Do you want me to stay?'

'No, you're fine. Thank you.'

Steve remained seated as Sheridan stood in the doorway, her arms folded. 'Before you say anything, I have to tell you that you're still under caution.'

'I understand.' Steve ran a hand over his head and Sheridan could see he'd been crying. 'Is Anna okay? Is she safe?'

'What do you want to speak to me about?' Sheridan answered bluntly.

Steve exhaled. 'Please keep Anna safe until you find Ben Harper. He's smart and if he managed to find me, then he'll find her and I swear to you, he'll kill her. He'll do it to get back at me.' Steve started crying and after a moment, he composed himself. 'I know you hate me and that's fine, it doesn't matter. But I want you to know that I love Anna. I've always loved her. I haven't always gone the right way about it and . . . I even . . . I even hit her when we were together. She probably never told you.' His voice was shaking with emotion. 'I hurt the only woman I've ever loved. I was a different person back then. When we split up, I was a total mess. I admit I became obsessed with her – obsessed with getting her back. I was so desperate to be with her, and I hated the thought of her being with someone else. But I do know that she's moved on and it's over. When she told me she'd had an abortion, I was so angry, I was angry that she'd lied to me and angry that she didn't even give me the chance to talk it through, make the decision together, instead of her doing it by herself.' He looked down. 'I remember getting home the night she told me, I just went mental and was screaming and shouting at myself, cursing her out loud. The old lady next door even heard me and was banging on the wall to make me shut up. I lost it, I completely lost it. But it didn't take away my love for Anna. It just hit me that there was no way we could ever get back together, and with all the shit going on with Ben Harper, I just wanted to get away, move to Scotland and try to start again.' He fell silent for a moment, before lifting his head to look at Sheridan.

'Once this is over, you'll see I'm innocent and I can get on with my life, but I really, really can't stress enough how much danger Anna's in. You *have* to find Ben, he might seem like a weedy little accountant living with his cats, but he's dangerous and it's all my fault that he wants to kill Anna. I can't protect her, but you can. Please don't let her out of your sight – not until he's caught. Promise me, Sheridan. If nothing else, please just promise me that.'

At that moment, her mobile rang. It was Hill.

Sheridan stepped back into the corridor, her eyes on Steve the entire time. 'Hi, Hill.'

'Sorry I know you're at home, I just wanted to let you know the officers searching the *Soldier Blue* haven't finished but they have found more photos of Anna, like the ones Steve was sent by Harper. And every one of them has a target drawn on it. They're going to send me the images, and we'll look at them in the morning. They're sealing the boat off for the night and will carry on in daylight tomorrow.'

'Okay, thanks, Hill.'

The drunk in the cell opposite started banging on his door and shouting.

'What's that noise?' Hill asked. 'Are you in the custody suite?'

'Yeah, but I'm just leaving. I'll see you in the morning.'

Sheridan went to close Steve's cell door.

'If Anna comes through this, please tell her I'm so sorry I've got her involved in my shit. And promise me you'll keep her safe.' Steve looked up at the ceiling. 'Talking of being safe, I never thought I'd like being in a police cell, but right now, I feel safer here than I do out there, until you find Ben Harper.'

Sheridan looked at him. She had so wanted to be right about him being the one who'd attacked Anna. But the man before her had covered himself in interview, he'd had an answer to every question and they all made sense. And Sheridan was furious about that. Was Steve really innocent? Had he been set up by Ben Harper or was he just an exceptionally good liar? She closed the door and left.

CHAPTER 56

Sunday 30 January

Steve was back in the interview room. Sitting across the table from him, Rob pressed the record button, while Dipesh sorted through his interview notes. Sheridan and Hill were set up in the room next door, monitoring.

'Steve, you said you visited Ben Harper a couple of weeks ago and he became violent, and you showed us the scratch at the back of your neck. What date was that?'

Sheridan had briefed Rob and Dipesh again on the line of questioning. Anna had remembered scratching her attacker on the back of the neck. If it really had been Ben who was responsible for leaving the mark, then Sheridan wanted to know if Steve had been scratched by Ben around the same time as Anna was attacked. Then Steve's account was very much believable.

Steve rubbed his forehead. 'A couple of weeks ago. Actually, it was the day before Anna's birthday. The Sunday . . . So, the 16th.'

'Bollocks,' Sheridan said under her breath in the room next door.

Rob continued. 'Was there a time recently that Anna could have scratched you on the back of the neck?'

Steve looked puzzled. 'Er . . . sorry, I don't understand.'

Rob repeated the question.

'No,' Steve replied, still looking confused.

'Were you scratched recently on your face?' Rob asked.

Steve smiled. 'Yes. But not by Anna. I was round at Sheridan Holler's house. Anna and I had been out for a drink, and she'd dropped her warrant card in my car, so I took it back to her the next day, and that's where she was, at Sheridan's. I picked up Sheridan's cat, and she scratched my cheek.'

'We found DNA under Anna's fingernails after she was assaulted. And it's the same DNA we found under the cat's claw.'

Steve sat back and crossed his arms. 'Yeah, so . . . ?'

'So, when you were arrested yesterday, as part of the booking-in procedure, your DNA was taken. If that matches the DNA we already have, how would you explain that?'

'What does that even mean? You still think I was the one who hurt Anna? Jesus, after all I've told you, you still think it's me?'

'Can you answer the question?'

Steve shook his head. 'I don't know, maybe when Anna was cleaning the blood off my face, some of it got under her nails. Is that possible?'

◆ ◆ ◆

Hill turned to Sheridan. 'Please tell me that's not fucking true.'

Sheridan's head dropped. 'It's true.'

Shit, she thought. Having prayed that this potential issue with the forensic evidence would never come out, Steve had now thrown an enormous spanner in the works and Sheridan knew the enormity of what it meant.

Hill stood up. 'Jesus fucking Christ, Sheridan. You know this is the only nugget we had to nail on him, or at least throw some doubt on his account. But *now* I find out that Anna could have got his DNA under her nail in *your* bloody house.'

'Anna had her nails done after that, it's unlikely she still had any of Steve's blood under there,' Sheridan protested.

Hill pointed at the screen. 'Unlikely . . . but not impossible. If this ever got to court, a defence would rip the shit out of this.' She sat back down. 'Trust me, unless Steve suddenly changes his whole account and admits everything, we've got *nothing*.'

There was a knock on the door and Hill opened it to see Bridie standing there.

'Sorry to interrupt. I just wanted to let you know that I've spoken to Steve's mate, Martin Styler, the soldier in Afghanistan. He confirms that the *Soldier Blue* is his, Steve's his mate and he's looking after the boat for him.'

Hill looked at Sheridan. 'So now we've got *less* than nothing.' She turned to Bridie. 'Anything else?'

'Martin does have a car, which he keeps in a garage while he's away. Apparently, he asked Steve to give it a run every now and then. I've got the details. There's a code to get into the garage, which I've also got. Do you want me and Dipesh to go out there? We've got the car keys.'

'Yeah,' Sheridan replied.

Bridie nodded at the monitor. 'How's it going?'

'It's going to shit,' Hill snapped.

Bridie slowly backed out of the room, before quietly closing the door.

◆ ◆ ◆

Rob took a sip of his coffee. 'Apart from Sunday the 16th of January, did you visit Ben Harper at his house any other time?'

'No, just that once.'

'Which rooms did you go into?'

'We sat in the kitchen. I didn't go anywhere else.'

'Did you at any time go into the shed or garage?'

'No. We literally just stayed in the kitchen.'

'You told us that last night Ben Harper came to the boat and threatened you.'

'That's right,' Steve said.

'Was the boat locked when you left to go shopping?'

'Yeah.'

'So how did Ben Harper get in if he didn't break in?'

'I don't know.'

'So, you're telling us that Ben has no key, but managed to get in, hide evidence connecting you to Anna Markinson's assault, and then screw in battens to prevent you from getting to the front of the boat, all before you got home. And then he threatened you with a gun and left?'

'Yes, that's what I'm telling you. Because it's the truth. I've got nothing to hide.'

'How long were you out shopping for?'

'About an hour or so.'

Rob looked at his mobile, which was on the desk on silent. A message from Sheridan: *Ask him if he's got access to another car*

Rob asked the question and Steve confirmed his mate Martin had a car which he asked him to take for a run every now and then.

Another text from Sheridan: *Has he driven it recently, and where is it?*

Rob asked Steve and he said it was in a garage and gave the details, but stated he hadn't driven it at all.

Her next message arrived: *Tell him he's a fucking dickhead*

Rob hid a grin and glanced up at the camera, knowing Sheridan was watching. She sent a final text telling Rob to conclude the interview. He looked at Dipesh, who gave a slight shake of his head to indicate he had no further questions.

'Unless there's anything you want to add, I think we'll leave it there for now.'

'Can you tell me if Anna's okay? I've been going out of my mind worrying about her.'

'She's stable.'

'Please make sure you keep a close eye on her. I know you've got a police officer outside the door. Please don't let anyone get to her. Ben could pretend to be a doctor or something and get in to hurt her.'

'I'm sure that won't happen,' Rob said. 'She's safe.' He made a note that Steve clearly didn't know that Anna had been discharged from hospital.

'What happens now?' Steve asked.

'We're just waiting for a few enquiries to come back, and then we'll let you know.'

CHAPTER 57

The team reconvened and went through the interview.

'Now we know why Steve's car wasn't picked up on ANPR when he was moving his stuff to the boat; he was using Martin's car.' Rob raised his eyebrows.

'But his neighbour, Mrs Dobson, didn't mention a second car, did she?' Hill said.

'No. So I guess Steve loaded his own car up, drove it to wherever he'd parked Martin's car, transferred his stuff and then continued the journey to the boat,' Rob replied.

'So, he's lying when he says he hasn't used Martin's car,' Hill said, looking at Sheridan. 'But apart from that, he's accounted for everything. We're just going to have to hope that we find something in Martin's car. But if we don't and the search team on the boat haven't got anything else, we're going to have to bail him out. Then we need to really focus on finding Ben Harper.'

'Fine,' Sheridan said. 'But I can't sit here waiting. I'm going out to Cheshire. I want to see how they're getting on with the search of the boat.'

◆ ◆ ◆

Sheridan walked along the towpath. It was bitterly cold, but bright in the morning sun which glinted off the water. It was so serene, and on any other day she would have taken a moment to enjoy the beauty of the moment.

Bridie and Dipesh had been to the garage, but Martin's car wasn't there. Sheridan spoke to Rob and told him to put another quick interview into Steve and ask where it was. Steve had stated that he hadn't been to the garage to date and had no idea where the car could be.

Bridie had tried to contact Martin Styler to check if he'd moved the vehicle before going to Afghanistan, but she hadn't managed to get hold of him.

Sheridan's heart felt heavy as she passed a young woman with a little girl, merrily feeding the ducks.

'Do you know what's happening? With all the police?' the woman asked.

'It's nothing to worry about,' Sheridan said.

'Do you want to feed the ducks?' said the little girl and held out her little hand, which was full of brown pellets. 'It's proper duck food, we're not allowed to give them bread. It's not dangerous for them but it doesn't give them any goodness. And ducks need goodness for their feathers,' she added matter-of-factly.

The little girl's mother smiled at Sheridan. 'She wants to be a vet.'

Sheridan smiled back and held out her hand, into which the little girl dropped the pellets.

'Thank you.' Sheridan felt a moment of peace from the simplicity of the gesture. She threw the pellets in the water and the ducks flapped and fought over them. She carried on walking and ducked under the police tape that cordoned off the canal boat, noticing one of the ducks had followed her along the pathway.

After showing her warrant card to the uniformed officer, Sheridan stepped on to the boat, poking her head through the door.

'How's it going?' she asked.

'We're almost done,' one of the search team replied. 'Not much to report, I'm afraid. We haven't found anything apart from the photographs of DS Markinson. CSI are almost done, too.' The officer nodded at Sheridan's feet. 'Who's your mate?'

Sheridan looked down to see her new duck friend had joined her and was pecking at her shoes. She looked back towards the woman and her daughter, now further on up the towpath.

'Come on, you.' Sheridan reached down and very gently tried to usher the duck away. The duck was having none of it and started quacking frantically, looking up at her. 'I'm going to call you Crispy.'

The officer on the towpath found it rather amusing as he watched Sheridan walk along the deck, holding on to the handrail. Followed by Crispy the duck.

'Be careful there, ma'am. Don't want you falling in,' the officer said.

Sheridan turned to face him. 'You'd love that, wouldn't you?' She grinned.

She stood at the side of the boat, looking down into the water, and Crispy flew up, landing on the roof.

'Please get back in the water, Crispy. I could do without you shitting all over my crime scene.'

Crispy quacked again.

'Don't suppose you've got a butty, have you?' Sheridan asked the officer.

'Yeah . . . but my wife made them and they're like, special.'

'Oh, come on, just a crust.'

The officer shook his head and walked over to a large black bag, retrieving his packed lunch and reluctantly tearing a piece of bread off, leaning over and handing it to Sheridan.

'Okay, Crispy. You're not supposed to eat bread but needs must.'

She threw the bread in the water and Crispy was down like a shot. Sheridan leaned over the side and watched him paddle out.

Her phone rang. It was Hill.

'What's the latest?' Hill asked. 'The clock's ticking, Sheridan. Have they found anything?'

'Not yet.'

At that moment, one of the search team popped his head out. 'We've found the money. Looks like a few grand. Apart from that, we're all done and so are CSI.'

Sheridan relayed this information to Hill.

'Okay, so that's the money Steve was meant to pay back to Ben,' Hill said. 'It doesn't add anything to our case, though. I'm going to have to bail him out.'

'Alright.' Sheridan ended the call. 'Shit,' she said, looking down as Crispy swam back towards the boat.

And then she saw it. Glistening in the sunshine.

Grabbing her phone she quickly called Hill back.

'Yes?' Hill answered.

'Don't let Steve go.'

CHAPTER 58

It was gone 12 p.m. by the time the underwater search team arrived.

Hill had joined Sheridan and stood beside her as a briefing took place on the towpath. One of the search team officers introduced himself, before saying, 'I understand we're looking for a gold pendant.'

'Yes.' Sheridan held up the evidence bag containing the broken gold chain. 'This was caught on the rope on the other side of the boat. If it's the necklace we're looking for then there's a gold angel pendant in the water somewhere, it might have fallen off. Do you think there's a chance you'll find it?'

'I can't promise anything, but we'll do our very best.'

'How deep is the water?' Sheridan asked.

'Only about five feet . . . Do you fancy going in?' the officer joked.

'Trust me, she would if you let her,' Hill quickly butted in.

'Bloody right I would. Anyway, thank you. We'll let you get on.' Sheridan smiled.

She stood back and the team started kitting up.

'How do you think it got there?' Hill asked as they sat on a bench further up the towpath.

'When we got here last night to arrest him, there was only one small side window open, the one facing out to the water. I think he threw it out of that window, and it got caught on the rope. Maybe that's when the pendant fell off.'

'We can't be sure it's definitely Anna's necklace.'

'I know. I sent her a picture of the chain and she's not sure. She'd only worn it for a few days.' Sheridan looked across the canal. 'We need that bloody pendant.'

◆ ◆ ◆

Half an hour later, the first of the underwater search team officers entered the water.

'It's a needle in a haystack, isn't it?' Sheridan said, despondently.

'Yeah,' Hill said, breaking off a piece of bread from the remains of the uniformed officer's lunch and feeding it to Crispy the duck, who had now settled in between them on the bench.

'If they don't find the pendant, we'll have to bail him out.'

'I know,' Sheridan replied. 'But if they *do* find it, then he's got some explaining to do.'

'Do you believe his story about Ben Harper being so dangerous?'

'I don't want to, but it all makes sense.'

'Ben's got no previous, he lives in a lovely big house, with a cleaner and a handyman, it just doesn't add up, does it?'

'No.' Sheridan fed Crispy another piece of bread.

They both looked up as the underwater search team officer emerged, his thumb raised in the air.

Sheridan was on her feet. 'Oh my God, he's only bloody found it.'

CHAPTER 59

Darkness cloaked the city by the time Hill and Sheridan arrived back at Hale Street, Hill having to tell Sheridan to slow down on several occasions. They walked into CID, where Rob, Dipesh and Bridie were all waiting for a full briefing.

'Our twenty-four hours is almost up, I'm going down to custody,' Hill said. 'Do you want to come?' she asked Sheridan, who nodded.

They were buzzed through to the custody suite and after speaking to the custody sergeant, he escorted them to Steve's cell.

The door was opened and Steve looked up.

'Hello Steve, I'm DCI Hill Knowles. As you may have been told, we can only hold you for twenty-four hours without charge, and we have now almost reached that.' She looked at her watch. 'By eight minutes.'

Steve stood up. 'So, am I being released?'

'As I was saying,' Hill continued. 'Once the twenty-four hours is up, we have to release you. Unless we apply to the superintendent for an extension. This only happens if a superintendent agrees that we are being diligent in our enquiries and have very good reason to hold you for longer. So, I'm here to inform you that you will be held in custody at this time.'

'What for?' Steve asked.

'We'll update you in due course,' Hill curtly replied, before closing the cell door and walking back down the corridor.

Sheridan stood for a moment, staring at the wicket on the door, which held the man she had always believed was responsible for attacking her best friend. There was still much to prove, but as she made her way back towards the custody desk, her head felt full and heavy. But her heart was lifted. This wasn't a moment of celebration, it was a realisation of what Steve was capable of. And it was a horror story. One that would stay with her, always.

The noise of prisoners shouting from within their cells echoed in her ears. Just then, three uniformed officers appeared, restraining a woman who was screaming her lungs out about the handcuffs being too tight, and that she couldn't breathe.

In front of the officers was Eve, the detention officer, who was escorting them into the female wing, raising her eyes at Sheridan. 'It's going to be one of those nights,' she said as the woman screamed even louder that she thought she was going to die.

Sheridan walked past the group and sat herself down in the custody office. The sergeant was calling through the next prisoner to be booked in and Sheridan didn't want to disturb him, but she did want to check through Steve's custody record.

The custody suite was busy, with cell buzzers going off, phones ringing and the radio crackling on the desk, the control room trying to inform custody that there were three more prisoners on their way.

Sheridan turned to see the door of the consultation room open and a suited man poking his head out. With everyone busy, Sheridan went over to him. 'Can I help you?' she asked.

'I need to get something out of my car,' he said.

'Okay, give me two seconds.' She peered into the room and saw the prisoner sat at the other end of the room, facing her, looking pissed off. But then most people looked pissed off when they were in police custody.

'Are you his solicitor?' Sheridan asked. It was a reasonable question, as she didn't recognise the man in the suit.

'Of *course* I am.' He shook his head, clearly indignant about being asked this question. He looked past Sheridan to see Eve coming towards them.

'Everything okay Mr Shamer?' she asked.

'I need to get some paperwork from my car.'

'Okay, no worries.' Eve opened the gate, and the solicitor left. But not before casting a belittling glance in Sheridan's direction.

'Dickhead,' Eve said as he disappeared. 'First time he's been in here and he's pissed us all off already. Rude little twat. And his breath stinks.'

Sheridan grinned. 'Maybe when he comes back you should offer him a mint.'

'I actually might do that. Anyway, what can I do for you?'

'I know you're busy, but I just need to have a look at Steve Templeton's custody record. How has he been?'

'I haven't met him yet, we've just done a handover, and I was off yesterday. The dayshift just said he's been quiet, not caused any problems.'

'Okay. Thanks, Eve.'

Sheridan read through the custody record and after a final briefing with her team, she headed home. Preparing herself for what she had to tell Anna.

CHAPTER 60

Monday 31 January

Sheridan walked into CID to find the place buzzing. The discovery from the day before had turned the investigation on its head, and now Rob and Dipesh were ready to head down to custody. Sheridan would have loved to be there in the cell to see the look on Steve's face. Instead she would watch on the camera. Would he kick off? Would he cry? Or would he shut down? Either way, he was about to have a bomb dropped at his feet. And Sheridan couldn't wait for his reaction.

As she took up her position in the room next door, Rob and Dipesh went to his cell and opened Steve's door. He remained seated.

'Am I being released?' Steve asked.

'No. And you need to listen carefully to what I have to say,' Rob said.

'Steven Templeton. I'm arresting you on suspicion of the murder . . . of Ben Harper.'

◆　◆　◆

The underwater search team hadn't found the angel pendant that Sheridan believed Steve had thrown out of the window. What they *had* found was a body. Ben Harper's body.

Wrapped in plastic and shoved in a large suitcase.

After it was discovered, the police realised that the rope the suitcase was attached to was on the wrong side of the canal boat. The vessel had been secured front and rear with ropes tied to the mooring pins on the towpath. The middle rope, which was often used when single-handedly mooring up, should also have been on the towpath side, not the canal side.

Steve had requested a solicitor, who, after being given formal disclosure by Rob and Dipesh, was now next to Steve in the interview room.

After the formal introductions, Rob began the interview, with Sheridan watching and listening via the monitor in the room next door.

'Steve, you told us that on Saturday the 29th of January, when you returned to the canal boat, *Soldier Blue*, there was a male on board, who you knew as Ben Harper, having previously known and met Ben on several occasions.' Rob looked up and noted Steve had his arms crossed. He continued. 'You told us that Ben threatened you with a gun. Is that correct?'

'No comment,' Steve replied.

'As you now know, we recovered Ben Harper's body from the canal yesterday. Did you kill Ben Harper?'

'No comment.'

'We know that Ben has been deceased for longer than two days, so we know you didn't kill him the night he supposedly turned up on the boat. So, Steve, I'll ask you, when did you kill him?'

'No comment.'

Even though it was clear that Steve wasn't going to answer any of Rob's questions, Rob still had to ask them.

Steve continued to reply 'no comment' when each question was put to him, until Rob appeared to have touched a nerve with his next one.

'Why did you try to barricade yourself inside the boat before the police arrived?'

'No comment.' Steve flicked a look at his solicitor, who was busy, head down, taking notes. 'I didn't try to barricade myself in,' he said angrily.

'When my colleagues arrived, you were screwing battens across the door leading to the front of the boat. And it was when these battens were removed they found the photographs of Anna, each with a target drawn on them. So, I put it to you that *you* took those photographs of Anna, not Ben Harper.'

'I didn't try to barricade myself *in*. I was trying to take the battens *off*. He put them there, not me.'

'Who?'

Steve waited for several seconds before responding. 'What's the fucking point. You won't believe anything I say.'

'Try me.'

'It doesn't fucking matter.'

'One final question for now. Did you make a phone call to DI Holler, impersonating a doctor, before telling her that Anna Markinson had died?'

Steve looked at his solicitor and then at Rob. 'Of course not.'

Steve refused to speak further, and the interview was concluded.

CHAPTER 61

Monday 7 February

It was three in the afternoon and Sheridan was at her desk, going over Anna's case.

Having been charged with the murder of Ben Harper and the attempted murder of DS Anna Markinson, Steve was remanded in custody by the magistrates, awaiting his first hearing at the Crown Court. The post-mortem on Ben Harper concluded that he was already deceased before being placed in the canal and had been dead for approximately two weeks. The timing of his death coincided with around the time that Steve had said he'd visited his house. The plastic sheeting, tape and rope that Ben's body had been wrapped in matched those that were taken from his shed, as were the weights that were missing from Ben's house. And the suitcase in which his body was stuffed inside.

Sheridan and her team still didn't know how Steve and Ben Harper knew each other, as Steve's account that they had become friends after he had split up with Anna didn't pan out. To date, the police had found no evidence of any contact between them, or anything to suggest that Ben had loaned Steve any money.

Steve hadn't admitted being the person who had made the call to Sheridan in the middle of the night telling her that Anna had died. But Sheridan was convinced he had somehow disguised his voice.

What didn't make sense was the similarity between *that* voice and the voice of the anonymous caller who had directed the police to Steve's location on the canal boat. That *couldn't* have been Steve.

There were still questions, and Sheridan knew that to secure a conviction they had to have a watertight case. And after everything she had risked and how hard the team had worked, she wasn't going to let Steve get away with what he'd done.

Anna was making a good recovery, and was desperate to gain her independence back. With Steve locked up, she was running out of reasons not to go home. She'd opened up to Sheridan about her feelings towards Steve and how she was trying not to blame herself for failing to see what he really was.

As well as building the case against Steve, Sheridan and her team were still working on the Dennis Canning murder. Frankie Yearwood's account that he'd been at home at the time Canning was killed had been ruled out, after Rob had discovered CCTV images of him leaving his house and not returning until later, giving him enough time to have committed the crime. But Rob and Sheridan had reviewed the image of the killer and agreed that although the build and height of the suspect was very similar to Frankie's, it wasn't conclusive, and with the attacker wearing a bala-clava, facial identification was impossible. Frankie's mobile phone had last pinged off a mast close to his house, five miles away from where Canning had been murdered. Rob had re-checked Bradley Penhaligan's custody record, which proved without any doubt that he had been in custody at the time, ruling him out as a suspect.

Extensive checks had been carried out on Milo Adams, making it clear that officially Milo Adams did not exist. Azriel Cass had maintained her account that she had only known him a short while and couldn't elaborate on any details about him. He'd vanished without a single trace. The anonymous female caller who'd stated that Bradley Penhaligan had killed Canning had called Sheridan twice more, but declined to say who she was. She had, however, continued to insist that there would be more deaths if Bradley wasn't arrested. The chief had continued to pressure Hill for a swift result, and had even suggested that the case was handed to Potters Road CID, but Hill had stood firm, as she always did, furiously protecting her team, even if she didn't share with them what the chief had suggested. Instead, she burdened the responsibility. The public response from the police requests for witnesses or information had been virtually silent and although Carrie and Vincent were kept updated, they showed little interest in the case, having continually aired their hatred for Canning.

The press had lost interest in the case, much to Hill's relief. But Sheridan and the team were determined to find the evidence they needed to secure a conviction. And they *had* to find Milo Adams.

◆ ◆ ◆

As Sheridan was about to get herself a coffee, her phone pinged with a message from Gabriel Howard: *How's Anna doing?*

Sheridan replied: *Really well thanks*

She had updated Gabriel about Steve's arrest and charges, but that was all she could tell him, not about how or where he'd been found. Which Gabriel understood.

Gabriel texted back: *And you?*

Sheridan: *I'm bashing my head against the wall with the evidence, but I think we'll get there*

Gabriel: *I'm here if you need anything*

Sheridan smiled and replied: *Actually, was about to grab a coffee. Fancy one?*

Half an hour later, she was sitting next to Gabriel on a bench in Sefton Park, removing the lid from the coffee that he'd bought her. In the summer months, the benches would be occupied by the flocks of visitors to the historical park, but now, in the cold of this February day, most of them stood empty. A light breeze whistled gently through the bare branches of the trees around them. Summer would bring with it the glory of the place, when the famous Palm House would be full of people admiring the beautiful nineteenth-century glass domed building that had in the 1980s fallen into disrepair, finally restored ten years earlier in 2001.

'Thanks for everything you did, Gabriel.' Sheridan threw him a smile. 'It wasn't your battle to fight, and yet, without you, we may never have caught Steve. Remind me again why you helped me?'

Gabriel sat back. 'One bad deed deserves another.'

'Very poignant. Didn't know you were a man of wise words.' She raised an eyebrow.

'I'm not.' He inhaled. 'Anyway, are you sure you've got enough evidence to convict Steve?' Gabriel asked, blowing the steam from his drink.

'Yeah, I think so. But it's never guaranteed that a jury will come back with a guilty verdict.'

'Do you need me to plant anything?' Gabriel said, turning his head slightly to see her grinning back.

'Don't bloody tempt me,' she said.

'So where was he hiding?' Gabriel asked.

'On a canal boat on the Cheshire Ring. You remember the keys you saw him getting from the wardrobe? Well, the blue ball that had the word "sold" written on it wasn't a ball, it was a painted cork float. Apparently, people put them on their keys so that they float in water if you drop them. And the full wording written on it was actually *Soldier Blue*, the name of the boat.'

'So Steve bought a canal boat?'

'No. It's his mate's.' Sheridan sipped her coffee. 'And the Allen key on the key ring was actually a miniature canal lock key.'

'Windlass,' Gabriel said.

'What?'

'Remember I told you, I used to go boating with my dad, he taught me all the terminology. The canal lock key is called a windlass.'

'Wow. How totally fascinating,' Sheridan said with a hint of sarcasm and Gabriel nudged her playfully.

She nudged him back and shivered involuntarily, cupping her hands around her coffee.

'Are you chilly?' Gabriel asked.

'Yeah, a bit.' She threw him a sideways look. 'And don't you dare do that fucking manly thing where you take your coat off and put it round my shoulders.'

'Why would I do that? Then *I'd* be cold.' He tutted loudly, hiding a smile.

They sat in silence for a moment, watching an elderly couple walk past, their overweight dog slowly wobbling behind them in a tartan coat.

'How's Anna doing? I expect it's a lot for her to take in, knowing now what Steve was capable of,' Gabriel said.

'It'll take time, but she'll get there. She's a tough cookie.' Sheridan sighed. 'He had it all worked out you know, every detail. And if we hadn't found Ben Harper's body, Steve would have probably got away with it. I've met a lot of liars in my career, but he's right up there. His account was so believable. He was so calculating in the way he tried to pin Anna's attack on Ben. He even had the gall to say that Ben was on the boat and threatened him with a gun. And the whole time, Ben was dead in the canal.' She looked at Gabriel. 'I don't know why I'm telling you this.'

'I think we've established that you can trust me, Sheridan.'

'Yeah, I guess I can.'

'Steve is a fucking liar though. You're right about that.' Gabriel wiped a dribble of coffee from his lip.

'I know,' Sheridan said.

Gabriel stretched his back out. 'It wasn't a gun.'

Sheridan frowned, taking in what Gabriel had just said. 'What do you mean?'

'It wasn't a gun I threatened Steve with.'

CHAPTER 62

Sheridan's mouth was still open, but no words came out. Gabriel calmly looked ahead and finished his drink, inhaling the cold winter air into his lungs. Giving her a moment.

Sheridan finally spoke. 'You. It was *you?*'

Gabriel shrugged his shoulders. 'Yeah.'

'Fucking hell.' Sheridan turned in her seat to look at him face on. 'Hang on . . . you were on the boat, so . . . Oh my *God, you* were the anonymous caller.'

'Yep.'

'How the fuck did you find him?'

'I remembered what you said about Steve saying he'd been at a pub in Cheshire on the night Anna was attacked. It stuck in my head, but it wasn't until a few days later that I realised the thing on his keys wasn't an Allen key; it was a miniature windlass. And the blue ball was a float with the name of the boat written on it. I know the Cheshire Ring really well, we went there loads of times as kids, and so I headed out there and spent every day looking for a boat that had the letters "sold" in the name. And that's when I found the *Soldier Blue*. Which as you now know is painted the same blue as the cork float.' Gabriel wiped his mouth. 'And then I sat back and watched. A few hours later, he came up on deck. It took me a minute to recognise him because he'd shaved his head, but I knew it was him. I never forget an arsehole. That's when I knew all I had to do was check out his routine, and once I'd figured that out, I made the anonymous call to the police.'

Sheridan shook her head slowly. 'How did you get on the boat and lock yourself inside?'

'If anyone can pick a padlock, it's me. So, I picked the lock, went inside, let myself out through the front door and then re-locked the padlock.'

'So, when Steve got back to the boat, what happened?'

'I told him that if I could find him hidden there, I could find him anywhere and that no matter where he went, I would always find him and that I'd be watching him for the rest of his life.'

'Why did you do that?'

'Because you told me he'd probably only get about ten years, so I wanted him to know that when he comes out of prison, I'll be watching him. Of course, at that point, I didn't know he'd killed Ben Harper.'

'Did you mention Anna? Or me?'

'Of course not. And I wore a mask, so he'll never recognise me.'

Sheridan sat back. 'So, if you didn't mention Anna, maybe he thought you were something to do with Ben. Steve actually used your visit to prop up his own story about Ben threatening him.' She smiled. 'I like that.' She shook her head. 'But I'm not happy that you went on the boat with a bloody gun, Gabriel.'

'I told you, it wasn't a gun. He just presumed it was because of the shape of it under my jacket.' Gabriel pursed his lips.

'So, what was it?'

'A drill.' Gabriel smiled. 'What do you think I used to screw the battens on with?'

Sheridan couldn't help laughing, before asking, 'Where did you get the battens from? Were they already on the boat?'

'No.' He looked at her. 'I'm a carpenter, I have a lot of wood.'

'Jesus,' Sheridan said. 'Did you find the photographs of Anna?'

'Yeah. And I knew you'd turn up a couple of minutes after I left, and I didn't want him to get rid of them. So, I barricaded the inside door that led to the front of the boat, to give you the time to arrest him before he ditched anything.'

Sheridan shook her head again. Thinking. 'Hang on, you didn't know about the photographs until you got on the boat, so how did you know to take the battens?'

'It wasn't my first time on the *Soldier Blue*. I got in a couple of days before, when Steve was out. That's when I found the pictures.'

Sheridan inhaled. 'You were the anonymous caller . . . but I didn't recognise your voice. How did you do that?'

'The same way Steve did it when he made the call to you to say Anna had died.' Gabriel reached into his pocket and took out a small black device. 'It's a voice changer. Pretty simple.' He handed it to Sheridan. 'Two can play that game.'

'Why didn't you just tell me when you first found Steve? Instead of the anonymous call and everything else.'

Gabriel put his hands on his head. 'Shit. If I'd told you sooner, would Ben still be alive?'

'No. He was already dead by then,' Sheridan said.

'Thank fuck for that, well . . . you know what I mean. The reason I didn't tell you at first, was because I wanted five minutes with him. I wanted to scare the living shit out of him and let him know, or at least make him think, that I really *was* going to watch him for the rest of his life.' He turned to Sheridan. 'I just wanted five minutes, and I wouldn't have got that if you'd got to him first.' He grimaced. 'Are you mad at me?'

Sheridan grinned. 'No, I'm not mad at you. But we can never ever tell anyone about this. And I mean *anyone*.'

'I know.'

Sheridan looked at him. 'Steve wet himself by the way.'

'I know.' Gabriel smiled broadly and they shared a fist pump.

'You were captured on camera after you left Steve's house that day. You were the jogger, weren't you?'

'Yeah. I take it you thought that someone jogging and wearing headphones hadn't just burgled a house?'

'Exactly. We dismissed you as a suspect based on that. Very clever.'

'Not clever, it's just illusion Sheridan. It takes two seconds to look completely different. And like I said before, it's about looking, not just seeing.'

Sheridan looked up to the sky. 'Thank you. For everything. I know Anna's safe now, Steve's not going anywhere for a long time, and I don't have to keep looking out of my window, worried that he's out there somewhere. I wasn't scared of him, but with Anna living in my house and my partner being there, I *was* scared that they were in danger. Not during the day so much, but certainly at night. I'd wake up in the early hours and stare out of the window, in case he was hiding in the shadows.' She felt her eyes fill with tears. 'I was terrified he'd hurt Anna again, or Sam. Fucking piece of shit.' She wiped a hand down her face.

'He wasn't watching from the shadows at night,' Gabriel said.

'You don't know that.'

'He wasn't watching your house at night, Sheridan.' He looked at her. '*I* was.'

Sheridan took a deep breath, holding back tears. 'Why?'

'So that I could be sure you were all safe.'

Gabriel was staring straight ahead and continued to look forward, even when he felt Sheridan's hand slip into his and squeeze it tightly.

Just before she stood up and slowly walked away.

CHAPTER 63

Anna put her key in the front door and pushed it open. Sheridan was behind her and saw Anna flinch as the police-installed alarm was triggered.

'Fuck. That made me jump,' Anna said out loud. 'You can get rid of that now.'

Sheridan entered the code and carried Anna's case into the living room.

'God, it feels good to be home,' Anna said, looking around. 'Cuppa?' she asked, picking up the shopping bag that contained the essentials: milk and wine.

'Let me do that,' Sheridan said. 'You need to watch that arm.' She nodded at the cast.

'I'll be fine, stop fussing.' Anna followed her into the kitchen and filled the kettle.

Sheridan refrained from trying to help, even though she really wanted to.

As they sat drinking their coffee, Anna talked about returning to work. She'd studied the Canning case and could find no further evidence. Once they'd discovered that Frankie had actually left his house on the night of the murder they'd hoped this would lead to something, but there was nothing to place him at the scene. Frankie had said he'd got the date wrong and couldn't remember what he'd done that night. All other lines of enquiry had been exhausted.

Anna hadn't spoken much about Steve and Sheridan knew she was trying to put what had happened out of her mind. And the Canning case had given her an opportunity to concentrate on something else.

Sheridan got up to wash her coffee cup. 'Have you got a spare key? I really should have one just in case I need to get in in an emergency.'

'What kind of emergency?' Anna asked, taking the wine she'd purchased from the worktop and placing it in the fridge. After kissing the bottle. Twice.

'Well, what if you get drunk and fall down the stairs. You're still on painkillers, so you really shouldn't be drinking, especially now you'll be on your own.'

'I'll be fine. But if you insist, there are spare keys in the little cabinet under the stairs.'

Sheridan went to the cabinet and emerged a moment later. 'There's only one spare here.'

Anna glanced at it. 'No, there should be two.' Anna went to the cabinet and looked through the few keys that were hanging up. 'That's weird. There's a key missing.'

They both stood looking at the solitary key. A few moments later, Anna put a hand to her head. 'Shit.'

'What?' Sheridan said.

'Steve must have taken one when he brought me home after we met for a drink. I fell asleep on the sofa, and he woke me up with a coffee, but he had time to take one of the spare keys.'

Sheridan thought for a moment, looking around the room.

'When was the last time you changed the password on your laptop? I've always known it as Sheridan Sherlock.'

Anna put her head down. 'I haven't changed it for years.'

'So, Steve knows it?'

'Yeah.'

Sheridan slowly shook her head. '*That's* what he did. He got into your house, logged on to your laptop, and found your conversations with Ben, just like I did. Ben worked from home. He was easy to find, you literally just have to google him and there's his address.' Sheridan sighed. 'Steve told us that him and Ben knew each other, but we couldn't find any proof of it. Now we know how Steve found him. He went to his house and either took him to another location, or killed him there. He took the plastic sheeting, tape and rope from the shed and the weights from the house, and the suitcase from the shed. That's also how Steve was so convincing about knowing Ben, like mentioning he had cats. He told us that Ben had asked him to go round to discuss the debt . . . but there was no debt. Steve only went there to kill Ben. Then once he had his mobile phone, he could see the texts between the two of you , so he knew which pub you were going to. And that's how he changed it from The Seven Horses to The Blacksmith. The quieter pub where he could attack you outside more easily. Just after he sent the text from Ben's phone cancelling the date.' Sheridan looked at Anna. 'It all makes sense now.'

'How do you think he knew the PIN number for Ben's phone?' Anna said.

'I don't know. And maybe we never will, unless Steve decides to tell us, which I very much doubt.'

'Christ,' Anna said. 'The night I stayed at yours for Maud's birthday, he turned up with my warrant card. He knew I'd be staying over, so I bet that was when he got into my house.' Anna instinctively looked around, as if expecting to see Steve standing there.

'But once he'd got into the house, looked at the messages on your laptop, why didn't he just put the key back and close the door when he left?'

Anna's shoulders dropped. 'Because you need the key to lock the front door from the outside. And he wouldn't have left it unlocked, because that would have looked too suss. But he took a bloody chance, I mean, what if I'd discovered a spare key was missing? The only person who could possibly have taken it would be Steve.'

Sheridan's jaw tightened. 'He planned to kill you on your birthday. So, he knew that when he took the key on the Friday, there was little chance you'd spot one was missing before he attacked you on the Monday. And if he *had* managed to kill you, then we would never have known that there should be two spare keys.'

Anna burst out crying; the realisation that Steve really had planned to end her life suddenly seemed very real. He actually *had* tried to kill her.

Sheridan immediately wrapped her arms around her.

She had worried that Anna had showed very little real emotion when she was told about Ben, although it could have been put down to shock. It had seemed like she hadn't registered everything about the attack and Steve. But now, it all came tumbling out, in wave after wave. She sobbed openly and cried out, 'Oh God Sheridan. I'm responsible for Ben. If I hadn't been such an idiot, this would never have happened. It's my fault.'

'None of this is your fault, it's all Steve and there's no way you could have seen any of this coming. So don't you dare for one minute blame yourself.' Sheridan held Anna's bruised face gently in her hands. 'Steve planned to kill you, and he almost succeeded.'

For the first time since the assault, Anna seemed able to talk openly and frankly about the attack. How, when she closed her eyes, all she could feel was someone behind her. And then the agony of the hammer hitting her. The flashbacks came thick and fast. And so cruelly vivid. She talked about how she desperately wanted to get back to normality and put it behind her. But Ben Harper's death, and its connection to her, weighed heavily. She knew Steve had been responsible for everything, but it didn't stop her feeling incredibly guilty over Ben's death. If they hadn't arranged that date, maybe he would still be alive.

'How does the team feel about it all?' she asked. 'About *me*?'

'They love you and they've worked their arses off to find the evidence against Steve,' Sheridan said.

'Do you think they'll look at me differently, now they know about the abortion and the fact that I never reported Steve for hitting me in the past?'

'No. They won't. You know how they feel about you, and this changes *nothing*. I promise you.'

'I'm going to have to face him in court and it will all be out there. How me, a police officer, became a victim.'

'Let's not worry about that for now. It'll take months and months to get to trial and we'll support you every single step of the way.' Sheridan smiled. 'I don't think you realise how much you're respected and loved, not just by me and the team, but everyone. When you were in hospital, we had uniform outside the door every minute of the day, to protect you, to watch over you. They all volunteered, without question and without being paid. So, don't you ever doubt how highly you're thought of.'

Anna took a moment to let that sink in. 'That's . . . amazing. Thank you for doing that.'

'It wasn't me. Hill organised it.'

It was gone seven in the evening by the time Sheridan got up to leave. She'd offered to stay overnight, but Anna insisted she was happy to be on her own, and promised to call if she needed anything, or changed her mind about Sheridan staying over.

After hugging each other goodbye, Sheridan stepped outside.

'I wonder if we'll ever find out who made the anonymous call that led you to Steve,' Anna said. 'I'd like to meet them.'

'Me too, mate,' Sheridan sheepishly replied, before getting into her car.

CHAPTER 64

Friday 11 February

Sheridan was sat next to Rob in CID when the desk phone rang. Rob answered it, looked at Sheridan and handed her the phone. 'Control room.'

'DI Holler.'

'Ma'am, lady on the phone, won't give her name, says she wants to talk to you about the Dennis Canning murder.'

Sheridan raised her eyes at Rob. 'Put her through.' She put the call on speaker and the team gathered round.

'Hello?'

'Is that DI Holler?'

'Speaking.'

'I've . . . called before about Bradley Penhaligan.'

'Yes, I remember.'

'I see you haven't arrested him yet. I want to help, because I'm guessing as far as you're concerned, he's not a suspect.'

'How would you like to help?'

'I'd like to meet you and . . . I'll bring the evidence you need.'

Sheridan's eyes widened. 'Like what?'

'Everything. Shall I come to the police station?'

'Yes, can you come this afternoon?'

'Okay. I'll be there at two. I'm bringing you a CD recording that will explain everything.'

The phone went dead.

Sheridan leaned back in her chair. 'CD recording? This could be really good . . . or she's a complete fucking crank.'

'To be honest, I'd take a crank at this point; we've literally got nothing on the Canning case,' Rob said, just as Hill walked in.

'What about the Canning case?' Hill said bluntly.

Sheridan told her about the call.

'Well, let's hope it really is something bloody useful, because the chief is still getting his bollocks in a twist over this case.'

'The problem is, it couldn't have been Bradley, it's physically impossible. He was downstairs in the bloody cells.' Sheridan turned to Rob. 'You double-checked it, didn't you? I mean it was definitely him?'

'One hundred per cent. He'd been nicked once before and his fingerprints, photo and DNA were taken. The second time, the day Canning was murdered, Bradley was booked in, and had his photo and fingerprints taken. It was *definitely* him, you can't fake your fingerprints. I also looked at the custody recordings and it's very clearly him being booked in. No doubt at all.'

'Maybe this woman's trying to set him up,' Sheridan said. 'The question is, why?'

CHAPTER 65

Sheridan and Rob were in the public enquiry office when the woman arrived and introduced herself as Glenda Harley. They showed her into a vacant interview room.

'So, Glenda, you say you have evidence that Bradley Penhaligan murdered Dennis Canning,' Sheridan said. 'Can you tell us why you believe this?'

'I was a journalist in 1974, and I was one of many who reported on the fire. It was a massive story, and had a huge impact on the local community. Every journalist within a hundred miles wanted to get close to the family, to get to know them. But to do that, they had to trust you. I was young and desperate to impress my boss. Being a woman gave me an advantage over the male journalists when it came to convincing people to trust me. I spent a lot of time with the family. Carrie was the one who struck me the most, she was so distraught about what Canning had done, but she still showed such great strength of character. She used to talk to me about her parents and how close they were, and how she relied on them to look after the children, Bradley and Elizabeth, when she was at work. Carrie was one of the first female fire control officers back then, she was young and keen, like me, and we seemed to have a kind of bond. She opened up to me about how she couldn't believe that Canning, a man she once loved, could set fire to her house and kill her parents and her daughter. He'd obviously planned to kill everyone inside, but as fate would have it, Bradley survived.'

Sheridan and Rob listened. So far, Glenda didn't appear to be the crank they'd envisaged. She was forthright, intelligent. They let her speak without interruption, because although much of what she talked about they already knew from the case file, it was clear that she wanted to tell the whole story. And they wanted to hear it.

'It was never discovered if Canning knew that Vincent's daughter, Melody, was in the house when he set the fire. He never said anything about it. But either way, Canning was hated, and I mean, really despised by everyone. Even me, I hated him. I'd never dealt with a case like that, and seeing first-hand how that family suffered, trust me, I despised the man. But I kept my feelings to myself when I met with Carrie and Vincent. I had to be professional. But I tell you, as much as I saw the hatred for him from the family, it was Bradley who seemed to harbour the most rage.'

'Bradley was only nine when the fire happened. Can a nine-year-old show that much anger?' Sheridan asked.

'No. When he was nine, he hardly spoke at all. It was when I met him ten years after the fire that I saw the anger in him.' Glenda shifted in her seat. 'The newspaper I worked for had an idea that we'd revisit cases where a family member had been murdered. They called it "Ten Years On". I was asked to get back in touch with Carrie and Vincent and see if they'd be willing to give us a story about how, after ten years, life had been for them. Carrie and Vincent refused point blank to engage with the idea. I remember sitting in their living room, and how they looked almost the same as they did when it first happened. The pain on their faces was as evident as the first time I'd met them. They'd tried to move on, but what Canning had done was always there. He'd destroyed them and it was quite clear that they were no further forward. Carrie knew that if she gave me an interview, there was a chance Canning would read it in the paper and revel in the fact that the family were still suffering.' Glenda cleared her throat. 'Anyway, I left them my contact details in case they changed their minds. It was a week later when I got a phone call from Bradley, saying he wanted to meet me. He was nineteen at the time, and so I agreed. He came to the office and the moment he walked in, all I could see was rage in his eyes. He had moments where he spoke calmly about how he felt, but his eyes gave away what was inside him.' Glenda paused, as if reflecting on her own words.

'Do you need a break or a drink?' Sheridan asked.

Glenda accepted a cup of water before continuing.

'Before I interviewed Bradley, I set up a camera to record everything. It was on a VHS recorder originally, but a few years later, I had it put on to a disc.' Glenda hesitated. 'I didn't tell Bradley I was recording him.' She swallowed. 'I thought maybe he wouldn't open up if he knew he was being taped. I never intended to use the recording, I just wanted it to refer to for when I wrote the piece for the paper.' She took the disc out of her bag and handed it to Sheridan, who slid it into the computer.

'It's a bit shaky, but you can see him quite clearly . . . and the sound is still there.'

Glenda nodded at Sheridan, and she started the recording.

On screen, the video showed a nineteen-year-old Bradley sitting with his hands resting on his knees, balled into fists.

Glenda asked him how the last ten years had affected the family and Bradley answered, saying that Canning had ruined their lives. His mother struggled every day to comprehend the loss of her parents and daughter. He talked of growing closer to her and Vincent over the years, and how they supported each other as best they could. But life couldn't move on, and Bradley wondered if it ever would. He talked with so much love about Carrie and how she was the perfect mother to him and his sister. He wept when he mentioned his grandparents and how no one deserved to die that way. He described how he'd escaped the fire and the guilt of being the only survivor had always haunted him.

The recording went on for half an hour, and as much as it showed his anger and grief, Sheridan couldn't see how any of what Bradley was saying had convinced Glenda that he'd gone on to murder Canning. The screen flickered and Sheridan pressed the stop button.

'Glenda, firstly thank you for bringing this in, but—'

'You need to keep watching.'

Sheridan pressed play.

The screen lit up again and Glenda's voice could be heard.

'Thank you, Bradley. I know that was hard for you; you were really brave.'

'What happens now?' Bradley asked.

'I'll write the column. We can meet up again so that you can look through it to make sure you're comfortable with what I've written. After that, it will go into the paper. How does that sound?'

'Fine.' Bradley put his head down and he suddenly looked distraught, put his hand to his face, and it was clear that he was crying. Then he lifted his head. 'I'm going to kill him.'

'I know you're angry and I understand that . . .' Glenda said.

'It's more than anger. I'm going to kill him one day.' Bradley wiped a hand across his face. 'He doesn't have a clue what's coming.'

'Bradley . . . Canning was sentenced to life imprisonment and is unlikely to ever be released. I worry that this pent-up anger is going to destroy you. You're a young man with your whole life ahead of you. Please try to find a way to let your anger go, it won't change what happened,' Glenda said.

'He might *not* be in prison for the rest of his life and if that's the case, then I'll be waiting for him. I'll hunt him down and he won't see me coming. Trust me. He'll have no idea.'

'I think you'll feel differently as time goes by.'

'Do you? Because *I* don't. You just watch. He'll be walking down the road one day, minding his own business, thinking he's going to live the rest of his days as a free man. But I'll be there, watching him, and then before he gets a chance to do anything, I'm going to slash his fucking throat.'

Glenda pressed stop on the recording.

Sheridan and Rob sat in stunned silence. The image of Bradley's face flickered on the screen.

Glenda took a sip of water. 'I saw on the news about Canning being murdered, and I remembered that I'd interviewed Bradley. It was twenty-seven years ago and obviously I couldn't recall exactly what he'd said. I didn't even know if I still had the recording. It was a few days later when it started coming back to me, and I remembered that he'd said he was going to kill Canning if he ever got released, but I couldn't recall the details. But I thought I should call the police, which, as you know, I did.'

Sheridan looked at Rob and then to Glenda. 'I can see how you'd think it was Bradley, but . . . we've eliminated him as a suspect. I can't say any more than that.'

'And now you've seen the interview, is he still eliminated from your enquiries?'

'Yes,' Sheridan said, sighing. Disheartened that even with this compelling evidence, they still couldn't change the fact that it was literally impossible for Bradley to be the killer. 'Did you end up writing the piece?' she asked.

'Yes, but I left most of it out. I just wrote about the sadness of the family, not the comments that Bradley had come out with about killing Canning. He was a young, angry man, and I didn't want him to be portrayed as he'd appeared in the interview.'

'Can I ask . . . ? You said before that everyone hated Canning, even you. You witnessed what the family went through and had a bond with Carrie. So why come forward and tell us all of this and show us the recording? You appear to have had some sympathy for Bradley back then, so why do you want him to be arrested?'

Glenda put her hands on the table, stretching out her fingers. 'If it was just about Canning and I believed that Bradley had got to him, I might not have come forward, if I'm totally honest. I would probably have destroyed the disc and spent the rest of my life living with that. Did Canning deserve what he got, to have his throat slashed, yes. Yes, he did.'

'So why have you come forward now?'

Glenda took a deep breath. 'Because when Bradley came back to read through the piece, he said something else, which wasn't recorded, but I remembered it when I watched the recording that you've just seen.' She looked at Sheridan. 'He said after killing Canning, he was going to track down Canning's family, friends, and anyone Canning had ever been close to. And he was going to kill them too. And that's the part I can't keep to myself because if he does what he threatened to do, I don't think I'll be able to live with myself. And that's why I told you that you might be running out of time and that there will be more killings.'

CHAPTER 66

Sheridan was in CID, reading through Bradley's custody record from the night Canning was killed. Bradley had been arrested at 5.30 p.m. and transported to Potters Road custody suite, where he was presented to the custody sergeant at 6.01 p.m. During the booking-in procedure he requested a solicitor, and his fingerprints and photograph were taken by the detention officer. Having previously been arrested, his DNA was already on the system and therefore wasn't taken again. He was then placed in his cell and given a cup of water. The solicitor, Geoffrey Long, arrived at 6.33 p.m. and was given disclosure by the arresting officer, who outlined the circumstances of his client's arrest. Bradley was then escorted to a consultation room where he met with his solicitor. At 7.26 p.m. the consultation concluded, and Bradley was taken back to his cell. The solicitor advised the custody sergeant that his client would be making a full and frank admission to criminal damage, and the solicitor stated he wouldn't stay for the interview and left the custody suite.

At 8.14 p.m., Bradley was interviewed by an officer from the custody investigation unit, fully admitted criminal damage and was placed back in his cell. At 9 p.m. he was charged and released.

Sheridan turned to Rob. 'Let's look at the custody CCTV, I want to see him being booked in. I know you've already checked, but I want to see for myself.'

Rob played the recording of Bradley arriving in custody. He could be seen clearly walking into the custody suite, where he was presented to the custody sergeant. Sheridan leaned in, scrutinising the images.

'That's definitely him.' She massaged the back of her neck. 'Let's see the rest of it. I want to make sure the timings are right, and he wasn't released earlier.' She looked at Rob. 'I know I'm grabbing at straws.'

She watched each recording of Bradley being taken for his fingerprints and photo, before being placed in his cell. Then being escorted to speak to his solicitor. Sheridan fast-forwarded the recording of the consultation to when Bradley was placed back in his cell.

'The timings work, don't they?' Rob said.

'Yeah. Bradley was in the cells when Canning died. So, it *has* to be Frankie who got to Canning. We need to be able to place Frankie at the scene. Him or Milo Adams. Or both of them.' She sighed heavily. 'Fuck's sake, we'll have to start all over again, we need to go through everything we've got.' She got up and squeezed Rob's shoulder before heading back to her office, deciding to raid the vending machine first. As she made her selection, she thought about the recording of Bradley in custody and couldn't shift the feeling that something was off.

Then it hit her.

She turned and ran up the stairs towards CID, Gabriel Howard's words echoing around her head: *'It's just illusion Sheridan. People see, but they don't really look. It takes two seconds to look completely different.'*

Then Eve the detention officer's comment about not having yet met Steve while he was in the cells.

'I haven't met him yet, we've just done a handover, and I was off yesterday. The day shift just said he's been quiet, not caused any problems.'

Rob looked up as she came thundering into CID. 'What's up?'

'Show me the recording again,' Sheridan said, catching her breath.

Five minutes later, she paused it, rewound and re-played it.

'There.' She pointed at the screen and Rob looked closer. 'Watch it again and keep a really close eye on Bradley's feet.'

Rob watched and a moment later, he looked at her, open-mouthed.

'Keep watching.' Sheridan nodded at the screen.

Rob concentrated on the screen and watched the recording over and over, until he saw it.

And then he slumped back in his chair. 'Well, fuck me.'

CHAPTER 67

Hill joined the team who were congregated in CID. Sheridan and Rob were standing at the front of the room, both still reeling from what they'd discovered.

Sheridan made sure she had everyone's attention before she began. 'Okay everyone, I'm going to play you the recording of Bradley Penhaligan in Potters Road custody on the night Dennis Canning was murdered. I want you to watch it and tell me what you see.'

She played the recording on the screen behind her and the team observed. When it ended, she turned to them.

'Did you see it?'

Vague expressions from everyone.

She played the recording again; this time she commented as it played.

'This is Bradley in the consultation room, facing the camera. Now, we know this is definitely him. Sitting opposite, with his back to the camera, is his solicitor. Bradley is wearing the foam slippers they give out to prisoners. Now watch as he puts his feet under the table.'

The team were glued to the recording.

'There. Bradley pulls his feet back slightly and if you look *really* carefully, you can just make out that he's now wearing shoes.' Sheridan looked around the room, before continuing.

'Now watch the recording again from the beginning,' Sheridan said, pointing at the screen. 'According to the custody record, this is Geoffrey Long, Bradley's solicitor. When he arrives, he's wearing glasses, a hat and a long coat down to his ankles, which he keeps on and buttoned up. He's also wearing black slip-on-style shoes. Bradley is wearing grey tracksuit bottoms and a grey sweatshirt. The solicitor takes the hat off and puts it on the chair in the corner, which as you can see, is only very partially covered by the camera. They sit opposite each other and start talking. Now, you see Bradley's feet go under the table, as do the solicitor's. A moment later, they've swapped footwear.' Sheridan took a sip of coffee. 'They talk a bit longer and then the solicitor stands up and steps backwards towards the door, which is obscured due to the camera angle. It's a blind spot. Now Bradley also stands up and goes to the door, so all you can see is his head and part of the solicitor's arm. Three seconds later, Bradley sits back down and so does the solicitor.'

'So, they swapped shoes? I don't get it,' Hill said.

Dipesh stood up and walked over to the screen and looked closely. 'They didn't just swap shoes. They swapped *places*.' He pointed at the screen. 'I don't know who that guy is, but it's not Bradley.'

'I know who it is,' Sheridan said. 'The only person in the family who didn't have an alibi that night. Bradley's cousin, Frankie. When Frankie arrives in the custody suite, he's wearing the long coat, because he's hiding underneath that he's got on identical grey tracksuit bottoms and sweatshirt. Him and Bradley are very similar in height and weight and by the looks of it, they've both had identical haircuts, hence Frankie wearing the hat when he arrives in custody.'

'Jesus fucking Christ,' Hill said. 'How is any of this even possible?'

'It's frighteningly simple,' Sheridan said. 'Bradley and Frankie were placed in the consultation room just before shift change at 7 p.m. They stayed in there, made the swap, and it's not until 7.15 that Bradley, now dressed as the solicitor, opens the consultation room door and speaks to the detention officer and the custody sergeant in turn. They've just come on duty and haven't met Bradley or the solicitor yet. Bradley, now playing the part of the solicitor, tells the custody sergeant that his client is going to give a full and frank interview, and he doesn't need to be there for that. Which, as we all know, is a little unusual but not unheard of. And that's when they let him out of the custody suite. The custody investigation officer, who has also never met Bradley or Frankie, arrives and just thinks he's interviewing Bradley. But it's Frankie, who then fully admits the offence of criminal damage and at 9 p.m. he's charged and released.'

Sheridan paused, taking a breath. 'Bradley left the custody suite dressed as the solicitor at 7.18 p.m., giving himself plenty of time to get to the Buckstop Café and kill Dennis Canning. Exactly the way he told Glenda Harley he was going to do it when he was nineteen years old.'

The room fell silent for a moment, as the whole team absorbed what they'd just witnessed.

'I really wish there was audio in that consultation room, because I'd love to know what Bradley and Frankie said to each other,' Sheridan said.

The whole team thought about this. Then, one by one, they turned to look at Rob.

CHAPTER 68

It was gone 7 p.m. and the team had stayed on, waiting for Rob to return with his wife, Jo, hoping she could lip-read the conversation between Bradley and Frankie.

Sheridan had checked Bradley's previous custody record from when he was arrested the first time, which showed that he'd only had telephone advice from the same solicitor, Geoffrey Long, who they now knew was Frankie. He had been contacted on the same mobile number as the night he made the swap with Bradley.

Dipesh carried a tray of coffees in, just as Rob and Jo entered. Jo went straight over to Sheridan and hugged her. 'How's Anna? I was so sorry to hear about what happened,' Jo said, before raising her eyes to the ceiling as she realised what she was saying. 'Well, obviously I didn't *hear* about it . . . but you know what I mean.'

Sheridan smiled. 'She's doing great, thanks Jo.'

As the team stood back, Sheridan showed Jo over to the computer and played the recording of Bradley and Frankie in the consultation room.

'As you know, Sheridan, this isn't an exact science. I can only read lips if I can clearly see the person's mouth.' Jo leaned forward.

Sheridan touched her shoulder and Jo looked at her. 'It's fine . . . just whatever you can see.' Sheridan smiled again and pointed out Bradley who was facing the camera. 'You'll only be able to see what *he* says, until they swap places, then hopefully you'll be able to tell us what Frankie says.'

'Okay.' Jo focused on the screen. 'They both feel nervous, I can see from their body language.'

Sheridan looked at Hill who raised her eyebrows, clearly already impressed by Jo.

Jo paused the recording. 'Okay, Bradley said, "They can't hear us. They're not allowed to listen. I told you that."'

Jo pressed play. 'Bradley just said, "It's okay, stay calm, remember what we practised." Then he says, "Yes, we will. Don't fuck this up."' Jo leaned in closer and rewound a segment of the recording. 'I can't tell what he's saying there, his head's down.'

Bradley then lifted his face and Jo concentrated on him. 'They don't seem to be talking, or Frankie's talking and Bradley's just listening.'

Several minutes passed and Jo advised the team that Bradley was just agreeing with whatever Frankie was saying. 'He just keeps saying "yes" or "no" and "I don't think so."'

Sheridan paused the recording. 'Okay, this is just before they swap footwear.'

Jo nodded. 'Okay, Bradley just said, "Do it slowly."' Jo's gaze was fixed on the screen. 'He just said "Bit closer."'

The team watched the recording they'd seen earlier and this time, the footwear swap seemed obvious.

'Bradley just said, "Have you got them on?"' Jo took a sip of coffee.

As they made the swap, Jo explained that she couldn't tell if they were speaking as they'd both gone off camera.

Sheridan paused the recording. 'Okay, this is Frankie, now sitting in Bradley's place.'

Jo pressed play. 'Wow . . . that's incredible. How did they swap so quickly? I didn't even see it.' She looked up at Sheridan.

'Practice, I expect,' Sheridan said. 'A *lot* of practice.'

Jo carried on watching. 'Okay, Frankie is really nervous, the way he keeps wiping his hands together, like he's got sweaty palms. He just said, "Yeah, I'm fine" and "I won't."'

'I'm guessing Bradley's asking him if he's okay and not to fuck it up,' Sheridan said and immediately realised Jo couldn't hear her comment. She shook her head slightly and looked apologetically at Rob, who just smiled. He was used to his wife's deafness and knew how to deal with it every day.

On the screen, Bradley, now playing the part of the solicitor, stood up and reached over just off camera. The next moment, he was wearing the hat. Frankie, playing the prisoner, remained sitting. Bradley opened the door to the consultation room and Frankie looked up, as Bradley turned back to him.

'Go get him.' Jo looked at Sheridan. 'Frankie just said, "go get him".'

Sheridan exhaled and the recording ended. 'Go get him, eh?' She touched Jo's shoulder again and sat next to her. 'Thank you so much, Jo. You really do have a bloody gift. I can't tell you how helpful you've been.'

'You're welcome.' Jo smiled back and Rob hugged her, kissing the top of her head.

Sheridan looked at Hill. 'Let's go and nick them both, shall we?'

'Absolutely,' Hill said, with a rare smile.

CHAPTER 69

Uniformed officers accompanied Dipesh and Bridie, who were tasked with arresting Frankie, while Sheridan and Rob went with uniform to arrest Bradley.

Frankie was transported to Potters Road custody suite, while Bradley was brought to Hale Street, neither of them having been informed of the other's arrest. They were both compliant throughout the arrest and booking-in procedure. They both declined a solicitor. By the time they arrived in their respective custody suites, it was deemed too late to interview them, and so they were bedded down for the night, having been advised they would be spoken to in the morning.

After such a long day, Hill sent the team home.

As Sheridan got into her car, she texted Anna. *Hope I'm not waking you up but had to let you know, you were bloody right, genius.*

Anna replied: *About what?*

Sheridan responded: *The Canning murder. It was family members. We've just nicked Bradley and Frankie. Interviews in the morning. I'm just heading home, you ok?*

Anna texted back: *All good. I'm at yours. Sam came and got me earlier, she's very persuasive.*

Sheridan replied: *She is. I'll see you soon.*

It was gone 11 p.m. by the time Sheridan arrived home, and as exhausted as she was, she sat up telling Anna about how Bradley and Frankie had swapped places in the consultation room.

'Bloody hell. You have to give it to them, that was really clever,' Anna said as she sat on the sofa, stroking Maud's head to try and stop her incessantly licking the cast on her arm.

'How could that happen?' Sam asked. 'Don't solicitors get checked out to see if they're legit?'

Sheridan rolled her shoulders and took a sip of coffee. 'Nope. I mean, if the prisoner asks for the duty solicitor, then we all know who they are because they regularly come into custody. But if they ask for their own solicitor and know the number, the custody staff will ring them and in they come.'

'Do they get searched?' Sam asked.

'Nope.' Sheridan paused. 'To be honest, I think this has high-lighted an issue in the system.'

'I've never heard about it happening before,' Anna said, shaking her head. 'They must have practised the shit out of it, to make the swap so quickly and then pretend to be each other, that took some balls.'

Sam looked confused. 'So, Bradley had been arrested once before, but only on minor charges – do you think he did that on purpose to check out how things worked in custody?'

'Yeah. Definitely,' Anna said. 'He'd have to have been in the cells and the consultation room before, otherwise he was working blind. Something that ingenious takes planning. A *lot* of planning.'

As Sheridan listened, tiredness was taking over, and she felt her eyes closing as she rested her head on Sam's lap.

'Do you want to go to bed?' Sam asked, gently stroking her forehead.

'No, I'm fine, you two keep chatting, I like to listen.'

Anna and Sam smiled at each other. They talked about the Canning case and Sam commented on how tragic the whole situation was, a family ripped apart. She said how she understood in some way why Bradley would want Canning dead. And how long he must have spent planning the murder with Frankie.

'It was still a massive risk though, to know what happens during shift change and how their conversation wouldn't be recorded. Ingenious,' Anna said. 'Really well planned.'

Sheridan suddenly opened her eyes and sat up.

'You okay?' Sam asked.

'Yes . . . I bloody am,' Sheridan said.

'You've just thought of something, haven't you,' Anna said.

'Yes, I bloody have,' she replied, smiling.

CHAPTER 70

Saturday 12 February

Bradley Penhaligan took a seat in the interview room and looked up at the camera, before taking a sip of water.

After the formal introductions, Sheridan began with her questions. And she got straight to the point.

'Bradley, did you murder Dennis Canning?'

'Yes,' Bradley replied. 'I did.'

Sheridan tried not to react. It wasn't often that a suspect admitted the offence so readily.

'Tell us what happened on Friday the 7th of January, this year.'

'I'd been watching him for months, I knew where he lived and that he went to the same café every day, usually about an hour before they closed. He'd sit on his own in the window with the same cup of tea. I'd been planning to kill him for a long time and I chose that particular day because it was my mum's wedding anniversary. Her and Vincent were celebrating it with my Uncle Roger and his wife, Marcia.'

'What's the significance of killing Dennis on their anniversary?'

'I wanted them to have two things to celebrate every year. Their anniversary and Dennis Canning's death.'

'Did Carrie or Vincent know about your plan to kill Dennis?'

'No. They had no idea . . . and they still don't know it was me.'
Bradley looked down. 'They will do now, though.'

'Okay, we'll come back to that,' Sheridan said. 'Going back to
the night of his death, tell us what happened.'

'I waited until he left the café, I walked up behind him, grabbed
his head, pulled it back and slashed his throat,' Bradley said, with
not a hint of emotion in his voice.

'What did you use to slash his throat?'

Bradley swallowed, hesitating before he answered. 'A penknife.'

'Where did you get it from?'

Again, Bradley hesitated, and Sheridan noticed his jaw tighten.
'It was a Christmas present from my mum.' He looked at Sheridan.
'When I was a kid.'

'After you killed Dennis, what did you do?'

'I went round the back of the café, through the alleyways and
kept walking until I got home.'

'You've been arrested twice. The second time was the night
Canning was killed. Tell us how you managed to get out of the
custody suite to go and kill Canning.'

'I swapped places with a friend who'd agreed to help me. I can't
remember his name.'

'Let me help you out with that. Your cousin, Frankie, is in
custody at another police station.'

Bradley sat back. 'Right. Well then you know that it was
Frankie who swapped places with me. I *made* him do it, I threatened to kill him if he didn't. And he knew I meant it.'

Bradley went on to describe that he had figured out how the
custody suite worked from the first time he was in there. How
he'd put the plan to Frankie who initially refused to be involved.
Until Bradley threatened to cut his throat. They had practised the
switch over and over until they perfected it. Frankie had been two
stone heavier than Bradley and as part of the plan for them to look

alike, he'd lost weight. They perfected each other's walk and Frankie had his hair dyed the same colour as Bradley's and cut in exactly the same style. Being cousins, they weren't dissimilar, but after the transformation, they looked even more alike.

'How did you find out about the blind spot in the consultation room?'

'The first time I got arrested, they put me in there to speak on the phone to my solicitor. While I was in there, I stood in the corner, a few minutes later, one of the gaolers came bursting in and asked what I was doing. I made a joke that I was trying to hide, and he told me to sit down so he could see me on the camera.'

'You said you were on the phone to your solicitor. Who was that?'

Bradley licked his lips and sighed. 'Frankie.'

'When you were in custody the night Canning was murdered and you asked for a solicitor, how did you get the staff to call Frankie?'

'I had a business card made up and put it in my wallet. When they asked me for my solicitor's name and number, I took the card out and read the details out to them. They called Frankie and he made his way to the nick. He was just around the corner. You know the rest.'

'How did you know about the shift change at 7 p.m.?'

'From the first time I was arrested. The time I was nicked then just happened to be before 7 p.m., so I knew the staff would change at seven. That's how I knew that when I did the swap with Frankie, it had to be at the same time, or the staff would know we'd swapped. We look alike, but we're not identical.'

Sheridan sent a text to Hill, asking her to check Bradley's custody record from the first time he'd been arrested.

'So, you got yourself arrested on purpose the first time, so you could check out the custody suite.'

'Yes.'

'And the second time, to give yourself a rock-solid alibi.'

'Yes. And I knew that if the plan was going to work, you needed my fingerprints on your system, so that the second time I was arrested, there was no doubt at all that it was *me* who was booked into custody.'

Rob wrote a note to Sheridan, for her eyes only.

He's very good

'Did Frankie know about your plan to kill Canning?' Sheridan asked.

'No.'

'He must have known why you had to make the swap, though. What did he think it was all about?'

'He agreed to do it after I threatened to kill him.' Bradley paused and puffed out his cheeks. 'Alright, I did tell him what I planned to do, but he didn't believe me. He didn't think for a minute that I was capable of something like that. I think he only went along with it to shut me up.'

'And when he found out Canning had been murdered, did you and him have a conversation about it?'

'No. We don't really speak that much.'

'You want us to believe that Dennis Canning was murdered just how you'd told Frankie you were going to do it and afterwards, you didn't talk about it? Come on, Bradley.'

'It's the truth. You can check our phone records, you can check CCTV, all of that, and you won't find any evidence of us having contact after I killed Canning.'

'I find that hard to believe. But . . . moving on. How did you find out that Canning had been released from prison?' Sheridan asked.

'Pure luck. I used to go back to the house, where the fire happened. I'd go every year on the anniversary, without fail. There's a bus stop opposite, and I used to sit on the bench and just stare at it. Then I'd lay flowers on the pavement. Then on one anniversary, the 23rd of December 2009, I was sitting there as usual, and I saw him. I saw Canning walking up the road. He didn't see me, and he just stood outside the house. I wanted to kill him there and then. But there were too many people around and . . . I didn't have a knife. So, I followed him and that's how I knew where he lived.'

'Did you tell your mum or Vincent that Canning was out?' Sheridan asked.

'No. They only found out when you went to their house to tell them he was dead.' Bradley rubbed the back of his neck and clicked his head from side to side.

Sheridan's phone lit up with a message from Hill. *Yes, he was in custody the first time during 7 p.m. handover.*

She didn't reply.

'After you killed Canning, did you plan to kill anybody else?' she asked.

Bradley cracked his knuckles. 'I take it you've spoken to the journalist woman? When I met her, I did plan to find everyone he had ever been close to. But as the years went on, I really just focused on him. I stopped thinking beyond that. After I killed him, I just wanted to get away with it and let us all get on with our lives. So, no, I wasn't going to kill anyone else. The planning it took to get to him consumed me. It's all I could think about for years, and if I'm honest, I'm tired. I'm really tired.' He closed his eyes for a moment. 'I never really believed that I'd get away with it. I thought I was bound to get caught, and I only tried to trick everyone so that my mum and Vincent didn't have the worry of me going to prison. That's why I never told them about the plan. I knew they'd try to talk me out of it. I hope now though, that even though I'll get locked up, they can rest easy that he's dead.'

'Before you cut his throat, did you say anything to him?' Sheridan said.

'Yes. I said, "This is for Carrie Penhaligan".' Bradley's eyes filled with tears, which he quickly wiped away. 'I have no regrets. Not *one*.'

Bradley had given his account, and it all made sense, it fitted. Just before Sheridan brought the interview to a close, she asked one more question.

'Does the name Milo Adams mean anything to you?'

Bradley slowly shook his head. 'No. Why?'

'It's just a name that came up.' Sheridan knew that Milo's phone records had been examined and there was no evidence to show that he, Bradley or Frankie had had contact with the man. Had she misjudged Milo? Could it really be that he wasn't connected to any of this?

Sheridan turned off the recording equipment and placed Bradley back in his cell.

Sheridan and Rob made their way up to CID where they updated Hill.

'Sounds pretty clear-cut. Although it's hard to believe that him and Frankie haven't had contact since the killing. We'll look into that and hopefully show he's lying.'

Sheridan's mobile rang. It was Dipesh.

'Hi mate, how's it going?' Sheridan said.

'We're on our way back. We've interviewed Frankie. Are you done with Bradley?'

'Yeah, full and frank admission to killing Canning. He told us everything.'

'Bit of a shocker about Frankie being there the night of the fire, eh?' Dipesh said.

'What?' Sheridan replied.

'Did Bradley not tell you that Frankie was there that night?'

Sheridan looked at Rob. 'No. He didn't.'

CHAPTER 71

Dipesh and Bridie walked into CID, where Sheridan, Rob and Hill were waiting.

Sheridan went over Bradley's account of what happened, how he planned the killing, and how he threatened to cut Frankie's throat if he didn't play the part of the solicitor and make the swap.

'Right, let's hear what Frankie had to say.' Sheridan settled back in her seat.

Dipesh told the team that Frankie had fully admitted to being a part of the plan to make the swap in custody, so that Bradley had the perfect alibi for when he murdered Dennis Canning. Frankie's version of how they planned and practised the swap, how they made themselves look alike, matched Bradley's version.

It had been halfway through Frankie's interview when he fell apart . . . and demolished Bradley's account. Not his plan to kill Canning. But his account of what really happened on the night of the fire.

Frankie and Bradley had been close when they were children. Like brothers. Often playing together and staying at each other's houses.

Frankie's parents, Marcia and Roger, were Jehovah's Witnesses. Their religion was drummed into Frankie as a child, and he often felt like he missed out on so much, including and especially Christmas, which was a holiday his parents would never allow him to celebrate. He was the only child in his whole school who was never given a Christmas present.

And that's why, on the night of the fire, he decided to change that. If he wasn't going to be given a present, he was going to take one of Bradley's.

And so, on the 23rd of December 1974, Frankie waited until his parents were asleep, took their spare key to Carrie's house and walked the short distance in the dark. Letting himself in through the back door, he crept into the living room, stopping for a moment to listen for any movement from within the house. He'd been there earlier in the day and seen the mound of gifts, carefully wrapped and placed under the tree. His heart had grown heavy at the sight. He knew his grandparents were staying over, looking after his cousins, Bradley and Elizabeth, and that Vincent's daughter, Melody, was on a sleepover.

In the silence of the house, he sat on the floor, picking up the gifts and reading the little labels until he came across one with Bradley's name on it. He felt the present through the paper, small and hard, his fingers squeezing and prodding it, and that's when he made the decision to open it.

When he saw it, his eyes fell on the most beautiful thing he had ever seen. A penknife. Its handle the colour of seashells and the blade sharp and new. This was the one. This was the present that he would take for himself and fantasise that it had been given to him by his parents, as if he were a normal child.

He didn't think about what would happen when on Christmas morning the gift had gone. He didn't think beyond putting it in his pocket and taking it home. As he studied it, he turned it over and saw the engraving:

Bradley. Christmas 1974

Shoving the wrapping paper and label into his pocket, he stood up.

And that's when he heard a noise. He stood deathly still, straining to hear where it was coming from. He realised it was at the front door, the sound of the letter box flapping. Thinking Carrie may have come home from her shift, he ran. He ran as fast as he could towards the back door, yanking it open and running away into the night to his home. Back to his bedroom, where he hid the knife under his mattress.

No one would ever know he had been in the house that night. He climbed into bed and fell asleep.

◆ ◆ ◆

'So, it was Frankie who left the back door open,' Sheridan said. 'That's why the fire took hold so quickly.'

'Yeah. And the noise he'd heard was Canning opening the letter box, before he squirted the petrol inside,' Dipesh replied. 'No one questioned why the penknife was missing, because the fire destroyed everything. Frankie didn't tell a soul what he'd done that night, but he always knew that the family might have survived if he hadn't left the door open. He was literally in bits when we interviewed him. He said he'd lived with the guilt his whole life. Then, a few years ago, Bradley went to see him because he was having problems with his car, and Frankie offered to fix it. It was while Bradley was there, rummaging in Frankie's garage that he found the penknife tucked at the back of an old toolbox. Frankie had scratched

Bradley's name off it but not the part that read 1974. Carrie had told Bradley after the fire, about the penknife and that she'd buy him one exactly the same the following Christmas, to make up for the one she'd believed had been lost in the flames. It was when he saw the one in the toolbox that he made the connection.' Dipesh took a sip of coffee. 'Bradley confronted Frankie, and he admitted what he'd done and begged Bradley not to tell anyone. He said if Bradley did tell Carrie or Vincent that he'd just deny everything. What he didn't know was that Bradley was recording the conversation on his mobile, and he played it back to Frankie and said if he didn't help him with the plan to kill Dennis Canning, he'd let Vincent hear the recording and Vincent would never forgive him.'

'Jesus.' Sheridan shook her head. 'Did Frankie say if Carrie or Vincent knew anything about the plan?'

'No. According to him, they knew nothing,' Dipesh said. 'So now we know what really happened.'

'Did Frankie say why he kept the penknife all those years?' Hill asked. 'Why not just throw it away?'

'He said it was the only present he ever got. Even though technically, it wasn't *his* present. He thought about getting rid of it loads of times but kept it as a reminder of what he'd done. Bradley took the penknife that day and Frankie never saw it again.'

'Bradley kept it and used it to slash Canning's throat,' Sheridan said. 'He said he'd used a penknife his mum bought him for Christmas.'

Hill stood up. 'Okay, let's put another interview into Bradley, now we know the truth.' She went to leave, turning as she reached the door. 'Great work everyone. Now the chief can stop getting his balls in a twist.' She gave them the thumbs up and left.

CHAPTER 72

Bradley was re-interviewed and admitted that Frankie's story was true. When Rob asked what he'd done with the penknife, he said that he'd got rid of it. He didn't need it anymore, now that Canning was dead.

As Sheridan walked Bradley back to his cell, he asked her if she would visit his mum and Vincent and tell them what was happening. Sheridan agreed and just before she closed the cell door, he looked at her.

'I did what I did for love. I just wanted you to know that.'

Sheridan gave the slightest of nods.

Bradley looked at the ceiling, his voice breaking as he spoke. 'I loved my sister, she was beautiful. So mischievous and full of fun. The same with my grandparents. They doted on us and none of them deserved to die the way they did.' He choked on his words, giving himself a moment. 'If I could turn the clock back, I wouldn't have been the one who survived the fire. The only one to get out. I'd have taken their places in a heartbeat. People do things for those they love, things they wouldn't normally dream of doing. Who'd have thought that someone like me, a scraggly little kid would turn out to be a killer? But I did it because I don't think justice was done. Canning should never have been released from prison. He should have died there. Old and lonely in a cell. When I saw him that day, standing outside the house, I knew I was going to kill him. I couldn't bear the thought of him being out there. I know he hated my mum when she got together with Vincent. That's why he did what he did, to get his revenge on her. It ruined her, she never got over it, and she never will. But now he can't hurt her anymore. There's no way he can try to get to her, because I think, given the chance, he would have found her, and I can't bear to think of what he might have done. I broke the law to get justice for her. But like I said, I have no regrets. I'd do it again, because I love her that much.' He turned and sat down on the bench. 'When there's no other way, when you have no other choice, but you need to get something done, you just do it. Even if it means breaking the law. You probably don't understand that.'

Sheridan stared at him for a moment. 'You'd be surprised,' she whispered before gently closing the cell door.

CHAPTER 73

Sheridan and Rob were sat in Carrie and Vincent's living room, having told them of Bradley and Frankie's accounts of the plan to kill Canning and what had really happened on the night of the fire.

Vincent held Carrie's hand throughout and both of them cried openly.

'We know all of this is a massive shock to you both, but we're here if you have any questions about what happens next,' Sheridan said.

Carrie was the first to speak. 'Is Bradley alright?'

'Yes, he's doing fine. He was very honest about what happened and that will all be taken into account when he goes to court.'

'How long will he get in prison?' Vincent asked.

'It's hard to say,' Sheridan replied, not wanting to say the word 'life'.

She explained that Bradley and Frankie would be charged and would then appear in court on the Monday. It was likely they would both be remanded in custody until their appearance at the Crown Court, and that if they maintained their guilt, the case wouldn't go to trial.

As they got up to leave, Carrie and Vincent thanked them and walked them to the door.

'Please call me if you need anything, anything at all,' Sheridan said.

'Thank you,' Carrie and Vincent replied in unison, with Carrie closing the door as Sheridan and Rob left.

She turned to Vincent, her face flushed red and her eyes raw with tears. 'I can't believe Frankie was there that night and Bradley never told us.'

'Me neither.' Vincent put his head down. 'I want to hate him, but . . . he was just a kid.'

Vincent led her into the living room, where he wrapped his arms around her and they sobbed together.

'What if they find out?' Carrie said, wiping tears from her face.

'They won't. Bradley won't break his promise.'

'What have we done?'

'We've done what Bradley wanted. We have to remember that,' Vincent said.

'But he's going to go to prison for years and years, maybe even for the rest of his life. Did we make a mistake?'

'Carrie.' Vincent gently held her face in his hands. 'When Bradley told us that he was going to kill Canning, you know as well as I do that nothing we could have ever said to him would have made him change his mind. He'd thought of nothing else since he was a teenager. All we did was help him try to get away with it.'

'Yes, and it didn't work. *None* of it worked. I really thought he'd get away with it, all that planning he did, all the times *you* got yourself arrested, so you could figure out how his plan might work. How he could make the swap and escape from custody. None of it mattered, he might as well have just killed Canning and called the police on himself.' She put her head down. 'How are Roger and Marcia going to react when we tell them what Frankie did that night, by leaving the back door open? They'll be devastated. Maybe we should just tell the truth.'

'Stop. Please . . . stop. If you tell them the truth, then they'll not only have to live with what he did, but that *we* knew all along about the plan. We'll have to tell them that we invited them to our wedding anniversary meal just so that we had an alibi for the night Canning died. Don't forget how much Bradley put into figuring that out, to keep you, me, Roger and Marcia out of this, to stop us being suspects. Please think about that for a moment. We need to make sure they never know that we were involved.'

Carrie sat down and Vincent sat next to her, his arm around her shoulder. 'I know you're right. I just need time to let it sink in that Bradley got caught,' she said. 'He'll be okay, won't he?'

'He'll be fine. Because he knows that you're free from Canning now. He did it because he loves you *that* much. We tried for years to talk him out of it, but he was never going to change his mind. He did what he set out to do. He always told us that he'd live with the consequences if he got caught. But remember, he did it for you. Don't let him down now.'

Rob turned at the end of the road and stopped at the traffic light. 'Do you know what doesn't make sense to me?' he said, glancing at Sheridan.

'What?'

'Bradley got himself arrested the first time so that he could check out how the custody suite worked. He then gets arrested the second time and makes the swap.' He sighed. 'I think there's more to it than that. I think Vincent was involved, and I think it was Vincent who checked out the custody suite, and that's why he got himself arrested seven times in a year. Because it would take that many visits to figure out how to beat the system. And Bradley couldn't get himself arrested too many times because then the custody staff would recognise him, and they might realise that Frankie had taken his place.'

Sheridan didn't reply.

'What do you think?'

'I think you're right.' Sheridan remained looking straight ahead.

Rob smiled. 'You'd already thought about that, hadn't you?'

'Yes,' she said.

Sheridan *had* already thought about it. And it had come to her while she had been listening to Anna and Sam talking about the case the night before.

'What do you think we should do about it?' Rob asked.

Sheridan hesitated, before replying. 'I think that family have been through enough. Don't you?'

'Yeah, I do. And I think maybe we never had this conversation. Our secret. Agreed?'

Sheridan smiled. 'Agreed.' She turned to him. 'Our secret.'

CHAPTER 74

Monday 14 February

Sheridan walked down the corridor, towards Hill's office. But Hill was already heading her way.

'I was just coming to see you. Bradley and Frankie have both been remanded in custody.'

'No surprises there,' Hill said. 'I was just coming to see you, too. They've found Martin's car, Steve's canal-boat mate. It was parked down a track about half a mile from the *Soldier Blue*.' Hill returned to her office, and Sheridan followed her.

Hill continued. 'The car's been searched, and they've found a door key, which I'm guessing is the spare one that Steve took from Anna's house. They also found what we think is Ben Harper's mobile phone and a voice-changing device.' She sat behind her desk. 'So that's pretty much everything now. If Steve goes not guilty, we've got a shitload of evidence to throw at his defence.'

Sheridan leaned against the door frame, her arms crossed. 'That's great news. We got there in the end, eh?'

'We certainly did. And you were right to trust your instincts about Steve. As always.' Hill sat back. 'We still don't know how he got into Ben Harper's house, maybe we never will.'

'It doesn't matter. We got him and I hope he rots in that prison cell. Fucker.'

Hill smiled. 'Yeah, fucker indeed.'

◆ ◆ ◆

After he finished writing the letter, Steve put the pen down and laid back on his bunk, reading his own words.

Dear Anna.

They probably won't let me send this letter to you, so I've given it to my solicitor. I want it read out in court so that you know that I'm not the terrible person you think I am. I'm going to plead guilty to what I did to you and for what I did to him. The reason I'm doing this is because I love you and I don't want to put you through a trial. I want to make this as easy for you as possible. I remember when we were together, you'd come home from work and talk about a victim you'd been dealing with and how they had to re-live everything in court. I don't want you to have to do that.

I forgive you for the abortion and I hope you meet someone one day that treats you the way you should be treated. You deserve a man who looks after you. I hope you find him.

Me? Well, it looks like I'll be here for a while. And I deserve to be.

Steve.

After reading the letter, he folded it up and put it under his pillow. Closing his eyes, he pushed out tears of anger. 'Fucking bitch,' he said under his breath, wiping his face with his sleeve. He wasn't really pleading guilty to save Anna from going through a trial. He was doing it because the evidence against him was so overwhelming and he couldn't stomach the thought of seeing her and Sheridan Holler's gloating faces in court.

As he lay there, he thought about how his plan had seemed so watertight. For months he'd been planning to move out of the house he rented to stay on his mate's boat. He'd emptied his bank accounts so he could live off the cash. He'd already planned to tell Anna he was moving to Glasgow. He'd told her this because there was a part of him that thought maybe, just maybe, she'd realise that he was moving on with his life and suddenly want him back.

But he had no intention of moving to Glasgow and had simply emptied his accounts so that he could stay off the radar. He would live on the boat, work during the day and then at night, he'd watch her house, slash the tyres on her car. Move the pots in the front garden, maybe smash a few of them, too. Throw a brick through her living room window when he knew she was home. All for one reason. To frighten her. To frighten her enough to realise she missed having a man around the house. But not any man. *Him.*

He'd had everything planned. And then the plan had changed the night she'd told him about the abortion. The night he took the spare key, while Anna slept on the sofa, after he'd plied her with drinks. He'd got into her house while she was at Sheridan Holler's, the day he'd taken her warrant card back. He knew she'd stay the night and that had given him the confidence to go to the house without fear of her coming home.

Once he was inside, he'd found her laptop and flipped it open, praying she hadn't changed her password. *Sheridan Sherlock.* It was then that he found the conversation between Anna and Ben

Harper, it was all there. The school Ben had attended as a child, his favourite teacher, his love of cats since his mum had bought him one for Christmas when he was nine. So much information he'd shared with Anna in their cosy little chats. All the information he needed. After putting the laptop back, he left. It didn't matter that he couldn't put the spare key back. Anna would be dead before she realised it was missing. A quick search of the internet and he'd found Ben Harper's home address. Getting into his house would be easy.

He purchased a bottle of wine, Ben's favourite, according to his conversations with Anna, wrapped it in tissue and boxed it up, writing Ben's name and address on the front. Then, taking his mate's car, so his own wouldn't be captured on any CCTV or ANPR cameras, he drove to Ben's house.

CHAPTER 75

Sunday 16 January

Steve pulled on to the drive. The fact that there were no cars parked outside gave him the confidence that if Ben was home, he probably didn't have any visitors. Ben didn't have a car, another fact that Steve had discovered after reading the online chats with Anna. He had a motorbike, which Steve could see parked in the garage through the open door.

He lifted the parcel from the passenger seat and walked up to the front door, which was opened a moment later.

'Hi, parcel for Ben Harper,' Steve said, his throat closing at the sight of the man Anna had been chatting to.

'Thanks.' Ben went to take the package.

'Can I ask you something?' Steve said, looking at the name on the box.

'Sure.'

'You're not *the* Ben Harper that went to Wallerton School, are you?'

Ben frowned. 'Yes.'

'I thought I recognised the name. We were at school together. You probably don't remember me, David Young.'

Ben pulled a face. 'Can't place the name, but . . . it was a long time ago.'

Steve laughed. 'I was a quiet kid. Spent most days on my own. But I remember *you*. We were in Mrs Valence's class together; she was a monster, everyone was terrified of her.'

'Oh God, yeah, I remember her. I was actually telling someone the other day about Mrs Valence, and how she used to have this evil stare like she was about to kill you.' Ben grinned. 'That's a blast from the past. So, anyway, what have you been up to?'

'Not much really. Got married, couple of kids, life's been pretty good. You?'

'Not married, no kids. Just never met the right one.'

Steve turned his hips from side to side and held his stomach. 'Sorry, I'm busting for a wee.'

'Oh, do you want to come in and use the loo?' Ben stepped back.

Steve followed him into the house. 'Thanks. Lovely place you've got here.' Steve noticed a cat asleep on the window ledge. 'You've got a cat. I love cats – we've got two of our own. Maud and Newman.'

'I've got three, they're spoiled rotten. The toilet's just through there.'

While Steve was using the toilet, Ben opened the parcel and pulled out the bottle of wine. And it was while he was rummaging through the tissue paper inside for a card or note that Steve came up behind him.

'I've no idea who this is from, do you have any details—' Ben was suddenly grabbed around the neck.

Steve had him in a headlock, his arm around his neck. Ben tried to grab his arm, but Steve was too strong.

'What's the pin number for your mobile phone?' Steve said, gripping tighter.

'I can't breathe . . . please . . .'

'Pin number and I'll let you go.'

'Four-four-seven-six-four-two.' Ben just about managed to speak.

Steve shuffled Ben towards the counter. 'Pick up your phone and type that pin number in.'

Ben still had one hand on Steve's arm and with the other he did as Steve demanded, while Steve watched him enter the pin number. The phone came to life.

'Now put it down,' Steve said and Ben dropped the phone on the counter. 'There's a good boy.'

And then he locked his forearm around Ben's throat until he stopped breathing.

As Ben's lifeless body lay on the floor, Steve went through the house. Finding the weights, he selected four medium ones and carried them to the car. He then went to the shed and grabbed the sheeting, rolls of tape, lengths of rope and a hammer. The hammer he'd use to kill Anna the next day. And then he spotted the enormous suitcase. It was perfect.

He dragged it into the house and eventually managed to place Ben's body inside and wheel it to the car. With adrenaline pumping through his body, he used every ounce of strength to heave it into the boot.

Returning to the house, he grabbed the bottle of wine and box he'd packed it in and left.

Once back at the boat, he waited until darkness fell, before getting Ben's body on board. Within the sanctuary of the boat, he took him out of the suitcase, wrapped him in the sheeting, and sealed it with the tape. Then he put him back into the case, along with the weights, before using the side anchor rope to slowly and carefully lower him into the canal.

Unsure if the weights were enough to keep the suitcase down, he knew he had to keep the rope attached for a while. Then, when he was confident that the body was going nowhere, he would later cut the tether and let Ben Harper rot in his watery grave. He thought he had control of everything. Of Ben and Anna. Even when Kathleen, whoever she was, had texted Ben's phone asking if he was alright, Steve knew how to word the texts to make Kathleen believe it was Ben responding. He made sure to mention the precious cats. It was perfect. He had an answer for everything, for every question the police had put to him. But then the plan fell apart when Ben's body was discovered.

◆　◆　◆

Monday 14 February

And now, as he lay on his bunk, tears of rage fell down the sides of his face.

The look on Sheridan Holler's face when he was arrested was always there when he closed his eyes, but he took some comfort when he recalled ringing her in the early hours to tell her Anna had died. He'd called from the hospital car park, having driven there in his friend Martin's car. He knew Sheridan would go straight to the hospital and he had watched as she walked into the building. Thinking her best friend was dead. At least he'd managed to put her through the pain of believing that, even if only for a short while.

He'd watched as Sam had later emerged from the hospital building alone, and it had taken everything inside of him not to follow her and run her car off the road. But the police had no idea that he was driving his mate's car, and he couldn't run the risk of being caught driving it. How he would have relished killing Sam. To take her away from Sheridan Holler. That would have given him so much pleasure. Sheridan Holler, a woman he hated as much as he hated Anna. Sheridan, the bitch who had somehow found him on the boat.

But *how* had she found him? Who had called the police? How had he missed the photograph of Anna that was found in his house? He'd Blu-Tacked them all to the wall in his bedroom, every one marked with a target. He'd lie awake at night staring at them. Screaming at her face that she was nothing but a child killer. Then hearing Mrs Dobson banging on the wall with her fucking walking stick and calling for him to keep the noise down. It was on one of those nights that he'd lost control and pulled the photographs from the wall in blind rage. He'd scrabbled to pick them all up, but he must have missed one. He'd been so careful with everything else. But they'd still found him.

As had the man in the mask who had appeared on the boat that night. Who the fuck *was* he? He'd appeared like an apparition and was then gone, slipping away into the night. Like he never existed. Like he had never been there at all.

CHAPTER 76

As Hill pulled on to her drive, she felt more upbeat than she had in a very long time. Two cases solved. The team had pulled together as they always did. Like family. Anna was recovering slowly from her horrific attack and would, in time, return to work. As Hill sat in her car for a moment, reflecting on what had been an emotional time for her and everyone else, she rested her head back just as her mobile rang. Her neighbour Gloria's number flashed up on the screen.

'Hello, Gloria.'

'Hill, are you home?'

'Yes, just.' Hill looked across the road at Gloria's house.

'I need you to come over, it's an emergency. I need your help. Come now.' Gloria cut the call off.

Hill grabbed the keys from the ignition and quickly made her way over, letting herself in.

'Gloria?' she called out, pushing the living-room door open, finding Gloria's chair empty.

'In here, Hill,' she said.

Hill walked through the living room and stopped at the kitchen door, where Gloria was standing over the cooker, stirring a massive pan, the aroma filling the room. 'Hello Hill, thanks for coming.'

'What the hell's going on? I thought it was some sort of bloody emergency.' Hill reached down and stroked Gloria's dog's head. 'Hello Barney,' she said.

Barney frantically wagged his tail.

'It *is* an emergency,' Gloria said. 'They'll be here in a minute, and I need you to set the table.'

'Who's *they*? And I'll have you know I've had a very stressful day, I've been up to my tits in work and I've literally just got home. So, I don't need you dragging me over here just because you've decided to invite someone round for dinner and you haven't even got the table set.'

Gloria turned around. 'You haven't got any tits.' She grinned, referring to the fact that some years before, Hill had undergone a precautionary double mastectomy, having discovered her family carried a faulty cancer gene.

Hill looked down at her own chest, readjusting her bra inserts. 'You cheeky old bat,' she said.

Gloria pointed past her. 'Less of the old. The placemats are in that drawer.'

Hill shook her head and proceeded to get the mats out. 'How many are coming?'

'There'll be four of us.'

'You don't know that many people.' Hill set four places.

'Yes, I do, *you* cheeky old bat.'

The doorbell rang. 'Can you get that?' Gloria said, having a sneaky taste of the food and smacking her lips. 'Lovely.'

Hill stomped through the living room, before yanking the front door open.

She stood there for a moment, a little taken aback to see Alan standing there holding a bunch of flowers.

'Hello, Hill. How nice to see you again.' He smiled.

'What's going on?'

'Gloria invited me round for dinner. Apparently, we're having Scouse.' He stepped forward. 'Are you going to let me in or do I have to eat mine out here?'

Hill turned on her heels and returned to the kitchen, leaving Alan to wipe his feet.

'What are you up to?' Hill said in Gloria's ear.

'I'm making Scouse, and you still haven't set the table.'

'I'm going home.' Hill walked out of the kitchen, passing Alan on the way. She carried on to the front door, just as Doreen was about to knock.

'Hello, Hill. I'm glad you're here. I've got a bit of a problem, and I really need your help.'

'It'll have to wait. I'm going home.' Hill squeezed past Doreen, then stopped. 'What kind of problem?' she asked impatiently.

'Come in, I'll show you,' Doreen said.

Hill put her hands on her hips and hesitated, before going back into the house.

In the kitchen, Alan was at the stove beside Gloria, inhaling the steam rising up from the pot of Scouse. 'That smells divine. My mum used to make Scouse, she always added a splash of brown ale.'

'I haven't got brown ale. So, it's lamb, spuds, carrots, onion and swede.' Gloria winked at him. 'And a little secret ingredient.'

'What's that then?' Alan asked.

'If I told you, it wouldn't be a secret.' Gloria tapped his nose with her finger.

Alan produced the flowers from behind his back and kissed Gloria on the cheek. 'These are for you.'

'Ooh, lovely.' Gloria beamed, reached up and cupped his ear. 'There isn't a secret ingredient, I just tell people that to make me sound interesting. Our secret?'

Alan smiled. 'Our secret,' he whispered back.

Hill was oblivious to their conversation as she watched Doreen rummaging in her bag.

'Right, what's the problem, Doreen?' Hill said bluntly.

Doreen finally produced a piece of paper. 'This. Can you fix it for me?'

Hill took the paper and read it. 'It's a parking ticket.'

'I know. Can you fix it? Like . . . make it go away?'

'No. I can't. You'll have to pay it,' Hill snapped.

'I thought cops could make these disappear,' Doreen said, tutting.

'No. That's magicians,' Hill said. 'I'm going home.'

'What about this one?' Doreen shoved another piece of paper towards Hill's face.

Hill snatched it from her. 'This is another parking ticket. How many have you got?'

'Fourteen,' Doreen said proudly. 'Do you think that's some sort of record? Maybe the papers will want to speak to me.'

'Right, dinner's ready, everyone.' Gloria opened the cutlery drawer. 'Hill couldn't be bothered to set the table, so you'll have to help yourselves. Did you bring the wine, Doreen?'

'No. I forgot. Shall I go and get a bottle?' Doreen was still rummaging in her bag for more parking tickets.

Gloria shook her head. 'Don't bother, your dinner will go cold. Honestly, you had one bloody job. Bring the wine, but no, you rock up empty-handed. You've got millions in the bank, you haven't paid your parking fines, and you couldn't be arsed to stop and get a bottle of wine. We'll have to have water, or there's some milk in the fridge.'

Hill stood in the doorway with her arms crossed.

'Are you staying? Or are you going to watch us eat from there?' Alan asked her, grinning.

'I haven't decided yet,' Hill replied bluntly.

Gloria dished up four plates while Alan and Doreen settled at the table with Barney underneath it, his tail swishing from side to side.

Gloria joined them. 'Happy Valentine's Day. To love and friendship.' She toasted her guests, and they lifted their empty glasses.

Hill left, closing the front door behind her.

'She has a habit of doing that, doesn't she.' Alan put his glass down.

'Oh, ignore her, she's a miserable old trout,' Gloria said through a mouthful of food.

'I think you two planned this.' Alan raised an eyebrow at the two old women.

'Don't know what you're talking about.' Gloria winked at Doreen. 'It just happens to be that we'd all be on our own on Valentine's Day, and we thought it would be nice to have some company, didn't we Doreen?'

'We did. Just an innocent get-together, nothing else.'

Alan picked up his fork and spoon and the trio continued to eat in silence.

A moment later, the front door opened, and they all looked up to see Hill walking into the kitchen.

Carrying a bottle of wine.

CHAPTER 77

Tuesday 15 February

Sheridan gave the vending machine a shove, as it had stolen her pound coin. 'You bastard,' she said under her breath.

'Robbed your money again?' Rob appeared beside her, grinning.

'It hates me. It actually hates me,' she replied.

'Guess what?' Rob said.

'What?' Sheridan shoved the machine again.

'Milo Adams has just handed himself in at Potters Road. And you're not going to believe what he's saying.'

Sheridan turned her head to look at Rob. 'Oh fuck, is it about the Canning job? Please tell me we didn't miss something.'

Sheridan pushed open the door of the Buckstop Café. The place was empty apart from an elderly couple sitting by the window. Azriel was sweeping the floor and looked up.

'We're closing shortly . . . oh, hello,' she said, recognising Sheridan.

'Hi, Azriel.' Sheridan looked around. 'Seems like things have quietened down.'

Azriel pulled a chair out for her. 'Can I get you a cuppa?'

'No. I'm fine, thanks.'

The elderly couple got up from their seats and after thanking Azriel, they left, and she flipped the sign on the door to closed. 'I'll be back in a sec,' she said to Sheridan, disappearing into the office and emerging a moment later, sitting opposite Sheridan and taking out a tissue to blow her nose. 'Sorry, I've got a stinking cold.'

'Apart from that, how are you doing?' Sheridan asked.

'Fine. You?'

Sheridan updated her with the fact that two arrests had been made in the case of Dennis Canning, although Azriel had already seen it all over the news.

'I couldn't believe it when I heard what he'd done. That poor family, what a terrible tragedy. I always thought that Dennis was just a lonely old man, I even felt sorry for him. It just goes to show you don't really know people. Now I realise why he never spoke and kept himself to himself. He didn't want anyone to know who he was.' Azriel shook her head. 'I have so many people through these doors, a lot of them like him. Not killers of course, but people on their own who just want to get out of the house and have a bit of company for a while. That's the main reason I keep this place open. It's more of a sanctuary than a café. A place where people can bring their troubles and sit with me and talk them through. I don't always have the answers, but I try.' She looked at Sheridan. 'You have to help people in this life, don't you?'

'Yes, and I think you're one of life's angels.' Sheridan smiled before asking, 'Do you have family?'

'No. I'm widowed, no children. That's probably why I love this place, it gives me company. I did have a cat, but he died a year ago. He was twenty-one.'

'Why don't you get another one?'

'I'd love to. I just don't seem to find the time to go and look at rescue places. I know it's a bad excuse, maybe I should just . . . oh I don't know, maybe one day.'

Sheridan's mobile rang and she saw Dipesh's number on the screen. She stood up. 'Sorry, Azriel, I've got to take this.'

Azriel nodded, picked up the broom, and carried on sweeping.

'Yes, mate?' Sheridan said.

'Sheridan, Tech Support have managed to get into Ben Harper's mobile phone.'

'Anything interesting?'

'Yeah. There's a recent text message that says, "The van's coming along nicely. Do you want to come and check out what I've done so far?"'

'Who's the text from, do we know?'

'Yeah. A guy called Josh Higgins. I've just spoken to him. He owns a small business, a local garage, and Ben took the transit van to him to the same day he bought it at auction. He's been working on it ever since.'

'Doing what to it?'

'Turning it into a camper van. All singing all dancing. Apparently, Ben was planning to drive it around the UK for a few weeks a year. He's always wanted to do that and felt the time was right.'

'Shit,' Sheridan said under her breath. 'And then Steve came along and fucked everything up,' she whispered, glancing at Azriel, who was now behind the counter, wiping it down.

'Yeah. Josh was really shocked when he found out what had happened to Ben. He had no idea, hadn't seen it on the news or anything. He said Ben was a really lovely bloke.'

Sheridan carried on looking at Azriel. 'Yeah. There's a lot of good people out there.'

'What do you mean?'

'Nothing. Just saying. Anyway, thanks for that Dipesh. I'll see you soon.' Sheridan ended the call and sat back down. Azriel joined her.

'I have some news, about Milo,' Sheridan said, watching Azriel's reaction and noting her face flush.

'Oh. Is he alright?' Azriel asked.

'He's in police custody. But yes, he's fine.'

'Police custody?'

'His name's not Milo Adams, and he's not Greek. His name is Afrim Marku and he's Albanian.' Sheridan didn't wait for a response. 'He came into the country illegally and got himself involved with a gang of car thieves. They offered him a hundred pounds to drive a stolen silver Mercedes from Liverpool to Manchester. On the night that Dennis Canning was killed, Milo left the café early, not because he felt unwell, but because he had to catch the bus to meet up with one of the gang. He was picked up in the Mercedes, which had false plates, and was driven to a remote area where the gang member got into another car, leaving Milo, or Afrim, to take the car to Manchester.' Sheridan paused. 'He's told my colleagues that he didn't tell you any of this because he didn't want to get you in trouble. When I spoke to him on the phone the first day we came to see you, I asked where he'd gone the night Canning was killed, and he thought we were going to find out about him driving the stolen car and he panicked. That's why, according to him, he ran and disappeared. He said he got rid of his phone so we couldn't trace him and he's been hiding out, although he won't tell us where he's been.'

'So . . . What will happen to him?' Azriel asked, and Sheridan could see she was holding back tears.

'He'll be dealt with for the stolen car and then I guess at some point, he'll be deported. He can seek asylum, but I can't guarantee he'll be successful, only time will tell. He has been compliant though and has given us the names of the car thief gang, which I have to say, is very helpful.' Sheridan leaned back in her seat and for a moment, neither spoke.

Then Azriel stood up and went to the fridge, where she took out a bottle of water, before re-joining Sheridan.

'I . . . I feel so sad for him. He's such a lovely lad,' she said, taking a sip of water, and Sheridan noticed her hands were shaking slightly.

'You had no idea who he really was?' Sheridan asked.

Azriel hesitated, before replying, 'No.'

'I just wonder why he handed himself in. We would probably have never known about him and the stolen Mercedes.' Sheridan ran a hand through her hair. 'I thought *maybe* it was because we've been contacting *you* a lot recently, asking questions about his whereabouts, and he wanted to keep you out of it. But, as you said, you haven't had contact from him since he told you he was going travelling. So, how would he know we've been asking you a lot of questions?'

Azriel took another sip of water and placed the bottle in front of her, twisting it around and peeling at the label. 'I don't know.'

'I guess . . . it's just one of life's mysteries and we'll never know.' Sheridan stood up. 'I can live with that.' She smiled down at Azriel. 'I'll let you finish up and get yourself home.'

Azriel swallowed. 'Home to an empty flat.'

'Go and get a cat.' Sheridan pointed at her, still smiling.

Azriel returned the smile. 'Maybe I will.' She walked Sheridan to the door. 'Thank you, Detective Holler. For everything.'

'You're a good person, Azriel. Take care.' And with that, Sheridan left.

As she got back in the car where Rob had been waiting, he turned to her. 'All good?' he asked.

'All good.' Sheridan clipped her seat belt in place.

'Back in a minute.' Rob went to get out of the car.

'What is it?' Sheridan said.

'I just can't leave it. I have to do it, Sheridan.' He closed the car door and went to the café door.

Sheridan watched as Azriel unlocked it and let him inside. *What the fuck are you doing, Rob?* she thought.

A minute later, Rob emerged and climbed into the driver's seat, a white paper bag in his hand. He reached inside and took out an enormous cream cake, handing the bag to Sheridan. 'That's your one.'

Sheridan pulled out her own cake. 'Why didn't you get enough for the whole team?' she asked, taking a huge bite.

'She only had two left.' Rob puckered his lips. 'Don't tell them we had one. Our secret?'

Sheridan took another bite. 'Our secret.' She wiped cream from her chin. 'It's not the first and I'm sure it won't be the last.'

'Cream cake?' Rob said.

'Secret,' Sheridan replied.

Azriel watched as Sheridan and Rob drove away and quickly wiped tears from her cheek. She stood in the middle of her café. Alone.

She thought of Afrim, the young man who she'd taken under her wing a year earlier when he had walked into the café, asking if she had any spare food.

She'd sat him down and listened as he told her he was a student, looking for work. His story was a difficult one, and one that Azriel had seen right through.

When she'd closed the café that first evening, she'd told him that she was willing to help him, but first, he had to be completely honest with her.

And with food in his belly and the kind face of the woman sat opposite him, he'd admitted that he wasn't a student. His name was

Afrim Marku, and he was an illegal immigrant. Born and raised in Albania. His parents had owned a grocery shop before they'd been murdered. And after their deaths, he'd fled the country and travelled to England.

Azriel had been so touched by his story that she put him up in her flat and let him work in the café.

They had come up with the name Milo Adams and given him a backstory that his family were Greek and he was travelling the world before deciding where to settle. In order to hide his accent, Azriel spent most evenings teaching him how to 'be more Scouse'. An accent he'd never mastered, but he tried.

After he had driven the stolen car to Manchester, Afrim confessed to Azriel what he'd done and then, with all the police activity around the café, Azriel had made him promise that he'd never be involved with the gang again and he swore to her that it was over. And then, to protect him, Azriel ensured he laid low, frightened that if it was discovered who he really was, he'd be sent back home. Afrim told her he'd only agreed to move the car because he wanted the money to pay her back for her kindness.

She *had* been kind to him, protected him as best she could. She'd let him hide away in her flat the whole time, praying he did as she said and stayed indoors, after destroying his mobile as she had told him to, so the police couldn't trace him to the location.

She recalled leaving to get to the café that morning, how he'd hugged her tightly and kissed her cheek, thanking her for everything she was doing for him. He was always affectionate towards her, but today had been different and now, as she headed home, she realised he was saying goodbye. He had planned to hand himself in, without telling her.

She pulled her coat collar up around her neck and walked home. Back to her empty flat.

CHAPTER 78

Hill walked into CID, ducking as something flew past her head.

'What the hell's going on? I've just come back from a meeting, and I can hear you lot from the other end of the corridor,' she snapped, then spotted Anna perched on Rob's desk. 'I thought you weren't back in until tomorrow. How are you feeling?'

'I'm fine, thanks Hill, just popped in to make sure Rob knows he's getting demoted back to DC tomorrow. Have you missed me?'

Hill stiffened up. 'I . . . yes, you've been missed.' She turned, hearing a whirring sound coming towards her.

'What the fuck *is* that?' Hill instinctively ducked down.

'It's the birthday present Sheridan and Sam bought me.' Anna smiled.

'It's a . . . helicopter.' The bright orange remote control toy hovered above her head, before suddenly veering off and crashing into the window.

'Yes, it's a helicopter. I told you that's what we'd got her,' Sheridan said, walking over and picking it up. 'Your turn,' she said to Bridie, placing the helicopter on the desk and standing back.

Bridie pressed the button on the control panel and the rotor blades sprung to life.

'Remember, you've got to land it perfectly on the target.' Sheridan pointed to the chair at the other end of the room.

The whole team watched as Bridie nodded. 'Okay, okay, here goes.'

The helicopter flew upwards and then changed direction. Just before it reached the chair it turned again and plummeted downwards.

'Oh, for heaven's sake,' Hill said loudly. 'This is a bloody police station, not a playground.' She marched over to the downed toy and picked it up. Putting her hand out, she walked over to Bridie. 'Give me that controller.'

Bridie handed it over and everyone looked away like scolded children, each trying not to laugh.

'Right.' Hill set the helicopter down on the desk. The team watched as she pressed the button and the craft took off. Gliding upwards and then in a perfect straight line, it headed towards the target, where it hovered before Hill landed it perfectly. 'Now, get back to fucking work.'

She handed the control to Rob and left, grinning to herself all the way back to her office.

CHAPTER 79

Wednesday 13 April

Sheridan was looking over towards the Albert Dock when Rob walked in, joining her at the window in her office.

'What time's Anna in?' he asked.

'Two. She's just doing a few hours until she's back full time.'

'So, I'm still acting DS for another twenty minutes?' Rob said, smiling.

'You certainly are.' Sheridan put her arm around his shoulder. 'You've been amazing, mate. Thank you for everything.'

'My pleasure.'

'And thank you for telling me that story about your dad. It made me realise that I'm not always right.'

'Yeah, but to be fair, you actually were right about Steve. And . . . I . . . made that story up.'

Sheridan removed her arm. 'What?'

'I made it up. I just wanted you to feel better about yourself.' Rob shrugged his shoulders.

'You dickhead.' She laughed.

'Who's a dickhead?' Anna said brightly, poking her face around the door.

Rob smiled broadly and went over to hug her. 'It's good to have you back. I kept your seat warm for you,' he said. 'Talking of which, I'd better go and clear your desk. I'll see you in a bit.'

When Rob had left, Sheridan sat at her desk and Anna perched herself on it. 'You're never going to guess who I've just bumped into,' she said, looking at the door to make sure no one was there.

'Who?' Sheridan said.

'Do you remember Gabriel Howard? You must do.'

Sheridan frowned. 'Gabriel Howard . . .' She tapped her forehead, as if trying to place the name. 'Oh, yeah, of course.'

'It was really weird to see him again. He said he'd seen on the news about the attack and asked how I was.' Anna shifted position. 'He's doing really well. Got his own carpentry business now.'

'Really?'

'Yeah, he makes bespoke wooden furniture. He showed me some pictures on his phone. He's really good.'

'Sounds like he's keeping out of trouble.'

'Yeah, he is. He asked how you were doing and said he sends his regards.' Anna yawned. 'Denise moved out, so he's living on his own now. He's in a good place though. He was really sweet when he was asking if I was recovering okay and was really glad when I told him Steve had been charged.'

Sheridan nodded. 'Maybe he's not so bad after all.'

'Seems that way.' Anna stood up. 'Anyway, I'm going to crack on. I'll see you in a bit.'

'It's good to have you back.' Sheridan smiled as she watched her leave.

She sat for a moment, thinking about Gabriel and how he'd come good. Without him, they may never have found Steve, and they were highly unlikely to have ever discovered what happened to Ben Harper.

She eventually got up and headed to Hill's office. Finding her on the phone, she hovered in the doorway until Hill waved her in.

'Alright, I'll let DI Holler know.' Hill ended the call. 'That was HR. They want to speak to Anna about having a course of counselling sessions.'

'Okay, I'll let her know. She's been doing okay though, and I spoke to the team this morning; we're all going to keep an eye on her.'

'Good. Anyway, what did you come to see me for?'

'I was just going to tell you Anna's in if you want to come through to CID. I'm off to get some cakes.'

'Of course. You always buy cakes when a case is solved, right?'

'Always.'

'I'll be through shortly.'

Sheridan smiled and was about go when Hill pointed past her. 'Close the door.'

Sheridan pushed it shut. 'What's up?'

'I'm going to say this, because I *have* to.' Hill stretched her legs under the desk and put her hands behind her head. 'The burglary at Steve's house, the photograph of Anna that was found on his bedroom floor, the flat tyre, the anonymous caller who led us to him, all of it.'

Sheridan felt her face flush.

Hill continued. 'I don't know *how* you did it and I don't want to know. Ever. Is that *absolutely* clear?'

Sheridan nodded once.

'Good, now get out of my office. And if you're buying cakes, I'll have a cream cone.'

Sheridan smiled, opened the door and turned into the corridor, just as she heard Hill call her back.

'Sheridan.'

Sheridan put her head around the door. 'Yeah?'

Hill grinned. 'Well played by the way.' She crossed her arms. 'Really . . . well played.'

EPILOGUE

Steve pleaded guilty to the attempted murder of Anna Markinson and the murder of Ben Harper. He was sentenced to life imprisonment, with a recommendation that he serve a minimum of thirty-two years before he was eligible to be considered for parole.

Bradley Penhaligan pleaded guilty to the murder of Dennis Canning. In his summing up, the judge took into account Bradley's early guilty plea and the tragic reasons for the murder. However, the judge also commented that due to the intricacies that had gone into the plan, it proved beyond any doubt that Bradley was one of the most calculating killers he had ever encountered in his courtroom. Bradley was sentenced to life imprisonment with the recommendation that he serve a minimum of twenty years.

Carrie and Vincent kept their word never to tell Roger and Marcia about their role in the plan to kill Dennis Canning.

They visit Bradley often.

Frankie Yearwood pleaded guilty to conspiracy to murder Dennis Canning. He was handed a fourteen-year sentence. Two weeks after appearing in court, he was found dead in his prison cell. He left a suicide note, saying he could no longer live with the guilt of what had happened on the night of the fire.

After his death, Frankie's parents, Roger and Marcia, made the decision to disassociate themselves from the Jehovah's Witnesses.

Afrim Marku did not apply for asylum and was deported back to Albania. He re-connected with family and now works on his cousin's farm. He never lost contact with Azriel and they speak often.

The angel pendant Anna was wearing on the night she was attacked was never found.

Anna attended counselling sessions and made a good recovery from her injuries. She returned to work full time.

She still has her helicopter.

Sheridan returned to the canal with Sam, where they waited on the bench, in the hope of seeing Crispy the duck.

After five minutes, he walked up the towpath and joined them. This time, he brought a friend.

Sam decided she should name her 'Pancake'.

Azriel still lives in her flat where, after long days at the café, she walks home alone. Home to her cats.

The three cats that Sheridan Holler convinced her to adopt.

The three cats Ben Harper left behind.

Gloria and Doreen are still working on their cunning plan to get Alan and Hill together.

Sheridan's team continue to have a betting pool on football scores. Hill is banned from entering.

Bridie has given up trying to explain the offside rule to Anna.

Doreen and Gloria wrote to the local paper, to see if they would be interested in interviewing Doreen about her having amassed fourteen parking tickets. The paper declined.

They are planning to approach local TV stations, once Doreen reaches thirty parking fines.

She currently has twenty-three.

Alan Rose is still waiting for Hill to accept his invitation to go out for a drink.

After retrieving a memory box from his loft, he found a pile of photographs from when he was at school. There, in one of the pictures, was Hill.

When he turned it over, he'd written the names of all the children in the photograph.

Including Hill's real name.

AUTHOR'S NOTE

Firstly, I just wanted to clarify something.

In this book, I have mentioned the time limit to prosecute a domestic common assault is six months. This book is set in 2011. The law changed in 2022 where the time limit was extended to two years.

I don't usually add an 'Author's Note' in my books, but for this one I felt I needed to. And this is why . . .

Some of you know that I joined Norfolk Police around 2001 and initially worked in the cells as a detention officer. It was a job I loved, and I had the honour of working with some amazing and dedicated officers and staff. It was a tough job, working in a busy custody suite. You had to be alert every moment you were on duty. Prisoners do strange and dangerous things when they're locked in their cells. Some are extremely violent, some are worryingly quiet, some are traumatised, others are suicidal and there are those who make you want to cry. I've mentioned working in custody here, because when you've read this book, you might ask yourself, could it happen? Yes, it could. Did it ever happen when I was on duty? No. I'll say no more.

I know that was a bit cryptic and now you just think I'm going loopy and saying weird things. Sorry about that. (Not sorry) x

Anyway . . . in 2004, I joined the domestic violence unit as a case investigator. My role involved working very closely with the victims, who were mainly women, but yes, there were male victims too.

I'll probably never be able to describe the feeling when you've been dealing with a victim, sometimes for months, trying to build their confidence, trying to help them regain some sense of self-worth and desperately trying to keep them safe. Then you come into work each morning and pray that they haven't been murdered. No words that I ever write, even as an author who writes words for a living, can describe that fear.

When I started this series, I knew one of the main characters was going to be a victim of domestic abuse, and Anna's story seems to have touched so many of you. Maybe you're a victim. I hope you're not. But if you are or think someone close to you is suffering, please talk. Please somehow find the strength to speak out. Do it safely, but please try to do it.

Anyone can become a victim. It doesn't matter who you are, what job you do, where you live. It doesn't matter if you're wealthy or poor. It can happen to anyone. Even police officers.

So, this is dedicated to the thousands of victims I met and worked with. To those who picked up the phone and made that call. Was it easy? No, of course it wasn't. It was probably the hardest thing you ever had to do. But you did it.

This is also in memory of the thousands who have been lost to domestic violence.

And to those who never got the chance to make that call.

ACKNOWLEDGEMENTS

And so, it's that time again . . . the acknowledgements. One of my favourite bits of this whole process. So, let's dive straight in.

I know I tend to mention as many people as possible here, but it's because, as I've said before, I'm just the storyteller.

First up? You the readers, of course. I can't thank you all enough for your unerring support. So many of you have messaged me to say how much you're loving the DI Sheridan Holler series. You buy tickets to events and stand quietly with my books in your hands, politely asking if I wouldn't mind signing them. Wait! What? Okay, let me explain. I'm always stunned when a reader thinks that asking me to sign the book they have spent their hard-earned money on is an inconvenience. No. It's not and it never will be. Ever. Without you buying the books, I don't have a job; publishers, agents, booksellers . . . everyone involved in this process, doesn't have a job without *you*. Please remember that. So, thank you. All of you.

Okay, next up . . . my rather bloody fantastic wife, Susie. You never cease to amaze me. I could go on and on about how wonderful you are, but you really should already know that. I hope I tell you enough. You make me laugh every day, even if you don't mean to. None of this would happen without you. And I wouldn't want it to.

In all seriousness though . . . this book really wouldn't have happened without you and your brilliant mind.

I do have a bone to pick with you though. When we were on the Norfolk Broads, you came up with an idea for a future book, then said you were tired and went to bed. I was then WIDE AWAKE and sat up for four hours in the dark writing down plot ideas on 400 Post-it notes because I couldn't find a notepad, and I didn't want to wake you. Next time, please come up with moments of genius during sociable hours. And one last request. Please stop getting your tongs out in public. (If you know, you know.)

Next up: the Doherty gang. Thank you all for your amazing support.

Breda Byrne: thank you for telling absolutely everyone you meet about me and the books. And I mean, everyone! And then you ring to tell us. You're wonderful. But you're still not getting paid.

Now I come to Supt Sonia Humphreys. Now you really do know for sure that I based Sheridan on you. I'm so happy that you managed to make the launch party for *Play With Fire*. Yes, it was pandemonium in our house the day before and the day after, but you'll have to blame Breda for that. She's always in charge of the food and drink. Wine . . . oh dear Lord . . . so much wine. I will say though, one of the highlights of the night was me telling people what an extraordinary police officer you are. Because you are. You are also a bloody nice human being. But please stop breaking things. Enough already. Anyway, thank you as always for your help on this book.

Next up: Fraser Ritchie, my CSI expert. Well, I really pushed you on this one, Fraz. But, as always, you came up trumps. I am so lucky to have you there when I need a weird or very technical CSI question answered. Thank you so much. I feel I now need to come up with stranger questions to see if I can make your head explode. Love to you and Gail.

Joanne Farrelly, senior probation officer: Jo, yet again you were there when I needed advice on sentencing. Thank you so much. Now . . . on to the next book . . . I'll be in touch, my lovely.

Paul Sturman: my firearms expert and all-round good egg. Cheers for all your advice, mate. How many beers do I owe you now? I'm so glad you're living your best life, after giving so much of it as a serving police officer. You deserve what you have now.

Now then, next up is: Sergeant Jo Walker. Where do I start, Jo? How long have I known you? It's well over twenty years and you're still out there, doing what you do best. You are an exceptional police officer, and I always loved working with you back in the day. And now, you're in the book. Why? Because I know that in real life, you'd be exactly as your character acts in the scenes where she appears. Calm, diligent and brilliant. Thank you for everything you do. Please stay safe out there, my friend. Oh . . . and . . . before you ask, because you always do . . . No. I'm not coming back to custody.

So, whilst writing this book, I randomly and rather bizarrely met several people who just so happened to be experts in the field that I was researching. I guess things just turn out that way sometimes. These are those people.

Firstly: Tracy Ford. I still get goosebumps when I think back to when we met. Randomly, while you were at work. I spoke to you when you were on a night shift and we chatted for ages. And I had no idea that you are profoundly deaf. You don't wear hearing aids, but you knew exactly what I was saying because you have an incredible ability to lip-read. I was so stunned when you told me this, and the fact that I was trying to find someone who could do that. And there you were. You taught me so much about how life is for you and if I'm honest, I'm actually getting really emotional now, writing these words, because I take so much for granted, every single day. Thank you for all your help. For your patience. For your strength. And for the beautiful and amazing person you are. I am totally honoured that you agreed to help me with some of the scenes in the book. I could not have done it without you.

Before I even started writing this book, I knew there was one scene that I was desperate to get right. No spoilers here, but Susie and I were in Liverpool city centre one day and I noticed she'd got chatting to a couple. I assumed they were old friends and went over to say 'hi'. But they weren't old friends, they were on a day out in Liverpool and were just asking her for directions. We got chatting, as you do, and I asked them if they were retired. And then they told me what jobs they used to do. I literally couldn't believe my ears. They were exactly what I was looking for. So, on to Lyn and Pete . . .

Lyn V Hutton: Ex Fire Service control operator.

Peter J Hutton: Fire Service station officer (retired).

I have few words that can describe how invaluable you have been in helping me with the scenes in relation to the fire. The fact that you were both in the fire brigade at the same time as my scene was set is incredible. I can't believe we met at a time when I needed both your expertise and there you were. Thank you for keeping in touch and for all your advice. Next time you're in Liverpool, please let us know and we'll meet up.

And now to Millie McNoon: critical care nurse. What a chance meeting that was! Millie, I needed someone who works in critical care and there you were . . . randomly in the same place as we were. Thank you so much for your time and advice. And thank you for all you do in such a demanding role. You are an angel. Literally.

Graham Bartlett: what can I say? You've made it into the acknowledgements again. Mate, thank you for your time on this one. You actually do know what you're talking about. Funny, that. I'd better get a bloody mention in your next bestseller. I mean it. I'm still gutted that you kept my tenner when I lost the bet in Brighton. You and those damned Brighton groins . . . or is it groynes? I don't know, but that was a cheap shot to get me to laugh. And I'm very disappointed in myself for not keeping a straight face. You won't get me next time.

The coven: you know who you are. I have a surprise for you all. Okay, so in our WhatsApp group we were all talking about what could happen to a certain character and you came up with the idea (I can't say what it is or which character, because it's a spoiler) . . . but . . . when you read the book, you'll remember. And so, thank you. Thank you so very much. Legends, one and all. Legends with chips and cats and tea not tea. I love you all, not in a creepy way.

Our dear friends: Lui and Maz Candiano. You are here for several reasons. One, we love you very much. Two, we love Milo the dog, even though last time we were at yours for one of our famous curry nights I went home with more dog hair on me than, well . . . a dog. Three . . . we wanted to surprise you. So . . . here you are with a little mention. Oh, and thank you for the cuttings, we've potted them and they're still alive. Well, I'm writing these acknowledgements in September 2025, so by the time you read this, we might have killed them off. Not on purpose, of course. Anyway . . . love you both.

Lynn Parsons: lovely Lynn, we can't wait to see you soon. Thank you for your continued support, love and friendship. I told you that Gloria and Doreen were going to get naughtier . . . and they have. What will they come up with next eh?

Heather Bleasdale: audio narrator. Heather, I am so happy that we finally got to meet you. Thank you so much for coming to the launches of *Play With Fire* and *Count The Dead* and reading the prologues to the audience. I had goosebumps listening to you. To hear you bring my characters to life and make it seem so effortless is mind-blowing. You will always be the voice of Sheridan and every character, because you are amazing.

Now to my agent: Broo Doherty. Book 5. I'll just say that a bit louder. BOOK 5!! Unbelievable. And when you rang us to say you loved it, yes we were bouncing. And now that Susie's ankle is fixed, she's bouncing more than ever. (God help me.) Thank you so much for everything. I know with you, I am in the very best of hands.

Vic Haslam: my editor. Okay, so we didn't work on this one together, but I'll let you off. I'm so happy for you and Adam, to have a new beautiful baby boy. (He won't be that new anymore by the time you read this, and he'll have probably grown out of his Sheridan Holler baby-gro . . . or grown into it . . . sorry about that, it was a bit big.) Much love to you and we'll see you for book 6.

Hannah Shaw. My other editor. You had a big pair of shoes to fill while Vic was away. (Not that Vic has really big feet, she has normal size feet . . . oh . . . I'll shut up.) Anyway, you stepped up and my goodness . . . you nailed it. Thank you so much for everything, you worked so hard, and you "get" Sheridan. You're brilliant.

To everyone at Thomas & Mercer: I am so blessed to have such an incredible team behind me. Thank you to the whole Amazon team for everything you do. What a family.

Russel McLean: my picky dev editor. You are fab and you know it. I always love working with you. You legend.

To my copy editor, proofreader and cold reader. You quietly work behind the scenes and I probably don't give you enough credit for that. I am immensely grateful for all that you do. Thank you.

To the cover designer, Dan Mogford. I get so many comments on the wonderful covers for the DI Sheridan Holler series. Again, you work quietly and without credit. So, thank you.

To all my wonderful followers on Twitter (yes, I know it's called X now but I'm not good with change). You have followed me for so long and always supported me. Don't think that I don't appreciate you all. I do.

My Instagram followers. What can I say? I still don't know how it all works, and all that flashy stuff just confuses me. However, we are getting better. Sort of. Although, I'm not entirely happy that Susie's tongs get more 'likes' than I do.

To the podcasters, bloggers and reviewers: thank you for all that you do and how hard you work. You are all legends.

To the wonderful team at Pritchards Bookshop, Crosby: Amy, Alex, Mitch and Angie. You all continue to be such advocates of the DI Sheridan Holler series, and I am forever grateful for all your hard work in making our launch events so amazing. Thank you.

Pete Frost: Messrs Fletcher & Frost bookshop, Mount Pleasant Road, Wallasey New Brighton. Wow. Okay, if anyone reading this is ever in the area, please pop in to see Pete. His bookshop is absolutely wonderful, and Pete is divine. Pete, thank you for your amazing support and friendship. I know I spend far too much time chatting to you and drinking your delicious coffee, but you have created a wonderful place at Messrs, and I hope you'll go from strength to strength. Now . . . get out of my pub.

Now to the lovely Rachael Slater. Rachael, you came to the launch of *Play With Fire* and entered the 'name a character' competition and won! I picked Milo Adams, because I just loved it and now . . . he's in the book! Thank you so much for your support, and for Milo. x

Another name I have used is Azriel Cass. Now, when Susie and I were on holiday in the Isle of Wight back in April this year (2025) we stumbled upon the most wonderful little restaurant called The Red Duster in Cowes. Wow . . . just wow. We fell in love with the place and couldn't keep away. The food is to die for, and the service is sublime. And that's where we met the lovely . . . Azriel Cass. As soon as she told us her name, Susie and I both looked at each other and said, 'We're having that.' And Azriel, you very kindly agreed that we could use it. So, thank you. Next time we're over your way, we are coming to see you. Please give our love to your dad, Liam. What a gentleman!

Now to the lovely (and rather clever) Heather Grainger. Heather, you came to the launch of *Count The Dead* in New Brighton and took part in the 'Murder in the Bookshop' event. And . . . you were the only person who guessed the killer was me! I promised to put you in these acknowledgements . . . and here you are! Thank you for being such a good sport and supporter.

There is an additional person who I should have thanked in *This Ends Now*. Ade McGraa (pharmacist). Ade, huge apologies that I forgot to include you back then. Thank you so much for your advice! And apologies for the weird question I asked you, even though you didn't bat an eyelid!

To Katharine Robinson. You will probably never know how many lives you have saved, how many families you have protected and how many victims of domestic abuse who will remember what you did for them. And continue to do. I'm honoured to call you my best friend and I love ya.

And finally. Okay, you can't judge me here, but I want to mention Crispy the duck. Because he's a real duck who decided to join Susie and I on our boat while we were on the Norfolk Broads. (Not *our* boat because we don't have one, just to be clear.) Anyway, Crispy was always on his own, he had a limp and a dodgy eye, and we fell in love with him. He then proceeded to walk up and down the boat most mornings and came back in the evenings for his supper. We're going back next year. We hope he's still there.

Right then, I think I've covered everyone (including ducks).

As I always say, you can see from the acknowledgements that I turn to a lot of people for advice when I write my novels. Sometimes, I decide to go off-piste a little, just because it works better for the story. So, any mistakes are mine.

I also sometimes make up road names and some places in and around Liverpool. Again, only because it works better for me. But Liverpool and the Wirral are wonderful places, and I only ever want to do them justice.

One last thank you and it's one I never got the chance to say at the time. To the firemen who carried my family from the fire in 1977.

ABOUT THE AUTHOR

© 2023 John McCulloch @ Studio 900

T. M. Payne was born in Lee-on-Solent, Hampshire, and now lives on the Wirral with her wonderful wife.

She is the bestselling author of the Detective Sheridan Holler series. Her debut novel, *Long Time Dead*, went to number one in crime fiction in both the UK and Germany. The second book in the series, This Ends Now, also became a number-one bestseller, as did her third and fourth books in the series, Play With Fire and Count The Dead.

She has spent most of her working life in the criminal justice system, starting out as a store detective (when she once got thrown in a river) before becoming a prisoner custody officer (when she once carried a prisoner out of the courtroom single-handedly after he started hallucinating butterflies).

She has worked in practically every London court, including the Old Bailey and Court of Appeal, and has been handcuffed to murderers, rapists, and dealt with some of the most violent prisoners to pass through the court system. In 2001, she joined Norfolk Police as a detention officer, working in the custody suite, before joining the Domestic Violence Unit as a police case investigator. In her fourteen years in that role, she dealt with thousands of victims of domestic abuse, with one of her cases earning her a chief constable's commendation. She now writes full-time.

T. M. Payne is crazy about animals and if you walk past her with your dog she will probably ask if she can pat it on the head. Or take it home with her. Or both.

She hopes to one day have seven dogs, fifteen cats and a penguin (or three).

She loves laughing, Christmas, playing golf (badly), walking along New Brighton beach (not walking her dog because she hasn't got one yet), snow, sunshine, sunsets, family and friends.

She dislikes beetroot.

Follow the Author on Amazon

If you enjoyed this book, follow T. M. Payne on Amazon to be notified when the author releases a new book!
To do this, please follow these instructions:

Desktop:

1) Search for the author's name on Amazon or in the Amazon App.
2) Click on the author's name to arrive on their Amazon page.
3) Click the 'Follow' button.

Mobile and Tablet:

1) Search for the author's name on Amazon or in the Amazon App.
2) Click on one of the author's books.
3) Click on the author's name to arrive on their Amazon page.
4) Click the 'Follow' button.

Kindle eReader and Kindle App:

If you enjoyed this book on a Kindle eReader or in the Kindle App, you will find the author 'Follow' button after the last page.